Served Hot
Baked Fresh
Delivered Fast
Knit Tight
Wrapped Together
Danced Close

Resilient Heart
Winning Bracket
Save the Date
Level Up
Mr. Right Now
Sergeant Delicious

UP IN SMOKE

—

ANNABETH ALBERT

carina
press

carina
press®

Recycling programs
for this product may
not exist in your area.

ISBN-13: 978-1-335-48472-7

Up in Smoke

Copyright © 2021 by Annabeth Albert

This edition published by arrangement with Harlequin Books S.A.

For questions and comments about the quality of this book,
please contact us at CustomerService@Harlequin.com.

Carina Press
22 Adelaide St. West, 40th Floor
Toronto, Ontario M5H 4E3, Canada
www.CarinaPress.com

Printed in U.S.A.

To Abbie Nicole,
one of the very best parents I know.
You inspire me daily.

UP IN SMOKE

Chapter One

Grangeville, Idaho

"I have a bad feeling about this." Shane wasn't kidding. Dread coiled low in his gut, tightening his abs, making it hard to sit comfortably on the hard plastic chairs in the waiting area.

"Quit being a baby." Tossing her long hair, Shelby trotted out her rarely used big sister voice. "You never know, you might love it."

"You said that about those fire chips too," he reminded her, memory of the incendiary potato chips making his mouth tingle.

Shelby was in a great mood this morning, especially considering it was prior to noon and this teeny airport didn't even have coffee. But then again, knowing Shelby, her good mood was probably precisely *because* it had been late night.

"Come on. At least smile. It's your birthday." She gave an exaggerated grin like she was coaching him through it.

Mimicking her, he dutifully pasted on the same smile he used with media and fans when they asked about his love life. "There. See?"

"That's not a real smile." She huffed out a breath, perfectly glossed lips pursing. This idea might be all kinds of stupid, but if they were about to die, at least she'd look pretty doing it.

"You're having me jump out of a perfectly good airplane. I'll smile when we're on the ground."

"I bet you smile before that." A guy a little older than him and Shelby made his way to where they sat. Long, purposeful strides, the kind Shane associated with cowboys and military personnel. Blond, shaggy hair that was just shy of needing a ponytail to tame it. Rugged stubbly jaw that was somewhere between lazy and beard. Hazel eyes with crinkly lines, like he laughed his way through life. Freckled, tanned skin that said he spent too much time in the sun. In short, he was gorgeous, but everything about the way he carried himself said he likely knew it.

"Hi again, Wilder," Shelby simpered, losing her sisterly bossiness in favor of batting her eyes and softening her mouth. Shane should have known that her sudden interest in taking him skydiving for his birthday involved a hot guy. She'd tried hard to drag her friend Macy along, but she'd wisely chosen to sleep in, unswayed by Shelby's latest obsession.

"Shelby. Thought I recognized your name on the itinerary. Glad you could come by." This Wilder guy had a great voice. Shane had heard enough DJs over the years to know Wilder could give most radio personalities a run for their money with his low, sexy voice that managed to be both light and sincere at the same time.

"I did. And I brought my baby brother, the birthday boy." Shelby motioned absently to Shane, eyes still locked on this Wilder.

"Happy birthday, brother." Wilder had another easy grin for Shane.

"I'm Shane Travis." He stuck out a hand because he couldn't trust Shelby with details like names. And he did have some manners. "My sister's been talking this up all morning."

"Fabulous. Shane, I'm Brandt Wilder. And there's no better way to spend a birthday than with your head in the clouds."

"If you say so." Shane could think of a whole list of places he might rather be than right here with Shelby's latest obsession, about to trust his life to a thin piece of nylon and this sky cowboy's expertise.

"Okay, so here's how it works." Brandt rubbed his hands together. "You'll watch a training video, then we suit up, and we do some practice exercises, then up we go for the tandem jumps. We already reviewed your waivers. My buddy Dallas, who owns this outfit, will have you in good hands, beautiful. I'll take the birthday boy."

"But I wanted to go with you." Lower lip coming out, Shelby pouted. She'd win of course. She always did.

"I know, darlin'. But we gotta go by weight and height. I'm the tallest—"

"Yeah, you are." She gave him a blatantly appreciative once-over that made Shane need to look away.

"Anyway, since I'm taller and stronger but not as heavy, I'll need to take your brother. We need to balance the weights." He gestured at another guy, who was shorter and older but ripped, with a rugged face. As far as consolation prizes went, Shelby hadn't done too badly for herself, but she still managed to pout all through the safety video and lecture.

For his part, Shane tried to pay attention. No way was

he about to die simply because he'd missed some critical tip. He had a show in two nights in Spokane that he couldn't miss. Thankfully, Shelby and Macy, who was an aspiring folk singer, were headed to a festival outside Bozeman. He wouldn't meet up with them again until Cheyenne. God bless the start of festival and outdoor concert season. If he was careful with his pennies, he'd be able to afford another winter in Nashville, pounding the pavement in search of his dreams. Maybe sell another song or two in the meantime. Life was too promising to go splat parachuting.

"Now we're going to check the equipment and practice body position." Dallas led them through getting suited up. Wind suits. Webbed harnesses. Helmets, like Shane needed the reminder his noggin was at stake.

"So, I'm gonna be right behind you." Brandt's silky-smooth voice slid over Shane's strung-out nerves, making it so his body wasn't sure what it thought of the other man's easy charm. Or his nearness as he slipped behind Shane, way too close for comfort. He smelled like the beach, salty and crisp with a hint of something botanical. "First thing we want to do check the harness fit."

"Uh…" Shane made a strangled sound as Brandt ran a blunt finger between the harness and Shane's shoulder.

"Relax, I'm a professional." Chuckling, he didn't remove his hands, instead continuing to check Shane's straps and each connecting point, stopping to review each place where they'd be hooked together. His spiel was probably meant to calm Shane down, but even his glancing touches were electric and had Shane tensing further.

He forced a laugh to cover for his discomfort. Couldn't have Brandt thinking he reacted to his presence in any way. "Somehow the fact that you're crazy enough to do this for a living isn't as reassuring as you'd think."

"Living? Nah." Brandt gave an easy shrug as he came around to Shane's front. "This is just a favor to Dallas. And you wanna talk crazy, I'm a smoke jumper. I leap out into active forest fires. This Sunday tourist hop is nothing."

Now that made sense. Naturally, Sky Cowboy wasn't gonna be happy on the parachuting equivalent of the bunny slope. Shane had heard about those smoke jumpers, the guys who risked their lives fighting wildfires, often with only their wits and a chainsaw. He was both impressed and slightly worried as a guy with that kind of danger tolerance might take risks Shane wouldn't.

"So, what you're saying is we're boring you."

"Not saying that at all." He turned his full megawatt charm on Shane before moving behind him again. "This is still a hell of a way to spend an afternoon. And it's a gorgeous view with the forests on all sides. I was thrilled to land the Grangeville assignment for the season."

"You're not local to here?" he asked to distract himself from Brandt's touch again, the way he stretched Shane's arms this way and that. The other guys were doing the same thing, but it didn't make it any more comfortable.

"Nah. No home base really."

"I feel that mood." Shane never knew how to answer the hometown question. Home for him was the stage, how he felt with his guitar, the friction of strings on his callouses. But a place? Nah.

"I just go where the forest service needs me most that year and try to enjoy the ride. Which is what you're gonna do." Brandt did something with the carabiners on Shane's harness, clipping them together, simple as that.

"You just sit back and let me worry about the details, and you enjoy the ride down."

Shane was none too sure that he could do that. He shifted his weight, not sure which he liked less, Brandt at his back or the rub of the harness. "Is this tight enough?"

"Nope. But that's because I'm not done checking."

"Check away." Shane stretched his arms wide, forcing himself to not to groan when Brandt's tightening efforts ended up with them sandwiched together, his warm torso flush against Shane's back. *Don't enjoy it,* he warned himself. The nylon flight suit the company provided was baggy, but even so, he was well schooled in keeping control over his body and responses.

"Your sister said you're a musician?" Brandt asked, as calm as if they were sharing a beer, not close enough to be sharing the same oxygen molecules.

"Yep." His voice was tight as his muscles.

"You and her ever perform together?"

"Some. We're kinda…oil and water." He gave his standard answer. Brandt was a big boy. He could find out for himself how unreliable Shelby was. And calling Shelby a musician was a stretch—she was decent at harmonies when she managed to show up but too impatient to master any of the instruments she'd dabbled in. She was, however, absolutely killer at moving merch, charming fans out of their credit cards with a smile and a flirty word. "And besides, she's having fun being her pal Macy's hype person."

"That's good. Fun's everything."

Actually, it wasn't, but Shane nodded nonetheless.

"Speaking of fun, show me what you learned from the video. How do you hold yourself in the air?"

Obediently, Shane stretched his arms out, loosening

his stance too, trying to relax like the video had said. "I feel like a little kid playing Superman."

"Don't we all, man. Don't we all." Brandt's deep chuckle rumbled straight through Shane. Damn. This was torture. Then the other man wrapped an arm around Shane, positioning his muscled forearm where Shane could see his fancy-looking watch gadget. "Now this is my altimeter. It tells me when we're at five thousand feet and ready to deploy the chute."

"Got it." Shane wasn't about to study that meaty arm any more than he absolutely had to.

"Okay, it's go time." Dallas's voice echoed though the room. Brandt quickly unclipped them, but as soon as he stepped away, Shane's pulse kicked up. Maybe he couldn't do this. Jump out of a plane? Who was he kidding? He was a ground dweller, through and through.

Right when he was about to turn away, though, Brandt grabbed his biceps. "Nerves hitting you? Trust me. You'll be just fine. I haven't lost a jumper yet."

Shane barked out a laugh. "Not exactly making me feel better."

"Listen, I can tell you all day about how awesome this is." Brandt looked him dead in the eyes, gaze serious for once, all his charm turned to raw intensity. "But until you do it, you're gonna think it's all BS. Sometimes you gotta take a leap of faith."

"Not very good at those," Shane admitted quietly as he stepped free of the other guy's grip. He couldn't keep meeting his eyes either. Too much power there, like a shot with an extra kick.

"Okay. You want me to tell Dallas you want out?"

A *yes* was right there on the tip of Shane's tongue, but then he heard Shelby's laugh ring out. She'd love it if he chickened out. Not only would she get bragging rights for all of eternity, she'd get what she'd wanted and get to go with Brandt. And for whatever reason, Shane hated that most of all. "Nah. I'm going."

He white-knuckled his way out to the small plane, spared a nod for the female pilot, and squished his eyes shut until Shelby jostled him into looking at the valley underneath them, the green canopy of the national forest contrasting with the pristine blue sky. Random snippets of lyrics danced through Shane's head, ways that he might try to describe this view. But then, right as he was settling into something resembling comfort, everyone started shuffling around, getting ready to go. The wind rushed in as the hatch opened, and a full-body shiver raced through Shane.

Then Shelby gave him and Brandt one last coy grin before she and Dallas were away, her *whoop* echoing across the sky.

"Ready? Here we go." Brandt nudged Shane closer to the open hatch. Shane wanted to say no, wanted to drag their clipped-together bodies back inside the plane, wanted to both hurl and yell. But in the end, all he could do was nod. *Only one way down.*

His knees had locked up even as his thighs trembled. Behind him, Brandt was sure and solid. He could push Shane out the hatch pretty easily, but he didn't. He was letting it be Shane's choice. And somehow that patience and restraint gave Shane a jolt of courage. One step into nothingness. That was all it took.

Brandt was right behind him, smooth as if they were on a dance floor, not open sky. And now they were falling. Falling so fast. Faster than a car on the interstate with the windows all down, faster than a dirt bike on a steep incline, faster than the whoosh down a water slide. There was no describing the feeling of the wind on his cheeks, the roar in his ears, the shout that probably belonged to him, the adrenaline that crashed through him as he tried to remember what they'd practiced about positioning. Damn. Hard to think.

Which was funny because that was the one thing he was good at. Shelby was forever teasing him about overthinking. But now, his brain couldn't even pull two words together as they rushed through the air. Brandt yelled something, but Shane was too busy hurtling through the sky to focus on it. And then he was pulled backwards, a hard yank as the parachute deployed. No more freefall. And the oh-my-God-about-to-die adrenaline quieted enough that he could look down, really look.

"Oh my word. It's…."

"Beautiful isn't it?" Brandt's voice was deep and rich, like warm honey over Shane's still jangling nerves. Now that the air wasn't rushing so fast, he could hear him better. Almost too much better, because it felt like they were soaking up each other's awe and wonder. Sharing something warm and tender and *perfect*.

"Yeah."

"Nothing like it." Brandt whistled low, a sound that hit Shane somewhere soft. "Never gonna get tired of this view."

"Me either." Shane almost didn't recognize his own voice, up this high, this far removed from everything that usually weighed him down.

"Hey, Superman. You want a turn steering?" Brandt didn't wait for Shane to reply, grabbing his arms, guiding his hands.

"Whoa. Wow. I'm doing it. Look at us." They swooped

gently from side to side, and it was quite possibly the best feeling Shane had ever experienced.

"Look at *you*. Didn't know your smile muscles even worked."

"Screw you. I can smile." Shane was feeling so good that he had to laugh.

"Well, then get ready. The landing crew will snap your pic as we land. It's your rock-star moment."

"Feels like it," he said right before Brandt took over and set them down softly in a clearing, barely even jarring Shane's knees. "Damn. That was…"

"It was something." Brandt was looking right at him, like he could see straight through Shane's layers, strip him bare. And Shane held his gaze, held the moment as long as he could.

Maybe… Should he say something? Offer to buy him a beer later? *Something* because no way could he let go—

"Brandt! Get over here." Shelby yodeled from down the field, and Brandt's head whipped around.

"Sorry." And just like that, Shelby won, like she always did, like Shane had known she would. Any thought otherwise was foolish. This had been a damn fine birthday memory, but that was all it was ever going be. Nonetheless, he felt it in his still-shaky bones. He wasn't ever forgetting what it had felt like for those few seconds to fly with Brandt Wilder.

Chapter Two

Eleven months later, outside Painter's Ridge, Oregon

There was a baby on Brandt's front step. And not a cute, sleeping in a wicker basket cherub that might signal that this was some sort of dream, even though it was the middle of the afternoon and he'd been up for hours. No, this was a loud, unhappy, red-faced infant in one of those little car-seat carriers with a pink blanket in its lap, and no adult keeper in sight.

Someone had rung his doorbell though. It had taken him a minute or two to get to the door because he'd been on a ladder, painting. And he never got company out here, so he'd figured it was a package and taken his time. But was it long enough for someone to slip away? Fuck. This only happened in old movies, right? No one in their right mind would ever leave a *baby* for him.

"Hello?" He swiveled his gaze across the scrubby property. *Thank fuck.* There was an older RV at the edge of the drive, and there racing back toward the house was—

A memory. Rusty laugh, tickling his ears. Short dark hair the color of polished walnut. Piercing blue eyes. It had been months, but Brandt hadn't forgotten the way those full lips had found their way to a smile, that sound of pure awe when the parachute deployed. Brandt might be easy-come-easy-go about most things in life, but there was no forgetting a moment like that one. But here? Now? Why?

Frowning, Brandt took a step toward the guy. *Sean? Scott? Shane.* Shane. That was it. Old West name, calling to mind a cowboy with a guitar and a horse with a too-serious name. "I know you."

"Yup." Shane nodded. He was hauling some sort of pink backpack over one shoulder. "Good you remember."

"What are you doing here? Show in town?" Brandt proceeded cautiously. He'd never had a stalker before, let alone one with a kid, but he also wasn't exactly an easy to track down person either. The possibility of this being some sort of freaky coincidence seemed small.

"Nope." Shane knelt in front of the fussy baby, gently rocking the carrier. "There. There. We're gonna get you changed and fed. Hang on a sec."

"Uh…" Brandt moved so he was between Shane and the front door. He was a friendly guy, but his arm and neck hair kept prickling, telling him to not be too fast to invite this blast from the past in. "Didn't know you had a kid. Wife back in the RV?"

Back at the sky diving school, Shane hadn't exactly given off wife-and-kid vibes, but it wouldn't be the first time Brandt was wrong in that regard. But Shane simply snorted, a sound of utter contempt.

"No wife. Not my kid." Shane's speech was clipped as he continued to rock the carrier, quieting some of the indignant baby sounds.

"Babysitting emergency?"

"You could say that." Shane's mouth pursed as he

looked up intently at Brandt. "If you remember me, you should remember Shelby, right? My sister?"

Sister. Sister. Brandt racked his brain, sorting through the last year of his life. Yeah, Shane hadn't been alone that day. *Oh fuck.* The sister. Long streaked hair. Adventurous but bossy. Kind of mean to her brother, which hadn't sat the best with Brandt, especially considering it was the guy's birthday.

"Yeah, I remember your sister. But that doesn't explain what you're doing here at my house now."

"Four days ago Shelby turned up in Portland, baby in tow. Next morning, she was gone."

"Hell. That sucks. You call the cops? I haven't seen her since that jump, man. Not sure what you're thinking…"

The baby gave another mad squawk. Baby. Shelby. *Oh, hell no.*

"Didn't figure you'd seen her." Shane continued to regard him coolly. "Had to track your ass down. Way more trouble than Shelby would ever go to."

"But why…" Brandt trailed off as he considered the baby on his doorstep again. "You're not trying to suggest—"

"Yep. She's yours. Congrats. You're a dad."

Brandt made an inarticulate sound as he sagged against the wooden exterior of the house, world going gray around the edges. *No fucking way.*

Shane had expected Brandt to be skeptical, perhaps even downright hostile. But he also hadn't known what else to do. It had been a hellacious three days, and he was running on almost no sleep, and now here was Brandt looking like he might be about to pass out. Stepping closer, Shane reached out a hand to catch him if he fell, but honestly he was so wrung out that Brandt would probably take them both out if he collapsed.

"Do you need to sit down?"

"Nah." Brandt glanced down at the step next to the baby like it might be a river of lava instead. "And no, no way. You've got the wrong guy."

"Your name's on both the birth certificate and the note Shelby left. She seemed pretty certain."

"I'm on the what?" Brandt rubbed his hair, which was even longer than when Shane had seen him last, spilling down his neck. "How is that even legal?"

"Not sure. Want me to show you?" He reached for the bag at the same time as the baby let out another unhappy noise. Shane rocked the car-seat bucket, but the trick failed to work. "Listen, I know this news is a shock. And I want to show you the stuff from Shelby. But she needs a bottle, I think. And changing. Is there any way we could talk inside?"

"Inside?" Brandt inched close to the door, like Shane and the baby might be about to storm their way into his house.

"Yeah. You know, that place where hopefully you have hot water?" Shane gentled his voice when Brandt's posture only got stiffer, more reluctant. "I swear, I'm not about to drop her on you and run. Promise. I only want to talk. And get her changed and fed. She's miserable."

As if she could understand, the baby squeaked, face getting pink again like she was building to an all-out wail.

"Okay. Okay. Here's the deal. You can come in. And we'll talk. But you dump the baby, and I'm calling the cops. You've got the wrong guy."

Of that they were in agreement, but Shane didn't have

a lot of options. He had no clue what the *right* guy for this situation would look like, but Brandt Wilder was not it. Messy hair. Dirty white T-shirt speckled with three colors of paint. Ripped jeans. Out here in the middle of nowhere at a house that wasn't even his, according to the intel that Shane had tracked down. Undoubtedly gearing up for another season throwing himself out of airplanes to fight wildfire. Yeah, he was far from ideal fatherhood material.

"Thanks," he said instead as he picked up the baby's seat and followed Brandt into the house, which was closer to a cabin, low with dark wood sides and a green roof, like the sort of building you might see at a summer camp. The front door led directly into a great room, an L-shaped space with sitting area, dining table and chairs, and open kitchen tucked beyond that. It seemed to be mid-renovation, toolbox on the counter, power tools on the dining table, half-painted wall behind the table, and sheets over the leather couches.

"Hot water's in the kitchen." Brandt's face was tight and wary. He hung back as Shane crouched next to the baby on the rug in the seating area. Luckily, she was only wet, so he was able to do a fast change using the little pad that came with her diaper bag. Figuring his chances of getting Brandt to hold her were nil, he put her back in the car seat long enough to wash his hands.

Working quickly while the baby continued to fuss, he made the bottle, which was a lot easier in this airy kitchen than in the RV. Still, he was hardly an expert. Some formula powder sprinkled on the counter, and he forgot the part about needing to put a finger over the top before shaking it up. Something about baby stuff made him feel all thumbs. As soon as the bottle was done, he rushed it and the baby carrier to one of the couches in the sitting area.

"Here." Brandt whisked the sheet on the couch away as Shane freed the baby again. Grateful, he took a seat. Sitting felt good after the epic journey he'd had. He'd made decent time while the baby had slept, but when she'd been awake, he'd quickly lost track of the number of stops it took to keep her calm. His throat was hoarse, like he'd performed back-to-back sets, and in a way, he had, singing endless songs to the baby because she'd fuss for the radio but quiet when he sang along.

Glug. The baby made an eager noise as Shane arranged her in his arm to give her the bottle. She was so tiny and helpless and never was he more aware of that than when feeding her. This part was fiddly too—he'd learned the hard way that angle mattered and that the mid-feeding burping was not optional.

"So. Tell me your story." Brandt took a seat in the large chair opposite of the couch, leaning forward with his hands on his knees.

"After Grangeville last year, Shelby and I went opposite directions. But she had some sort of sinus infection she couldn't shake, and when I saw her again a few weeks later in Cheyenne, she was miserable. Congested, upset stomach, headaches. From what she said the other night, that's how she knows you're the dad—she was too sick with the sinus thing to party, and then she kept getting sicker, not better."

"That sucks." Brandt's voice was guarded but not unkind.

"Yeah. And rather than go to a clinic or something smart, she decided to leave Macy on the festival circuit and go hang out with my mom instead and try to get better."

"And where's your mom? Maybe she'd be a help?" Brandt sounded all too eager to make this someone else's problem.

"Mom is the last person, maybe even after you, that I would trust with a baby. And calling her is not an option. There are few phones at the commune she's currently at in southern Oregon." Shane kept his voice level and matter-of-fact, no time to dwell on his disappointing parents and their inability to settle down, even now. "I'll go to her if I have to, but she's even less reliable than Shelby when it comes down to it."

"But Shelby stayed there?" Brandt frowned as Shane paused to burp the baby. The baby book Shelby had left had a whole section on feeding, but it didn't adequately describe the way this kid could rival a trucker with her loud burps, half of which brought up some of the formula. He remembered at the last second to grab one of the little light blankets for his shoulder.

"Apparently. I mean I knew she was there over the winter, getting her inner hippie chick on, but I didn't know she was pregnant because I was in Nashville most of the fall and winter." Shane refused to feel guilty about not checking in more. It was hard enough to reach his mom at the commune, and if he'd felt relief that Shelby was at least not out stirring up more trouble, well that was his business, not Brandt's.

"Why'd you come back?"

"I've had good luck before with the festival and rodeo circuit in the Northwest. Nashville just wasn't paying off yet." Shane didn't want to go into how there he was one of hundreds of hungry young country star wannabes, broke and desperate. So far, his only claim to fame was selling a couple of songs to B-list acts, but even that was hit or miss. At least in the Northwest, he could make a buck. And maybe his big discovery would come out here anyway. "I was in Portland for an audition for one of those reality talent show contests, and that's how Shelby knew to find me."

"What I'm struggling to follow is why leave the baby with *you?* I mean, no offense, man, but you're not exactly instant daddy material either."

Shane wasn't going to dispute that. He had no real clue why Shelby would trust him with this other than the fact that he was always the one batting cleanup on whatever her latest mess was, this one included. "She was pissed about fighting with my mom and the commune leadership. What's surprising is that she lasted this long there. She's allergic to routine, and I doubt they had enough excitement for her. And Macy just booked a Canadian tour. No way was Shelby gonna miss that. I thought she was taking the baby though, until I woke up and she'd split."

"But she left a note you said?"

"Yeah." Shane fumbled with the now-sleepy baby to get the note and the birth certificate from the bag. Damn. He was exhausted too. He'd kill for a nap himself. Just thirty minutes even. These had been some of the longest days of his life.

"Here's the note." He passed over both pieces of paper. "And as you can see, the commune midwife put your name as the dad. Apparently, Shelby thought your last name was cooler than Travis, decided to use it for the baby."

Brandt blinked a couple of times. "She named the baby Wilder?"

"This is Jewel Pearl Wilder." Shane made the baby wave her arm. "I know you don't believe me. Hell, I don't want to believe me either."

"You're not wrong," Brandt muttered, folding forward again. "And you seem like a stand-up guy in a bad spot. But there's been a mistake. I swear there was a condom. I'm not an idiot."

"You found a magic brand with a hundred percent guarantee?" Shane countered, staring him down. But his snark was undone by a huge yawn. "Look, if alcohol and Shelby were involved…"

"I wasn't drunk." Brandt frowned, hands clenching and unclenching. "I was scheduled to jump the next day with Dallas. I was mildly buzzed, if that. Which is how I know for sure that the kid's not mine."

His certainty hit Shane like a punch to the solar plexus, stealing all the wind and adrenaline he'd been running on the past few days. *Whoosh.* Gone. Leaving only utter exhaustion. If Brandt wasn't the father, then that left him few options, each more horrible than the next.

"Fuck," he whispered, drawing the word out. Then he remembered he was holding a baby and cursed again. "Shit. Sorry. I'm… I don't know what to do."

Hell, he could barely keep his eyes open and here was Brandt so sure he wasn't involved, and it was all too much.

"Police?" Brandt asked. "Missing person report? If she's in danger…"

"She's not in danger. She's with Macy. Likely in Canada by now. And like it or not, she's still my sister. Police…they'll want to charge her with something bad."

"Yeah." Brandt nodded and looked away.

"And they're likely to haul in a social worker to take the baby. I'm a single guy with no address other than that beat-up RV. Like you said, no one's trusting me to keep an infant. So, after I read the note, I figured the best plan was to track you down first." His eyes started to burn, the audacity of his own stupidity having him closer to tears than he'd been in years. "See if… Hell. I don't even know now what I was thinking. Not like you're in a much better position than me to keep the kid from the system."

"I get it." Brandt surprised him by slipping from the chair, coming to crouch next to the couch and putting a hand on Shane's knee. Damn. He must be in rough shape if Brandt thought he needed comforting. "Trust me, I know better than most how rough the system can be. I don't want you to have to make that call either. I truly don't."

"Gonna have to." Shane bit his lip and squeezed his eyes shut. No way was he crying in front of this man. But the second his eyes shut, exhaustion started winning again, and another yawn escaped his lungs. Didn't help that the baby was snoozing away, bottle finished and her little warm body in his arms working as some sort of sleeping potion.

"Not right this minute." Brandt's voice was as soft and comforting as a towel right from the dryer. "You're going to rest a few. I'm gonna sit right here and watch her while you sleep. Promise I'm not going anywhere. We'll all hang out while you rest. I've been where you are, strung out on no sleep to the point nothing made a lick of sense."

"Okay." It spoke to how exhausted Shane was that he was agreeing to this plan. Not like he had much choice. He was in no shape to drive, that was for sure. Maybe when he woke up, some new solution would present itself, one where this wasn't all on his shoulders. He knew better than to count on Brandt Wilder for help, but right then, he was all Shane had.

Chapter Three

Brandt knew exhaustion. He'd seen it enough in himself and his fellow smoke jumpers. He well knew that wall where a person simply had no more to give. No energy to even eat or hydrate. It was a special level of hell when sleep was hours away and putting one foot in front of the other was a herculean task. He'd heard from his friends with kids that parenthood could be like that too, taking everything one had to give and pushing the limits on how far someone could go without rest.

Shane was at the point now, eyes shut, skin even paler than usual, shoulders slumping, head falling forward as if it were too heavy for his neck. His grip on the baby hadn't loosened, but Brandt wasn't sure what would happen when sleep finally claimed the poor guy in earnest. Thinking fast, he lined up his arms with Shane.

"Let me take the baby. You don't wanna drop her," he whispered.

"Mmm. Okay." Shane made a sleepy noise as he handed her over.

Miraculously, she didn't wake up, didn't even make one of those unhappy noises she seemed so good at. Sitting back on the rug, Brandt adjusted the tiny package in his arms. She was small and warm. Maybe ten pounds, less than a lot of Brandt's power tools and definitely less than most of his smoke jumper gear. The weight was nothing at all, and yet, the baby also felt like the heaviest thing he'd ever held.

It had been years, possibly decades, since he'd last held a baby, and he tried to create a mental checklist. Head support. Little blanket for warmth but not close to her face. What else? With a jump, he had a very clear list to work through to ensure a good outcome, but here he had only very foggy memories. He didn't dare risk putting her back in her little carrier. She didn't seem to like that place, not that Brandt could blame her.

"I wouldn't want to be strapped into a plastic bucket either." He laughed softly at himself for talking to a baby.

On the couch, Shane snorted like he'd heard the joke, then shifted around, stretching his long body out, head on the throw pillow against the arm of the couch. Brandt had the strangest wish for a quilt, something to cover him with. *What the heck?* He wasn't exactly the caretaker type. He'd provided a safe place for buddies to crash countless times, and never once had he thought about ways to make things cozier for them.

"Wake me in ten," Shane huffed into the pillow.

Brandt was doing no such thing. As long as the baby stayed sleeping, Brandt could sit here, let Shane rest. The painting would keep. Eventually, he'd need to worry about food, but that seemed far less pressing than getting Shane some rest. Asleep, he looked far younger. More vulnerable too. Brandt had to look away before his sympathies got the better of him. Rest, then maybe Brandt could feed him before…

Before what? Could Brandt really turn him out? Let him sort out what to do next on his own? He wasn't sure

there was any other option. There was no way this was
Brandt's kid. He might love sex, but he'd always been
more cautious than most of his friends, getting tested on
the regular, never skipping proper condom use. Shane
might be right that they weren't one hundred percent fool-
proof, but he'd made it to thirty with no issues.

Until now. A soft voice pricked at the edge of his consciousness. Hell. Could he live with himself if they didn't
at least do a paternity test? And then there was the little matter of the birth certificate. He hadn't signed anything, but could he be legally liable for this kid? Shifting
the baby, he looked again at the birth certificate. Yup.
That was his name. And his birthday, which Shelby had
known because they'd been flirting, that way strangers did in bars, sharing random tidbits. She had been
all into astrology with some app on her phone and had
found his Valentine's birth date hilarious and cute, calling him cupid like she was the first one to use that joke.

Fuck. Maybe he was going to have to get this cleared
up, get his name off the birth certificate at least. He
moved to fish his phone out of his pocket, but the action jostled the baby, who squeaked, an adorable baby
mouse noise. Shane had her in a little pink-and-white
cotton sleeper with a zipper, and when she stretched, her
legs kicked out, little kitties on her feet bopping Brandt's
forearm. His chest did a weird electrical surge past a soft
place he'd almost forgotten he had.

"Shush, shush," he soothed, rocking a little in place,
hoping she'd drift back off. Which she seemed inclined
to do, but as she resettled herself in the crook of his arm,
her head turned, revealing a large reddish-brown birthmark on her neck, right below the hairline on the left side.

"No way," he breathed out. He knew that mark. With

his free hand, he rubbed his own neck. He kept his hair on the long side mainly out of laziness, but he'd also been teased enough for the mark as a kid that keeping it covered was a nice bonus.

Hereditary birthmarks, he typed on his phone. Was that even a thing? Huh. Apparently so. Most weren't, but some were, and whatever the case, it was damn spooky how much the baby's spot looked like the one he'd presumably had since birth too. It fucking sucked that there was no one he could ask about his either, but it was there in what few kid pictures he had.

"Hey there, beautiful." He looked at her again, trying to see any resemblance beyond the birthmark to the couple of pictures he had of his younger self. Hard to say whether that heart-shaped bow to her lips was the same as that upper lip divot that was hell to shave for him. Ditto trying to figure out if she had the same slope to her nose or curve to her ears.

Trying to hold her and his phone at the same time was a major challenge, especially now that she was squirmier. Even as he tried a variety of different holds, his eyes kept drifting back to her neck. The resemblance was eerie enough that he found himself doing some research on paternity testing too. Expensive, but he had some savings. It took days though for results, even rushed.

Damn it. Looked like maybe this was his problem after all. At least temporarily. No way was he sending Shane packing until he knew for sure that this wasn't his kid. And even if the paternity test showed he was in the clear, his stomach cramped at the idea of letting the system sort out the fate of this little bundle. Shane was in over his head, that much was for sure, and now Brandt had no choice but to join him in these murky, uncertain waters with no clear answers. There were few things he hated more than serious discussion, but as soon as Shane woke up, they were going to have to *talk*.

Shane woke up slowly to the scent of something meaty and spicy. His stomach growled even before his eyes opened. His legs cramped as his feet connected with something solid. He wasn't in his bed, that much was sure. Too narrow. Too—

"Baby," he gasped as awareness slammed into him. He was at Brandt Wilder's house, having more or less collapsed on the guy, leaving Jewel to a guy who'd been rather clear he wanted nothing to do with this whole situation. How could he be so reckless?

"Hey. Easy there." A strong hand landed on his shoulder.

"Wilder." Shane blinked a bunch. "Where's the baby?"

"Think you can call me Brandt." Brandt laughed low as he came around the couch. Empty handed. "Seeing as how we're in this mess together."

"We are?" Shane swept his gaze around the room. Baby. Baby. Where was Jewel?

"Baby's right there." Brandt pointed at a blanket rimmed with pillows on the floor, halfway between the seating area and the kitchen, and Shane scrambled to his feet, almost landing on his knees, in his rush to go and find Jewel.

"She's awake?" Relief surged through him so fast he almost puked. But Jewel was fine. Lying on her back, kicking her little kitty feet in the air. "How long did I sleep?"

"Couple of hours. I figured we'd wake you when she fussed, but so far she hasn't much, not even when I set her down so I could heat us up some food. I don't know what age they start rolling, hence the pillows."

"Smart." Still practically shaking with relief, he scooped Jewel up, held her close. "She hasn't rolled yet on me, but safe is good."

"She might need changing, but I thought I'd leave that to your expertise since she wasn't putting up a fuss. Ditto the bottle. Not many things I won't try, but I'm scared I'd get the temperature wrong."

"I hear that. I had to look up the temperature thing myself. She was not amused at the delay." He went ahead and dragged the bag over to where she lay, settling himself down next to her. Brandt had put her on a thick folded thermal blanket and there was a little wooden animal near her. "What's this?"

"Thought she might want something pretty to look at." Brandt gave him a crooked grin. "Smoke jumper buddy of mine whittles and gave me that bear as a thank-you after I saved his ass from a tree."

"Wow." Shane picked it up and admired the handiwork before moving the baby to the changing pad. "Not sure whether I'm more impressed at the woodworking or that you thought ahead to baby entertainment."

"I always think ahead to fun." Brandt chuckled as he retrieved two plates from the cupboard.

Not wanting to ruin this surprising hospitality, Shane bit back a quick retort about how everyone knew Brandt was all about the party. Shane had been so focused on keeping Jewel alive that extras like something for her to look at had been beyond him. Hell, even sleep had been beyond him until he'd had help.

"Thanks for letting me rest," he said as he left the baby on the blanket and washed his hands at the sink.

"You needed it." Brandt clapped him on the shoulder again as he passed behind Shane to stir something on the stove. "And now you need food. Also, we should talk."

"Not gonna lie, I could eat a rusty old Ford right now. I'm not even sure what day of the week it is right now or the last time I had food that required a plate."

"I'm not a foodie by any stretch of the imagination, but I can do better than a bag of chips and some jerky." Brandt set the two plates on the table. "This is black beans and sausage I made the other night. I wasn't sure how much cooking time the small thing would give me, so it's toast on the side, not biscuits."

"Toast is fabulous." Taking a seat at the table, Shane narrowly avoided moaning at how good the food smelled. He waited for Brandt to join him, then was about to dig in when an angry wail sounded from the floor. "Heck. She's probably hungry too."

Reluctantly, he pushed himself up to retrieve the bottle from earlier, trying to move past disappointment over the missed food to do what had to be done. "I'll wash this and make her formula."

"And then I'll feed her while you eat. We can work in shifts." Another way too easy smile from Brandt, who had no idea how hard this was, day in and day out.

But Shane also wasn't going to turn down help while he had it. "Appreciate it."

"No problem." Brandt settled back down at the table with the baby and took the bottle from Shane, easy as if they'd been doing this for weeks. "Am I doing this right?"

"Angle your arm up a little more." Shane demonstrated with his own arm. "If she's more upright, less gets puked up later."

"Got it. Now eat."

"Trying. This is really good." Shane tucked into the beans while Brandt adjusted the baby and the bottle, finding a position that worked for him. He was more of a natural than Shane, that was for sure, as Shane had ended wearing most of the formula the first time he'd tried. "And why the sudden helpfulness? Thought you were pretty clear on not getting involved before I fell asleep."

"Yeah. Well…" Brandt drew the word out. "I did some thinking. And research. I'm on the birth certificate, and while that shouldn't have happened without a paternity form, a court might have something to say about my name being there, especially if the kid goes into custody. It's going to take a paternity test and a court order to get me removed from the birth certificate, assuming the test is negative."

"And if it's not?"

"Then it's not, and I deal. No kid of mine is going into foster care if I can help it. I grew up in the system. Aged out. There are some good people in child protective services. I even know a few. But it's not the life I'd want for a kid."

"I'm sorry."

"Eh. It was a long time ago." Brandt tried to wave away Shane's concerns and ended up with an indignant squawk from Jewel.

"Better burp her now if you don't want a shirt full of formula," Shane warned, getting up from the table to retrieve the light blanket he'd been using for his shoulder.

"Look at my neck." Brandt tilted his head as Shane handed over the blanket.

"Pardon?" Shane couldn't see any baby spit up from here, but he wasn't sure he trusted himself to touch the other guy as he still remembered how electric Brandt's touch had been checking the parachute rigging that day.

"I want to show you something and can't with my hands full. Move my hair."

"Okay." This was beyond surreal. Food. Help. And now an invitation to touch the guy. Brandt's hair was softer than it looked, like corn silk, and try as he did to not let his fingers linger, his body still took notice of the warmth of his smooth skin. He almost forgot he was supposed to be looking for—

"See it?" Brandt asked right as Shane hissed in a breath. Shane had a large birthmark shaped like an oversized, perky comma. Little darker and bigger, but Shane had seen that mark before.

"Yeah. Looks like the one on the baby. Wow." Shane sank back into his chair.

"Okay. Not just me that sees the resemblance." Brandt moved Jewel around, awkwardly patting her to burp her.

Shane was still too stunned at the birthmark to offer baby advice, but he managed a laugh when the baby made one of her trucker burps.

"Damn, lady. That's loud." Brandt laughed too. "And that's good I guess that you see the birthmark similarity. Means I'm not losing my mind."

"No. It's definitely weird coincidence. That why you want the paternity test now?"

"Yeah. I looked up hereditary birthmarks. And apparently they are a thing. Rare, but common enough that I'm not gonna rest easy till we know for sure. I'll go to my grave swearing there was a condom and that it was a one-time thing, but I can't argue with my eyes here."

"Speaking of eyes, did you notice the baby's?"

"Huh." Brandt peered down at Jewel. "Sorta gold-green-brown?"

"You look in a mirror lately?" Shane was not going to confess to half-written lyrics waxing poetic about moss-colored eyes and clear blue skies. "I might be remembering high school biology class wrong as to which colors are dominant, but that's closer to your shade than blue like Shelby and me."

"Okay. Wow." Brandt readjusted the baby, offering her the bottle again. "She's bald though."

"Not sure there are many babies with a full head of shaggy blond hair." Shane laughed before eating more dinner. "Were you a bald baby? Got a picture?"

Brandt shook his head. "Not many. Foster care, remember? I've got a little book that I might show you later, but most of the pictures are school age."

"Not the same thing, but I can sympathize a little as our folks were terrible about things like pictures. We moved so much that I learned to not get sentimental about much. The couple of baby pictures I remember seeing, Shelby had a lot of dark hair."

"Yeah." Brandt's mouth twisted. "So. Paternity testing. And a lawyer to figure out options. I've got a message into a buddy who's married to one. How sure are you that Shelby's not in danger? I'm good with not reporting her missing to the authorities, but I've heard about post-baby mental health issues. And there are other dangers."

"Shelby said she's going to Macy. I believe she'll do that, even if she's not answering her phone. Macy and I aren't tight, but I left a text asking her to let me know if Shelby doesn't show. And to tell Shelby to call me, not that I expect Shelby to listen."

"Okay. Keep trying to reach her." Brandt nodded like

he was the one organizing this plan. Shane's back muscles bristled, but arguing over who was in charge was probably not the best use of their time. Instead, he left his chair to go reclaim the yawning baby.

"Here. Your turn to eat." He waited until Brandt had a chance to microwave his plate before continuing. "As far as post-partum depression, I read a little bit about it in the baby book. And I suppose it could be a factor, but a lot of this is typical Shelby behavior. She gets serious about cleaning up her act for a spurt, then it's right back to hard partying and bad choices."

"I know plenty of people like that." Brandt scooped up some beans with a piece of toast, and Shane tried hard not to notice his long fingers or his lips. He forced himself to focus on settling the baby in his arms, trying to see her with fresh eyes, trying to find more of Brandt in her little face.

"Also, she's not threatening self-harm in the note and is pretty clear where she's headed. Honestly, I'm not sure what the cops would do with this other than charge her with child abandonment."

"Yeah." Brandt frowned. "Probably don't want that. But keep me posted what you hear. I'd hate it if we missed some sort of cry for help."

"Will do. And agreed." Shane liked that *we* far more than he should have, liked not being alone in this dilemma. Hell, simply having someone to tell the story to was a relief, as was getting a second opinion about how to deal with Shelby and the question of whether to involve the authorities. Brandt still wasn't his first pick for father material, but right then, he was all Shane and Jewel had. It wouldn't be smart to trust him to see this through, but Shane also wasn't walking away from his help.

Chapter Four

"Now what?" Brandt considered Shane across the table, trying to read his reaction to Brandt's new willingness to get paternity testing. Shane wasn't the easiest guy to read, impassive expression and tense body language appearing to be his default. However, now that Brandt had agreed to be part of this mess, he wasn't entirely sure how to proceed, which was a feeling he didn't much care for. And might have been why he felt the need to needle Shane. "I mean, what was your plan for after you found me? Drop the kid and get back on tour?"

"I'm not on tour at the moment." Shane flushed and his tone said that might be a sore subject Brandt should steer clear of. "And no, of course, I wasn't gonna leave her on your doorstep or anything dramatic like that. I'm not Shelby."

"On that we are most clear." Brandt's voice was dry, but his memory was vivid with the way Shane had smelled that day in Grangeville, the way he'd felt against Brandt, the exact timbre of his laugh. He'd done countless tandem jumps over the years, and never had one affected him like that.

"Honestly, I didn't have a plan beyond getting here. Couldn't really let myself think beyond that. I just knew we couldn't stay in my RV in Portland much longer." Shane shifted from side to side, yawning at the precise moment the baby did too. "Lack of sleep and food had my brain fuzzy. I keep trying to follow the schedule in the baby book, but Jewel doesn't seem to have read the same manual as me."

"I imagine not. Reading's what, a six-month skill?" Brandt had to laugh at the idea of this poor over-his-head uncle trying to put this itty-bitty baby on a schedule. Hell, Brandt had worked with plenty of grown ass adults who couldn't keep to a routine.

"Probably." Shane snorted. "Anyway, I guess I better find an RV campground around here for the night. My kingdom for the chance to do a load of baby laundry. And my shirts."

"I've got a washer here." For reasons Brandt didn't entirely understand, his back tightened at the thought of Shane and the baby leaving. "And an extra room. You can stay here tonight. Tomorrow, we'll deal with the lawyer and a lab for the paternity test, go from there."

"Thanks. I'm not too proud to take that offer."

"I've got you. Two sets of hands is always better than one." Brandt had been alone so much of his life that he often lost sight of that fact himself, but he was pretty good at recognizing when others needed help.

"Tell me about this place." Shane patted the baby, tone a little more relaxed now. "I tracked you down through the sky diving outfit in Grangeville. Finally got someone on the phone who believed me that I wanted to send you a thank-you note. Guy on the phone said you were helping a friend?"

"Sort of a mutual help situation." Brandt set aside his ire at Dallas's staff for giving out his personal information. There'd be time enough to get mad about that later. "I'm with Painter's Ridge air base this season, and I needed to find a place on the cheap. Tourist season drives all the rental prices around here sky high."

"Grangeville didn't want you back?" Shane was conversational, not accusatory, but Brandt still had to clench and unclench his fists before replying.

"Didn't say that. Was time to move on, that's all." Brandt was not getting into the specifics on his nomadic lifestyle with Shane, even if the guy might be one to understand how his feet always got itchy if he stayed too long in one spot. "I hadn't done an Oregon season in a few years, wanted to see some friends in the area. And when she heard I was coming back, the widow of an old-timer asked if I'd have interest in helping her get this place ready for market. It's rural but an easy drive to the air base and Painter's Ridge, and also close enough to Bend."

"Nice deal." Shane whistled low as he rocked the baby side to side. She was awake but drowsy after the bottle, little eyes fluttering shut then popping back open every time Shane stopped the rocking.

"Yup. It's a sweet property, but it'll fetch Maggie a better price in a tight market if it's fixed up. Nothing me and my tools couldn't tackle, so we struck a bargain."

And it was highly satisfying work, painting rooms that hadn't been refreshed in years, fixing little imperfections in drywall and such. It wasn't the first time he'd made such an arrangement, and he was grateful for the choices like this that allowed him to have a fair bit in savings.

"I see. Think she'll have issue with you having…company?" Shane pursed his lips. Brandt supposed *company* was one way to describe them arriving on his doorstep unannounced and upending whatever plans and assumptions Brandt had about his life and how it was supposed to go.

"Maggie's in Seattle with her adult kid and grandkids now. She wouldn't care about you guys staying. She only said no parties, but that's not my style anyway."

Shane raised an eyebrow at that.

"Okay, not my style *now*. I'm thirty. Old enough to go to others' parties and want to go home to my own bed after." He grinned at Shane, who didn't grin back. Man, for a musician, he certainly could be uptight. "And like I said, I don't drink much during the fire season. Beer here and there. Nothing harder. If I'm gonna be jumping, I need a clear head."

"I respect that." Shane transferred the baby to his shoulder, which was cute, her little body hanging on his wide shoulder like this little flowerpot gnome one of Brandt's foster mothers had had. He'd have to try that hold next time it was his turn, save his elbow from getting so stiff.

"I wasn't always so careful about mixing partying and being on call," Brandt admitted as he stretched before clearing their plates. "But I've seen enough tough situations, had enough close calls that I value my own neck a little more these days."

"Good." Shane's gaze swept over Brandt, like he was sizing him up as a fatherhood candidate. And Brandt didn't like how much he cared what Shane concluded. He wasn't usually someone who cared about others' opinions. Brandt lived his own life and let others live theirs and that was that. But somehow Shane's opinion *mattered* and that rankled.

"What do you need from the RV for the night?" His

muscles were restless after all this talking, needing a purpose.

"If you hold her, I'll grab her little cot thing and the laundry." Shane stood and handed over the baby before Brandt could protest that he wanted to do the work. When Shane headed outside, he and the baby wandered down the hall beyond the kitchen that led to the bedrooms. He tried that shoulder position Shane had used. Pretty nifty.

"Okay, miss. Let's check the spare room." Talking to the baby still felt a little new, but after watching her while Shane napped, he'd determined that narrating to her was strangely settling. Not having both hands free was another thing to get used to. He'd seen those baby harness carrier things that some parents wore. Maybe he could suggest one to Shane.

In the meantime though, he settled for tossing a set of clean sheets and a comforter on the spare bed. Making the bed might be beyond him right then, but he could at least make sure Shane had what he'd need. Luckily, this had been the first room he'd painted, so the fresh paint fumes were minimal, and it was a nice clean ivory color despite its dated furnishings.

Shane arrived back in a few moments with a full laundry bag and a collapsible baby bed that resembled an upside-down pup tent but stiffer with mesh sides.

"Wow. That does not look comfortable in any way." Brandt continued to hold the baby while Shane set the small bed on the floor of the spare room. "And I've slept in some truly bizarre places over the years."

"Well, it's what Shelby left with her. And the baby book says not to let them sleep too much in the car seat carrier." Shane sounded freshly exhausted again, like his nap had already worn off. "Why don't you try setting her in it? On her back. Sometimes it works."

"And then she'll sleep the night?" Crouching, Brandt set her in the bed, moving slowly like he was transferring an armful of eggs. Instinctively, he kept a hand on the baby, waiting until she snuffled her way back to slumber.

"Ha. You wish. And I mean that. You might want to sleep with earplugs. She'll howl the house down about two or three. And probably a few other times before morning." Shane started making up the bed, and Brandt went to help him, two of them making quick work of the sheets.

"Okay, here's what we're gonna do." He kept his voice decisive as he snapped the bottom sheet into place. He had a feeling that poor, tired Shane needed someone else to step up and take charge. "We'll tag team baby duty tonight. You'll put the laundry on, then try to sleep as far as she'll let you, but that second wakeup, bring her to me. I'm typically up early anyway, and I can let you get a little more sleep that way."

"You sure?" Shane glanced up at him with grateful eyes before smoothing the comforter over the sheets.

"Yeah. If she's truly my kid, I'm gonna need to figure out this stuff in a hurry. And even if she's not, you're in a tight situation." Brandt truly did believe that. For all that he was a little grumpy, Shane had an air of trust-worthiness about him, the sort of solid guy who could be counted on. "Helping you for a couple days while I'm off in any event isn't any skin off my back. And maybe it keeps you from needing to call the authorities a little longer. That's important to me."

"Me too." Shane nodded solemnly. "I appreciate it. And I'm sure Shelby would too."

"Your sister isn't the reason I'm doing this." He met Shane's impossibly blue eyes, holding his gaze. Something passed between them, more electric than simple understanding. More potent. Almost dangerous. They were both in over their heads here, but Brandt needed to be careful he didn't risk anything he couldn't afford to lose.

Shane had forgotten what sleep, multiple consecutive hours with actual dreams, felt like. The sun filtering in through the slats in the blinds warmed his face, waking him gently. No baby, but this time he didn't panic.

He'd had a bizarre early morning handoff to Brandt that he only had foggy memory of, Brandt appearing at his door even before Shane could go hunt him down. In a different T-shirt and loose track pants, he'd smelled like some sort of pine soap. Of course, Shane's body would choose that detail to remember along with how pathetically grateful he'd been for the rescue.

The baby had taken forever to settle back down at two, only to wake again at four something. And now it was a little after eight, the luxury of four straight hours of sleep having Shane stretching and humming. He felt almost human. Fresh clothes from the laundry and a shower would complete the transformation, but first he needed to go search out Brandt and Jewel.

The laundry room door was open as he passed. They'd been a two-man comedy show the night before, standing over the machine and debating whether baby clothes could go in the same load as Shane's shirts. Seeing as how everything had various baby fluids on it, they'd come down in favor of the efficiency of a single load, but with an unscented detergent Brandt had unearthed from under the sink. He'd mumbled something about

sensitive skin, like he was any more of an expert on babies than Shane.

It had been a first, doing laundry with another person,
almost like they were a team. Brandt had even transferred
the clothes to the dryer after Shane had fallen asleep the
first time. Shane knew better than to get used to the help,
but he also wasn't above enjoying it while he had it.

"Brandt?" he called as he entered the main part of the
house, stopping short at the scene in front of him. Brandt
was sprawled on his back on the couch, eyes closed, chest
rising and falling like he was sleeping, but one hand dan-
gled down, rocking the baby who was strapped into her
car seat. Her eyes batted open then closed again, drowsy,
but not unhappy for once.

"You broke Brandt," Shane whispered to her, battling
the strangest urge to take a picture. And not simply because the scene was adorable, but also because Brandt
was way too appealing asleep with his muscular arms
poking out of his shirt and his scruffy jaw and his full
lips, gently parted…

Yeah. Shane wanted a picture of *that*. Yet instead of
giving into the impulse, he went into the kitchen. Brandt
had done a nice job with the beans the night before, but
Shane had learned early on to fend for himself with food.
He found a canister of good coffee, and assuming Brandt
drank it, he started a pot. Glancing back at the sitting
area from time to time, he checked in on Jewel while he
fixed some eggs and bacon. He made a mental note to
pay Brandt back for the groceries. The guy hadn't been
expecting Shane to drop into his life like this, and honestly, Shane would give a lot to not have needed to.

The coffeepot hissed as it finished brewing, and
the eggs finished at the same time as the bacon. Shane

wanted to believe it was a good omen in a life with far too few of them lately.

"Coffee?" Brandt came awake with a start, one of those guys who had the talent of going from dead to the world to bolt upright in three blinks. "Smells great."

"Good. I didn't know how you take it, but it's ready if you want a cup."

"Hot, strong, sweet, and plentiful enough for seconds." Brandt's laugh was almost as deep and rich as the brew.

"Noted." Shane could apply those same adjectives to describe Brandt himself, something that made the back of his neck heat. Same as all those months ago, he didn't want to be attracted to Brandt, didn't want the way his body reacted to the other man, but he seemed powerless to stop it. He plated the food as Brandt poured two mugs of coffee. Cozy. Like the laundry and making the bed the night before.

"Wanna take bets as to whether Little Miss lets us eat?" Handing Shane a mug, Brandt scooped up a plate and took it to the table.

"Dish duty." Shane took the bet with a smile. "I say she's gonna howl. If I'm wrong, I'll do the dishes."

"Sounds good. We've got an appointment with the lawyer at ten."

"Okay. You're sure you want me to come along?" Shane didn't want to assume. Heck, in Brandt's situation he might want to be alone at the lawyer simply to complain about the audacity of someone showing up with a kid on his doorstep.

"Yeah. The lawyer said there's a medical lab nearby. It's a cheek swab for the baby, so no big poke, but I don't want to take her without you. And like it or not, you're in this thing too."

"True." Shane didn't want that either, didn't want to be here, didn't want to be responsible for something so tiny and important, not when he didn't even have his own life together. "I'm still pissed at Shelby. I never babysat or anything like that. Hell, this might be the first baby this young I've held."

"No younger siblings or cousins?"

"Nah. Only the two of us. And we've got cousins, but they're somewhere on the east coast. Never really met. My folks were the branch of the family tree others tended to want to prune off."

"I hear that." Brandt saluted his with his coffee cup. "I suppose I've got extended family, but they didn't care to get involved when I was in foster care, so I've never felt the need to go tracking them down. Not gonna be one of those teary commercials for that genealogy website."

"Yup. Same. Like it or not, I guess we're all Jewel has." The truth of that statement hit him like a boat anchor, pulling him back under, away from the good mood he'd been in since waking up.

"Guess so." Brandt closed his eyes as he exhaled hard, as if he too were overwhelmed. Which he likely was. This was a lot to hit a person with out of the blue.

Even if the testing showed Brandt was the father, was Shane really going to be able to walk away from them both? The heavy feeling in his gut said that like Brandt, he was stuck. No bolting town. Yet again, he'd be the one cleaning up after Shelby, proving he was the better person. And that meant working together with Brandt to do what needed to be done and figuring out a way to ignore the way the air crackled every time Brandt so much as smiled his direction. The baby had to come first.

Chapter Five

"Jewel's not exactly a low-maintenance girl, is she?"
Brandt had to laugh as they finally departed for the lawyer's office. He was used to going from dead asleep to on the road to the air base in under five minutes, but the baby traveled with her car seat, which had a snap-in base that Shane had had to retrieve from the RV. Then there was the diaper bag and a lunch box Brandt had dug up to hold bottles ready to go. Right as they'd been about to close the backseat door, Shane had produced a little light blanket to drape over the car seat to block the strong morning sun. It was no wonder that they were cutting it close to the appointment time. Luckily, the rural road that the house was off of was only a ten-minute drive to the center of Painter's Ridge and only a little farther to the air base.

And how weird did a car seat look in the back of his old Jeep? Strange enough having someone else in the passenger seat, especially someone who wasn't a coworker. Not to mention someone as distracting as Shane. Brandt was used to buddies he could largely ignore, not whatever this strange pull was that Shane had over him.

"Trust me, I've toured with some *real* divas before. At least this tiny one sleeps a lot, stays in her seat, and doesn't require praise every five minutes." Shane laughed, a rare sound from him. His laugh always had a hitch, like he was surprising himself too.

"Okay. You've got a point. Could be worse." Brandt joined him in chuckling.

"Yup. She could be a teenager. I wouldn't want to relive Shelby's teen years for anything."

"Yeah," Brandt agreed weakly, stomach churning because that tiny baby in his rearview would indeed someday be someone's opinionated, fashion-conscious, nonstop-eating teenager. This wasn't simply a baby, a weekend sitting adventure. This was a *person*. A person who was going to grow and change and have needs, wants, and preferences. A person who would need parents. And the universe in all its wisdom thought that role should fall to Brandt? *Lord help us all.*

"Did you ever see yourself as a dad?" Shane asked, almost as if he could read Brandt's discomfort. "Down the road, I mean. Assuming you met the right person…"

"No. Never. Not after my childhood. That's why I was so careful with condoms. Always." Brandt turned into Painter's Ridge, following the directions he'd been given for locating the law offices in the small downtown. Nearby Bend was bigger, but there was something quaint and familiar about this small community that Brandt had always appreciated.

"Ah." Shane made a thoughtful noise as he stretched. "I was just thinking that this might be easier if it was something you'd always wanted, but more a matter of timing."

"Trust me that I'm the last guy someone wants as a husband and father." No one was lining up to commit to a guy who moved on as often as Brandt, and who had his fetish for dangerous hobbies and occupations.

"I feel that."

"You?" Brandt's own musical tastes were more diverse, running heavily to metal and alternative, but his impression of country was that it leaned heavily to the blond, wholesome, and saccharine. "And you're young. No white picket fence and hound dog with two kids in the future for you?"

"Nah. I won't say in interviews, of course, but I'm not the wife type." Shane met Brandt's eyes as they stopped for a traffic sign.

"Ah." Message received. Brandt had figured that might be the case, but he didn't like to assume. "Not going to find judgment from me. I'm—"

"Think this is the place." Mouth a thin line, Shane pointed to a quaint downtown building. The set of his jaw said this was not a conversation topic that he was eager to resume. Which was just as well. Brandt tended to keep his personal life private, but he'd been about to match Shane's cryptic disclosure with one of his own. Probably for the best, though, that they keep their focus on the kid, and not on the fact that these sparks between them might not be a total illusion.

"Look." After finding a parking spot, Brandt turned toward Shane. "I might not be eager to be a dad, but I'm not gonna run from my responsibility either. Just want to say that before we go in there."

"Good. And I'm the one who dumped this in your lap. I can put something toward the lawyer—"

Brandt held up a hand. "I've got some savings. Let's see what she says."

Brandt's buddy was a grizzled late thirties smoke

jumper with more beard than face, but his wife, Cameron, was an elegant blonde with short hair, a sharp business suit, and an enviable way of cutting to the chase. She led them to a well-lit corner office with a little couch where Shane sat with the baby. Brandt took one of the leather side chairs while she reviewed the situation in concise terms, taking notes on a shiny tablet.

"Because there was never an acknowledgment of paternity form, getting you removed from the birth certificate shouldn't be too hard if the paternity test is negative, but I'm going to level with you—I'm expecting it to be the opposite."

Brandt nodded. That was the view he'd been coming around to more over the last twenty-four hours as well. The birthmark was hardly a definitive DNA test, but the coincidences kept adding up.

"And given the abandonment, what we need to be moving toward is a custody order for you." Cameron clicked her stylus for emphasis, leveling a shrewd gaze at him. "Otherwise, Mom can show up at any moment and reclaim the kid and potentially make visitation a nightmare for you."

"Don't want that." He hadn't thought much on that possibility—the idea that he was the father, but that he could end up cut out of decision making. But now that she'd said it, he didn't much care for that notion at all. He glanced at Shane, who was also frowning as he patted the baby.

"With Shelby anything's possible. Get the official document."

"Okay. Good." Cameron turned back toward Brandt. "So, you'll want to be able to show that you're better positioned to provide a stable home than other options if and when this goes to court. What's the plan for living arrangements? For example, do you have a room for the baby? Childcare? The court will look at all those factors."

Fuck. Now there was a whole list of items he'd been avoiding thinking too hard on. But he supposed he had little choice but to make some sort of plan.

"I'll call Maggie after this, let her know what's happening, but she promised to not put the place I'm renovating for her on the market until after I'm done needing it for the season. There's a little room I could put a crib in. I'll get something sturdier than that cot she came with."

"So that's good." Cameron nodded, but her face remained solemn. "But, Brandt, I know exactly how many hours you work. The plus is that you can probably get the baby on your health insurance with a minimum of paperwork, but you're going to have to be able to show reliable childcare, especially if the custody case runs into snags."

Yeah. That was a tricky question. He had no idea what daycare even cost, let alone how to go about finding a good one. He'd been in some horrible ones himself. Then there were babysitters and nannies, but how to locate ones who were both decent human beings and affordable? Mary Poppins didn't exactly make house calls in Central Oregon.

"Let me think—"

"I can help out." Shane's voice was resigned but firm, like he'd been thinking on this and finally come to a conclusion he wasn't sure he liked.

"You?" Brandt raised an eyebrow, trying to give him space to gracefully back out if he was only offering out of obligation.

"Yeah. I'm still the uncle regardless of what that test

shows, and I'm the one Shelby left her with. I might not like it, but I feel responsible."

Ah. Yeah. Obligation was the thing driving him all right. Brandt wasn't going to hold him to that offer, admirable though it was. "Don't you need to get back on the road?"

"Nah." Shane shrugged, but still didn't seem precisely eager. "Right now, I'm between bookings. I parted ways with the agent I was using to get a lot of gigs, and tracking down opportunities myself has been…challenging. I can take some time to help you. Like I said back at the house, I guess we're all Jewel has. I can't walk away from that."

"Okay. Appreciated." Eager or not, this might be the best offer Brandt was getting, and he wasn't dumb enough to turn it down. "That would help a lot while I try and figure out a plan."

"Yes, you'll want something more permanent," Cameron agreed as she looked up from her notes. *Permanent.* All that coffee sloshing around in Brandt's stomach turned sour. God. He wasn't ready to think like that.

"Yeah," he said faintly, still trying to keep up with how fast his life was changing. "Daycare. Something."

Frowning, Cameron set her tablet back on the desk. "I'm going to be honest here and take off my attorney hat and talk to you as a wife and mother. Smoke jumping and parenthood is a hard combo."

"Rich says you're a saint for putting up with it." Brandt smiled at her, even as his gut turned more caustic at her words.

"I am." She didn't laugh. "Standard nine-to-five daycare isn't going to work for you. A nanny might help, but this is going to be difficult no matter how you slice it. Single parenthood and smoke jumping may not be compatible."

"I'll make it work." On that, Brandt was determined. Shoulders tensing, he sat up a little taller. He was a smoke jumper. It was in his blood, and the only family he knew was in the wildfire fighting community. "I'm not walking away from this kid, but I'm not giving up my life either."

"Maybe Shelby will make it back," Shane offered, but there was no real hope to his voice.

Cameron nodded. "In an ideal world, the mom will return and be an acceptable primary parent, and I'll get you an equitable visitation schedule, but ideal rarely materializes."

"Don't I know it." This whole damn thing was so far from ideal he had no idea what he was even hoping for anymore.

"And I'd be remiss if I didn't tell you that right now, at two months, the baby is highly adoptable, especially if we could get Mom on board quickly. Private placement. Find an open situation with some visitation—"

"No." Shane cut her off before Brandt could, a pained sound that echoed in Brandt's soul.

"Yeah, no way. That's not gonna happen."

"All right. Then we'll work on that custody order and get a rush on the paternity test results. Now, Uncle Shane, what are your plans if the paternity test clears Brandt of responsibility?"

Shane blinked repeatedly, baby deer caught in the headlights, needing someone to bail him out. "I…"

"You can stay with me while you figure it out." Brandt was so far from maternal it wasn't funny, but no way was he going to watch Shane flounder. Not when he could do something about it. "You're willing to help me out.

The least I can do is return the favor. I don't want you to rush into a placement simply because you don't think you've got options."

"Thanks." Shane swallowed audibly and his eyes shone with relief. Like the night before, a current passed between them. An acknowledgment. They might be all the baby had, but they were also all each other had. An unofficial team now. Partners of sorts, simply trying to find a way forward.

"We're going to make it through this." Brandt forced some conviction into his voice, saying the words they both needed to hear. And maybe he didn't quite believe it yet, but he'd made it out of deadly no-win situations more than a time or two. Surely one little baby wasn't going to be his undoing.

Shane almost missed Brandt coming back into the waiting area at the medical lab office where they'd gone for the DNA test. Giving a sleepy baby a bottle was a recipe for drifting off himself, but he managed to look up right as the door to the lab area swung shut.

"We need to go shopping." Brandt was remarkably peppy for a guy who'd just had both a cheek swab and a blood draw. Jewel had only needed the cheek swab, but she'd protested that enough that Shane had taken her to the waiting area while Brandt got his needle stick.

"Whoa. What happened to you being the low maintenance one?" Shane joked to cover how much he didn't like medical stuff himself. Brandt was much more easygoing in general, but especially about this sort of thing. Damn good thing they hadn't needed Shane's blood. Passing out on Brandt would be embarrassing, especially since he'd been far nicer than he needed to be, saying

Shane could stay even if the paternity test showed Brandt wasn't the dad.

"Not shopping for me. For the little diva." Brandt gestured at the baby. "Cameron gave us a list of what social workers look for if they have to do a home visit, and besides that, the baby didn't exactly come with a lot of gear."

"You poor guys." The female med tech in blue scrubs who had followed Brandt out had evidently learned at least part of the story from Brandt, who was nothing if not chatty and charming. The woman even went as far as to pat Brandt's arm. "If I were you, I'd hit up the used store down the street—tons of gently worn kids' clothes and toys at a fraction of what you'd pay retail. And as a single mom, I can say to start with the basics. Don't go nuts. You can always fill in as you go if the baby ends up staying longer."

"Good tips." Brandt turned the full wattage of his smile on the young woman, who blushed. His smile didn't dim any as he turned back to Shane. "You up for it?"

His body was more than up for whatever Brandt wanted when he smiled like that, but he made himself ignore the sudden hot surge that raced through him.

"Yeah. Not having to park again is good." He placed the now-empty bottle back in the diaper bag as he shifted the drowsy baby in his arms. "We can stick the car seat in the car, and I'll keep holding her so she stays asleep."

"Sounds good. And first thing on my list is some sort of harness thing to save our arms. One of those hands-free carrier things."

"A sling. You want a sling," the tech offered. "Make sure it's sized for...*tall* guys."

Shane supposed that her appreciative gaze included him too, but he was more uncomfortable than flattered. He'd let Brandt handle the flirting and made his way to the door as Brandt collected a few other tips on their way out. They dropped off the car seat, and Shane used another light blanket to shield Jewel from the sun as they walked. The downtown area of the little town was only a couple of streets, but the brick storefronts coupled with the almost unreal blue tint to the sky made it feel like a 1950s movie set.

The store was a large, open storefront in an older building with racks and racks of clothes organized by kid sizes in the center and toys and baby equipment around the edges of the space. The sole clerk was busy at the front counter with two moms who had several kids of varying small ages with them. Their presence freed him and Brandt to browse unattended.

"She needs more sleepers." Shane pointed to a rack of small garments as Brandt grabbed a plastic shopping basket. "They're far easier to get her in and out of than anything else Shelby left with her."

"Sure. Let's get her some that are…" Brandt trailed off, mouth pursing.

"Less pink?" Shane raised an eyebrow. Brandt was totally that rough and tumble type guy to be threatened by lace and bows.

"Sturdier. That's the word I was looking for." Brandt joined him in riffling through the rack. "I don't have an issue with pink, but dark colors, denim, thick fabrics, those would handle baby mess better."

"I'm pretty sure that they don't make canvas onesies or cargo—"

Brandt cut him off with a happy noise. "See? Overalls!"

"Do babies have a waist measurement or is it by pounds or what?" Shane inspected the tag on the teeny pair of blue denim overalls.

"She's not a puppy where the chow rations are by weight." Brandt held the overalls up to the baby in Shane's arms, shook his head, then grabbed a slightly bigger version. Still teeny though.

"She might not be a puppy, but she could be another animal." Shane rolled his shoulders as he too tried to find a way to relax. Brandt's obvious enjoyment was contagious, and Shane wanted some of that fun. He held up a fuzzy brown sleeper. "She could be a little bear or—"

"A dragon." Brandt added both Shane's sleeper pick and another one in green with a little hood and tail.

"Maybe we're enjoying this too much." Shane tossed in two cheap, plain sleepers for when they ran out of funny ones.

"Probably." Brandt shrugged. "But why not? I mean I didn't ask for this, not gonna ever do it again if I can help it, but if I'm here, caught in a tight spot, so why not find a way to have a little fun? Either way, I gotta deal, but my way, at least I'm not miserable."

"Good point." Shane wished his own moods could shift so easily, wished that fun and lightness came as naturally to him as Brandt.

"I do." Brandt bumped Shane's shoulder, the contact far more electric than he undoubtedly intended. Oblivious, he moved on, tossing a pack of assorted small blankets in the basket. "See? I'm getting more spit-up rags, but now she can be a dragon while she pukes on you and forgets how to sleep at night."

"True. Look! She *can* be a puppy, after all." Shane added one more sleeper to the pile.

"In my house, we welcome all species." Brandt wandered over toward a display of cribs and various baby-holding devices like swings and high chairs.

"I bet you do." The remark came out a little flirtier than Shane intended, which might be better than judgmental and grumpy.

Brandt, though, didn't seem to care about Shane's tone, if he'd even noticed. In the car, he'd been rather easy about the news that there wouldn't be a wife in Shane's future, but that didn't mean he'd welcome Shane trying it on with him. Not that that was Shane's intent. He'd only revealed that much to Brandt because he'd asked, and Brandt seemed like the sort of guy to value a straight shooter.

Which Shane was. He might be discreet on tour and with what limited press he encountered, but he was generally honest with the people in his life who mattered. And besides, even if it had been a less than comfortable conversation, Shane had wanted to know now if it was going to be an issue as they worked together for the baby's best interest.

"Okay. So now for a crib. What are we thinking?" Brandt turned to him like Shane might have an opinion that mattered when it came to where babies slept. But simply being consulted, that was nice, the warm feeling of not being all alone. And he was so used to being the responsible one, the one in charge, that it was nice to get to share some of that.

Shane scanned the prices of various options, eventually pointing to a box with a picture of a white crib with wide slats. "This one is cheaper than some but safe and with a better mattress than the cot. If you get it, you might have enough to also get a swing or something for the great room."

"Sold." Brandt's decisive nod was strangely sexy, the way he knew what he wanted and went for it.

"My goodness aren't you the most adorable thing." The store clerk had finally taken notice of them, coming over to stand next to him, and it took Shane a moment to realize that she meant the baby in his arms, not him. "How old is the little princess?"

"Two months." Shane adjusted the blanket so the woman could take a peek.

"What else can I help you find?" She had frizzy hair and kind eyes, but also seemed like the sort of shrewd business owner who sensed a big sale.

"We'll take the crib. Next on the list is a harness thing—sling." Brandt gave her the same smile he'd given the med tech with the same predictable result of the woman tripping over herself to help Brandt select a baby carrier.

"Pink, pink, or pinker?" Brandt paged through a colorful display of pouches and slings, turning his grin back on Shane. "It needs to fit you too."

"Whatever she won't fall out of." Shane looked away before that grin could work its magic on his insides again. "I grew up with Shelby's hand-me-downs, especially when funds were tight. You're not going to scare me away with some florals."

"Aww. You guys are so cute." The clerk, who was still hovering too close for Shane's taste, did a fake swoon with one hand on her chest. "How long have you been together?"

"About two days," Brandt said absently, eyes still on the rack of slings.

A sputtering noise escaped Shane's throat. "We're not together."

Brandt looked up at that, not nearly as put out as Shane would have thought. "Sorry. Misunderstood. Yeah, we're not a couple. He's the uncle."

"Still sweet." The woman continued to smile at them, perhaps even more so, as like with the med tech, she couldn't seem to resist flirting with Brandt. "Let's find you what else you need."

They left with an eye-popping bill, a crib, a swing, enough outfits for a whole season of a Hollywood TV drama, and even a few toys and board books. The clerk had talked Brandt into those with a cheerful "Babies grow fast!"

Shane had opened his mouth to say that they might not be around to see that if Shelby changed her mind, but then he thought better of it. And he didn't know what do with the weird prickle the reminder had triggered. Almost like dread, which was ridiculous. He should *want* Shelby to return. Or for the paternity test to show Brandt was the dad and for him to settle on some permanent childcare arrangement. Shane should want the responsibility off his shoulders. But instead he was...wistful.

Babies did grow. She already seemed a little bigger. And as exhausting as this all was, he also felt that press of time pushing forward. Snippets of lyrics about change and time danced in his head, things he'd want to write down later.

"That should do it." Brandt wasn't burdened by his melancholy, laughing as they loaded the last of the stuff in his Jeep. And damn, was he ever attractive in the mid-day sunlight, light sheen of sweat from hauling everything to the car. His hazel eyes were almost gold in this light. Messy hair. That grin.

Forget the baby. *Brandt* was the most adorable thing. And every single time he laughed like that, Shane's urge to be stupid only intensified.

Chapter Six

"Hell." Brandt cursed low under his breath as the collection of slats collapsed yet again. And of course, that was right when Shane came back in the room, perfect timing to witness the crib getting the better of him.

"Still stumped?" Shane crouched down next to him.

"I'll have you know that I've rebuilt a chainsaw on the fly. More than once." He shuffled the instructions for the crib, like that might make this easier.

The baby was asleep in her cot in the spare room, which gave them this narrow window of time to set her new room up. Shane had pushed the twin bed against the wall and moved the dresser, while Brandt had—in theory—tackled the crib. *Divide and conquer,* he'd said, overly optimistic about his own abilities to juggle all these parts. Usually it wouldn't be an issue. Today though, everything kept distracting him.

"I have the right tools. But there are a lot of little pieces." Brandt refused to admit defeat. "I'll get it."

"I think this will go faster if we work together. I'll hold and you do the screwing."

"That's what she said," Brandt joked without thinking. Not surprisingly, Shane arched an eyebrow, mouth quirking in something short of a smile. *Oops.* God, after this mess, Brandt might never be able to joke about sex again. "Sorry. Anyway…let's try that idea."

"Sure." Shane grabbed one of the big crosspieces and held it steady. "Paint looks good in here. You did this room too?"

The ivory was the same as the guest room, the sort of neutral color that always enticed buyers, but the clean and fresh look did make the small room seem more spacious.

"Yup. I was working on the sunroom when you arrived with the baby." Brandt got the first few screws in without issue. Shane had been right—the extra pair of hands were a decided help.

"Sorry. We ruined all your plans." Sighing, Shane looked away even as his hands stayed steady.

"Nah. I'll get the painting done." His voice was light because two more crib pieces screwed together, and finally, a rectangle shape was achieved. Victory would be his.

"I can help. I'm probably not as handy as you, but I'm not opposed to work." Shane was way too appealing when he was firm and direct like this. There was an old-fashioned air to that trustworthy vibe he gave off that made him feel like some classic movie hero. "Tell me what you need."

Now that was a dangerous question. Because the more time they spent together, the more Brandt *needed* to know what made Shane tick, what could make all that careful sincerity unravel, what might drive them both wild. But that need was best given wide berth, like encountering a bear on a hiking trail. Back away slowly and try not to show he was rattled.

"I'll let you know," he said quickly.

"How did you get so handy anyway? You've got quite the toolbox."

This time Brandt stopped himself before a flirty retort could escape. *Be serious for once.* "I scraped the tools together over the last decade. Sales. Estate auctions. Trades from people needing work done. Started with a drill and screwdriver set my last year in foster care before I turned eighteen. I was in a group home. The couple that ran it were all about life skills and had us helping to rehab the old building that housed the facility."

"That sounds like it could be interesting." Shane's tone was deliberate, like he was trying to avoid passing judgment on Brandt's experiences, and that sort of care was appreciated, made Brandt keep talking.

"It wasn't bad. I was in worse situations at other times, that's for sure. I showed a knack for fixing things, I guess. So I got the drill as a birthday present that year." As far as memories went, it wasn't a terrible one, the big cake and the other kids in the group home gathered around, pile of homemade cards and the unexpected gift. "And then when I moved out, I was able to get some construction work here and there while I started getting my certifications for firefighting."

"You always knew you wanted to work in wildfire?"

"Nah. I wanted to be a regular firefighter. Same as other little kids who get obsessed with first responder jobs, I guess, but I never outgrew it."

"Bet you were a cute kid." Shane didn't look up from the piece he was steadying which was just as well as Brandt had no clue what to make of the compliment.

"I don't know about that. Anyway, then I found that the city wasn't really for me. Too loud. Too crowded. Moved to a smaller area, and one of the community college classes I took was about wildfire fighting. I got work that summer on a line crew down near Klammath Falls. Met some smoke jumpers while working a fire and that was it. I knew what I wanted to do."

"That's awesome. The first time I took the stage was like that. Scared out of my mind, but still right where I was meant to be. Never wanted to do anything else after that."

"Man, now I wish I'd heard you at that music fest near Grangeville." Actually, there were other things Brandt regretted more about that weekend, things best not explored right then. "Shelby said you're something on stage."

"Something." Shane laughed, that rattly one that made it seem like him enjoying this conversation was a surprise to them both. "I suppose she's right. I'm not the best showman, though, not compared to the big names. I struggle at doing small talk with the audience, but I'm working on that. However, when I start to sing..."

"The earth moves?" Brandt teased as he secured another board in place.

"Well, it does for me at least. Not sure about the audience. Performing's the best feeling in the whole world for me though."

"Best?" Brandt raised an eyebrow, same as he would with one of his buddies. "Better than sex? Because I love skydiving, and at its best, it beats out mediocre sex, but good sex...that's still the winner."

"For you maybe." Shane surprised him by not joking back, but instead going serious. "Not sure I'd know."

Brandt had to blink at that. Repeatedly. "You mean the not into women thing? Because last I heard straight sex didn't have the monopoly on amazing."

"I'll take your word for it. I don't exactly have the experience to compare." Shane fumbled the piece he was holding before he recovered, voice going firmer. "I'm not like Shelby. Or my dad, who never can keep it in his pants. I saw how they were, and that wasn't for me. I'm not into random hookups, and the road is hell on friendships, let alone anything more."

"You're a virgin?" No way. The guy was far too good-looking for that. And sure he was a little serious and grumpy, but some people dug that.

Shane's mouth twisted and his forehead wrinkled. "I guess you could call it that. At the risk of TMI, I've had some hot make-out sessions, but for one reason or another, it never went further. Usually because one of us was leaving town in a hurry."

"Wow. I can't imagine…" And that right there was a lie and not a particularly well delivered one. Because Brandt could picture in technicolor detail, a hot and heavy make-out session with this guy. What he couldn't imagine though was that Shane had never ventured beyond that.

Rolling his eyes, Shane shook his head. "Well. Of course *you* can't."

"Hey now. I have restraint. Sometimes." For example, there was that whole part of himself he seldom indulged. And he was ready to tell Shane that, admit that maybe Shane wasn't the only one lacking in some vital experiences. He secured the last support for the crib and took a step toward Shane. Dangerous. Potent. Like the last moment before exiting a plane with a parachute. Probably ill-advised, but he needed—

Waaaah. The baby cried right as he took that step, and Shane looked away in a hurry.

"I'll go get her. We can introduce her to the new crib." Shane's eagerness to get out of this conversation was more than clear, even if he was cute, wanting to show their work off. Still, Brandt couldn't help but feel like a moment had been lost. And foolish as it was, hell if he didn't hope another chance came along sooner rather than later.

Jewel hated her new room. Oh, she'd been adorable at first, lying on her back in the crib while Brandt danced the little soft toys they'd bought around her, trying to encourage her to reach and grab. And she'd been sweet, hanging out in her new swing while they managed to eat a quick dinner. But now it was three a.m. and she was angry. There had already been more wakeups than any night Shane had had her, and that was saying something.

"Come on, baby. Time for sleep." Shane jiggled her from side to side, throat rough from humming to her. He'd tried everything, including re-reading the baby book while pacing with her.

"Want me to take over?" Brandt appeared in the doorway to the room. And *damn*. He looked way too good sleepy. Even with sharing dinner, Shane had managed to avoid more deep talk and had also given Brandt and whatever this strange energy was between them an extra-wide berth. But apparently the universe wanted to tempt him even more because here Brandt was all shirtless, fuzzy chest and ripped muscles on full display.

He smelled good too, like he'd showered with that pine soap before bed. And Shane was somehow supposed to concentrate on the baby with him this close?

"You've got work tomorrow. I've got this."

"No, you don't." Brandt's voice was both sleepy and

matter-of-fact. Not nearly as cranky as Shane felt. "But I've got an idea. Hang tight."

Shane nodded like he had much choice in the matter. Brandt disappeared only to return a few minutes later carrying the rocking chair that had been in a corner of the sunroom.

"Babies are supposed to like this, right?" Brandt's grin was far too chipper for the hour, and he plopped down in the chair before Shane could thank him for the gesture. "Hand the diva over."

"I can—"

"I know you can. But you're dead on your feet. Let me."

"Okay." Shane couldn't keep fighting him. He passed over the fussy, squirmy baby who almost immediately quieted as Brandt settled her against his chest. Figured. Shane would give a happy sigh if he got to cuddle those warm muscles too. "Don't let her fool you. She'll quiet then howl as soon as she hits the crib."

"So we'll rock a spell." Brandt shrugged. The guy was undoubtedly oblivious to how he looked like something out of a diaper ad—gorgeous dad, sweet baby, perfect picture. A line of a song danced through Shane's head, as elusive as sleep.

"Go sleep," Brandt ordered, shifting Jewel so he could point at the doorway.

"Passed sleepy a couple of hours ago," Shane admitted, perching on the edge of the twin bed. Exhausted energy surged though him, the same jangly nerves that made it hard to sleep after a late show.

"What? You need a bedtime story or something?" Brandt's voice was light and warm and made Shane want to tease back.

"Sure. Tell me a story. Make it a good one, something I can use for a song."

"Worthy of a song?" Brandt shook his head. "Tall order. Let's see though. Country songs, those are all about achy breaky hearts and regrets right?"

"Something like that." Shane was enjoying this far, far too much, and he made himself more comfortable on the small bed, pulling his legs up and sitting back. "Guess a lot of my songs are bittersweet, moments that passed by, wondering about what could have been, dealing with what never was. But also legends, the sort of epic stories that simply need a song. I bet you've got a few tales like that."

"Hmm." Brandt made a thoughtful noise, like he was actually thinking about this. "Legends, huh? Me, I'm not song material, but I'm gonna tell you about my buddy Roger. He deserves a song."

"Okay." Shane's pulse sped up. Somehow he knew he was getting a story Brandt didn't often tell. Something special. And he wasn't sure what he'd done to earn Brandt's trust, but he'd take it.

"It was my rookie smoke-jumping season. I'd done a couple of seasons with line and engine crews, putting in my hours, and damn, I was proud to get that call. Headed to California in a beat to hell Toyota, barely enough for gas money and some food. No plan beyond that. Young and stupid."

"I get that. I've been there more than once, arriving in Nashville with little more than a prayer I wouldn't be living in my car." Shane stuffed a lumpy pillow behind his head. "That's why I turned a few good checks from selling some songs into that old RV. I needed to know I wouldn't be waking up with some cop's searchlight in my eyes, telling me to move along."

"Yeah, you get it. Southern California prices are like that too. I was prepared to spend the season in a tent if I had to, just to get the chance to jump. But first day of training, this freckle-faced kid comes up to me, says they're one dude short for making rent on an apartment near the air base." The chair creaked as Brandt rocked, slow and steady. "Terrible place, five of us squashed in there, but Roger, he'd done the math, knew we could afford food and stuff if we split it."

"So you said yes?"

"Not at first. Didn't have much to put up toward the deposit, but Roger was determined. That was just how he was. No way in hell was he getting cut from training either." Brandt gave a low rumble of a chuckle as the baby snuffled, then settled again. "They said seven pullups, he'd do double. And laugh. They said eighty percent on a quiz, he'd go for ninety-nine. Some people would grab a beer after training, but never Roger. Head down. He was gonna be the best damn rookie ever."

"Sounds like a serious guy." Shane could relate to that sort of focus. Maybe not on academics, but on his music, especially early on, that drive to be better than simply good.

"He was. But funny thing, so was I back then." Brandt's voice took on a far-off quality as he patted Jewel, still rocking. "Everyone else would go out, but we'd be there reviewing procedure manuals. Early morning run? We were first ones in line. Late night equipment inventory? Both our hands were in the air."

Shane had to shake his head. There was no question that Brandt was a hard worker, but seeing him as an eager beaver young person took a little more imagination. "Wow. I've got a hard time picturing you as that much of a go-getter."

"Yeah, well, I was. And somewhere along the way he became the best friend I ever had. Saved my neck more than once, but I did the same. All season long."

"Glad you had him." Was it possible to be jealous of someone he'd never meet? Brandt's use of the past tense was a major clue that this Roger was no longer around, but still Shane's jaw tightened.

"Me too. Looking back now, maybe I took him for granted. Never once told him…" Brandt trailed off as the baby squeaked.

"I bet he knew." Shane held back a yawn. This story was too fascinating to miss even if his eyes were still growing heavy.

"Maybe. He was the guy I most wanted to be." Brandt adjusted his hold on Jewel, who was almost but not quite asleep. "Even visited him out in Colorado that winter, where he was from. Met his mama and the girl he wanted to marry. I wanted his family, that was for sure."

"Yeah." Lord, how Shane knew that mood. Wanting a family that stayed put in one place, owned a home, didn't leave on a whim, parents who didn't fight, siblings who stayed out of trouble. "Been there."

"Anyway, when you write that song about him, you say how fearless he was. Never met a tree he wouldn't climb or weather he wouldn't jump in. Worked hard. Loved his family and his girl hard. Solid guy. You remind me of him, a little."

"Thanks." He didn't quite know what to make of that. This story was sad and tender, a tribute of sorts, and he was already holding his breath for the inevitable ending, even before Brandt looked down at the hardwood floor.

"We lost him that next August. Him and a few other good ones."

"What happened?" He didn't like making Brandt relive a painful memory, but the songwriter in him needed to know, to understand, to be able to make sense of this pain.

"He and his crew were behind a fireline, doing their damnedest to slow the spread before the winds worsened. He was hell with a chainsaw, man. You should have seen him…" Brandt exhaled, long and heavy. "Anyway, winds shifted quicker than anyone was prepared for. They did their damnedest to outrun it, him leading the way, but then they had no choice but to deploy their fire shelters. Wasn't enough."

"I'm sorry." The words were inadequate to the ache in his chest, the way his hands opened, wishing Brandt were close enough to touch. He knew loss, but not like that, not bone deep, the sort a person never came all the way back from.

Shrugging, Brandt stood with the baby. "Part of the job. Part of life. Maybe I wasn't quite grown until that day. But that was also the moment when I realized life was too short to not live it. Go out there. Have fun. Don't forget to play and enjoy it because the end might come before you know it. Don't put it off."

Brant punctuated his mantra by gently laying Jewel in her crib. She didn't cry, but Shane was perilously close to losing it himself. Tired. Emotional. This gut-wrenching story. A glimpse into Brandt he wasn't sure he wanted because now he had to see him as so much more than a partying sky cowboy good time guy. He wanted to ask about the emotions underscoring the story, if it had all been friendship and brotherhood or if there was something more there, at least on Brandt's side.

"Brandt…" He started to find his way to the questions he wanted to ask, pausing to yawn as Brandt came and crouched next to him, setting a blunt finger against Shane's mouth.

"Shush. Enough story time. You're already mostly asleep. You rest now. Diva's gonna wake up, and I'll probably be gone. Early start for my crew."

Stretching, Brandt pulled a cover from the end up the bed up and over Shane. Damn. The guy was going to get an hour or two of sleep at best, and here he was, taking care of the baby. And Shane.

"Sorry—"

"Don't be."

But Shane was. Sorry for Brandt, for his younger self, for the losses he'd had to endure. Sorry he'd never meet that Roger or the kid Brandt had been. His eyes fluttered shut as he tried again to hold emotion in.

And he had to be sleeping already because he could have sworn those were Brandt's lips ghosting over his temple. It was a sweet dream, thinking Brandt might care like that, thinking there could be something here. And he knew it had to stay a dream, couldn't be real for a whole host of reasons, but right then, he was going to snuggle into the pillow and pretend for a moment that he lived in a world where Brandt Wilder had just tucked him in.

Chapter Seven

"So how was your weekend?" Hartman, the jumper-in-charge on Brandt's crew, was all conversational as they walked toward the hangar after finishing the morning briefing. Poor guy had no idea exactly what a weekend Brandt had had.

"Uh…" He did a fast calculation, trying to decide what to reveal. He hadn't really thought through telling people, but he also wasn't one to lie. And Hartman was a good guy, younger but not brash, the sort who honestly did want to know as opposed the type of leader who only made small talk to fill silence. Might as well get it out there. "Apparently I have a kid now."

"No shit?" Hartman's head swiveled like one of those dashboard dolls. "Like one just turned up on your doorstep?"

"More or less." Brandt stretched, letting the crisp morning mountain air fill his lungs. Gorgeous clear blue skies, totally at odds with his jumbled thoughts. In the distance, the mountains loomed large, white tips and craggy silhouettes, unchanging, unlike Brandt's life.

"Damn. How old are you anyway if you've got a kid searching you out?" Hartman's words were light, the sort of ribbing all the guys gave each other. Nonetheless, they stung. Never had he felt every one of his thirty years more than sitting there in the lawyer's office trying to make a plan for the baby.

"Screw you. I'm not that old," he shot back, giving as good as he got before he softened his voice. "It's a baby. With an AWOL mom. Long story. But I'm gonna need to sort out insurance paperwork at some point I guess, if the paternity test results prove the kid's mine. Rich's wife is helping me with the legal stuff."

"God bless Cameron."

"Seriously." Brandt might still be smarting from her comment about smoke jumping and single parenthood being incompatible, but he couldn't deny that she'd also been a huge help. "She even had a list of what all I might need for the baby."

"Baby, huh?" Hartman shook his head, expression as incredulous as Brandt still felt. "Linc can probably help you with the paperwork situation. He's…discreet. Won't gossip about your new addition."

"Thanks." They were a couple of weeks into training, but he'd already picked up on Hartman and Lincoln Reid, one of the instructors, being a couple. Intra-crew hook-ups happened on the down low occasionally, but longer-term relationships like what they had going were rarer. The two were nothing other than professional, and Brandt figured if he had to tell someone, he could do a lot worse.

"Cameron did some wills for us." Hartman gave him a serious stare. "I know no one ever likes to think about shit like that, but if you've got a kid now, have her do one for you too. Update your life insurance as well."

Brandt knew better than most how fast life could change, and there it was again, that same uncomfortable feeling as when Cameron had talked about the realities of the smoke jumping life. He'd make this work. He would.

"Good tip." Things felt too heavy now, like trying to haul an extra pack with their gear. He didn't much like that, so he made himself laugh. "You leaving everything to the dogs?"

Luckily for him, Hartman seemed to pick up on his need for lightness. "Don't be ridiculous. We're leaving it to a human. Who will then take care of the pack."

"Huh." Who would Brandt leave Jewel to? Shane? Could he count on him that way? He was there for the lawyer and late nights, but Brandt was under no illusions of this being permanent. His head swam as he went through his vast and varied friend network. Who could he count on when the chips were down? Not liking how few names he came up with, his gut churned.

"You okay to jump?" Hartman grabbed his sleeve as they reached the hangar. "It's understandable if your head isn't in the game, but you gotta tell me now, so I clear you staying back with management. We're taking the rookies up with us and can't afford distractions."

Brandt shook his head, trying to clear it. No way did he want to miss some airtime. "Nah. I'm good to go."

"Excellent. Let's do this thing." Hartman's strides took on new purpose before he stopped and pivoted back to Brandt. "Oh, and Wilder?"

"Yeah?"

"I've got a ton of nieces and nephews. You let me know if you need anything. I can probably track down hand-me-downs or recs for things like sitters and doctors."

"Will do. I've got childcare right now. The baby's uncle is staying to help." That niggle of *how long* was back, a pesky branch scratching against the window of his brain.

"That's good." Nodding, Hartman picked up speed again. Blessedly, he didn't inquire further into Brandt's situation or Shane's presence, not that Brandt had a lot more insight on either. "Okay, let's find those rookies."

The rookies were still sweaty from an early morning run, and most were eager to get their first jump reps in. The one assigned to Brandt was almost as tall as him with short, punk hair, but it was her shaking hands Brandt was more concerned with.

"So, I'm nervous," she announced defiantly, like Brandt was waiting for an excuse to kick her off the jump list.

"Really? Never would have guessed."

"Don't play dumb." Her voice was more irritated than uneasy now. "I know everyone's waiting to see if I wash out."

"Nah." Brandt wasn't here to be a self-esteem coach, but he also didn't want to bring her down further.

"Jimenez let on that there's a betting pool on rookie odds."

Busted. He shrugged though, not going to let her bad mood ruffle him, not when the weather was so good and their turn to jump coming soon.

"Every year there's something like that. But I know stubborn when I see it. You've got that on your side."

He did know stubborn. And all day he'd been trying to outrun that late night story time with Shane, the rawness of his emotions by the time he'd finished. He hadn't talked about Roger in years. Something about Shane, his solidness, his dogged determination, unearthed memories he'd buried a decade ago.

And Odell here, she pulled loose other Roger memories, like how he'd never once let fear win. Brandt had to admire the way she clenched her jaw and set her shoulders. "I'm not giving up."

"That's the attitude." He could see the plane off in the distance. Wouldn't be long now until they were in the air themselves. "Here's our ride."

They fetched their gear, got prepped for the tandem jump, and were in the air in short order. Odell was as nervous as predicted, but she settled in the presence of Hartman. Brandt tried to focus on the here and now, but he kept getting hit with memories of that jump with Shane. Funny how he'd had hundreds of jumps, maybe even up to four digits now, and that one moment stood out so vividly. He needed to stop obsessing over Shane and absolutely needed to stop doing risky things like tucking him in at night. A physical pull was one thing, but he couldn't go getting attached. He knew better.

So he firmed his own spine, pushed Shane out of his head and tried to make the jump a success for Odell, enjoying her *whoop* of success as they landed.

Hours later, he was still buzzing from the jump, but also weirdly restless. Eager to get home in a way that wasn't his normal. He might not be as hard-charging as some, but he was still dedicated to the job in a way that nothing else in his life came close to. He pulled long hours and he loved it, so this new side to himself, the part that was eager to see Shane and the baby, was more than a little disconcerting.

As he let himself back into the house, he caught a few chords of guitar music and followed the sound to the great room, where Shane sat on one of the dining chairs in front of the baby swing they'd bought Jewel. She was awake but calm, kicked back as the thing gently swayed. The dining table was covered with sheets of paper with blocky handwriting and a couple of notebooks.

"What's this?" he asked, voice more unsure than he liked, mainly because he had no fucking clue how to greet Shane. Kissing him senseless wasn't the answer, even if Brandt's body wanted to argue otherwise.

"Live music for happy hour." Shane strummed another few chords, smiling at the baby in a way that showed a glimpse of what he must be like on stage, looser than normal and infinitely appealing. "I think she likes it."

"Cute." And it was. So cute it made Brandt's chest hurt with the sweetness of it all.

"Besides, I believe I promised you a song." Shane's lopsided grin truly was going to be the death of Brandt, taking that unexpected sweetness and amping it up, like flipping on stadium lights. And there Shane was, not only remembering their conversation from the night before but following through on it. Dependable as the sun. Fuck. Brandt was doomed.

Surrendering to his fate, he plopped down in one of the other chairs. "You're really gonna write one?"

"That is what I do." Shane raised an eyebrow, blue eyes gleaming in the early evening light. "I'm a songwriter. Tell me a good enough story and I'll find the song."

Their eyes met, and the memory of the night before danced between them. An acknowledgment maybe of the trust Brandt had shown, but also a confirmation that Roger mattered. Shane had heard, truly *listened*, and he'd understood on a level that not many could.

Brandt's throat went tight. "Thanks. I...that means something. You trying."

"Told you I would." That solidness again. The sense that this was someone Brandt could count on, maybe even trust, when he didn't count on anyone other than himself.

"Yeah." Brandt's voice came out far too husky, even as he tried to remind himself all the ways that he should not, could not rely on this man. "Gonna show me what you've got?"

"Not yet. It's too new." Shane quickly flipped over two of the sheets of paper, pink flush staining his neck and cheeks.

"I feel that." And he did. Because this whole thing was new. Having a kid. Having someone around he could depend on. This attraction. And honestly the scariness of instant parenthood was nothing compared to whatever this thing with Shane was, but hell if he wasn't going to stick around and try to earn that song.

Chapter Eight

"Asleep at last. And clean." Shane stuck his head into the sunroom at the back of the cabin.

"Bet the tub time tuckered her out." Brandt didn't look up from his painting work. He had music on softly, something punk with a good bass. Brandt's strokes of white paint kept time with the singer's baritone, showing more internal rhythm than Shane would have given him credit for.

"Tub is being generous," Shane couldn't help but tease. "That, my friend, was a bucket."

"But it worked, right?" Brandt gave a pragmatic shrug. They'd reached a point where cleaning the baby with a damp cloth wasn't quite enough, but they lacked the infant bathtub recommended by the baby book. Undaunted, Brandt had produced a shallow plastic basin, which they'd put across the kitchen sink, both of them testing and retesting the water before lowering Jewel in. Shane had held, Brandt had scrubbed, and somehow both of them had ended up wearing more bathwater than Jewel. Brant had ended up the wettest, so he'd headed for a dry shirt while Shane had attempted bedtime. And now here they both were, asleep baby, and Shane having no clue what to do with his restless energy.

"Need a hand with the painting?" Shane tried not to sound too eager because Brandt seemed to be enjoying his solitary painting work. Shane probably could have left him to it, but for once, it was early enough that he wasn't quite ready for sleep himself. He'd gone in search of Brandt for reasons probably best not examined right then. Sure, they'd had a few days of successfully coexisting, but it wasn't like they were TV watching buddies or anything like that.

Frowning, Brandt studied him carefully, and Shane half expected to be shooed away. Instead, Brandt finally shrugged and handed him a roller. "I'm assuming you know how this works?"

"Uh. Not so much. My folks were never in one place enough to paint."

"Fair enough. It's not that hard." Brandt demonstrated rolling off the excess paint on the tray and finished up his tips with, "Steady, even strokes. That's the trick."

Only Brandt could make the word *strokes* sound so dirty. Heat crept over Shane's skin, prickles of awareness of how close Brandt was standing. He smelled good, too. Like soap and sweat, like a guy who'd put in his hours on the job and then found the energy for more work now. Shane wanted to lick the strong cords of his neck, see if he tasted salty.

Trouble. He'd taste like trouble, and Shane damn well knew it. And still he wanted, to the point that he had to turn away, focus on the half-painted wall.

"What was the longest you were ever in one place?" Brandt asked as they worked. "None of my business, I know. But sometimes I forget that I wasn't the only kid who never got to settle at one school."

Shane's chest pinched, some soft place again feeling

for Brandt's rocky childhood. At least he'd had his parents and Shelby. His past wasn't the best, but it was better than nothing. "Think we made it two school years in Boise once." Those had been better years than most, but he'd never fully relaxed, even then, knowing the next move was coming. "My dad was a roadie for a rock group you've probably heard of when my folks met. Neither had relatives they were close to, so it's not like we were ever going to be a perfect Christmas card of a family."

He smeared the paint a little too roughly on that unhappy thought, so he had to focus on evening it out and almost missed Brandt stepping closer as he deftly helped Shane avoid a nasty drip.

"I feel that lack of extended family. Part of why I changed my last name was because I figured if none of them wanted to be involved in the foster case, I didn't need that link to them. Screw them."

Letting his roller drop, he whirled toward Brandt. "You changed your name?"

"Yup." Brandt didn't even look up from his work, smoothing the paint evenly like a name change was no more of a deal than swapping pairs of jeans. "I wanted something Western but not super cowboy. Original last name was plain as dirt. And people my first season on the line crew kept calling me the wild one, so when I got enough cash together for a name change, I made it official. Made sense to my nineteen-year-old brain."

"I can see that." God knew Shane had had his own share of iffy logic at nineteen. And Wilder did suit Brandt, on some core level, both declaration and warning that he lived harder than most. "But it's more than a little funny that Shelby got so smitten with your name, decided to give it to the baby."

Brandt gave a harsh laugh. "Ironic that. I never intended to pass it on, that's for damn sure. So your folks never did pick a place and stick there?"

Shane didn't miss Brandt's readiness to switch the conversation topic back away from himself, but strangely, he was enjoying talking way more than usual. He didn't share most of this stuff, but Brandt was the rare type to understand Shane's unconventional upbringing, empathize without falling into pity like so many did.

"Hell no. My parents tried settling down when they had Shelby, but itchy feet kept getting the better of them both. Neither of them could keep a regular job more than a couple of months. Dad would chase get-rich-quick schemes with buddies all fall and winter, then head out on the road in the summer with whatever group would have him."

"Guess that's how you got the music bug?" Brandt was too close again as he refreshed the paint in the rolling pan. Too near. Too warm, his mere presence raising the temperature in the room a good ten degrees.

Shane tried to turn his attention to the painting and memories of those first few times he'd held a guitar, but it was hard with every sense tuned to Brandt. "I don't remember ever not wanting to make music. There were always musicians and instruments around. We never had enough for formal lessons like piano, but I picked up enough early on as far as reading music. Guess encouraging me was one of the better things they did."

"That's more than something." Brandt nodded sharply, and Shane could see the flash of a kid who maybe hadn't heard enough kind words. "Bet they're proud of you now."

"Ha. I wish. I mean maybe. Dad always did idealize

the music scene life. I know it grates on him that a bad back caught up with him and he lost out on roadie work."

"But he's still alive?" There was a certain softness to Brandt's tone that Shane didn't miss. He might act all tough, but some wounds went soul deep.

"Yeah. They're both still alive. And I'm not discounting that they do love us. But he's still miffed that I don't want him managing my career, so we don't talk much." This time Shane managed to keep the roller under control as he summarized some of the more contentious years of his life.

"Sounds like a smart call on your part. Keep things professional." Brandt's voice was easy as he did some touch-up work with a brush. Unlike most people, he seemed content to accept Shane's reasons for not wanting to work with his dad. And that made Shane's shoulders ease.

"That's one way to look at it. Not his," Shane admitted. God, there had been enough arguments between them before he'd finally struck out on his own. But something deep inside him needed to be the one in control of his destiny. Singing his own songs. Making his own choices. Not tied to his dad's highly unpredictable reliability and stuck chasing a rock-and-roll dream that wasn't his. "Last I heard, Dad was shacked up with some too-young waitress and working at a night club in Cheyenne. He and Mom finally split for good after a number of dramatic separations when I was in high school. Anyway, to your original question, I suppose the west is as much home as anywhere else for me."

"I hear that. Guess you could call this region home for me too. Most of my growing up was California, ended up going north to Oregon on my own. Then it's been all over the west, chasing the next fire. Even did a summer in Alaska a few years back."

"That sounds fun. Bellingham's about as far north as I've been. That was a good gig."

"I bet." Brandt rolled his shoulders.

They were both about as ill-equipped for this sudden caretaking role as two people could be. But there was also a deeper sense of connection here, one Shane didn't often get. It was rare, finding someone who understood how instability burrowed under a kid's skin, left scars, and made it hard to relate to people who'd had that picket-fence life.

And that understanding made his stomach wobbly and his hands way shakier on the paint roller than he'd like. Maybe they needed to be done with the personal truth telling.

"I'm going to need to go into town tomorrow. The baby's getting low on formula." Yeah, that was it. Keep to the practical.

"Finding parking for your rig is going to be a challenge. I'm going into work later tomorrow because of a meeting with Cameron. If you take me out to the base, you can have my car to run errands."

The practical became markedly less comfortable with the news of another lawyer meeting. "Cameron needed you to come in?"

"Yeah. Sorry. Should have said that earlier. She called while you were putting Jewel down. She's expecting the paternity test results first thing in the morning, so she wants to discuss next steps depending on what it shows."

"Oh. Wow. That was fast."

"Yep. I paid a pretty penny to get it expedited, but probably better to know sooner."

"True." Shane's voice was soft and faint. He had no clue what he was hoping for anymore. All he knew was that those first few days completely on his own with Jewel had sucked and he didn't want to return to them. Having someone to share the burden with was good, even if Brandt was possibly less suited for parenthood than Shane's own parents. But he wasn't doing half bad as a pinch hitter, and his efforts sure beat Shane alone with no backup.

"Hey." Brandt set his brush back on the paint tray before coming to stand next to Shane. "I meant what I said. I'm not kicking you out. Even if I'm not the dad, I want you to stay until you've got a solid plan."

"Thanks." Shane had to swallow hard. Brandt's eyes were too serious right then. He truly was a better guy than he had to be. Maybe a better guy than Shane would be if the situation were reversed. "I appreciate it."

"No problem," Brandt said, even though it totally was, opening his house to a baby and her sleep-deprived uncle. "And thanks for the help in here."

"Put me to work. I like to earn my keep." Shane meant the words to come out lightly, but as usual, he underestimated his own solemnness, and the words came out closer to a plea. *Please. Find a use for me. Please. Need me.*

"Understood." Brandt nodded, then broke into a grin. "You might want to find some crap clothes though. You're almost wearing more paint than the wall."

"I am?" It said something that Shane hadn't even noticed how much of the room they'd finished or how messy his hands and arms had become.

"Yeah. You've got a big drip right here." Brandt reached out, wiping something on Shane's cheek. Now he truly was too close, the energy from that unexpected connection transforming into something warm and crackly. And Brandt must have been oblivious because he didn't yank his hand away, instead lingering, stroking his fingers down Shane's jaw.

He needed to step away, needed to break this spell, but instead he put down roots, heels as good as stapled to the hardwood, riveted to this moment. And he wasn't totally naive. He knew desire, knew how its notes dragged out like the sultry song playing on the radio, and he knew how someone's face shifted right before they kissed another person. He saw the mistake coming, but hell if he was going to dodge Brandt's lips.

Chapter Nine

Kissing Shane would be stupid. Not to mention dangerous. And for a guy like Brandt who regularly hurled himself out of airplanes, that was saying something. But for all Brandt loved to chase adrenaline, he wasn't generally reckless or out of control. Sure, he took risks, but almost all were calculated, situations he fully intended to triumph over.

This was different. He might get pushed on his ass. He'd probably regret it. He had absolutely no illusions of this being a good idea. But he couldn't not kiss Shane. The skin along his jaw was rough under Brandt's thumb, each bristle a fresh spark of electricity. He leaned in slow, half expecting Shane to shove him away, end this idiocy before it even started.

Instead, Shane exhaled, a soft huff, like he too had done the math and decided to stay right where he was, losing odds and all. His lips were achingly soft, such a delicious contrast to his stubble that Brandt had to groan at the first glancing contact. Ordinarily, he'd hold something back, keep the first kiss light and teasing. Easy enough to brush off if it were underwhelming or not as welcomed as he'd thought. With Shane, however, there was no holding back, only tumbling straight into a desperate, all-in devouring.

And there wasn't even a whiff of underwhelming. No, every single thing about Shane was *over*whelming. Intense, just like his eyes. He was so serious a lot of the time, and he kissed with the same gravity, like there was nothing on earth more important than this kiss. He kissed like not even a tornado could tear them apart, paint-streaked hands coming to rest on Brandt's shoulders, strong grip. Steady in a moment when Brandt felt on the verge of flying apart. He might be the one who'd heedlessly barreled into the kiss, but Shane was its conductor, the one who took all Brandt's frantic energy and transformed it into something more refined, more tender.

Shane let Brandt plunder his mouth, but his own explorations were much gentler and more deliberate, like he was trying to show Brandt a different way. And it worked, settling Brandt down, making him more aware of each sensation. The rasp of Shane's tongue against his. The surprising fullness of his lower lip. The warmth of his mouth. The coolness of the night air coming in the window. The strength in his hold on Brandt. The solidness of his body.

He yanked Brandt closer, close enough that Brandt could tell that he was as turned-on as Brandt was. Hell, he wasn't sure he'd ever been this hard in his life. He both needed them to find a horizontal surface pronto and wanted this right here to never end. He could kiss Shane for days and still have kissing left to do. Little discoveries he wanted to make like—

Waaah. The sunroom door was wide open, and the baby's cry echoed off the empty walls. Shane sprang apart from him like they'd been caught casing a bank. No way was Brandt waiting around to see the guilt in his eyes or hear all the reasons why they couldn't do that again.

"My turn to get her," he said gruffly on his way out of the room. "You can leave the rollers here. I'll clean them after. And there's soap that will remove the paint in the hall bath."

But naturally, Shane couldn't leave it at that, and he appeared with a freshly scrubbed hands and a new bottle while Brandt was still finishing changing the diva. He was still slow at this part, the wrestling her in and out of tiny garments. Still distracted by that kiss, he'd grabbed the bear sleeper Shane had picked out and accidentally put her legs in the arms. However, he had that mistake sorted out and she was down to only a couple of hiccups and unhappy noises when Shane came into the room.

"Oh, I see how it is. The work is done, so now you can be Mr. Popular with the refreshments." Forcing a laugh, he quickly settled in the chair before Shane could claim it. Brandt would make jokes from here to eternity if it meant avoiding being the one making a hasty retreat with his tail between his legs.

"Nah. She likes you better anyway." Shane swept his gaze over Brandt as he handed over the bottle. Brandt had pulled off his paint splattered T-shirt before picking up the baby, and he didn't miss the quickly shuttered appreciation in Shane's eyes.

"How do you figure? You're better with the tiny snaps and stuff on her outfits." Brandt settled her against the crook of his arm, getting the right angle for the bottle. Lately she did this adorable thing where she'd rest her little hands on the bottle. Made him smile even as he tried to will this conversation to its inevitable conclusion. "And she's with you all day."

"Exactly. You're the exciting one." Shane shook his head like he couldn't quite believe Brandt was playing things this casual. He'd probably underestimated Brandt's desire to outrun anything approaching an uncomfortable talk. And the last week had been too damn full of them to start with. Last thing he wanted was to dissect that kiss, turn the memory from scorching hot to charred earth.

"I do aim to bring the good time." More of that forced lightness.

However, this time Shane groaned instead playing along. "Are we seriously not going to talk about what happened?"

"Do you want a repeat?" Brandt looked him up and down, as purposeful as one could get from a rocking chair while trying to feed a baby who was sucking back formula like a small wolverine. Still, he knew what he wanted. And more importantly, what Shane so clearly did not.

"Hell no. That would be a terrible—"

"—idea. Yeah, yeah I got that message." A muscle in Brandt's jaw twitched. It stung, the way Shane had recoiled. "If we're not knocking boots later, there's nothing to talk about. We were both tired. It was a lapse. Won't happen again. End of story."

"Yeah. Can't do it again." Shane made a pained noise as he paced away from Brandt. Figured. It had been months since Brandt had been laid, and far, far longer since he'd made out with another guy. Shane might not be the first, but it wasn't like Brandt made a habit out of this either, no matter what Shane thought.

"Yep. Agreed." Brandt wasn't one to beg. Ever. And Shane had a point here as well. The baby had to come first. Brandt couldn't go mucking up their childcare partnership just because his dick was more than a little lonely. It, like the rest of him, could just deal. "See you in the morning."

"Night." Shane stalked away, leaving Brandt hoping like heck he didn't leave in the night. Or in the morning after the lawyer meeting. Fuck. The paternity test. He'd let it slip out of his mind for a while, but now it was back again, churning dread. And he didn't even know which outcome he feared more at this point. The baby was warm and soft in his arms, little snuffling sounds as she fell back asleep. What if this was her last night here?

Unsettled, he rocked her long after she slept, still not sure he recognized this version of himself, the one that wanted Jewel and Shane to stick around a little longer.

Brandt had called it. The morning was as awkward as he'd predicted. Shane had dealt with the middle of the night wakeup on his own and was bleary eyed as Brandt stepped around him to get his coffee. The appointment was at eight, but the early summer sun had long been up. Which Brandt knew because he'd been up, too. Forget the rare chance to sleep in. His brain had churned all night with thoughts of the paternity test results and that kiss. Not to mention the way the two things intersected. He wasn't sure he'd blame Shane if he chose to head out rather than stay on.

"You still want the car after the lawyer?" he asked before taking a sip of coffee, bracing himself for both the bitterness and Shane's possible rejection of the offer.

"If it's not too much trouble." Shane set his own cup in the sink, then walked over to where the baby was lying in her swing. "Better to have too much formula than to run out in the middle of the night."

"Word. Get two of those canisters." Brandt went in search of his boots by the door while Shane scooped up the baby and moved her to her car seat.

"Will do. You'll need to tell me what time to pick you up." Shane's voice was still stilted, weirdly formal, and he was giving Brandt enough physical space to park a 747 in.

"Nah. Never know exactly when we'll finish up." Having Shane pick him up felt almost too domestic. The car sharing was only practical, but someone waiting on him…that was maybe too weird in a week of strange occurrences. "I'll snag a ride with Hartman or another jumper who lives outside of town."

"Okay." Still hanging far back, Shane grabbed the baby's bags. "I packed the bottles and the diaper bag already."

"Thanks. She looks cute." He followed Shane's lead and gave him far more room than needed as they exited the house. The little diva did look extra adorable in one of the playful sleepers they'd picked out for her, and for once, she was awake and happy.

"You were right." Shane snapped the car seat into its holder in the back of Shane's SUV. "She's an excellent dragon."

"Yup." But was she *his* dragon? His kid? That truly was the question, and thinking on it kept Brandt quiet the whole way to the lawyer's office. They had to park down the street, and Brandt grabbed the baby in her car seat before Shane could try again to get the bags and the baby both.

"You want me to wait out here with her?" Shane asked as they entered the law firm offices.

"Nah. This affects you almost as much as me." He

waved Shane ahead of him as Cameron came out to greet them and lead them back to her office.

"Morning!" She gave them a bright smile before picking up her tablet. "Have you checked your email yet or you want me to be the one to click?"

Brandt had filled out the paperwork with the paternity testing lab so that both he and Cameron got notified of the results. And he supposed he could have logged on first thing that morning, put an end to all the suspense, but part of him had held back.

"You do it." He sat forward in his chair, hands on his knees. A shudder raced through him before he could pull it under control. The air had that certain stillness to it that big moments always brought. His life was about to change forever, either way. His stomach churned and he had to study the carpet, not look at either Shane on the couch or Cameron at her desk.

"The result was definitive that you are not excluded as the father." Cameron looked up from the tablet as Brandt struggled to make sense of what she'd said.

"What does that mean?" His heart hammered. This was always much more dramatic on those reality TV legal shows.

"Scientifically speaking, that means that the probability of paternity is 99.99% or higher."

"Ah." He made a noise of understanding even as his head buzzed like he'd taken a hard landing parachuting. *Paternity.* That meant father. Dad. He was a dad. And he'd kind of known, but that was different than *knowing* like this. Ninety-nine percent or whatever certainty.

"And legally, that means that the court will likely consider you the father and not allow attempts to change the birth certificate to say otherwise. If state agencies get involved at some point, they too are likely to see the result as definitive of paternity."

"Wow." He worked his jaw, up and down, side to side. *The father. Him.*

"Do you want a moment?" Cameron tilted her head, eyes full of concern. Over at the couch, Shane's expression was much harder to read, eyes shuttered, shoulders tense.

"I'm good. I'm just...wow. Wow." The earlier stillness was gone, replaced by a wave of adrenaline that left him sweating and feeling both like he could run a half marathon and he needed a nap.

"I know. It's big news." Cameron rolled her chair closer so she could pat his hand. "Now, knowing that, do you want to move on a custody order?"

She was right to get back to business, but the abrupt shift was still enough to make him blink a couple of times. "How necessary is that?"

"Given the circumstances here, I'm going to say very. You want to protect your rights in case the mom comes back and wants to assume sole custody. Neither of you has heard from her?" She glanced at Shane.

"I had a cryptic message from Macy that she's with her in Canada, but no contact from her directly." Shane rolled his shoulders like he was trying to shrug off the weight of his sister's actions. Brandt might not have siblings, but it had to sting, her not replying to Shane's messages. "For what it's worth, I'm not a lawyer, but I'm with Cameron here. There's no telling what Shelby will do. Having something in writing is probably only smart."

"Yeah," Brandt agreed even if he didn't want to. It might be the necessary choice, but he hated the idea of the courts involved at all, hated the thought of them all up in his business.

"Okay, I'll get started on that paperwork then." Cameron clicked around on her tablet as the remainder of the meeting was all logistics—getting proof that he'd added the baby to his insurance at work, arranging for other documents that he'd need, and discussing further steps. The details were almost more than Brandt's overloaded brain could hold.

"You gonna be okay to work?" Shane asked as they left the office, Brandt with Jewel in her seat and Shane with the bags again.

"Of course." Brandt sped up once they reached the sidewalk, like adding more purpose to his strides could show he had a handle on things.

"That was a lot—"

"I'm fine." Brandt pulled up short and spun to face Shane. "Honestly, it wasn't that big a surprise."

"Yeah. Still though, this is a big deal." Shane moved his hand like he might be about to pat Brandt, but then returned it to his side.

"No kidding." Damn. Brandt was being an ass simply to cover how rattled he was. He shifted the baby to his other hand and took a big breath. "Sorry. I'm…"

"Processing. I get it. And I know things are weird between us right now, but I'm not dumping Jewel on you and running."

"Appreciated." Then because that sounded a bit short, he dropped his voice. "I…need the help."

And he did. No way could he do this on his own. Swallowing his pride was tough, but he had to admit he needed Shane. He was damn fortunate that Shane was such a stand-up guy and not rushing to get back on the road.

"I'm gonna do my best." Shane's tone was solemn, and Brandt didn't trust many promises, but he believed Shane that he wasn't about to bolt. Shane looked away, like he was uncertain about where they went from there, but then he pointed at the window of the little coffee shop they'd stopped in front of. "Hey, what's that?"

A flier advertising an open mike night Friday hung near the door inviting local acoustic musicians to sign up for a slot.

"I think the coffeehouse does it every so often." Brandt seldom made it to Painter's Ridge's small downtown, but the place had good muffins. "You should go tomorrow, get out. Assuming there's no callout, I should be back in time and can watch the diva while you go."

"You sure?" Shane's eagerness was more than a little cute, like Brandt confronted with a chance for some unexpected airtime. He kept glancing at the flier, like it might evaporate before he got a chance to sing.

"At least one of us should get a Friday night. Go on, go put your name down. I'll hold the bags." He held out his free hand. Shane transferred the bags, then hurried into the place. He was back a few minutes later with two steaming cups.

"Okay. I got signed up. Figured I owed them a purchase, so I got you a sweet, black Americano. That close enough to your usual?"

"Yep." Brandt's chest was strangely tight as they made their way to the car. He wasn't used to others thinking of him, that was for sure. Wasn't sure he liked it. Or rather, he might like it too much. Frowning, he tossed

Shane his keys. "Here, you drive, so you can see how to get back to town."

"Sounds good." Shane waited while Brandt clicked the car seat into the holder. This working together thing was like the coffee, almost too good, too easy to get used to. But it was nice to be settling back into companionableness after the morning's initial awkwardness.

"You know, things don't have to be weird," he said as he slid into the passenger seat.

Shane said nothing aloud, but his pointed look could have written a term paper on all the ways that Brandt was wrong.

"We made it work just now," he pointed out, as he stretched. Speaking of weird, it was bizarre to be on this side of his car. "We'll be like roommates."

"You make a habit of playing tonsil hockey with roommates?" Shane's voice was dry as the local lava rock in August.

"No. I don't." Too bad Shane had already backed out of the parking space because Brandt was damn tempted to kiss that judgmental tone away. Hell, he hadn't even been attracted to a roommate since… Yeah. Not letting his brain hit rewind back to those memories again. But the point remained that he'd shacked up with plenty of buddies and none tempted him like Shane. "And I'm not saying I wouldn't go there again with you if you wanted, but I need reliable help with the kid more than I need a hookup partner."

Shane snorted at that. "You might want to check your condom stash before you put yourself back on the hookup market. Just saying."

"Jesus. Don't remind me." Brandt had to groan. But

Shane's joke was also good because it cut the tension. They'd make this work. He'd see to it.

Roommates. It wasn't the worst idea, even if his body was clamoring for him to kiss Shane senseless again the moment he got the chance.

Chapter Ten

"You sure you're going to be okay?" Shane snapped his guitar case closed, but he didn't move toward the door.

"Me. A tiny baby. A couple of hours. How much trouble do you figure we can get into? Think we could make it to the casino at Warm Springs?" Brandt grinned at him. He'd taken a fast shower when he'd come in from work, and his shaggy hair was still damp. Shane wanted to run his fingers through it, get all the tangles out, feel the silky softness against his hand.

"Baby might be better than either of us at blackjack." Shane tried to joke back, but he ended up pacing over to where Jewel was currently chilling in her swing, the one place they could count on her being happy for longer than three minutes. "I feel bad leaving her because she was fussy all day then napped way longer than usual."

"Shane." Brandt came closer than he'd been in days. Too close. He set his strong hands on Shane's shoulders, but instead of yanking him into a kiss like Shane's tortured libido wanted, he steered Shane in the direction of the door. "A week plus of baby duty has made you loopy. We'll be fine. You go have fun. Wait. Is that bad luck? Break a leg."

Shane couldn't help but smile. "Thanks. I think break

a leg is more for theater, but I'll take the luck. And okay,
I'm going. Thanks for letting me borrow your car again."

"No problem. You don't want to park your rig downtown on a Friday night. And text if you're gonna break
curfew, Junior." Brandt's laugh was deep, rich, and oh
so welcome after the past few days.

Roommates. Shane shook his head on his way to the
SUV. The dude seriously thought he could kiss Shane
like he had, like the stars might tumble to the ground
around them unnoticed, and then declare them capable
of platonic coexisting? No way. Shane wasn't buying
it, not when that kiss haunted his every quiet moment.
Feeding the baby. Doing dishes. Showering. Breathing.
No matter what he was doing, he could still taste Brandt,
still feel how solid his shoulders were, still hear his gasps
and groans.

Damn it. Move on. Outside, traffic picked up as he
approached the more populated parts of Painter's Ridge,
but inside, his head was still a mess. It was just a kiss.
He'd had others. *But none like that,* his brain taunted.
And of course, it had to toss in the memory of Brandt
saying he'd go there again if Shane wanted. Fuck. He
wanted. Lord, did he want.

After he found a parking spot, it was an easy walk to
the coffee shop. It was more crowded than it had been the
day before, but still a relatively small crowd that spilled
out the back of the place to a modest patio with a small
stage in the corner. The night was perfect for relaxing
outdoors, clear and cool mountain air but not cold, especially with the sun not quite set. It was mainly older couples, but a few families and younger friend groups too.
The way the late-teen kids kept jostling each other said

that they were there to watch a friend take a turn at the microphone. Remembering those days made him smile.

Not that he'd had the friend group, but he'd certainly had the days when any audience, any gig was a huge milestone and when the pressure to make it wasn't a thing. Felt nice, being back in that position, no expectation for the night other than to play a song or two. It was too late for coffee, but he ordered an Italian soda to give the place a little business.

"You playing tonight?" The barista was younger than him with hipster glasses and a pierced nose. He was cute, but Shane's body apparently had a one-track mind lately that compared everyone to Brandt and found them lacking.

"Yep. Got a slot in about thirty minutes. Figured I'd check out some of the other music first."

"You look familiar." The barista cocked his head. "Did you play the Brownsville country festival last summer? One of the side stages maybe?"

"That I did. So early in the day, I wasn't sure much of anyone noticed." He laughed. Being recognized was still rare and always a little odd.

"Kinda cool, you deciding to play for us."

"Kinda cool, you having a stage." Shane gave him a smile as he collected his drink and found a table. Another time, another city, and he might continue to chat up the kid, but his fixation on Brandt had him decidedly off his flirting game. The coffeehouse hadn't had as many takers for their open mic night as some places, so they were doling out ten minute or two song slots that night. He waited through a middle-age dude with a banjo and then a painfully young girl with first-timer nerves and a paper-thin voice.

"You did real good," Shane said to her as she passed his table. She blushed all the way up to her pale hairline and hurried back to her parents, who were in matching shirts and had that sort of unconditional proud and wholesome vibe that Shane had little familiarity with. Would Jewel grow up that loved? That supported? He hoped like heck she did.

The baby was still on his mind when his name was called. Figuring the crowd might lean a little more folk than country, he'd decided to open with a cover, a favorite oldie that straddled the genre line. It was one he'd performed hundreds of times, but before, the girl in the song had always stayed vague. But as he sang, he kept thinking about Jewel, all those hopes he had for her and that tightness in his chest every time he thought about leaving.

Another layer of emotion that hadn't been there a week ago, and it gave him something new to draw on as he went into his other song, one of his that he'd written over the winter in Nashville. He loved the familiar covers, but there was no thrill quite like doing his own material. And he could tell by the applause and his own racing pulse that he'd nailed it. Maybe this whole baby-watching thing agreed with him.

"Hey, man. Great set." A guy around Shane's age greeted him as made his way back to his table and his guitar case. The guy had a ponytail and vaguely familiar eyes. "My brother told me the place had a real one tonight. We saw you in Brownsville. You've got something."

Ah. The flirty barista's older brother. That made sense. Kinda cute, the kid being excited enough to tell his sibling.

"Thanks. Appreciate it." Shane let the guy give him a handshake after he stowed the guitar.

Uninvited, he took the other seat at Shane's table. On the stage, a young duo with guitars was murdering a perfectly good seventies ballad. "You in town for a while or just passing through?"

"Both maybe? Why?"

"I'm in a county cover band with a regular gig at a steakhouse in Bend. I'm Tim by the way. And we had to take this weekend off because our lead singer is battling some vocal cord issues."

Shane made a sympathetic noise. "Sucks."

"Yep. If you wanted to sit in with us next week, I can speak for my buddies and say we'd be honored to have someone of your level." Tim's eager tone made Shane's ego take notice, made him itch to play again.

"Been a minute since I've played with a full band, but sure. I'm interested. Gig pays?"

"You get your dinner comped plus we split a fee." Tim's crooked grin said it wasn't a big take, but Shane was used to that. "And there's a tip jar. Not much, but we're not asking you to jam for free."

"Okay. Let me see what I can arrange as far as my schedule. Let's make this happen."

They talked awhile longer, worked out some logistics while Shane ate a sandwich as a late dinner. He left all amped up. An actual gig. It had been a while. After he got things set for the baby, he might need to think about getting on with a new booking agent because he sucked at landing things for himself. But this thing sounded promising. A little cash wouldn't hurt either.

Damn. This had been a fine night. He had his usual post-show buzz after only a couple of songs and the promise of that gig. And with the promise of some pay on the horizon, he picked up a four-pack of some decent beer at a local microbrewery he passed on his way back to the rural road that led to Brandt's place. Despite the bar having live music and a rowdy tourist crowd, he wasn't tempted to linger.

Strangely, he was eager to tell Brandt his news and maybe share a beer if he was awake. Hoping Jewel at least was asleep, he let himself into the house quietly through the side door near the kitchen and set the beer on the counter. No baby in her swing, but a passed-out Brandt was on the couch, snoozing away. A quick check revealed the baby sleeping in her own room, a veritable miracle.

When he returned to the living area, his breath caught as he looked Brandt over. His hair was dry now, and even scruffy and asleep, he was the hottest thing Shane had ever seen. He'd lost his shirt at some point, probably to baby puke, and his chiseled chest with its light dusting of hair looked like something off a book cover in the soft light. That want from earlier was back, double strength.

There was a blanket on one of the chairs, so Shane spread it over Brandt, returning the tucking-in favor. A low, sweet spot pinched in his gut as he straightened the covers.

"Hey." Brandt's eyes blinked open. "What time is it?"

"Not even ten, old man." Shane laughed as he crouched next to the couch. "Brought you a cold one, but maybe you should try to sleep through?"

"Hell, nah. I'm awake now." But Brandt made no move to sit up, and Shane too was rooted to the spot. His hand reached for Brandt's hair and brushed it off his neck, need finally winning out.

Silky. Slippery. Like the slippery slope that had him leaning closer until the warm huff of Brandt's breath brushed across cheek. Brandt turned into the contact, and there they were face-to-face. Easy as that. And he could no more resist kissing Brandt than he could turn off the music in his own head. He didn't know how to experience the world without song, and he didn't know how to shrug free of this hold Brandt had on him. Didn't know if he wanted to either.

Brandt's cheeks were scratchy, but his lips were soft and warm, welcoming him with a sigh like Brandt had been holding his breath, waiting for him to make a move. And he sure was enthusiastic in kissing back, active but not overbearing. The kiss felt like they were dancing, with Brandt content to let Shane lead, even as he put his own style on each move.

He tasted sweet, like falling into a steaming cup of cocoa on a frigid day, and his hands were warm and strong as he pulled Shane closer, cover falling to the floor. Shane could spend the rest of his life caught up in this kiss, absorbing each of Brandt's rumbly groans, dying a little when Brandt sucked on his tongue, and fluttering away on surging energy with each pass of their lips.

Shane's knees dug into the rug, and his aching cock brushed against couch, but still all he could do was kiss Brandt over and over. Lips and tongue and teeth and grasping, needy hands.

"C'mere." Brandt tugged on his shoulders, trying to pull him onto the couch. And Shane was powerless to do anything other than give Brandt what they both needed.

Chapter Eleven

"C'mere," Brandt repeated. The angle was shit for hauling Shane up to the couch, but luckily, Shane didn't make
him ask a third time. Rising up, he let Brandt tug him
right back down, this time onto the couch. Onto him.

"*Oof.*" Brandt made a noise that wasn't quite human
as he urged Shane to settle on top of him. It was like his
body had had a missing Shane-shaped piece for days
now, and the second Shane stretched out over him, everything clicked back into place, world that much brighter
and clearer.

"Good?" Shane balanced one arm above Brandt, keeping some of his weight off. Brandt wasn't having any of
that though, and pulled him the rest of the way down,
until they were as pressed together as two people could
get.

"Fuck, yes." Brandt stretched up for another kiss, but
Shane wasn't quite as pliant as before, and his back was
tense under Brandt's hand.

"Think we might break the couch?"

"Fuck the couch." Couches were replaceable. This
moment wasn't. He wasn't kidding himself that this
was anything other than another ill-advised collision

for them, but hell if he wasn't going to make the most of something this good while he had it. "Kiss me."

And Shane did, with humbling tenderness and care. Even his tongue was deliberate, each sweep seemingly calculated to drive Brandt out of his head, reduce him to nothing other than this aching need. His body surged, arching up against Shane, who was right there, pressing him back down. Felt so good that he had do it again, more purposefully this time, rocking against Shane simply to feel that solid weight against him. It was a rush, like the heady yet reassuring sensation every jump when the parachute deployed and yanked him back. Felt like an unspoken conversation. *Yes. Yes, I've got you. Yes, it's safe to let go and enjoy the ride. I've got you.*

Shane ground down hard enough to have Brandt groaning before pulling back slightly. "Is this—"

"Good. So good," Brandt answered before Shane could get the question out, shifting his legs so that their cocks more directly aligned. That got a soft moan from Shane, too.

"Yeah it is." Good. Brandt didn't want to be the only one unraveling here, and Shane getting more into the grinding while kissing thing was next level good, the way their bodies learned to move together as they kissed and kissed.

Breathing hard, Shane skated his lips across Brandt's jaw, lighting up nerve endings until his tongue teased Brandt's earlobe. And that was electric enough to have him shivering, but nothing compared to the way Shane's mouth on his neck produced full body shudders.

"Fuck. Do that again." He tilted his head to expose more of his neck for Shane.

"Don't wanna leave a mark—"

Brandt made a frustrated sound. "Fuck that noise. My hair can cover. Mark away."

"Yeah?" Shane raked his teeth against Brandt's skin, a slow torture followed by the heat of his mouth. He repeated the gesture, firmer now, openmouthed kiss that sent shockwaves down Brandt's torso and made his cock throb. "You like that? Me biting you?"

"Uh huh. And how." Brandt leaned even more into the contact, shameless preening to get more of that delicious attention. It was entirely possible he might get off from simply Shane's mouth on his neck and his denim-covered cock rocking against Brandt's. And then Shane went and upped the ante, big hand sliding up Brandt's side, thumb scraping against his nipple.

"And this?" Shane's voice was all husky now. Intimate. His voice was always sexy, but Brandt wanted to hear him like this always, like each word was for Brandt and Brandt alone.

"Gonna kill me." He wasn't lying. Either he was going to come gangbusters or he was going to die right here on this couch, but man, what a way to go. He wasn't complaining.

"Good. 'Cause you're killing me too." Shane smirked down at him an instant before his mouth reclaimed Brandt's and drove the last of the sense from his brain.

"Fuck yeah." Shifting again, he opened his legs more, hooking the outside one around Shane, pulling him even closer, more friction, more weight, more of this pressure so good he almost couldn't stand it. Shane must have felt similar because he moaned and the motion of his hips sped up.

"Damn. The way you amp me up. It's been a minute…"

"Yeah. Me too." He didn't care if Shane didn't believe him. It had. Longer than that since he'd felt this out of control, this needy, and yet this free to let go. He used his leg and hands to urge Shane faster and harder.

"Oh, hell. That's…"

"Right." And it was. So right. So perfect. Every kiss, every thrust of Shane against him. Then Shane shifted, more pressure against Brandt's aching cock, and perfect redefined itself again. "Move like that again."

Shane groaned, low and lusty. "If I keep this up, I'm gonna…"

Oh yeah. No better feeling than knowing Shane was as kiss-drunk as him and maybe even more on edge. "Do it."

"Yeah?" Shane nibbled Brandt's neck again, seemingly determined to take Brandt with him. The cotton of his shirt dragged against Brandt's bare torso, making him shudder.

Brandt stretched, getting Shane's mouth on the sensitive spot where his neck and shoulder met. "Want it. You so riled up…love it."

"Mmm. Sure as fuck am worked up." Shane punctuated his words with a hard suck against Brandt's superheated skin. He'd wear his hair down for a week if it meant more of the delicious contrast of Shane's hot, soft mouth and his raspy stubble.

"Fuck. Do that again and you're gonna take me with you."

"Yeah I am." Moving faster now, Shane captured his mouth for a kiss that was so all-consuming, Brandt almost levitated, back bowing, but Shane was right there, holding him down, grounding him even as Brandt's body readied for flight.

"Shane. *Fuck*. Shane," he mumbled between kisses that were increasingly artless.

"Yeah. Come on. Come on." Eyes closed, Shane sounded like he was praying. And Brandt had already been right there, but the pleading did it, hearing Shane so close to coming apart.

"*Yes.*" The climax rolled through him, more diffuse than usual, like the pleasure was reaching new places, like summer rain in the canyons flooding hidden cracks and crevices. His cock pulsed and his head buzzed. Holding Shane even tighter, he reveled in his harsh grunt as he too stiffened, face first tense then slack, transformed. So beautiful that it was humbling and all he could do was cling.

"Damn." Shane's chuckle sounded dazed.

"Oh fuck." Brandt had to laugh as his breath returned to normal. "I haven't come in my pants in a decade."

"Thank God for that washer of yours." Groaning, Shane sat up, taking all that warm weight with him and Brandt had to resist the urge to yank him back down.

"Yep. And the shower." Immediately, he had the vision of Shane wet and soapy. He liked it, wanted to know what Shane looked like naked, wanted to explore and touch and taste. He might as well have not come for all the eagerness his body still had. "Think I could talk you into joining me?"

Shane made a pained face. "Brandt…"

"If that's your 'we need to talk' voice, I'm gonna need that beer you promised me." Brandt went ahead and sat up himself. Playtime over.

"It's in the kitchen, but I need to clean up first." Shane's blush would be adorable if the man weren't so freaking confounding.

"Good idea. Me too. See you in a few." He quickly washed up and changed pants in the master bath. The cleanup process could have been way more fun if Shane had been on board with the shower plan. Damn. Brandt needed more, even now. Shane might want to pretend this hadn't happened, but Brandt sure as fuck wasn't forgetting a single moment. And if he had his way, there would be lots more moments in store.

"Here. Opened one for you." Now in flannel pants and a T-shirt, Shane greeted him as he returned to the kitchen. The bottle of local brew was damp with condensation as Shane handed it over. "Hope this one's good. I told the woman working the counter at the brewery to find me something on the darker side."

"Somehow I'm not surprised that even your beer is brooding." Brandt shook his head before taking a sip. It was darker than his usual, rich in assertive hops, but not bad. Kind of like Shane himself, a shift from light and easy and forgettable towards unique and memorable.

"You saying I'm moody?" Frowning, Shane shrugged. "I mean, I'll own it, but I don't think that liking to think things through makes me a total drag."

He sounded like a guy who'd had that trait thrown in his face before, and Brandt could almost hear Shelby making that accusation.

"Nah. It's smart. You'd be good in the field." He studied Shane closer. He wasn't an adrenaline junkie like Brandt, but he had the steadiness that would make a good first responder. "You'd make a good spotter—the guys in the air who direct their crews. Even tempered, cautious attitudes save lives."

"Yeah. That's me." Leaning against the counter, Shane

gave a small smile before taking another sip of beer. "I like to look before leaping."

"But you've gotta admit, that leaping a few minutes ago was sure as fuck fun. We should do that again."

"No, we shouldn't." Shane pursed his mouth, eyes going sharp and pained. "That was…what did you say last time? A lapse. A big one, but still a lapse. And that one's on me. But we can't make a habit of it."

"Sure we can." Brandt plopped down at the nearby table.

Even as his expression stayed reluctant, Shane took a seat opposite him. "I've got a stack of reasons saying we can't."

"Okay, let's hear them." Brandt leaned forward as Shane recoiled backward.

"What?"

"You've got reasons. Maybe I've got answers." Stretching, Brandt kept his tone casual, trying to keep his intense want for a repeat at bay. "Because the way I see it, there's more reasons in favor than not. But let's see what's got that brain of yours in a tangle."

"We should focus on the baby."

"She's asleep," Brandt countered, playing with the label on his beer. "I'm not suggesting we let her yodel while we get our freak on. But we're adults, and if we want to make the most of naptime, we can. Next?"

"I'm Shelby's brother." Shane nodded sharply like that was his trump card.

"I'm aware. And?"

"I don't like… I'm a crappy consolation prize, you know? And I'm not sure I like coming in second to start with."

Head tilting, Brandt had to blink at that. "You think I'd rather be with Shelby?"

"I'd say the proof of that is asleep in the other room." Shane regarded him coolly before taking a swallow of his drink.

"And I'd say you can stow your jealousy." Brandt kept his voice even. Nothing was going to be served by him getting worked up. "No offense, man, but anyone who'd leave their kid with their ill-prepared younger brother isn't someone I'm interested in shacking up with. Sure, she's cute and fun, but that doesn't mean she wins out over other options."

"But—"

"Look. I'm not sure your ego needs the win, but that hookup with Shelby? It was before I met you the next day." Even now, he could still feel the thrum under his skin, how alive he'd felt simply talking with Shane. "After we jumped together, I couldn't get you out of my head for a while. But you were both leaving town, so it didn't much matter."

"You thought about me?" Shane's mouth quirked like he was thinking about smiling and trying to hold it back.

"Fuck yeah." Brandt went all in on trying to earn that smile. And he won a soft, shy grin for his honesty, Shane's dark lashes fluttering against his pink cheeks.

"Me too," Shane whispered.

"See? Another reason down. What else do you got?" He leaned back in his chair, letting the warmth in his chest spread to other body parts.

"You wouldn't be worried that hooking up with me might get back to your buddies?"

"Nope." Brandt met him level stare for level stare.

"What is your deal anyway? Bi? Pan?" Shane twirled

his half-empty bottle between long fingers. "You don't strike me as the type who's out, but you also don't seem particularly freaked out by what just happened."

"I've been in too many truly crappy situations to get all worked up over what makes my dick twitch. Honestly, I did the whole mixed-up feelings thing in my teens and twenties, trying to figure out why it was some guys but not others but still plenty of women. And then Roger died, and fuck it. Never said a word to him, but my heart knew."

"Yeah," Shane said softly.

"Does it matter if it has a label? I like what I like, and I'm not here to defend it to anyone. Life's too damn short to worry about what others might think."

"I get that. I'm not exactly out on the road either. Country and folk music is way more welcoming than it used to be, but a lot of these events are in super rural communities, so I keep to myself mainly. And *fuck*. Of freaking course it would turn out that you've got more experience than me." Shane's laugh was belly deep and warmed Brandt even more than the beer.

"Did I say that?" Brandt joined him in chuckling. It was nice, talking openly like this. "Actually, I've done a lot of looking, a little kissing, some touching, but not a ton beyond that. And that, my friend, is exactly why we should let ourselves do what we already did even more."

"How do you figure?"

"Maybe we've both had limited opportunities to explore some of this. And I get that neither of us wants something heavy or permanent, but it can be more than a one-off hookup. More room to try stuff, maybe stuff you've been wanting for a long time." Brandt opened his palm, a welcoming gesture.

"Hmm." Shane made a thoughtful noise.

"What do you say? You can't tell me you're not curious about a repeat or ten." Brandt wasn't one to pressure, so he tried to keep his posture and tone neutral, but damn if he didn't want—*need*—Shane to see the benefits of continuing to hook up. His pulse pounded. Once wasn't nearly enough.

Chapter Twelve

Shane was curious all right. Curious about what the rest of Brandt looked like under his clothes, what he'd feel like skin to skin, what other noises Shane could coax from him given more time. And he was curious in the general sense of the word too, curious about what it might feel like to kiss someone more than a handful of times, curious about the vast real estate between the one-night stands he was so opposed to and the sort of permanency he knew wasn't for someone like him. Time to explore. Damn but Brandt was tempting as hell.

"I can be curious but also recognize a damn bad idea when I see it. I can't stick around indefinitely." The beer bottle was cool and slick against his sweaty palms. "I don't want a messy parting. And I'd like to be able to see the kiddo. Visit."

He'd been thinking about that while he'd been singing. He might need to get back on the road eventually, but he wasn't going to give up this baby. He'd be the fun uncle. Or at least the guy with cool souvenirs from far-flung towns.

"Of course. You're family to her." Brandt nodded like this was a given, easing some of the tightness in Shane's back. "And contrary to popular belief, it's possible to be adult about a little fling. You'll move on when you're ready to, and I'm not gonna be the static line, snapping you back. I'm not really high on drama."

"You're a good guy," he allowed. And Brandt was. Shane was the one who had brought drama to his doorstep, and Brandt had been nothing other than responsible. He was way more than the party-happy sky cowboy Shane had assumed at their first meeting.

"Yeah, I am. And so are you." Brandt saluted him with his nearly empty beer. "Way I see it, we're two good dudes with itchy feet who need to stay put for a spell. Why not enjoy it?"

Why not indeed? All Shane's reasons were melting away, one by one, leaving only this aching need for more. More kisses. More time together. More discoveries. "How would this work, anyway? We make a to-do list of everything we haven't tried yet?"

"You're way too organized." Brandt laughed, deep and rich, and set down his beer. "Or we could ditch the list. See what comes up. I'm not saying we have to fuck either if that's something you're intent on saving for someone special."

Ha. Shane had given up on that notion several years prior. His music dreams had won out over his romantic ones. He wasn't ever going to be in one place long enough to fall in love. He wanted more than a one-off, but he also was a realist. And a human, one with needs and wants, even if he usually tried to keep them under lockdown.

"I didn't say that was off the table." He tried to mimic Brandt's cool disinterest and failed miserably as he searched for the right words. "But I need to tell you, when I think about fucking, it's not… I'm not…usually—"

"I wanna get fucked." Brandt cut him off with the

bald statement, matter-of-fact delivery like he was discussing pizza toppings.

"Uh…" Shane somehow managed to cough and blink
at the same time, a combo that left him lightheaded.

"Careful there." Brandt pushed back from the table,
came around the table to rub Shane's shoulder. "You
might want to scoop your jaw off the table while you're
at it. I figured I might as well be direct and save you all
the hemming and hawing, but we don't need you leak-
ing neurons."

"Sorry. That's…" It was close to impossible to think
with Brandt so close, big hand right there, pressing down.
Crazy hot. That's what it was, but he wasn't sure he was
ready to reveal how turned on the notion made him.
"You seem rather sure for someone who hasn't tried it."

"Dude. You think I reached thirty and never encountered my prostate?" Brandt scoffed, and Shane didn't
need to glance up to know that he'd rolled his eyes. "I
don't need a partner to know what I like. Hell, I'd say
you're missing out if you haven't played around at all."

"I didn't say…" He exhaled hard, words escaping him
because Brandt had added his second hand and started
a gentle but effective massage. "It's more that my fantasies run to…"

"Fucking ripped smoke jumpers? Maybe if I ask
nicely?" Brandt was grinning like a puppy with a ten-
nis ball when Shane glanced up. Damn. His usual easy
grin was hard enough to resist, but him like this, silly
and flirting, was damn near deadly.

"You're pretty hard to resist." Shane didn't even try
to hide his chuckle.

"Yep. All this and I come with toys. I've got this one
prostate massager…" Brandt trailed off with an affection-

ate sigh. "You can try it, tell me after whether it doesn't make you stoked about fucking."

"Toys?" Shane's brain short-circuited on the image of Brandt reclining on a bed, legs spread, using a toy. God. His brain couldn't decide what it wanted to see first. "Damn. Warn a guy."

"I'm not opposed to showing—"

Raaah. For once, Jewel wasn't all-out wailing, but her awake-and-unhappy battle cry was enough to put an end to all those sexy images.

"Hold that thought." Brandt immediately dropped his hands as they both hurried back to the crib. Brandt reached Jewel first and lifted her out of the crib. "You're way too awake for this late. When are you going to learn that sleeping is fun?"

"Lies. And this is Shelby's kid. Sleep is for the weak." He laughed as he clucked the baby under her chin. "Heck, she's your kid too. We're lucky she's not base jumping off the side the crib yet."

"True. It would serve me right to get a pint-size adrenaline junkie." Brandt positioned Jewel like she was flying, then made a face. "Can you get a diaper ready? And a fresh sleeper?"

"Sure." Shane went to the top drawer of the dresser. They'd put a little pad on top to change the baby. Sleepers and diapers underneath. In theory. All he came up with was her puppy sleeper. "Did you use up the diapers while I was gone?"

"What? No. At least I don't think." Brandt bounced her from side to side. "Didn't you get some when you got the formula?"

"No. Because I'm an idiot." Shane smacked his head.

He should have realized how low they were getting. "She goes through them way faster than I thought."

"It's okay. We're all learning on the job." Brandt was far less pissed than a lot of people would have been, shifting the baby so he could pat Shane on the shoulder. "It's late, but I'm gonna bet that big convenience store near the highway in Painter's Ridge has something. But we can't leave her wet in the meantime."

"No." Shane searched the drawer again, like a diaper might have magically appeared in the last thirty seconds.

"I've got this. You hold her." Brandt thrust Jewel at him. Damn. Just when Shane thought Brandt couldn't get sexier, he went and got all confident and take-charge again.

I want to get fucked. The words kept echoing in Shane's head. Brandt was going to be his undoing. Big, cocky dude who wanted to get done? Yes, please. Sign him up, pesky reservations and his natural cautiousness and all.

Brandt returned a few minutes later with two faded T-shirts, a roll of duct tape, and a piece of plastic, like the sort used for painting drop cloths.

"What the…" Shane's head tilted, and he could have sworn the baby repeated the gesture.

"Cloth diapers are a thing, right? Like historically, little cave babies didn't have name-brand diapers."

"Guess not." Shane had to laugh, jostling Jewel in the process. She made a little hiccup, like she was testing the idea of laughing herself.

"So, here's what we're gonna do. I'm gonna McGyver up a diaper. Then you can give her a bottle while I make a run to the convenience store. Hopefully, then we're back in business until tomorrow when we're doing a run to that warehouse store in Bend. Bulk diapers and wipes."

"Sounds good." What truly felt good was all that *we* talk, Brandt's easy assumption that they were in this together and that they'd go shopping together.

"Aren't cloth diapers supposed to have pins?" he asked as he watched Brandt fold one of the shirts.

"You're thinking of cartoons. I thought about some binder clips or something like that, but I don't want to scratch her." The tenderness with which Brandt wrapped the baby up in the folded shirt was truly something to behold, his big hands so gentle as he deftly secured the whole thing with a layer of plastic and tape. He put her in one of her little shirts to keep warm before handing her back to Shane. "There. That should do her."

"Excellent." He headed for the kitchen to make the bottle. "You good to drive?"

"On less than a full beer? Yeah. I'm fine. I've driven these roads on thirty-six hours without sleep before. Not recommended, but fires don't work nine-to-five."

"Yeah." Shane licked his lips, feeling strangely shy, like they shouldn't leave their earlier conversation entirely unfinished. "Brandt…"

"You don't need to decide anything tonight." Mind reading was apparently another of the Diaper Wizard's tricks. "I have a feeling it's gonna be another night of taking shifts with the diva. Just tell me if you're in the mood for something. This doesn't have to be complicated."

"Yeah." The lie made Shane's hand tense on the bottle. It was already complicated because he didn't only like kissing Brandt. He liked *Brandt*. Liked his ingenuity and forthrightness. Liked how he hadn't run from responsibility. Liked his fun side even. *Complicated.*

Yup. And yet, here he was doing complex math trying to figure out when next they might both be awake while the baby was asleep.

"Did you have a fun outing with your adoring fans, Diva?" Shane softly teased the baby as he rocked her on the couch. She did seem pretty tuckered out after their shopping trip to Bend. She'd worn the puppy sleeper and had received enough stranger smiles to leave him slightly exhausted. But not *too* exhausted. All day he'd been counting down to this nap.

"That's the last of it." Brandt's muscles flexed as he showed off, hauling both a box of diapers and a giant four-pack of formula. Shane had lost the rock-paper-scissors game for who had to deal with a fussy baby and who got to unload Brandt's SUV.

And only Brandt could make warehouse shopping sexy. Shane didn't consider himself particularly out of shape either, but there was something about watching Brandt haul heavy items that had a low hum of arousal following Shane all day like a tune he couldn't shake and wasn't sure he wanted to. Brandt leaving the ball in Shane's court as to what happened next was both frustrating and touching. Not that Shane wanted Brandt to go for a hard sell, but part of him wouldn't mind if Brandt wanted to push him against the nearest wall and plead his case with his mouth.

"I'm going to try to set the diva in her crib," Shane whispered as he carefully got off the couch with the sleeping baby in his arms.

"Good luck," Brandt called softly back. And his wish must have worked, because for once, she let Shane do the transfer on the first try.

When he emerged, Brandt had made two glasses of lemonade and was finishing up two sandwiches.

"Figured you were probably as hungry as me." Brandt gestured to the food, like it was no big deal him thinking of Shane like that. And maybe it was the hunger. Maybe it was the exhaustion from dealing with Jewel amid navigating the big box store. Maybe it was how Brandt's hair looked in the afternoon light, a hundred shades from blond to brown, long strands fluttering around his rugged face. Or maybe it was that Shane's body had finally had enough of his brain's indecision.

Whatever it was, his feet carried him over to where Brandt stood by the counter. So much for his low-key pining for Brandt to make a move. Fuck that noise as Brandt would say. He could make a move too. He was perfectly capable of taking that one extra step, invading Brandt's personal space.

"Thanks," he said, voice already husky simply from being this close. Brandt smelled extra good, more woodsy than usual. "I think she'll sleep awhile."

"So, what you're saying is it's naptime?" Brandt hooked a finger in one of the belt loops on Shane's jeans, pulled him even closer, so their thighs rubbed, let Shane crowd him the rest of the way against the cabinets.

"And we're both adults." Shane gave him a long, considering look before brushing the hair off Brandt's face, giving in to the urge to bury his hands in the silky strands again.

"That we are." Brandt met his gaze. He could have easily closed the mere inches separating their mouths, taken over and kissed Shane, but there was a certain playful curiosity in his eyes. "You taking suggestions for how we fill the time?"

"No." Shane didn't let himself smile because catching Brandt off balance was fun.

Predictably, both Brandt's eyebrows went up. "No?"

"Nope." Releasing Brandt's hair, Shane sank to his knees in a smooth motion. "I already know what I want."

"Oh, now that *is* an idea." Brandt traced Shane's lips with his thumb, hissing softly when Shane nipped at his fingers.

"Like it?" Shane danced his fingers across Brandt's belt, stopping right at the clasp.

"Definitely not opposed." Brandt bumped his hips forward. Subtle he was not. This time Shane couldn't help the smile.

"Good." Shane undid the belt, then stroked the outline of Brandt's cock through his pants. "I know you said we don't need to make a list, but if we did…"

"This might be at the top of mine." Brandt groaned low as Shane freed his cock. And damn, the novelty of a cock that wasn't his own in his hand was enough to send all Shane's blood rushing south. Brandt's cock was close in size to his own, making Shane want to line them up, jack them off together. Later. Because there would be a later, because he was done fighting this. And also because right then, he was more concerned with exploring.

Cataloging all the tiny differences between them made a shiver race up his back. Brandt was more ruddy, more thick veins on the shaft, sexy to trace with his thumb. Like Shane, he was cut, but his cockhead was more oval, more of a defined ridge as it flared out, bold and assertive as the man himself. He stroked Brandt with his fist a few times, trying to decide what to try first with his mouth. He'd played this out in his head enough in the last week that actually being here was a little overwhelming.

Tentatively, he opened his fist and traced the thickest vein with the tip of his tongue. The skin was velvety soft even as Brandt's cock was hard enough to pulse against Shane's palm. And simply that much contact was enough to have Brandt moaning again, a muffled sound like he was biting his lip. His hips thrust forward again, clear request for more. Shane could do that, using the flat of his tongue now, all along the shaft before he found a spot on the underside that made Brandt shudder and curse.

"Oh fuck. Yeah. That."

"You like?" Bolder now, he made his way to the cock-head finally, laving it all over. The tip had a drop of clear fluid waiting there. Salty. Sexy, knowing he'd coaxed that from Brandt. He liked it enough that he licked at the slit more until another drop slipped onto his tongue.

"Hell yeah." Brandt stroked Shane's hair, not directing or pushing, but there, a solid, warm presence making Shane feel even more connected to him. "I'd say you're a natural, but damn, why don't you practice some more?"

"Willing victim, huh?" Shane laughed before licking some more.

"Taking one for the team." Brandt's tease ended on a strangled groan as Shane finally took the head fully in his mouth. "Oh, God. Do that again."

"This?" Shane repeated the action, sucking harder this time, still careful to not go too low. Gagging would be the opposite of hot. He'd sucked his own fingers while jerking off enough to know that deep throating wasn't going to be in his bag of tricks quite yet.

"Yeah. More." And maybe Brandt understood that Shane was being cautious with depth because he wrapped a fist around the base of his cock. With his other hand still in Shane's hair, it was almost like he was feeding it to Shane, which was such a turn-on that it made Shane's cock throb against his fly.

In porn, the guy doing the sucking often jerked off, but Shane wasn't sure he was that coordinated. And besides, he wanted to focus both on Brandt and on memorizing every single detail about this experience. The weight on his tongue. The salty taste whenever he did something that Brandt particularly liked. The feel of Brandt's jeans against Shane's torso.

"Harder. Love that." Brandt's whispered praise made Shane redouble his efforts to turn Brandt on. He discovered that he could use his tongue while sucking if he was careful about his teeth. Brandt seemed to like that tongue action a lot, hand speeding up along with his moans. "Fuck. Fuck. Close."

Shane pulled back enough to groan himself. "Yeah, you are. I want to taste it."

"Tested." Above him, Brandt nodded, eyes glassy but serious. "Before season. Promise."

"Good. Gimme." Even more eager now, if that were even possible, he channeled all the anticipation racing through him to his mouth, moving faster now, finding a rhythm that worked in tandem with Brandt's motions. Spit ran down his chin and his tongue lost coordination, but it was worth it, earning Brandt's moans.

"Shane. God. Just…" Brandt was breathing hard and his hand tightened in Shane's hair. Shane pushed up with his tongue, milking the shaft. "That. There. Oh, *there*."

Then Brandt was coming, and it was such a rush, knowing he'd caused it, that it almost tipped him over too. It was a lot too, multiple spurts, and swallowing was a trick, enough to keep his own orgasm at bay. So fucking hot though, the sounds Brandt made, like he was fighting a losing battle on being loud.

"Fucking hell." Releasing Shane's hair, Brandt hauled him up next to him. "No way are you convincing me that was your first."

"Beginner's luck?" Shane grinned at him before grabbing one of the lemonade glasses and taking a healthy swallow.

"Taste that bad?" Brandt laughed, pulling him close enough to kiss, but pausing right before their lips touched.

"Nah. Different. Not bad." Sex was weird. He'd been desperate to taste it right before Brandt came, but then after, it was less turn-on and more odd, the lingering flavor. But then Brandt was kissing him, and he was less about dissecting the experience and more acutely aware that he was still painfully turned on.

"Okay to touch?" Brandt palmed him through his jeans, fingers already messing with Shane's belt.

"Please." Like Shane was gonna stop him, not when he was this hard and aching, but he appreciated the ask.

"I got you." Brandt withdrew Shane's cock, big grip different from Shane's. Rougher. Callouses in different spots. More active thumb. Different. And so fucking amazing that he had to groan.

"Damn." He shut his eyes as he let his head fall onto Brandt's shoulder. "That's good."

"Yeah, you were. Fuck. Not sure I've ever shot so hard."

Shane had to laugh around a moan at how his cock pulsed at each bit of praise.

"Your mouth is so sweet." Brandt found his lips for another kiss, one that left Shane trembling, right on the edge. Ordinarily, he liked being the one in charge of a kiss, but here he simply surrendered himself to Brandt, to this kiss, to his strong hands, and his dirty words. "Can't wait for my turn."

"Mmm." The mere thought of Brandt on his knees had Shane moaning. Brandt's strokes were slow and steady, keeping him riding the edge between almost and too much.

Brandt made a thoughtful noise and loosened his grip. "Maybe…"

"Not…too worked up." He wasn't sure Brandt would even get a lick out before he shot, he was that tense with need and want. And as soon as Brandt tightened his fist, his hips started moving, fucking Brandt's hand, no more waiting.

"Next time." Brandt laughed and licked Shane's ear. "Gonna suck you so good. I wanna taste it too."

"Fuck. Fuck." Just like that, Shane was coming, head full of thoughts of Brandt's mouth, him gulping Shane down with the same hunger and enthusiasm he did everything else. His knees wobbled and his vision swam and he wanted the climax to last forever. Finally, he slumped against Brandt.

"That did it, huh?" Brandt chuckled, a certain fondness in his voice that hadn't been there before. "Image of me blowing you?"

"Smug bastard." Shane dug his shoulder into Brandt's chest, mostly because he could, because this felt so damn good. "Like your ego needs the boost."

"Come on." Brandt squeezed him tighter before releasing him to tuck his dick back in. He headed to the sink, looking back over his shoulder. "You gotta admit that's a hell of a use of naptime."

"Yeah, it is." Unable to stop his grin, Shane straightened his own clothes. Everything put away, he took another drink of lemonade. The sweet tart flavor was heaven for his dry mouth, and he couldn't help the happy sound that escaped.

"So, think you'll be up for more?" Brandt's voice was casual. Almost too casual, like he was having to work to not sound too eager. Shane liked that thought, liked him invested in this thing.

"Yeah." He could have been coy and went for a *maybe*, but he didn't have it in him, not when he wanted more already. And not just more orgasms, but more of this, bumping shoulders and sharing laughs. And his list of things he wanted to try with Brandt just kept growing. "Bring it on."

Chapter Thirteen

Brandt was getting too domesticated. He shifted around in the passenger seat of his SUV as they approached the air base, both trying to wake up and trying to not get to comfortable with this new arrangement.

"Thanks again for letting me have the car." Shane parked in the back of the lot, same as he had last time. He was more awake than Brandt had expected considering the early hour. The baby was still in her fuzzy sleeper and had dozed back off in her car seat.

"No problem." The bigger problem was figuring out whether he should give Shane an affectionate goodbye. It had been several days and this thing between them still defied classification. They'd shared a number of super-heated make-out sessions and mutual orgasms, but they each slept in their own beds. He supposed that made them roommates-with-benefits, but he also liked Shane far more than a lot of casual hookups. In the end, he settled for squeezing Shane's knee. "I've already told Hartman I need a ride home. Have a good practice."

"Thanks." Shane was headed that afternoon to a band rehearsal for the group he was sitting in with that weekend. He wasn't sure what the parking situation was in the neighborhood where the band met, so Brandt had volunteered the SUV.

"You think the diva is gonna let you get some reps in?" Brandt glanced back at the sleeping baby. She sure was cute snoozing like that, but when she was awake, she had a way of demanding every ounce of attention they both had to give.

"Hey, she likes it when I sing." Shane's smile was enough to make Brandt forget where they were, make him bump Shane's shoulder.

"Maybe you're okay." He was undoubtedly more than passable—simply the humming he did around the house showed way more natural ability than Brandt had, that was for sure.

"Yeah, maybe I can carry a tune." Chuckling, Shane rolled his eyes. "But I asked Tim—that's the band leader—about bringing her, and he said his girlfriend will be around if I need a hand."

"That works." Brandt couldn't help the frown though. What did Shane know about these people? Had this girlfriend person ever even held a baby? And since when did he become so cautious? He'd never once had the reputation of being nervous.

"Don't worry." Shane returned his leg pat. "I'm not letting our girl out of my sight."

Our. The word was a lot less scary than it would have been two weeks ago. "Good."

"But right now, you better hurry. We don't want you in trouble. Jewel needs you employed."

"I'm on it." And he was. Head back in the game. He might have savings, but he did love his job, and the baby hadn't changed his obligations there. He trusted Shane with Jewel, and honestly, he wasn't sure who he'd trust

more. Shane was there in the middle of the night, sometimes even before Brandt. Shane would take good care
of her, even with this band gig of his. And how weird
was that? Being all proud of Shane for finding himself
a chance to sing this weekend.

Brandt had gone so long with no one to brag on, only
his own drive to push him, that this caring was decidedly different. And it went deeper than remembering
that Shane would need to eat too and making extra food
or taking turns handing off a fussy baby. He cared when
Shane seemed a little down, celebrated his good news,
and felt way more alive than he had in years, simply from
spending time together. He could jump out of a hundred
planes, and he'd still be less freaked out than he was over
whatever the hell was happening in his life.

Hours later, Shane was still on his mind as he worked
with Hartman and some other jumpers on equipment
inventory and repair. A number of jumpers, especially
younger ones, found this part of the job boring, but
Brandt had always taken it very seriously. They were
all one frayed connector away from not making it back
from a jump. He was known as being good at this, spot-
ting weak points that others couldn't see, fixing things
some would have trashed, but that day his brain kept
wandering away from the task at hand.

"What do you think, Wilder?" Hartman held out an
older pack. "Think this will hold the season?"

"Hmm. Yeah. Should be good. This kind of fabric
can take a beating and not give." Brandt still studied
it closely though, looking for any snags or wear like
stretched seams or other weak points. And yet again, his
head flitted to the baby, picturing her in a little pack. The
sling they'd purchased was serviceable, but too stretchy

for his tastes and not quite as long as either he or Shane needed. "Huh. Maybe…"

"Maybe?" Hartman prompted when Brandt trailed off.

"Nothing." His skin heated even as he made a mental note to acquire some fabric. Maybe Shane would appreciate an additional option when he was out and about with the diva. Hartman kept looking at him, so he finally went ahead and added, "Was just thinking that this material would be good for a baby carrier."

"That's right. Forgot you have dad brain now." Hartman laughed as he continued to check out the stack of packs. "How's the kid doing?"

"Wait. Wilder has a kid?" One of the younger jumpers, a kid from Montana nicknamed Bronco, made an exaggerated face, like his eyes were about to fall out. "Other than himself?"

"Fuck you." Brandt flipped his middle finger at Bronco. "Yes, I have a baby."

"Oops. Sorry. Didn't think before asking. Didn't mean to put you on the spot." Hartman frowned.

"It's okay. I'm not keeping her hidden." If his buddies found out about Jewel or even about him and Shane, so be it. Life was too short to worry about big secrets.

"Got a pic?" Rich asked, coming up next to Bronco. "Cameron says she's a cutie."

"I…uh…" He didn't have many actually. Taking pics didn't come naturally to him, as he wasn't particularly active on social media, and despite his large circle of acquaintances, he wasn't the type to spam the group chats with pics. He'd taken one on Sunday though of Shane strumming his guitar to Jewel in her swing, thinking he'd message it to Shane so he'd see how sweet they looked together. He supposed he could show that one, but he was strangely unsure about sharing what felt like a private moment.

"No pics?" Bronco apparently wasn't done teasing him. "What kind of dad are you?"

"Okay, okay," he groaned, not willing to admit he was the kind of newbie father who didn't know he was supposed to fill his camera roll with kid pictures. Fine. Let them see Shane. He'd work on getting better at picture taking, but not for Rich and Bronco. No, he wanted to get better at capturing memories for Jewel herself, so she'd have a few to look back on, not have the same lack he did.

To his surprise, when he pulled out his phone, though, there was a message waiting from Shane. He clicked it, hoping nothing was wrong, hating how his pulse sped up.

Look who's smiling, Shane's message read, and it had a close-up of Jewel, who indeed seemed happier than usual, gummy expression that might be generously called a smile.

"Oh. Here's a new one." He held out the phone so the guys could see. "Looks like she's learning a new trick."

"Oh, that's a fun age." Rich clapped him on the shoulder. "But just wait until she's older, man. That's the smile of a girl who is definitely gonna want a pony."

"Or a tattoo," Bronco added.

"I suppose we'll see." Certainty he hadn't had before rushed through him. He wanted to be there to see what made her smile, to hear her wants, to tell her ink was forever and horses took a lot of hay. He still had no clue what he was doing with this dad job, but he wanted to try to get good at it. He pocketed the phone until a while later when they took a break as they wound down for the day. He walked away from the building, taking a quiet moment for himself to text Shane.

Thanks for the pic. How was practice?

Shane's reply came before Brandt needed to head back inside. Not bad. I'm starving though. Going to start some dinner soon.

Me too. Save me some? I shouldn't be too much longer, he texted back and was rewarded with a quick return text from Shane.

Will do. I'll grab an apple now so we can eat together.

Yup. Brandt truly *was* one hundred percent domesticated now because he couldn't wait to get home, see Jewel's new trick and hear about Shane's day. And that made him one hundred percent screwed.

"I'm home."

The moment the door shut behind Brandt, Shane's senses tingled with fresh awareness. *Home.* This wasn't actually a home for either of them, more like a temporary way station, but the way Brandt said the words, all light and happy, made Shane long for something he wasn't sure he'd ever had, even as a kid.

"Good. Food's almost ready." Stirring the pot of meat sauce, he tried to push that longing aside, focus back on the practical. The noodles were done and drained, and he had a bag of prepackaged salad mix for the side. This might not be *home*, but he could at least get them fed.

"What smells good?" Brandt came up behind him at the stove. He stood closer these days. Not precisely affectionate, but also nowhere close to just-friends distance. Then his hand came around Shane to rest on his abs, making it hard to breathe from how good Brandt felt behind him, warm and strong.

"Me?" he joked, tipping his head back. Brandt might be more into having his neck kissed as an orgasmic thing, but Shane also wasn't going to turn down some nuzzling from Brandt's bristly cheeks. "And maybe the pasta."

"That too." Brandt inhaled deeply before nipping at Shane's ear. "Can the spaghetti wait?"

"Thought you were hungry?" Shane's voice dropped to a husky whisper as Brandt worked that hand of his under Shane's T-shirt.

"I am." He pulled Shane closer, rubbing against his ass, making Shane want to feel that hard length other places too. Spinning around, he looped his arms around Brandt's neck.

"Maybe—"

"Aah! Aaah!" Jewel did this new thing she'd been doing, a sort of chirp that meant she was awake and thinking about crying. It was cute, her growing repertoire of noises and expressions, but he also had learned that the sound meant an all-out wail wasn't far off.

"And hold that thought." Brandt scrubbed at his hair before heading over to scoop her up. The baby immediately stopped crying, because of course she did.

"You've got the magic touch. She's been fussy all afternoon. Her sleep got messed up with the band practice, so I guess it's payback."

"Oh, I don't think she's out to get you." Brandt held Jewel out like she was part of the conversation. "Are you, Diva?"

"Funny." It was hard not to appreciate Brandt's silliness and all that brought to Shane's life.

"I try. I'll go change her if you want to serve the food?"

"Sounds like a plan." Shane grabbed plates while Brandt headed back to Jewel's room. He reemerged with the baby in a fresh sleeper right as Shane set the food on the table. Brandt dragged Jewel's swing over to the table, setting her up next to him.

"Let's see if this works so we can eat. Looks great." Brandt's smile made the effort of making a real meal more than worth it. "Tell me about band practice?"

"It was good." And this was weird, having someone to tell about his day, someone like Brandt who nodded expectantly, like he actually wanted Shane to continue. "Jewel liked Tim's girlfriend because she made silly faces for her. And the band's not bad. Good people. They've been playing together a long time, all locally. And all covers, but luckily I speak fluent classic country."

"That take talent or just twang?" Sparks of gold danced in Brandt's eyes.

"George, Johnny, and Waylon just rolled over at your sass," Shane countered before taking a big bite of pasta. Jewel squawked like she too was registering her objections.

"Nah. I'm just teasing." Brandt lifted Jewel back out of her swing. "I've heard plenty of country. Just because my tastes run more eclectic doesn't mean I don't appreciate the oldies."

"I'd believe eclectic. Your radio presets are all over the map. Reminds me of our house growing up—always music, never the same thing twice."

"Well, some of that is bouncing around, having to find new stations in new places." Brandt shrugged like moving from place to place was simply a given. He popped

a lettuce piece in his mouth while bouncing the baby. "How'd you choose country anyway? Didn't you say your dad was more into rock?"

"He is, but back when his joints would let him live the roadie life, he'd pretty much go with what was paying. We did a summer in an RV, out on tour with a big-name country duo. It's not really overstating it to say I fell in love that summer, at least as much as a nine-year-old can." Shane closed his eyes, almost able to hear the iconic love songs the duo was famous for, hearing Shelby's tween laugh. "I memorized all the songs, bribed Shelby to be my audience."

"Aw. Bet you were a cute kid."

"Maybe." He didn't know what to do with the way Brandt's face had softened, didn't like how it made his insides quiver. "But what I really love about country is that it tells a story. It's a storyteller's genre."

"Isn't that most music?" Brandt transferred Jewel to his other arm.

"Sort of. With country, it's more that the stories are all fundamental emotions and truths, and the audience is eager to come along on the journey. Don't get me wrong. I can do some pop too, but there's something raw about country. The rush of tearing my heart out, I guess."

"See?" Brandt did an exaggerated eyebrow raise. "Knew you had a secret adrenaline junkie side. You go for those emotional thrills."

Shane had to laugh at that, but he wasn't wrong. "Yeah, that's one way of putting it. Anyway, my dad thought the money might be there in pop or rock for me, but I've always had my heart set on the country charts."

"Gotta make your own road." Brandt saluted him with his water cup. "I respect that."

"Thanks. Not sure he does, but that's okay." Shane stabbed his spaghetti harder than necessary.

"I've never had to wrangle anyone's dreams or hopes other than mine, so maybe my opinion doesn't count for much, but the way I figure it, you've got to live life for yourself first. No one else is gonna make your goals a reality."

"Truth." Shane had to swallow hard because he wasn't sure he'd ever felt so *seen* before. He had no clue what to do with all the big things Brandt made him feel. But before he could decide on a better reply, the baby started fussing again. "Here, let me take her so you can actually chew."

He walked around the table to fetch her from Brandt, who handed her over with an easy smile. "You be good for Uncle Shane, Miss Diva."

"Ha." Shane stood to bounce her some more. She'd eaten shortly before Brandt came in, so he doubted it was hunger making her so cranky.

"Too bad she's fussy. I kinda wanted to see that smile. Thanks for doing the picture. I appreciated that."

"No problem." He hadn't been the surest about texting Brandt at work, but the moment had felt too good not to share. "And I discovered after we were back home that I can make her do it, but…"

"You're blushing." Brandt waggled his fork in Shane's direction. "What goofy thing has she got you doing?"

"Nothing." Shane's face was hotter than if he had a dozen floodlights on him.

"Nah. You're lying, and this I gotta see. Make her smile."

"Okay, but no laughing." Shane might not have Brandt's knack for goofy shit, but he wasn't above trying all manner of things to get Jewel calmed down. "You try spending all day with an infant. You'll do wacky things too."

"I believe you. And maybe I haven't said as much, but I appreciate it, you taking the time to help."

"Thanks." And somehow Brandt's understanding and gratitude made it easier to make a fool of himself. "All right. Let's see if this works again. Hey, Jewel? You want to mash?"

Bouncing the baby around, he launched into "Monster Mash" complete with different voices, and sure enough she gave a gummy grin at his antics.

"This is no joke the cutest shit I've ever seen." Shifting in his chair, Brandt pulled out his phone.

"Hey, what are you doing? No pics!"

"Trust me. She's gonna want a pic because I'm fully intending to tell her the story of her first smiles for Uncle Shane." Brandt's expression got that far-off look again. Oh, yeah. That was right. This was a guy without baby pictures or many mementos of his own to share with his kid. Shane could understand the impulse to do better for Jewel.

"Okay." Shane resumed singing, trying to ignore the camera so Brandt could get a good pic of them. "She likes this other song too…"

He went into "She'll Be Coming 'Round the Mountain," for which he'd made up Jewel-specific lyrics, which got her smiling and Brandt laughing so loud his eyes crinkled.

"Damn." Brandt whistled. "If you're that good at silly songs, I bet you're killer with a band."

The urge to show off for Brandt was strong, something he'd never had before. He loved having an audience when he was on stage, sure, but he'd never wanted to sing for one specific person before. But now he did, wanted Brandt to see him at his best. "Come see me this weekend?"

"Yeah?" Brandt dropped his gaze from Shane's face to the baby. "Isn't the gig at a bar?"

"No, it's more of a steakhouse with a Western vibe. Family place. They've even got mini golf. I drove by on our way back here. Big, open space. Shouldn't be too hard for you to sneak out if the diva's fussy."

"Sounds a lot better than staying home."

"Good." A look passed between them, an understanding of sorts that this was something more than a purely casual friend invite. This wasn't like the early days when he'd beg anyone he knew to come out, and maybe Brandt knew that because he nodded at Shane, eyes solemn. This thing between them was like the early summer weather, warm but also fragile, rapidly shifting from moment to moment. Impossible to plan for, but still worth enjoying.

Eyes still serious, Brandt's mouth curved, and the smile worked like a tractor beam, making Shane step toward him. He wanted—

Rah. Rah. Whatever he'd had in mind, the baby had other plans.

"Hey now. None of that." He half laughed, half scolded because what else could one do with a tiny baby? It wasn't like she was blocking his romantic urges on purpose.

"Here, let me take a turn." Done eating now, Brandt pushed away from the table. "You go find those cookies we got at the store. I have a feeling we're going to need them."

And they did. Jewel just did not want to settle down

for the night. No signs of illness or true distress, but her crankiness knew no bounds. She was happy enough while one of them was holding her, and Brandt's trick of making the soft toys dance for her worked as a distraction while Shane did the dishes. However, she started up again after her last bottle when Shane tried to put her to sleep in her crib for the night while Brandt took a shower.

"How's it going?" Towel around his neck, Brandt poked his head into Jewel's room where Shane was pacing with her. *Damn.* The man looked downright edible damp, face glistening, chest muscles flexing under a thin white sleeveless T-shirt, strong legs in loose shorts.

"So much for that thought of yours from earlier." Shane spared him an appreciative look before the baby squawked again. "Or sleep."

"Switch." Not waiting for Shane to agree, Brandt held out his hands. "Let me try the rocking chair."

Groaning, Shane handed her over if only so he could stretch his back. "I tried that, but she wakes back up as soon as she hits the crib. Patting her back in the crib works too, but she cries as soon as I stop."

"New plan. You sing. I'll pat. Then you sneak away first, then me." Brandt nodded decisively, a glimpse into how he probably was in the field. Cool head, quick decisions, not afraid to think outside the box for solutions.

"Like a stealth mission?"

"Hey, whatever works, right?" Brandt shrugged as he swayed with Jewel.

"Okay. But no more goofy songs. Those wake her up." Strangely, he was more self-conscious singing an old favorite than the kid songs. He had to start with humming, warm up to forgetting that Brandt was right there, and sing like he did when it was only him and Jewel. But then he fell into the familiar song about a tired singer, notes falling easily now as Brandt lowered the drowsy baby to the crib, patting her back. He kept singing, that song fading into another, softer now as the baby's eyes finally fluttered shut and stayed that way.

Still singing, he crept from the room, staying in the hallway to finish the song. Right as he hit the ending notes, Brandt tiptoed out of the room, triumphant look on his face.

"It worked." Shane smiled at him. The hallway was dark and seemed narrower than usual with Brandt right there in front of him, smiling mouth and intense eyes and all those acres of muscles, right there.

"Yeah, it did." Licking his lips, Brandt backed Shane against the wall. "You tired?"

"No," Shane whispered, voice hoarse from singing and from want, sheer overwhelming want.

"Good. 'Cause I had this idea in the shower…"

"Yeah?" Shane gave in and pulled Brandt the rest of the way against him, thigh to thigh, chests brushing, warmth unspooling in his gut. "What's that?"

"You seemed to dig the idea of seeing my toy collection. Maybe you'd want to see me show off which ones I like?"

"Yeah." Shane could barely manage an articulate noise as warmth turned to heat turned to fiery lust. "Show me."

Chapter Fourteen

Brandt had been willing to pray to whatever sleep gods governed two-month-olds, he was that desperate to get a chance to be alone with Shane before they both passed out from exhaustion. Thankfully, his idea had worked, maybe a little too well because the ache lingered from listening to Shane sing sad, sleepy songs. He could still hear that perfect baritone as he led Shane down the hall toward his bedroom. A cappella, no guitar, no band, only the same strong, clear voice Shane had used for the silly songs, but stripped down to pure emotion. Old tunes, but new feelings in Brandt, ones he didn't know how to cope with.

But he did know how to kiss Shane, how to push him against the hall wall, not even waiting for his room or a bed to kiss him hard. All those strange, new feelings wiggled their way into the kiss. Raw. That was what Shane had called country music and raw was exactly how Brandt felt, like a scrape he couldn't reach. Vulnerable in a way he didn't like much.

What he did like though was Shane's mouth under his, hot and willing. Shane tasted like cookies, almost too sweet, the way he pulled Brandt in, met him kiss for kiss. He'd let Brandt plunder his mouth before returning the favor, a give and take that left them both breathless and clinging to each other.

"Been wanting to do that all day." Brandt rested his head against Shane's, not willing to move away, even to catch his breath.

"Me too." Shane found his mouth for another kiss, this one more aggressive as he took control of Brandt's mouth.

"Damn." Moaning, Brandt started a slow grind against Shane that only revved him up further.

"Fuck." Laughing low, Shane stilled Brandt's hips with a firm grip. "Are we getting off in the hall here or are you going to make good on that promise?"

"Oh, I can make good." Brandt captured his hand and dragged him the rest of the way to his bedroom.

"I bet you can." Shane moved like he was going to steal another kiss, then broke away to chuckle and point at the bed. "Hopeful much or do you always leave your toys around?"

Brandt's skin heated. He'd turned down the dimmer switch for the lights and pulled back the covers. And yeah, he'd laid out lube, three toys, and some condoms and a towel for easier cleanup.

"Told you. I had this idea in the shower." His voice was a little defensive because he wasn't used to this level of eagerness from himself. "Almost got off to my fantasy, but I decided to wait for you."

"Waiting is hopefully the more fun option." Shane licked his lips. Maybe Brandt wasn't the only one super eager. That helped.

"Hell, yes."

"Now, tell me about your…collection." Shane kept turning pinker and pinker the longer he looked at the bed.

"None of that shy act." Laughing, Brandt wrapped him up in a hug from behind, sliding a hand down Shane's torso. "Your dick says you're plenty into my toys."

"I'm into *you*." Shane tipped his head back against Brandt's. "Still not sure about trying a dildo or something myself, but hell, thinking about you with any of these has me ready to shoot in my jeans."

"Can't have that." Palming Shane through his jeans, Brandt lightly squeezed his hard cock before releasing him so he could point at the various options. "Mmm. You wanted to know the difference between them. This smaller one vibrates. Helpful for hands-free action. This other one has fun ridges and an angled tip to hit the sweet spot. And this bigger one is for when I want to feel full."

The last one was more phallic than the other two, which were more like fun plugs with flared bases. The bigger one was blue silicone, with a distinct round head, long shaft, and then longer curved base that allowed for easier gripping for fucking himself. He had another with a suction cup base, but that was more of shower toy, not as suitable for showing off. And showing off was exactly what he wanted to do. The thought alone of Shane watching him with any of these had his cock throbbing.

"And that feels good?" Shane hadn't moved his eyes off of the big one. "Full?"

"Uh huh. And how." Brandt reached around Shane to pick it up, show him the heft of it. "This the one you want to see?"

Shane inhaled sharply as he trailed a finger down the length of the toy. "Yeah. Please."

"So polite." Chuckling, Brandt dragged the chair he usually tossed his shirts on over near the bed. "You have a seat here so you can see all the action."

"You've seriously thought this through." Shane took the chair, legs spread, outline of his hard cock still prominent. His T-shirt was still twisted from the hallway make-out session, and Brandt came behind him and tugged at the fabric until Shane got the hint and removed it. He could keep the jeans on, but Brandt hadn't had nearly enough time to admire his lean yet chiseled chest with the barest dusting of hair and dusky nipples.

"You're not the only one with a creative imagination." Stepping back in front of Shane, he pulled off his own shirt.

"Apparently not...*damn*." Shane started out teasing but finished on a groan as Brandt's shorts hit the floor.

"You like?" Brandt preened a bit, coming close enough that Shane could touch if he wanted. Which mercifully he did, dancing his fingers down Brandt's chest to rest right above his cock.

"You know I do." Holding Brandt's gaze, Shane gave his cock a few firm strokes before releasing it. "Now get on that bed before I change my mind about what we're doing here."

"Look who's bossy now." Not truly put out, Brandt scrambled to the center of the bed, leaning back on a stack of pillows and angling himself so that Shane would have a good view of his ass.

"Hey, I never promised to be a silent audience." Shane leaned forward, eyes intense as he swept them over Brandt's naked body.

"Good. Talk me through it." Brandt didn't mind one bit if Shane wanted to get talky. Or bossy. He fucking loved it when Shane took over a kiss, and this was no different, the heady rush of giving up some control. "Tell me what you want to see."

"Show me how you warm up on your own." Shane reached out and tapped Brandt's foot. He was almost but not quite close enough to touch more of Brandt and the friction between wanting his touch and wanting to give him a show, amped Brandt up further.

"Alone, I don't have much patience," he had to admit, running his hands down his torso, quick journey straight to his cock.

Shane gave a dry laugh. "Somehow I'm not surprised."

"I go right for jerking it, but not too tight or fast yet." He kept his fist loose, enjoying the slide of his hard cock against his calloused palm. "A little tease is good. Gets me harder."

"Hard is good."

"Yeah, it is. You hard now?" Brandt asked even though he could still see the lump in Shane's jeans. But he wanted to see even more. "Get it out."

"I think you're forgetting who's giving the orders," Shane complained even as he lowered his zipper and withdrew his cock. Brandt liked the feel of it against his when they rubbed off a lot, but he also liked the chance to admire it from a distance. Long. Thick. Smooth. Wider near the base, less of a flared head than Brandt, but still so fucking sexy. Shane gave himself a stroke as he returned to his take-charge voice. "You keep touching."

"Oh, I will. The more I touch, the more turned I get. There's a certain level of horniness…hard to describe, but it's like my ass wakes up, demands some of the attention." A blush crept up from his chest, a new level of warmth. He'd never tried to explain this to anyone else before.

"It awake now?" Shane nudged Brandt's foot again, urging him to spread his legs. And fuck, Brandt wanted that, wanted to be on display for Shane, wanted him looking at Brandt's ass like it was the eighth wonder of the world.

"Uh huh." His ass clenched reflexively the more Shane stared him down. "You looking at me like that does it for me."

"Good. Show me what you do next." The tip of Shane's cock was damp and Brandt wanted to taste it almost as much as he wanted to keep the show going.

"Sometimes I go slow, play around with my balls and outside of my hole." He swept a hand over his balls, pausing to tug them lightly. "But more often, I go ahead and get the lube."

He grabbed the tube. It was half full, so Shane probably had a good idea of how often Brandt played like this. But instead of embarrassed, all he felt was emboldened. Damn right he liked playing with his ass and Shane liked watching, and the intersection of the two wants was perfection. Already, he was harder than he could remember being.

"So much rushing," Shane chided as he leisurely stroked his own cock, far slower than Brandt could ever manage. "It's a wonder you don't jump out of the plane at two thousand feet."

"Ha. Fair point. But it's hard to go slow when I know how good it can get." Slicking his fingers up, Brandt started tracing little circles around his rim, trying for the tease, but already wanting more. He pushed a finger in, and immediately his hips rocked upward, seeking.

"Tell me. How's it feeling now?" Shane's whisper was seductive as fuck, commanding but curious too.

"Tight. Alive. Like I want more." His own voice was

needier now, little moans escaping as he worked his finger deeper.

"Do it. Can you do two?"

"Ah…" He'd been about to add the second on his own, but having Shane direct him was hot as fuck. His ass pinched as he scissored his fingers a little. He pulled his legs back more so he could go deeper. "Yeah. That stretches. But it's good. So good. Hard to keep this position though which is why I love the toys. Easier to reach."

Withdrawing his fingers, he quickly put a condom on the largest of the toys and lubed it up.

"Sure you're ready for that one?" Shane's hand sped up a little and his breath hitched. "It's big."

"You're bigger." Brandt wasn't going for flattery. Shane was wider than the toy for sure, probably a little longer too, and damn Brandt couldn't wait to have him inside of him.

"True." Shane's rough breathing said he'd liked the compliment, but he somehow managed to sound vaguely interested not dying for it like Brandt.

"You like that thought, don't you? You fucking me."

Still with the too-calm tone, Shane gripped his cock tighter. "You know I do."

Maybe showing off wasn't the best use of Brandt's time. Need rose up in him, other fantasies he'd waited far too long to make reality.

"Do you want…"

"Not this time." Shane's voice was far more even than Brandt's. His smooth control only served to make Brandt that much more determined to see him unravel. "I want to see you take that toy. Want you to come on it."

"Damn. I'm regretting not making you sit closer. Wanna touch you."

Giving a dirty chuckle, Shane gestured at the slicked-up toy. "I think your hands are about to be a little busy..."

"Fuck right." Spreading his legs wider, Brandt positioned the toy at his rim. "So, everyone's a little different, at least judging by porn. Some go fast. Some go slow, ease it in, little by little."

"I don't even have to guess which camp you're in."

"Guess I am predictable. Get through the stretch part so I can fast forward to the part where I'm all full and the pressure on my gland is so good. That's when I like to linger a little, edge until I can't stand it."

"Do that." The hard edge to Shane's voice made Brandt's cock throb. "Get it in there, show me what you like."

"Yeah." Brandt pushed the toy in, steady like he liked, not so fast as to court a harsh sting, but enough that his body shuddered as it tried to adjust to the intrusion. His rim burned, but already the fullness was chasing that sensation away, replacing it with deep pleasure. He lacked Shane's way with words, but it didn't much matter because all he could do was moan softly anyway as he went deeper.

"Fuck. You're so fucking hot." Shane was leaning back in the chair now, stroking his cock, one hand flicking his nipple. Brandt wanted to do that for him, preferably with him buried in Brandt's ass, moaning just like that at how good it felt.

"Tell me," Brandt demanded as he rocked his hips to take the toy a little deeper.

"Turns me on, watching you open like this, taking it so good. Give yourself more." Finally, Shane's voice had more waver to it, more proof that he was as close to the edge as Brandt.

"Trying." Brandt's eyes screwed closed as he delved deeper, letting awareness of Shane fade so that it was simply him and the toy, doing what he liked.

"That's it." Shane's voice cut through his pleasure fog, but instead of making him tense, the praise made him melt further. "I want you to find that spot. The one you keep raving about."

Brandt had been close before Shane spoke, and his command was all it took for him to angle the toy upward, pressing into his prostate now. "Aaah. There."

"Jesus. Your eyes rolled back in your head. So fucking sexy. Do that again."

Shane didn't have to ask him twice. Brandt started fucking himself in earnest then, long, deep strokes that had him panting. "Fuck. Yes."

"You ever come without a hand on your dick?" Leaning forward, Shane rubbed Brandt's foot, a grounding touch, a welcome reminder that he was more than a detached audience member.

"Couple times." Brandt loved the memory of those solo sessions, but no way was he going to last that long now. "Not…usually…patient."

"Not surprised there." Laughing, Shane resumed stroking his cock, voice all confident. "Bet I could make you wait."

Brandt wanted to drown in Shane's confidence, let his demands carry him higher than he could go on his own. "Hell yes you could."

The thought of coming on Shane's cock had him reaching for his cock, needing to chase the edge that much faster.

"No. Not yet." Shane's harsh command stilled Brandt's

hand. "Get closer. So close you're gonna die if you don't touch your cock."

"Fuck. You don't ask for much." Even as he complained, Brandt still moved his free hand away and started fucking himself faster with the dildo, hard thrusts that had his back arching and thigh muscles shaking. "Right…there…now. Please. Now."

"That's it. Beg me." Shane's hand sped up, the tip of his cock glistening with fresh moisture that he spread around with his thumb. Watching him might be enough to get Brandt there, but he was still greedy and impatient.

"Please. You come too. Please."

Shane shook his head like he was about to say no, then his whole body tensed. Oh fuck yes. He was unraveling exactly as Brandt had hoped.

"Do it. Stroke that cock for me. Come." Shane didn't really have to add that last command because Brandt already was. Didn't even take two full strokes of his fist before he was shooting creamy ropes all over his abs. His ass spasmed around the toy, another layer of pleasure that coaxed another few spurts when he pressed deeper. Shane must have liked that because he was coming too, even before Brandt withdrew the toy, groaning and arching away from the chair before slumping back.

"Dear God that was maybe the hottest thing I've ever seen." Shane's come had landed both on his own stomach and Brandt's leg, and he fumbled for his shirt on the floor, using it to clean them both.

"Live action porn?" Brandt stretched as Shane swiped at his stomach.

"And then some." Shane glanced down at the bed, and for a second, Brandt was sure he was about to stretch out next to him, but instead he gave the barest shake of his head and stepped back.

"Damn." Brandt hid any conflicting feelings under a laugh. No way was he begging Shane to cuddle. "Now I need a second shower."

"Yeah, you do." Shane's mouth quirked, again like he wanted to say more than he was. "Tell you what, you go first, leave me some hot water, then I'll shower and see if I can sleep. I'll take the first wakeup, get you some consecutive hours before you have to work tomorrow."

"You taking pity on me because I'm all fucked out now?" Brandt waggled his eyebrows and kept his voice easy because the alternative was a level of neediness he never let himself have. If he wanted a cuddle and to drift off together, that unfamiliar impulse was on him, not Shane.

"Yep." Shane moved his gaze toward the door, but his feet stayed rooted next to Brandt.

"Not gonna fight you on it." Stretching, Brandt faked a yawn. He meant more than the order of the showers. He wasn't gonna fight to make Shane feel something he didn't.

"Good. You get some rest." And then Shane went and undid every last one of Brandt's resolutions when he brushed a kiss over Brandt's forehead. Just that one moment of tenderness, that little gesture, was enough to have Brandt wanting with fierceness he wasn't sure he'd ever had before.

"You too," he managed, eyes burning as Shane pressed another kiss to his mouth. His heart might not have enough padding for this fling of theirs, yet no way was he stopping before Shane did, before he got to experience every possible moment.

Chapter Fifteen

"What the heck are you up to?" Shane pulled up short at the sight of Brandt at the dining table with a sewing machine in front of him and fabric and scissors strewn over the tabletop. He'd already been in a good mood from band practice, and it showed in his light tone.

"Sewing." Brandt continued to feed fabric through the machine. They'd had a fast baby handoff when Brandt had come in from work and Shane had needed to leave, but clearly he'd been busy in Shane's absence.

"I see that." Still in a teasing mood, he offered Brandt a grin. "Since when do you sew?"

Shane walked over to where the baby was in her swing, doing her new trick of holding on to a little soft toy and watching whatever Brandt was doing with wide eyes. She might have Brandt's birthmark, but she had Shelby's cheeks and her long thin fingers, which made Shane's chest tight when he thought too hard about it.

"How do you think our gear gets repaired?" Brandt made a dismissive gesture before he turned the fabric with the ease of someone who did this often. His competence was weirdly sexy, the way he effortlessly juggled talking with Shane, working the foot pedal, and guiding the fabric. "Hell, yes I can sew. But I could do that before smoke jumping too."

"Oh?" Lifting Jewel out of the swing, Shane took a seat on the floor with her near Brandt's chair at the table.

"Yeah. One of the foster homes I was in had a mom who liked to quilt. She showed me some of the basics of hand sewing and how machines operate. Nice place. Had to move on when she got pregnant with twins, but the sewing lessons stuck with me."

"I'm glad you had that for a while." Shane's jaw flexed. The image of young Brandt, moving on yet again, made a melancholy tune roll through Shane's head. He tried to match Brandt's casual tone, but it was tough when he wanted to rail at the system that had let Brandt down over and over. "What are you making now?"

"Well, I like the sling we got for holding the diva at the resale place, but it pulls at my shoulder and is almost too short for either of our torsos. I had the idea that some of the industrial material we use for packs would make a better sling, so I deconstructed the first one and am having a go at it."

"Go you. Super dad." He meant it too because not only had Brandt coped with Shane being out of the house for a few hours, but he'd managed to craft for the kid. Damn impressive.

"Huh. I guess I am. The dad I mean." Brandt sounded slightly amazed at this turn of events.

"Yeah, you are." Shane was more and more able to see Brandt in that role. He was damn good with Jewel, never leaving her entirely to Shane when he was home and always attentive to her needs. "Just wait until she starts talking. And now you're going to be the only dad on the playground with a parachute-worthy sling."

"Talking? Playground? I'm over here trying to take it one day at a time." Stopping sewing for a moment, Brandt glanced down at Shane and the baby, lopsided grin but worry in his eyes. "There's still no guarantee that your sister is going to stay gone. And beyond that, I don't want to think too far down the road."

"Me either. And I tried Shelby's phone again," Shane admitted. It hadn't been because he was overwhelmed or because Brandt was doing a bad job. He was concerned about her, and Jewel learning new tricks only underscored how long she'd been gone. "Texted her the pic of Jewel smiling. And then later, I tried calling. No reply."

"That's worrisome." Brandt's frown mirrored the weight on Shane's soul whenever he thought about Shelby. "I'm still concerned this could be some sort of post-baby depression. I wish there was some way to know if she was safe."

"Me too. I know she's alive because Macy says Shelby will be in touch when she's ready. I like to think Macy would at least text if she was in a bad way." Shane had known Macy a number of years, ever since he first started getting gigs on the festival circuit as a teen. She could be flighty and temperamental, but she did seem to care about his sister. He hoped.

"Yeah. I hope so. Speaking of Shelby, I talked to Cameron." Brandt's mouth twisted as he mentioned the lawyer. "She's working on those court papers. If your sister's not going to communicate with either of us, I probably have no choice but to file, but damn, I wish there was another way."

"Me too." Shane huffed out a long sigh and buried his face against the baby. The heaviness of the conversation was getting to all of them—baby squirming, Brandt looking like he'd gone a few rounds with a monster truck, and Shane feeling like no one was going to come out a winner in this thing. Time to change the subject. Forcing a smile, he brightened his tone. "Let's see this sewing project of yours. Gonna model it for me?"

"I think you like me showing off a little too much." Brandt waggled his eyebrows at Shane.

"After the other night? Hell yes." All damn day he'd been haunted by the memory of Brandt's face as he'd climaxed, the way his big body had bowed and the sounds he'd made. He'd needed Jewel to sleep, and soon, so he could indulge in another mental replay. "But let's stick to a G-rated show right now."

"You got it." Standing, Brandt pulled the new sling over his shoulder before scooping the baby off Shane's lap and settling her in the pouch. "I think she likes it."

After tightening the sling, Brandt gave a spin, which had Jewel grinning.

"Having been strapped to you, I can testify to it being a little fun." Shane gave him a pointed look, one that had color rising up Brandt's neck. Knowing he remembered the parachute jump that fondly made Shane's insides warm and melty.

"Yeah, it was." Brandt held his gaze until Shane was the one blushing and looking away as Brandt added, "And hey, it's been almost a year, right? Do you have a birthday coming up?"

"Soon. No big deal." Shane had never been the type for a party, even when younger, leaving the yearning for a big crowd to Shelby. "Jewel will be three months then too. Make a fuss over that, not me."

"We'll see. Maybe I should get you your own toy." Brandt's eyes sparkled as he laughed.

"I think you've got plenty of options for both of us." And damn, now Shane really wanted the baby to sleep so he could watch Brandt with a different one maybe. Or replace the toy with his own fingers or better yet, his cock. His list of things he wanted to do with Brandt kept growing, not shrinking.

"Damn right I do. And I'm dying to—"

Jewel let out a fussy noise, like she'd had enough of both the sling and their flirting.

"Someone says our chances of getting lucky tonight just went down." Shane headed to the kitchen to make the bottle.

"Good thing she's cute." Following him, Brandt added some bouncing to his steps which seemed to work to distract Jewel. "And so are you."

"Me?"

"Oh yeah." Somehow Brandt managed an appreciative once-over even while trying to calm the baby. "What's your favorite flavor of cake?"

"Choc—*wait*." Shane wagged a finger at Brandt, trying to channel some of Brandt's playfulness into his ambivalence over birthdays. "No way. I said I don't want anything."

"Fine. Have it your way." Brandt shrugged as he accepted the bottle, but Shane had a feeling the subject wasn't truly dropped. "Are there more cookies left?"

"Yeah, I'll get you one if you want to do the feeding." After grabbing the cookies from the pantry, he followed Brandt to the couch and waited until the baby was happily cuddled up with her bottle in the crook of Brandt's arm before holding the cookie so Brandt could take a bite.

"Thanks." Grinning up at him, Brandt kissed Shane's

hand before sneaking another bite of cookie. "We make a good team."

"We do." And therein lay Shane's biggest problem. They had a good thing going, but good things never lasted.

"Damn fine day for a jump." Bronco bounced on his feet like a hyper puppy and was about as good at listening. "And some actual work."

"Word." Brandt might not be jumping around, but he was psyched to get to head deep in the forest to deal with clearing out dead timber that had been flagged as a potential summer hazard after some damage in a lightning strike. The clear blue sky awaited their jump, and he was ready for the chainsaw workout.

"Hey, training is work," Hartman reminded them both as he checked the straps on one of their gear packs.

"Sure it is, but you know what I mean. This one actually counts for something more than training reps with the rookies." Bronco conveniently forgot that he'd been one of those rookies not long ago. He also had far too much excitement for this early in the morning. Hell, neither Shane nor the baby had been up when Brandt had crept from the house. His head pounded like he was going to need another hit of coffee to keep up with Bronco's energy.

"I get it." Yawning, Brandt stretched out his back before strapping into his pack. There wasn't any time for that coffee now as the plane would be ready any moment.

"Cross-check Bronco," Hartman ordered him as they finished gearing up. Double-checking each other was a big part of their pre-jump routine, but Bronco still groaned as Brandt examined each of his connection points and the condition of his pack.

"Tighten this connector," he recommended, pointing at a spot near Bronco's groin. Dude was touchy enough about being checked that Brandt wasn't going to do it for him, but he sure as hell was going to wait until Bronco did it himself to Brandt's satisfaction.

"It's fine, but whatever." Bronco's tone was somewhere between impatient and whiny. It was going to be a damn long morning if he kept this shit up. "Being a dad is making you all overprotective."

"If it keeps you alive, you'll be damn grateful." Hartman shot Bronco a harsh look.

"Sure thing." Bronco still rolled his eyes as soon as Hartman turned away. He was a handful, and Brandt wasn't looking forward to babysitting him most of the season.

"Here comes our ride." Hartman gestured at the tarmac. "Let's take care of business and be home for dinner."

"Amen." Brandt was already looking forward to that. Last night, after Shane had come in from band practice, they'd had a nice chat, but the baby had taken forever to settle again. Eventually, exhaustion had won out, and they hadn't ended up fooling around despite all their flirting. Which was fine. Brandt was an adult. He could live until they finally managed another hookup, but he'd be lying if he didn't admit he was craving the taste of Shane's mouth something awful.

And his conversation. Talking with him, both joking around and more serious stuff, had become one of his favorite things. He'd missed him when he'd been at practice last night, but tonight he'd be home and had promised to do something with chicken for dinner. Bronco might not recognize this new cautious, domesticated self of Brandt's, but that was okay because Brandt was still figuring it all out himself.

Once they were in the air, thoughts of Shane fled, replaced by the business at hand. The din of the plane and the jostling of his crew was familiar. Grounding. No matter what else changed, he had this. Reid was acting as spotter for them, and he kept frowning as new weather data came in. "Not crazy about these wind conditions."

Hartman nodded, an entire conversation happening between him and Reid in body language alone. Their close bond was as enviable as it was frustrating.

Giving up on trying to read their faces, Brandt asked, "You want to call it?"

"Nah." Hartman's tone was casual, but his eyes were sharper than usual, posture a little straighter.

"Let's circle again first, but you'll want to keep your heads about you to avoid getting treed." Reid had a meaningful look for all of them, but his gaze lingered on Bronco.

The kid held up both hands. "Hey! Why does everyone assume I'm the risk taker?"

"Because you are." Brandt might have reached the end of his patience already, and they weren't even on the ground yet.

"Hey now. Tone it down." Hartman frowned at Brandt, unspoken message that Brandt was older and supposed to be better than petty squabbles.

And then there was no time for arguing as the plane swung back around and the decision was made to go for it. Gear first, then them, timing both practiced and absolutely critical. Brandt waited for Reid's signal before leaping. No hesitation, only appreciation for the blue sky and the rush of freefall that never grew old, even as he executed his training for positioning and the release of his chute. Below, the green canopy of the forest broken up by rocky sections waited to greet them.

Despite the great visibility, the trick was going to be making the landing zone in this wind. The air fought against all his steering efforts, yanking him this way and that. The ground was rushing up, too fast, and he was going to wind up in a tree if he couldn't course correct.

And there were too many of the suckers, big ancient trees stretching up, dizzyingly high and close, wide branches waiting to snag his chute. Inches. He was inches from dangling off one of those widow-maker limbs.

Not today, fucker. He flexed his whole body into a last-ditch course correction, avoiding the trees, but with only seconds to prepare for a hard, teeth-rattling landing.

"Damn, that was close." Dazed, he rubbed his thighs and rolled his shoulders, trying to make sure all his parts were still in working order before he stood up and untangled himself.

"You're telling me." Hartman shook his head. His face was dusty, like he too had taken a jolt. "Some of the gear ended up treed. Lucky it wasn't your ass."

"Damn right." Brandt looked in the direction Hartman was pointing. Sure enough, the chute for their biggest gear pack had ended up tangled in an angry-looking tree. "Fuck. At least it's not one of us."

"Yeah, but someone's gonna have to fetch that down." Bronco looked around, like another crewmember might materialize from the rocks.

"I'll do it." No time for games, he headed to the tree in question. Like all of them, he was good at tree climbing, even big fuckers like this one. But he wasn't ten feet up when the tree creaked. Damn. It was drier than it looked. "Fuck. I don't trust this tree."

A year ago he would have kept going, would have secured their gear because a single creak wasn't enough to scare him off. But now the creak echoed through his bones, an ominous sound that stood between him and the easy evening he had planned. Several smoke jumpers had suffered vicious falls the last few years, and he inhaled sharply. What was he willing to bet here that this tree would hold? His neck? His future? Jewel's?

That last question did it. Nope. He climbed back down so he could reassess his approach.

"Oh, stop with the overprotective bit. It's getting old." Huffing noisily, Bronco shoved by him. "You keep dithering. I'll get it."

"No, you won't. Wait a damn minute." A minute. That was what Brandt needed. A chance to come up with a better plan that wouldn't put any of them in danger. But Bronco was already scampering up, ignoring both Brandt and Hartman, who was gesturing furiously for Bronco to get down. He reached the branch where Brandt had turned around, reached up.

Creak.

"Don't—"

Didn't matter whether it was him or Hartman who yelled because the whole mess, Bronco and branch, both came tumbling down.

"Bronco!" Brandt rushed over, Hartman right on his heels.

Bronco lay in a heap, groaning softly. "Fuck my life."

"How bad is it?" Crouching down next to him, Brandt stopped him from sitting up.

"Don't move." Hartman joined him in pushing Bronco back down. The risk of head or spine injury was too great to not take every precaution. "Let's check you out. Wilder, can you radio in that we've got an injury? They'll probably want to send in the backup team and get us a medical evac for Bronco."

"Got it." Brandt went for the radio that was back with their other gear, the stuff that wasn't currently treed.

"I'm fine." Bronco was well enough to keep hassling Hartman as he checked him out. "Just my fucking arm. And maybe my ankle."

Hartman made a skeptical noise. "You in good enough shape to pack five miles out?"

"If we go slow…" Bronco hedged.

"I'm on that evac," Brandt promised Hartman before Bronco could try again to convince them he was okay. He got a message into base before returning to Hartman and Bronco.

"They'll have an ETA for us shortly on both the evac and a second crew."

"Fuck." Bronco's curse had as much wounded pride as pain behind it. "I hate them sending in someone else to do our job."

Hartman made fast work of splinting Bronco's arm. "Maybe next time you'll listen to me and Wilder and then we can all do our jobs."

"It was only a slip. Wilder was being a fucking—"

"Think about your words," Hartman warned before Brandt could defend himself. "You sure you want to be starting shit when we still need to haul your ass out?"

"Sorry." Bronco managed to sound a little more contrite.

And damn, that could be Brandt himself lying there,

putting up a fuss about being packed out. His stomach quaked at how close he'd come to falling.

His insides stayed all jumbled up the whole time they got Bronco ready for the helitack crew for a medical evacuation. They had to pack him out to a flatter clearing, and bile kept rising in Brandt's throat every time he thought about being the one on the stretcher. A decade of doing this, and his in-case-of-emergency contact form had stayed blank. Two weeks with a kid and suddenly he was thinking hard about adding Shane's name to the sucker because the thought of him waiting at home with the kid had him ready to hurl all over again.

"You okay?" Hartman asked in a low voice as they waited for the evac chopper. "If you're not feeling well, I can send you with him."

"I'm okay. You were right though, close call." Too close. He wasn't going to rest easy any time soon. He wasn't going to run from the work that still needed to be done though, nor was he going to leave Hartman alone with the replacement crew. Besides, five of them could get the job done fast, even without Bronco. "I'll be happy when we're done, that's for sure."

"Yep. We'll get you home for supper." Hartman laughed like he still couldn't quite believe how eager Brandt was to get back to his kid these days.

And honestly, neither could Brandt. This parenthood stuff wasn't for wimps either. That moment when he'd fought the air, trying to avoid the trees, still lingered with him, as did him pulling back from the climb. A few weeks ago, neither thing would have rattled him, but now all he could think about was how damn fine the line was between strutting out of a job and being carried out.

Hours later, no one strutted, but they all did make it

back to base in one piece, sun still shining like it hadn't been a long-ass day already. It had taken all of them to safely retrieve the gear from the tree, no more injuries, and then they'd had the actual work to get done, too.

And as for the rest of his mood as he finished up, all the loose ball bearings rattling around his chest, maybe home was all he needed. Weird how his craving wasn't for a beer or a hot shower, but for time with Shane and the baby. He might not understand the how or why, but under his weariness and exhaustion was the bone-deep certainty that Shane's nearness could help, a terrifying craving he couldn't shake. And worst of all, maybe he didn't want to.

Chapter Sixteen

"You look like hell." Shane supposed there were nicer ways to greet Brandt, but the guy truly did look terrible as he came into the house—dusty and sweaty with a deep frown and slumped shoulders.

"Yeah. I imagine I do." Brandt leaned heavily against a cabinet. Shane jiggled the baby in his arms, not wanting her crankiness to add to whatever Brandt was dealing with.

"Tough day?"

"You could say that." Head tipping back, Brandt closed his eyes. His dirt-streaked fists clenched and unclenched. The scent of the chicken Shane had browned to go with some baked potatoes filled the kitchen, but Brandt's desperation cut through Shane's hunger, made him shift Jewel so he could squeeze Brandt's arm.

"There's food, but if you want to shower first, I can set it to warm instead."

Brandt opened a single eye. "If that's not too much trouble…"

"Of course not." After a long, frustrating day, maybe Shane had been looking forward to the baby handoff, but no way was he pushing the kid on Brandt when he looked like that. "You go shower."

"Thanks." Brandt didn't take too long cleaning up, emerging in sweats and a T-shirt with a towel around his neck right as Shane was plating the food. He'd stashed the baby in her swing, and he handed Brandt a plate before she could start squawking.

"Damn, I'm hungry." Brandt started eating before he even reached the table, and Shane didn't force him into conversation as he packed away the food. However, they were both only half finished when Jewel started beating the air with her tiny fists.

"Hey, sweetie. You want out?" Brandt abandoned his plate to go crouch next to the swing, voice still exhausted but also strained, like he was making the effort to be tender even if it cost him more precious energy.

And Jewel responded as soon as Brandt lifted her out, ceasing her fussing long enough to cuddle against Brandt. He even managed to coax a few smiles from her while Shane made the bottle. She sure did seem to love being close to Brandt, and Shane didn't blame her. Even with Brandt tired and stressed out, Shane still appreciated his presence beyond the baby help.

Brandt took the baby and her bottle to the couch, where he settled down with a groan. "I don't mind holding her while you eat."

"Thanks." Shane ate quickly to outrace guilt over Brandt being the one to deal with the baby. Grabbing Brandt's plate, he headed over to the couch area. "Here. Let me have her so you can eat the rest of your plate."

But when he reached the couch, Brandt and Jewel both had their eyes closed. Brandt had turned so his long legs stretched out along the length of the couch. The empty bottle sat on the floor and the baby had snuggled into Brandt's chest, snoozing away.

"Oh." Shane started to back away, but Brandt blinked a couple of times.

"'M sorry. Sleepy."

"So is Jewel." Setting the plate aside, Shane carefully took her from Brandt. "You rest here. I'll see if she'll sleep in the crib."

"Thanks." Brandt's eyes fluttered shut again as Shane retreated with the sleeping baby. Settling her in the crib took some coaxing and back patting and a few songs, but finally she was deeply asleep enough to allow Shane to creep out of the room.

And almost run into Brandt, who was staggering toward his room. "Oops."

"Sorry." Brandt rolled his neck.

"Don't be." Shane gave in to the urge he'd had ever since Brandt turned up so exhausted, moving so he could rub Brandt's shoulders. "Think you can sleep?"

"Maybe." Brandt stretched into the contact, not so subtly inviting more. "Not sure. Guess I'll try."

"Okay." Shane continued the massage, working Brandt's tense muscles with his thumbs and palms. "Let me know if you need anything."

"That feels good," Brandt whispered softly, like any sudden movement might make Shane stop. Or like the admission cost him, acknowledging his needs even this much.

"You want more?" Not waiting for a reply, Shane moved to Brandt's neck, more deliberate now, trying to sense what Brandt needed most.

"If you want…"

"I want," Shane said firmly, dropping a kiss on the back of Brandt's strong neck. And he did want, and not as a sex thing. More like Brandt was hurting and he wanted to help. "You want to lie down for it?"

"Maybe." Brandt's eyes darted around like a bed or couch was likely to show up in the middle of the hall. Shane steered the tired guy toward his room, where the big bed would give him more room to work and where Brandt could safely collapse.

"Shirt off," he ordered as they reached the bed.

"One of your bossy moods, I see." Brandt managed a tired smile before pulling the shirt off and stretching out on his stomach.

"I'm probably not the best at this," he admitted as he knelt next to Brandt on the bed. "But I want to try, so tell me what feels good."

He resumed rubbing Brandt's shoulders, digging his fingers into a particularly tense knot. He didn't have a ton of experience with either getting or giving a massage, but he tried to aim for what he figured might feel nice.

"That," Brandt groaned as Shane traced the long line of his spine with his thumbs. "You can go harder. I won't break."

"This?" Shane worked the area around Brandt's shoulder blades, pressing deeper as Brandt relaxed further into the mattress with soft groans that increased the more Shane tried. With feedback like that, experimenting around with different pressure and strokes of his hands was fun.

"Fuck." Brandt released a lusty moan as Shane found a particularly good spot on his upper back. "I'd say we should hire you out to the rest of the crew, but I might get jealous."

"You? Jealous?" Shane paused long enough to kiss

Brandt's neck again, a soft little reward for admitting he didn't want Shane touching others.

"Trust me." Brandt gave a rough chuckle. "I'm amazed too."

"Better be careful or we're going to fully domesticate you." Shane gave him a playful swat on the ass before he straddled Brandt so he could put more weight behind his hands for the massage.

"Funny. And fuck, I was thinking exactly that when…" Brandt trailed off on a groan that was more pain than pleasure.

"When?" Shane prompted, softening both his touch and his tone. "It's okay if you don't want to talk about it, but I'm here if you do. I get crap days."

"Crap day. Yeah. That's one way to put it."

Shane waited him out as he kneaded Brandt's meaty shoulders. And sure enough, Brandt did have more to say. "There was a lot of wind today. Made our jump… challenging. Then there was an injury. Which happens. Part of the job. But…"

"It rattled you?" Shane was guessing, but he could tell from how battered Brandt had looked when he'd arrived home that it likely had.

"Yeah. Ordinarily, it wouldn't." Brandt tensed under Shane's touch, undoing all his earlier work getting Brandt to relax. But this was important too, getting Brandt to keep talking. "But I kept thinking about if it were me. Who would tell you and the baby?"

"Huh. Yeah. We'd want to know." Shane stilled, hands resting lightly against Brandt's warm sides. Inside though, his chest went tight and cold. He hadn't thought about this before, the very real risks of Brandt's job, what that might mean for Jewel. For him. For what they had going here, even if they didn't want to name it. "Maybe you could give someone my number? At least until you get other childcare arrangements."

He hoped that didn't sound too desperate, but his need to know Brandt was safe outweighed his ego's need to play this cool.

Luckily though, Brandt didn't fight him, instead nodding into the pillow. "I'm gonna do that tomorrow."

"Thanks." Resuming the massage, Shane swept his hands up and down the broad planes of Brandt's back, head still churning with the risks Brandt faced every day. "Was…was the injury bad?"

"Could have been. Damn fool risk this kid took. And he is a kid. Younger than you even." Brandt tensed again, frustration clear from his tone.

"I'm not a kid," Shane protested, digging into Brandt's lower back a little harder than he probably needed to.

"No, that was a compliment." Brandt sighed like he enjoyed the rougher touch and wiggled more into the mattress. "You're more mature than I was at your age, that's for damn sure. Anyway, Bronco fell from a tree. Avoided a concussion by the skin of his teeth. Broke his wrist and I'm not sure what else."

"Damn." Shane whistled low to try to cover the shudder that raced through him.

"Yeah. Fuck. Could have been me."

"But it wasn't." He was going to cling to that fact, hold it close so he had any hope of sleep himself that night. Brandt was safe and in one piece and here, and that counted for a whole lot right then.

"Someday it might be." Not letting Shane have his delusion of safety, Brandt had a far more pragmatic tone. "That's the thing. None of us ever know when shit's

going to get real. Roger didn't. Or any of the other buddies I've lost over the years."

"That's hard." Shane wasn't sure what else to say.
Roger's loss still ate at Brandt. That much was clear from
the pain every time he mentioned his name, and nothing
Shane could say was going to bring back Brandt's friend
or make the risks he faced any less.

"So fucking hard." Brandt's voice cracked, and Shane
stopped rubbing to stroke his sides more gently. "I almost
can't think on it. Most of the time I don't."

"I get that. Some things are almost too much to let
yourself dwell on." Shane hadn't suffered many real
losses like Brandt, but he had his share of heartache,
memories that hurt when he poked them.

"Yeah. And the thing is, I don't even like this kid that
much." Sighing heavily, Brandt stretched like he needed
Shane to keep the massage going. "Yet, here I am all torn
up over him breaking a wrist."

"You're getting soft," Shane teased as he returned to
massaging Brandt's strong shoulders and upper arms.

Brandt laughed exactly as Shane had intended, some
of his tension draining away. "Fuck you."

"Nothing wrong with letting yourself feel stuff."
Shane traced the curve of Brandt's biceps with his thumb.
He was such a fucking liar, giving advice he couldn't
take. "Emotions don't have to be big and scary."

"Says the guy who practically opens a vein every time
you sing, even to the baby."

"You think so?" Shane's ego hummed at the compliment.

"Can't wait to see you tomorrow with a band." Brandt
sounded sleepy again, but also warm. Almost sultry.
"And yeah, all those feelings...the stuff I try not to think

about, you manage to make it almost pretty when you sing."

"Maybe that's the trick. Take the stuff that hurts and do something with it." Shane shifted against him. Brandt might think he was brave for being able to show emotion, but the reality was that sitting with his feelings made his whole body revolt. He *needed* that release of grabbing his guitar or doing something, anything. "And it's not always singing. Sometimes I punch a pillow or do push-ups until my arms wanna fall off."

"I wondered how you kept in shape. Rage pushups?"

"Sometimes. Whatever works." He punctuated his advice with digging his thumbs into a particularly tight knot under his neck. "But I can't run from all emotions. Not sure I want to, honestly. Feelings suck, but then I write the perfect line…"

He couldn't help his dreamy sigh. He'd had a great writing day when Jewel had napped. The song for Brandt's friend was almost done, and he had the start of a few others going too. With any luck, even if he couldn't guarantee his own singing success, he could sell one of these songs, get a little breathing room on his finances.

"Dude, you talk about songwriting like most of us do sex." Brandt sounded more in awe than complaining.

"Hey, when it's good, it's good." Shane softened his touch because Brandt was sounding sleepier and sleepier.

"This is good, too. Damn." Brandt's groan was low and lusty, and Shane had to shift away so that Brandt didn't catch on to how turned on Shane was. The guy needed sleep more than he needed a horny Shane rubbing up on him. "Didn't realize how much I needed this."

"Good." Shane swung off Brandt's ass and pulled

the covers up over him, smoothing them in place over Brandt's back.

"Fuck." Brandt's voice was down to a rough, sleepy whisper. "Really want to return the favor, but I keep almost drifting off."

"Do it. Let yourself sleep. It's what you need now. You can owe me one later." Shane continued to rub his back through the covers lightly, a grown-up version of how he'd put the baby to sleep earlier. "I'll just sneak out if you start snoring."

"Maybe..." Rolling toward him, Brandt cracked his eyes half-open.

"Yeah?"

"Nothing." Looking away, Brandt sagged back against the pillow. "Only that you don't have to go. You can sleep here."

"That what you want?" Shane stretched out next to him, his front to Brandt's side, holding him close as he dared.

Brandt took a lengthy pause, several breaths before his head dropped against Shane. "Maybe."

"Then that's what I'll do." Shane kissed Brandt's messy hair and held him close. Brandt was already halfway to sleep, and it wasn't long at all before he relaxed even more in Shane's arms, softly snoring. Shifting restlessly, Shane willed the rest of his erection to go away. This wasn't about sex, not tonight. It was about what Brandt needed, about making him feel better after a fucked-up day, and about giving him what little comfort Shane could.

And strangely, sleeping without sex was way more

intimate than if Brandt *had* wanted to get off first. And way more deadly to Shane's heart, a possibility that kept him awake long after Brandt drifted off.

Chapter Seventeen

"Okay, baby. Let's do this thing." Brandt triple-checked the position and tightness of the sling before taking his hands away to close his car door. He'd dropped Shane off at the steak house's back entrance, then he and Jewel had taken their time getting set to go watch. Fresh bottle. A change. A ride in the sling instead of the bulky car seat. Surprisingly, Brandt liked wearing Jewel, liked her close, and liked how she smiled for him when he looked down at her. Shane might have the magic touch with his singing for her when she was fussy, but Brandt loved how the sling could have a similar calming effect.

All in all, he was feeling like the super dad Shane thought he was, and he stood up a little taller as he reached the hostess station on the expansive porch of the Western-themed building which vaguely resembled an upscale barn in styling.

"Welcome." The blonde woman working the hostess station had a smile and aggressively helpful demeanor worthy of an insurance commercial. She grabbed two menus before Brandt even had a chance to speak. "Waiting for your wife before you grab a table?"

"Uh…no. No wife. Just us." Smiling back, he gestured at the baby.

"Awww." The hostess did the whole fake-melting thing that some women liked to do around small children and animals. She also didn't hide her slow perusal of his ring finger either. "Table for one, then. Er...two. You going to want a high chair?"

"She's not sitting up yet enough for a high chair." Brandt laughed and patted Jewel. From his scouring of the baby book, Shane would know the exact month babies started sitting independently, but Brandt at least knew enough to not put her in something without back support. Planning ahead for sitting on the patio to hear the band, he'd dressed her in the dragon sleeper with the hood.

"She seems pretty happy right where she is." Having finished examining Brandt's hands, the woman returned her gaze to his face, far flirtier glint to her eyes. And on a different night, Brandt might flirt back, have a little fun, but tonight his attention was already on the small stage where the band was setting up.

"Hopefully, she stays calm until the music starts." He followed the woman as she wove her way between tables full of families and couples enjoying the start of their weekends with lots of platter-size steaks and cocktails in mason jars.

"Oh, you came for the music? This group is usually fun. I'll get you a table with a decent view."

She finally arrived at a tiny table off to the side. Table for one, indeed. Maybe he should have invited Hartman and Reid or some of the other guys to come out and hear Shane sing. Weird as being so conspicuously single here was, though, he also was strangely reluctant to share Shane with his coworkers. Not because he feared their judgment, but because he wasn't sure he could hide all his mixed-up emotions and wasn't really ready for any razzing in that department, didn't want them cheapening…whatever the fuck this was.

"Enjoy the music." She gave him another lingering smile.

"Thanks. I'm…friends with the singer they've got tonight." He was, right? If nothing else, he and Shane had to be friends at this point. Fuck buddies didn't share massages, didn't hold someone all night simply because they had a bad day, and didn't wake up early to make sure Brandt had coffee and food for another long day.

"Excellent." She gave him a last flirty glance, and a more determined guy than Brandt would have probably come away with her number, but Brandt wasn't that guy, not tonight.

Instead, he was the guy who bounced his kid in the sling and ordered finger food easy to eat one-handed with a baby on his front. Hell, it was only him and Jewel. No one else to care if they got three appetizers and no main dish. And this way, he could maybe save some food for when Shane got his break between sets. While they waited on his order, he made the silverware dance for Jewel. She loved when he got silly with her soft toys, and his antics earned him another gummy grin.

The band finished their warmup before his food arrived, and the drummer found a lively beat, her ponytail bouncing with her efforts, before the bass player stepped forward.

"Hey there, beautiful people. I'm Tim with Cowboy Up." All the musicians gave a friendly wave, and Shane too stepped forward. Damn, he looked good up there. Fresh dark-washed jeans and a close-fitting Western shirt with pearl buttons. And his guitar all shiny under the lights. He had a big grin for the audience as Tim continued, "Tonight we're joined by Shane Travis, and we're gonna play some of your old school country favorites. Let's get this thing started."

They launched into an oldie Brandt remembered from several different long drives, staple of radio stations all over the west, but somehow Shane breathed fresh life into the tired classic, sweet baritone carrying the tune and making the crowd tap their feet and turn their heads. By the second song, several couples were dancing near the stage, and Brandt bounced the baby in time to Shane's crooning.

By song three, his food had arrived, and he spent several songs juggling the baby, the food, and his pride at watching Shane slay it. Then Shane launched into a love song, some cowboy pining for the girl he couldn't have, and Brandt had to set his food aside and simply *listen*. God, the way this man could make him ache, make him jealous of the girl in the song and the audience both. He both wanted to bottle Shane up, keep him all for himself, and to see him in some huge stadium on the big stage his talent deserved. It wasn't simply how Shane could hold a note or how perfect his pitch was. Rather, it was that deep down feeling he inspired, the way Brandt believed him, believed each word like Shane was singing for him and him alone.

When the set break arrived, Brandt was so ready to see Shane up close that he had to deliberately direct his attention to the diva as Shane approached the table so he wouldn't see how damn sappy he'd made him.

"You made it the whole set." Shane settled into the chair opposite Brandt and swiped a chicken finger.

"We did. The diva is actually behaving. I think she

likes all the people to look at." He turned so that the baby could see Shane.

"Maybe she does like my singing." Shane reached over and clucked Jewel under the chin. His speculative gaze though was all for Brandt, and it was adorable how a guy that fucking talented was all bashful like Brandt might have not appreciated the music.

"You're not terrible." Brandt wasn't above making Shane squirm, but he couldn't help grinning while he teased.

"High praise." Shane's eye roll said he was on to Brandt's game. He stole some more fries and drank half a glass of water in a single go.

"Told you last night." Dropping his voice, Brandt leaned forward, a sudden seriousness replacing his joking. "You make me feel…fuck. Way more than I want to. Don't know how you do it."

"I try." Shane's little pleased smile made the honesty more than worth it, and something powerful passed between their eyes. Reminder of the night before maybe, how close he'd felt to Shane in those moments before he'd fallen asleep. But it also hearkened back to that song, to how Shane made him feel like he sang only for Brandt.

"Well, you're damn good at it. See? An actual compliment." Brandt tapped his boot under the table, electricity going up his calf when Shane bumped him back.

"Thanks." Heat flared between them, and he wasn't sure how he was supposed to make it another few hours until they could be alone, until Shane could be all his again.

He was debating how best to communicate that powerful need to Shane when the diva started fussing. Rocking from side to side to quiet her, he sighed. And smiled because what else could he do?

"I'm not sure if she's gonna make it the whole second set, so if I disappear, I'll see you at home."

"You don't have to wait up." Shane had already arranged a ride home after the gig from Tim and his girlfriend. He lightly kicked Brandt's foot again, jeans catching his ankle. At thirty, he wasn't supposed to get this turned on from footsie games, and narrowly repressed a groan.

"Oh, I'm waiting up." He held Shane's gaze until Shane started turning pink.

"Damn. Way to make sure I pack up in record time."

"Good." Brandt nodded. He'd hold that promise close while he put the baby to bed. And showered. Because hell yes he was waiting up. All the way up.

"Get some rest." Shane laughed wickedly before glancing over at the stage. "I better get back."

"Good luck." Brandt waved him away. "Make 'em weep."

He meant it too. As much as he didn't want to share, he also wanted every person in that restaurant to feel what Shane made him feel, to appreciate every note, to understand what a fucking gift they were getting. And then he wanted Shane to hurry home.

Shane loved to sing. Loved being on stage, loved making people dance and tap their feet, and loved making them feel things, like Brandt said. But there was a new sort of specialness about singing to Brandt and Jewel, knowing he was making Brandt specifically feel something. There was a power there, but also a connection, one he wasn't sure he'd ever felt before.

"This next one is going out to a special little girl." Knowing Brandt was likely leaving soon, he'd changed up the song order. Tim and the group liked this sappy classic ballad about the passage of time, but Shane had never much seen the appeal until Jewel. She changed every day, more awake and alert now than a few weeks ago, squirming around more, not quite full rolls, but closer and closer. Like her gassy grins that had become real smiles, genuine laughs undoubtedly coming soon along with other milestones.

It was weird, cheering Jewel on but also wanting time to freeze so he could memorize exactly how she was in this moment. He put all those conflicting feels into the song, finding Brandt and the baby in the crowd and letting everything else fall away. Brandt was standing now, close to the building, swaying a little with Jewel still in the sling. In a minute, he'd slip away, but right then, Shane held close to his presence.

Not unlike how he was treating Brandt in his life in general. Knowing it couldn't last, but soaking up all the good memories in the meantime. Guarding his heart but knowing it was likely a battle he'd already lost. Hell, even tonight, seeing Brandt juggling Jewel in the sling and his food all alone, another chunk of his heart had melted away.

Even after Brandt left, he kept harnessing his emotions to power through the set. The way Brandt made him feel. The tenderness Jewel inspired. The push-pull of a life spent largely on the road. All of it. The music might be classic covers, but he made each his own.

"Last one for y'all for the night." Tim stepped forward again, waving at the crowd, which had thinned somewhat from the dinner rush to couples with drinks and desserts. "I want to see y'all shaking it on the dance floor. And make sure Shane hears how much you wanna see him next weekend."

That got a hearty round of applause. Tim probably did it to help his case for Shane to come back, but it still felt damn nice, being appreciated. His shoulders rose, right along with his voice, the audience's approval giving him a fresh burst of energy that lasted until they were done and packing up.

"Wow." The drummer, a thirty-something cowgirl named Elaine who trained horses during the week, whistled low as she counted out the take for them to split. "Double the tip jar. Props to your voice."

"Eh." Shane shrugged, more comfortable with praise when it came on the stage than one-on-one like this. "It was all of us. We really jammed."

"Damn right we did." Tim slapped him on the back.

"Are we gonna see your face again next weekend?" Elaine asked.

Shane glanced at Tim, who nodded. Shane wasn't about to turn down another gig, so he nodded along with him. "Looks like it."

"Good." Tim handed out the cash as they all ate a hurried post-show dinner before heading out. "Let's get you home to that baby."

More like home to Brandt, but Shane wasn't sharing that with the group. Instead he kept his anticipation private, let it build over the miles back to Brandt's place, let the quiet thrum of arousal he'd had all evening turn into a deeper need until he was bounding up the steps to the house, letting himself in quietly in case Brandt was asleep, but hoping like heck he was awake.

And he was, all freshly showered with damp hair and

nothing but sweats on, kicked back on the couch with a magazine. "You made it back."

"I did." Shane set down his guitar and other belongings and headed over to Brandt. "I figured you might have given up on me, headed to bed."

"Oh, I'm heading to bed." Brandt unfolded himself from the couch so that he stood right in front of Shane. He hooked a finger in Shane's belt loop, hauled him closer, like Shane needed the enticement. "Soon."

"Good." Shane breathed deep, letting Brandt's shampoo and soap fill his senses, more of that delicious anticipation. He was about to go in for a kiss when the magazine fluttered to the floor. "What were you reading?"

"Smoke jumper journal. There's an article about a buddy I know from California in there. Saved his whole crew in one of those fires last year near the bay area. His wife sent me a copy."

"Cool." Shane's pulse sped up at the reminder of how dangerous Brandt's job was, how slim the line between hero and cautionary tale.

"But I'm done now." Brandt moved his hands up Shane's torso, toying with his pearl-snap buttons before leaning down to nuzzle at Shane's neck. "You smell good."

"I shaved before my gig. And you smell nice too." Shane met his gaze, dragging that moment right before they kissed out, enjoying Brandt nipping at his neck and jaw. "You're cute all eager."

"Yeah, but I'm not so hard up that I can't wait if you're exhausted or want a shower or—"

Brandt might be able to wait but Shane couldn't. A shower might be polite, but hell if his body was slowing down after all this waiting and anticipating. He slid his mouth over Brandt's, a slow, deliberate claiming. He liked being the steady rock to Brandt's impatience, the thing that silenced all his usual motion and energy. And damn did it feel good, the way Brandt clung to him as Shane explored his mouth. He knew now more of what Brandt liked, the harder sucks and deeper tongue swipes, and he used all those tricks to get him moaning.

"Well, okay then." Brandt looked adorably dazed as Shane released his mouth to catch a breath. "Good. We're on the same page."

"We are." Shane gave him a pointed look before resuming the kiss, deeper now, more purposeful. Part of his brain wanted to slow down, seduce and tease, but the other part kept pointing out that the couch was right there. It had been days since they'd had this. He tried to steer Brandt back to the couch, but he planted his feet, preventing Shane from toppling them both to the cushions.

"Not here." Brandt jerked his head in the direction of the hall.

"No?" Shane asked even as he let Brandt tug him toward the bedrooms.

"We need a bed for what I've got planned. That is, if you're up for one of my ideas…"

"Oh, I'm up." Shane brushed against him so he could feel exactly how up certain parts of Shane were. "And your last idea was so good I swear I can still feel the aftershocks. What's this one?"

"How would you feel about trying fucking?" Brandt had a lopsided grin as he hauled Shane even closer against him. "I figure if toys were good, your cock might be even better. But only if you feel like that's something you wanna try."

All Shane's blood rushed south and his voice came out all breathless. "You want me to fuck you?"

"Hell yes." Brant's gruff voice and easy grin had Shane vibrating like a too-tight guitar string. *Hell yes, indeed.*

Chapter Eighteen

"But only if you're comfortable." Brandt's heart was hammering, far more than he'd thought possible over this question. "I don't want you to look back and regret your first time."

"I'm not going to. Promise." Shane moved in to kiss him, a soft brush of their lips, the sealing of a deal.

"Good." As much as Brandt had fantasized about this over the years, he wanted to make Shane's sexy dreams come true too. And he hated the thought of Shane not being here and of him moving on, but at least he could send him off with hot memories, not pages of regrets. "Don't want to end up in some angry song."

Shane laughed. "Don't worry. If I put you in a song, it'll be a good one."

"Deal." Him? In a song? Not likely, especially not the sweet ballads Shane was so damn good at. Brandt went ahead and ducked into his bedroom before they could accidentally wake the baby with their talking in the hall. Shane followed, bending to toe off his boots before straightening with a chuckle.

"What?" Shane pointed at the bed, which Brandt had haphazardly made after his shower. "You didn't set out the stuff? I'm disappointed."

"I didn't want to add pressure by being too…eager." Brandt went ahead and grabbed the condoms and lube out of the nightstand and pulled back the covers before tossing them on the bed.

"Well, you can be as eager as you want now." Shane brushed Brandt's hair out of the way, fingers tickling a moment before his lips arrived, hot and possessive on Brandt's neck. "And lose the pants."

"No please?" Brandt teased the best he could with Shane's mouth wreaking havoc on his nerve endings.

"You need sweet talking?" Shane traced Brandt's waistband with his thumbs.

"Probably not." Impatience won out as usual, and Brandt went ahead and shoved his pants off. "And I want you naked too."

"Oh, I'm planning on it." Shane started on his shirt buttons, but Brandt batted his hands out of the way so he could do it.

"Good." There was something super sexy about him being the naked one while Shane was still fully dressed. Unwrapping Shane slowly made Brandt's skin prickle with fresh awareness. Once he had Shane's shirt open, he couldn't resist sweeping his hands up and down Shane's torso and dropping a kiss under his collarbone. "I haven't seen near enough of your skin."

"Who's the sweet talker now?" Shane had closed his eyes, stretching into Brandt's touch.

"Still you." Brandt sent Shane's shirt to the floor before turning his attention to Shane's belt. "Damn. Your singing tonight…"

"You liked?" Shane sucked in a breath like Brandt needed help working the buckle. Nice to see the eagerness, but Mr. Endless Patience could wait a second.

"You know I did." Brandt kissed his mouth firmly, only pulling away when Shane tried to take over the kiss. "You're going places, man."

"Thanks." Bashful eyes and soft lips, Shane looked away.

Not about to let him get away with the humble act, Brandt captured his face in his hands to gently turn him back for another kiss. "I mean it."

And then they were kissing again and all Brandt's resolve to not let Shane take over fled as Shane used his nimble tongue to leave Brandt moaning. Breathing hard, he pulled away before he could forget his plans.

Hell, he was so ramped up that his hands shook as he undid Shane's belt. As he pushed the pants down, he followed their path to the floor, falling to his knees in front of Shane.

"What are you up to?" Shane tangled a hand in Brandt's hair.

"This." Brandt touched the tip of his tongue to Shane's cockhead, more tease than lick. Like Shane, this was still fairly new to him, but damn did he like it. The smell. The taste. The sight of Shane's cock, hard and flushed jutting towards him. When their positions were reversed, Shane was so good at being patient, taking it slow and letting the pleasure build.

Brandt was not.

"Fuck. Warn a guy," Shane groaned as Brandt did what he *was* good at—sucking deep and fast. He loved the weight of Shane's cock on his tongue, the way it filled his mouth and chased out all stray thoughts except for the question of how to take more. He moved his hands to Shane's hips, fingers digging into his ass, encouraging Shane deeper.

Felt like leveling up on some video game, going hands free and letting Shane thrust while he tried to figure out the breathing part. Apparently, he wasn't doing too badly because Shane kept groaning and cursing under his breath.

"Damn. You're getting too good at that." He tried to shove at Brandt's shoulder, but Brandt wasn't having any of that.

"You wanna get off this way and try for doubles?" He grinned up at Shane before licking up his shaft, mouth poised to go deep again.

Predictably, Shane laughed and shook his head. "Afraid I'm gonna last five seconds and not give you that pounding you're craving?"

"Maybe." Brandt went for honest. He'd heard enough stories of first times being over before they started, and he wanted this good for them both.

"Bast—*oh*." Shane started off laughing and finished on a moan as Brandt went as deep as he possibly could, holding his breath like he was jumping off the high dive. And the rush was almost as good, Shane surging forward, him powerless to do much more than relax enough to take it without gagging. But Brandt fucking loved this, the challenge to see how long he could stave off the need to breathe while going for bonus points with some tongue action. Maybe it was his adrenaline junkie nature, but he wanted even more, wanted to see how much he could take. He used his hands to urge Shane to fuck his mouth more, entire body thrilling to his every groan and curse.

"Fuck. Brandt. Close."

"Do it." He pulled back only long enough to get the command out. Fuck what other people might think about swallowing. He'd always liked come, liked the look of it painting skin, liked the taste of it, and he was desperate to get Shane off, to feel him shoot in Brandt's mouth.

Going deep and fast again, he didn't slow down, not even when Shane started to shudder, moans becoming broken pants. Shane thrust deeper and Brandt let him, welcomed him going fast and hard especially when his cock pulsed. Once. Then again. And again, his flavor filling Brandt's mouth. The elation that cascaded through him was almost as good as if he were the one coming. Finally, he let Shane pull back and swallowed quickly before licking his lips. Yup. He loved everything about this and couldn't help his grin.

"Damn." Shane flopped back on the bed. "You miscalculated. I'm dead."

"You are not." Brandt stretched out next to him, lightly tickling Shane's flat stomach. "But if you're gonna nap on me, I'll just get busy with one of my toys…"

"Hell no." Just like that, Shane was back awake, rolling so that he was pinning Brandt to the mattress. "Like I could sleep through that. And ever since your little show, I've wanted to be the one to play."

"Have at it." Raising his arms, he wriggled, trying to offer himself up. Shane took the hint, kissing Brandt's jaw, then spending a lot of time torturing Brandt's sensitive neck until he was rocking his hips. But Shane ignored his rising need, instead going even slower than usual, stroking Brandt's arms and chest before his mouth followed suit.

His kisses felt good. Warm. Not nearly enough, but each was like another log on the fire, especially when Shane used his teeth. Licking was nice and all, but Brandt lived for those love bites, wanted to wear Shane's marks.

"You sure you're the dead one?" he groaned, stretching again, trying to bump Shane lower. "Because you're killing me here."

"So impatient." Shane raised his head to meet Brandt's gaze. "Thought you were all about me having fun?"

"I am. But maybe fun could mean my ass gets some attention?"

That got a laugh from Shane and him scooting lower. His breath ghosted over Brandt's cock before he nipped at Brandt's hip. "Say please."

"Please." Brandt's voice dropped further as Shane licked all along the crease of Brandt's thigh, fingers dancing over his balls. "God. Now."

"Mmm. I like it when you beg." Shane rewarded him with an openmouthed kiss on his balls, gentler here but no less electric.

"I've noticed." Fumbling around, Brandt managed to reach Shane, find his cock hard again.

"Yep." Laughing, Shane rolled out of Brandt's touch and reached for the lube. Giving up any pretense at being cool, Brandt spread his legs and drew his thighs up.

"You can go right to two. I can take it." Already his body was thrumming, simply from Shane slicking up his fingers.

"Don't make me gag your bossy mouth." Shane stared him down, commanding tone doing delicious things to Brandt's insides.

"Hmm. I'd let you tie me up."

"Of course, you would." Shane's tone was fond, like Brandt's willingness to try new things was an inside joke between them. "And I might take you up on that. Later."

Raising his eyebrows, Shane held his gaze as he rubbed slick circles around Brandt's rim. Only one finger, but he had long, blunt musician's hands, and when he finally took pity on Brandt and slowly pressed in, Brandt couldn't hold back a needy noise that was more whimper than moan.

"Oh fuck. Like that." He rocked up, trying to take more, get Shane's finger where he wanted it most. "A little deeper."

"This? Right here?" Forehead furrowing like this took intense concentration, Shane pressed more deliberately, feeling around until Brandt's whole body arched off the bed.

"That. Right there. Feel that spot?"

"Yeah." Shane kept working it, thrusting his finger against it before withdrawing and returning with two fingers. Bit more of a pinch and stretch, but it was worth any discomfort to get that increased pressure against his prostate. Then Shane went for bonus points, leaning forward to lightly bite Brandt's stomach.

"Oh fuck, you bite me like that again, I'm gonna shoot." The pleasure was almost too good. He knew what he wanted, and he made a frustrated noise. "Want you in me. Want to come on your cock."

"Luckily, I'm in favor of that plan." Shane pulled back, reaching for the condom box. "Help me with the condom?"

That was sweet, the uncertainty in Shane's eyes. And Brandt sure as hell wasn't going to ruin the moment with a joke about how he was hardly the condom expert. Instead he grabbed a foil packet, but first he spent a minute stroking Shane's cock.

"Yeah, I've got you." He rolled the condom on, a shiver racing through him because getting Shane ready to fuck him was that sexy. Adding more lube, he jacked Shane a little more before releasing him.

"This how you want it?" Shane gestured at Brandt's position on the bed. "Or you want to flip?"

"Flip. That's how it usually is in my head…" That much was true, but he was also rolling to avoid the strange flutter in his stomach every time he met Shane's intense gaze. He wasn't sure he could handle fucking and watching Shane both.

"Good." Shane had an easy smile as he watched Brandt flip over onto his knees. "I want to make your fantasies come true."

"Ditto." A lengthy reply was more than he could manage because Shane had moved behind him now, and the brush of his thighs against Brandt's was distracting as hell. As was the pressure as Shane lined up his cock and slowly pushed forward. So slowly. "Fuck. Not that slow."

"Don't want to hurt you." Shane's voice was strained.

"You won't." Shane's cock was bigger than his fingers for sure, but it wasn't painful, just more of an insistent pressure and not nearly deep enough.

"Okay…" This time when Shane pressed, Brandt rocked back, making Shane's cock slide further in. And that was far better, the stretch replaced with the fullness he loved from his toys, the glancing contact with his gland a welcome addition.

"That's it. Give me more." He loved how warm Shane was and not simply the cock in his ass, but also his legs against Brandt's, a solidness that toys were never going to duplicate. And toys didn't moan like Shane or have hands that roamed all over his back and sides.

"This?" Shane's next thrust was more forceful and his pelvis bumped Brandt's ass.

"Yessss." Eyes squishing shut, Brandt groaned. It was

almost too much, too full, too slick, too much movement, but also not quite enough. "Harder. Need…"

Shane took another few thrusts, changing angles with each, until he found the one that had Brandt panting and dropping his head to the mattress. "Better?"

"Fuck. Yeah. More." This was like the blowjob again, surges of adrenaline, the desire to push himself, to take more, to completely lose himself in the sex. As it was, all his senses were full of Shane, his smell, his warmth, his little groans and praise.

"Damn. You feel so good."

"Better than that powerful imagination of yours?" Brandt kept his eyes shut, letting himself relax more into the motion, hoping that this felt as fucking amazing for Shane as it did for him.

"Yep." Shane's laugh was a little pained. "And you being still able to talk means I'm not doing quite good enough."

Seeming to come into his own more, Shane sped up, a new deeper rhythm that nailed Brandt's prostate each thrust.

"Fuck. That. Like that." Shifting his weight, Brandt worked a hand under himself. He wanted this to go on and on, but his natural impatience was rising again too. He wanted to amp up all the good sensations, see what happened when he got closer to coming.

Shane made a tsking noise. "You can do that this time, but sometime, I wanna make you come on nothing but air."

"You can. You will." As it was, it didn't take much at all from his hand to have him dangling over the edge. He wasn't sure he'd ever been this hard before, this ready.

"You want that?"

"Yeah. Make me come. Go fast." So close. He was so close. Felt like he was a bonfire awaiting the right match, energy crackling through him.

Shane groaned. "I go fast and I'm gonna go too."

"Good. Do it. Please. Wanna feel you lose it."

Shane's voice was it. That was the match. Brandt needed to feel Shane come apart, needed his increasing groans and erratic thrusts, needed the way his fingers were digging into Shane's side and the way he slammed deeper now, no more cautious movements.

"Cl—*oh*." Shane made a sound like he was going to speak then broke off into a primal groan that Brandt felt roll through his own body, his thighs, his ribs, his chest, until the energy was too much and that bonfire finally ignited. Heat roared through him now as he came all over his barely-moving fist.

"Fuck. Coming. Coming. Shane."

"*Yes*." Shane thrust deep and held, tight enough that Brandt could feel his shudders. Brandt slumped against the mattress, not giving a damn about the mess and letting Shane worry about the condom because he was well and truly fucked.

"Damn," he groaned as Shane landed next to him. "Did we really go at the same time?"

"More first timer's luck?" Even Shane's voice was warm and smiling as he dropped a kiss on Brandt's shoulder.

"Fuck. If that's us as beginners…" Brandt trailed off, chest tight. They might not get the chance to reach expert status. And he wasn't ready to think about this ending, not yet, didn't want to consider a world where they didn't get to do this over and over again.

"Yep." Shane stroked Brandt's back, voice soothing

but also playful. "We've got natural talent, but we may need a lot of practice."

Some of Brandt's tension released. Practice. That was it. Keeping going. "A lot of reps. It'll take time, but we can do it."

"I've got faith in us." Shane laughed sleepily.

"Me too." Brandt supposed that they needed fresh showers and to do something about the bed. Later. Right then, he wanted Shane to keep petting him while his brain raced with everything he still wanted to try with Shane, all that practice. Shane might be teasing, but he wasn't. His body pulsed, an achiness that wasn't merely the obvious physical effects of a thorough fucking, but a deeper ache of needing something he couldn't even name.

Chapter Nineteen

"Rise and shine." Brandt's voice tickled the edges of Shane's consciousness, the scent of coffee and something sweet further coaxing him awake. He blinked, then blinked again because there was Brandt, wearing the baby in the sling and carrying a tray with food. The sun filtered into the room. He'd slept all night in Brandt's bed and apparently deep enough to miss the morning baby wakeup.

"Damn. Breakfast in bed?" Struggling to sit up, he rolled the kinks out of his shoulders. And if he was feeling creaky after their exploits the night before, Brandt had to be feeling it even more. "Shouldn't I be the one doing that for you?"

His skin heated. They'd stumbled their way through a joint shower and remaking the bed before collapsing in it together, but Shane had a feeling that more experienced lovers might be a little more attentive.

"Ha. Maybe this is me being sweet to ensure you get more *practice* in." Brandt waggled his eyebrows at Shane. He certainly didn't seem worn out from the sex. And the fact that he wanted a repeat was even more encouraging.

"Hell, I'd give you more practice without the food

bribe." He moved so Brandt could set the tray down. Luckily, he was still in the flannel pants he'd grabbed before the two a.m. baby wakeup. Brandt too had found clothes at some point—cargo shorts and T-shirt advertising the skydiving outfit in Idaho.

"Well, I figured your voice might need something more than coffee this morning after the long gig last night. And somehow a glass of juice for you turned into pancakes before the diva decided she'd had enough of the swing."

"Well, thank you. And thank you, Jewel." He smiled at Brandt before dropping his gaze to the baby, who seemed both awake and happy in her sling. "Are you gonna eat too? There's plenty here."

"Let me grab a fork and my plate." Brandt slipped away only to reappear moments later with his own coffee mug and plate. Shane helped him juggle so that he could set Jewel between them on the bed where she kicked her feet and practiced her smiles. This was almost unbearably cozy, both of them sitting up in bed, eating and admiring the baby, who was in an especially cute mood. She was heavier now with big chubby cheeks and plump little fists, which were better at grasping things by the day.

"Wonder how long until she can have some real breakfast?" Brandt asked.

"According to the book, another couple of months." Of the two of them, Shane had done more baby research, but Brandt was better at winging parenting. And they'd both quickly figured out that babies had their own schedule. She might not be eating, but Jewel was definitely interested in their food, wriggling more purposefully than usual. "Look at this! I think she's gonna flip."

"See?" Brandt preened and lightly tickled Jewel. "My kid has talent."

"She does. You gonna strap her in for a jump before she can walk?" Laughing, Shane bumped his shoulder before gesturing at Brandt's shirt. Today, the memory of their jump was warm and sunny, not bittersweet, the last few weeks having mellowed him considerably.

"Never. Eighteen. I won't talk her out of it, but it's got to be her choice." Brandt's eyes popped wide as if Shane had suggested playing in traffic. Him as an overprotective daddy was too cute. "There's other stuff I want to do with her while she's little. Silly things...never mind."

Brandt's hesitance was also appealing, making Shane grin. "Come on. You can tell me."

"Okay, but it's sort of sappy. Like the sort of things kids get to do with their dads. Fairs. Amusement parks. Go-carts. Haunted houses. Fishing. That's a dad thing, right?"

"Yeah." Shane's chest was so tight it was a wonder he could speak at all. And oh how he ached for Brandt's younger self who hadn't had much of that. And maybe a little pang for his own upbringing, where there had been adventures, but not a lot of traditional memory-making activities. "You're gonna be great at this."

"Thanks." Brandt met his gaze, eyes more solemn than Shane had seen, like getting it right truly was important to him. And Shane wanted to see that, him taking Jewel places, giving her the gift of a dad who cared enough to put in the time. Right when his heart was almost too full to stand, Brandt's mouth curved into a slow smile. "I've got some pretty good help right now, though. Makes it easier."

Shane matched his smile, something tender and big

and terrifying all at once passing between them. "You're easy to help."

The moment was too sweet. He had to look away, turning his attention instead to Jewel, who was still in the center of the king bed, between them. She was still kicking and wriggling, determined expression on her tiny face as she swung from her back onto her belly.

"Oh, wow! She did it!" He turned to Brandt, whose whole body language had brightened, broad grin and proud eyes as he scooped up Jewel and held her high.

"Go, Jewel!"

As Brandt cheered, a song unspooled in Shane's head, perfect lyrics for a perfect moment. That urge to see the future intensified. He wanted to see these two laughing together for all sorts of milestones. And not simply the big ones either, the ones that an uncle might drop in for like holidays. No, he wanted all the little moments like these too. Everyday miracles.

And even without writing it down yet, he knew this was his best song yet. If he didn't keep it for himself, this could be one to keep him in gas and food all winter. *Winter.* Damn. It was barely summer. Where would he be come winter?

Why not here? It was an impossible wish, but for a second, he could see an alternate universe, three shimmery and hazy shadows, hands linked. But it wasn't like Brandt was asking him to stay. Wasn't like they were a real couple, a genuine little family and not an amicable arrangement born out of crisis and practicality.

"What's that look for?" Still holding Jewel, Brandt turned toward him.

Oops. Busted. Shane tried to school his expression

away from all his churning emotions. "Nothing. Just had a few lines for a song pop up in my brain."

"Damn." Brandt whistled like Shane too had performed some new feat. "I love how you can do that."

"It's just how my brain works." His heart trilled as Brandt continued to smile at him.

"Play for me later?"

"Maybe." Worry made his voice more distant. Brandt had seen him sing, sure, but he hadn't heard any of the new stuff yet. Shane wasn't sure he was ready for what his latest songs might reveal. But he also didn't want to ruin this moment by shutting Brandt down, so instead he pointed at the baby. "Hey, you should record her trick."

"Good idea." Setting Jewel back on the bed, Brandt fished out his phone from his pocket, then frowned. "I've got a message from work."

"Callout?" Shane started stacking their plates, mentally bracing himself for Brandt's departure.

"Not exactly." Brandt's mouth twisted. "They need volunteers for a demo next week for a school-age kids' group. Some sort of exploration club."

"Sounds more fun than a fire." Safer too. Shane didn't like the way his heart had sped up at the thought of Brandt rushing off to danger.

"Yeah, bosses knew I wouldn't turn this one down." Brandt tapped away on his phone before looking up again. "Hey. You want to come?"

"Me?"

"Sure." Brandt managed to sound like this was no big deal, like it was adding an errand to Shane's day, not offering for him to meet Brandt's friends and coworkers. "The message thread says that some of the guys will have families there. Rare chance for their kids to see them in action. Cameron will probably be there with her and Rich's kids."

Family. He wanted to be that for Brandt with an intensity that stole some of his oxygen. And no way could he let on to Brandt how much the offer meant. "Guess I'll see how the diva is that day, if it's not too close to one of her naps."

"Dude. When did our lives start revolving around naptime?" Groaning, Brandt flopped back against the pillows.

Shane seized the change in subject like a life buoy, putting on his best attempt at a flirty smile. "I dunno but I've got some ideas for today's nap…"

"Save that thought." Brandt laughed and sat back up. "First some painting, but then I've got plans."

"You do have good plans. Last night was…" He trailed off, not sure he had an adjective good enough for those memories. Hell, he could write a whole album of songs and it wouldn't be enough.

"Yeah, me too." Brandt's happy sigh filled in the blanks and also went a fair way to reassuring Shane that he hadn't done terrible. But then Brandt's expression turned strangely vulnerable, almost like he was having some of the same doubts. "You okay? I mean as far as first times go…"

"Fishing for compliments again? Need me to tell you that I saw Jesus?" Shane teased him because the alternative was to get all sappy, and neither of them needed that. And Brandt wasn't the type to ordinarily seek extra ego stroking. Unless… "Or you worried I'm about to get a tattoo of your name?"

Maybe Brandt was afraid of Shane getting sex-drunk and getting too attached. And no way was Shane admitting that that was a real possibility here. For all he was turning out to be a great dad, Brandt was still the guy who was allergic to commitment and wasn't likely to find Shane catching feelings that funny.

Or maybe Shane was wrong there, because all Brandt did was laugh. "Apparently my name is pretty popular. I picked good. It'd look damn nice as a tattoo."

"Ha." Shane forced a chuckle and shook his head to clear away the parade of tattoo possibilities, Brandt's name in a heart, all middle school crush style. "You barely got me to jump out of a plane. Needles aren't happening."

"Never say never." Brandt gave a pragmatic shrug before picking the baby up.

"Truth."

It was. He couldn't say never, just like he couldn't seem to shut off this rogue streak of hope running through him, the little voices whispering *maybe* and *someday* and *why not*.

"I hear your girl is coming today." Hartman's tone was conversational, but Brandt still whipped around, glad it was only them walking toward the hangar.

"Girl?" Brandt didn't have one of those. Wasn't remotely interested in getting anyone significant of any gender or even dating. Not when things were so damn good with Shane. The whole last week had been one big high. He couldn't even remember when Shane had last slept in his own bed, and no way could Brandt miss going out when staying in meant memories that filled cracks he hadn't even been aware he had.

"Your baby?" Hartman frowned as he stopped walking. "The one that's been making you all distracted and doubled your coffee intake? Thought I heard Rich say someone was bringing her to the demo today."

"Oh. Yeah. My…the baby's uncle." Damn it. He was undoubtedly going to have to introduce Shane today, and he really needed a better explanation for his presence beyond babysitter. It wasn't fair to Shane to minimize his role in Brandt's life, but hell if Brandt had the right word for it, especially on the fly like this. "He's staying with me, helping out."

"That's right. I thought you'd mentioned that before. How's that working out?"

Amazing. Incredible. Shane was the one with the poetic vocabulary, not Brandt. "Okay. We…get along."

"That's good." Hartman nodded, then stepped closer, lowering his voice further. "Wilder? Brandt?"

"Yeah?" He matched Hartman's whisper.

"You know you can talk to me, right? I'm sorry about mentioning the baby where Bronco and the others could hear, but if there's something on your mind, I'm here to listen. As a friend, not your coworker or the jumper in charge."

Oh. Maybe Brandt wasn't doing such a good job of playing it cool. And if anyone could understand Brandt's mixed-up state, Hartman might. At least he wasn't likely to judge Brandt for harboring feelings for Shane.

"Thanks. It's complicated. Do you think—"

"Are we ready?" Rich chose exactly that moment to pop his head out of the hangar.

"Yup." Brandt wasn't even sure what he'd been about to ask. It wasn't like Hartman had a Magic 8-ball and could predict how long Shane might stick around. And there wasn't any test for Brandt's feelings, no scientific way to judge whether this was simply a byproduct of all the proximity or whether this might be something real. Confession might be good for the soul, but in this case, it was probably just as well that they'd been interrupted.

He followed Hartman into the hangar, where a number of their fellow jumpers were gathered. A few of the supervisors were there too, and Hartman spared a last speculative look for Brandt before he went to stand near Reid as one of the senior trainers addressed them.

"We'll all greet the visitors, but then Reid and some of the others staying on the ground will give the visitors a tour of the facilities while the designated jumpers take the plane. After the plane circles back around, the jumpers will parachute in and show off some climbing and chainsaw skills. Easy day, but let's keep it safe."

"Will do." Brandt answered along with his fellow jumpers. They spent the next chunk of time laying out gear to show the visitors so they could watch a few of them gear up for the jump. Brandt and Rich agreed to demo, getting ready while Hartman did the explaining.

Shortly after they finished setting up, Reid and the supervisors led the group in. About twenty or thirty kids, assorted adults, and then a few families he recognized like Cameron and her kids, and some blond tweens waving at Hartman—undoubtedly some of his many nieces and nephews. And there was Shane and Jewel next to Cameron, both of them smiling at something Cameron was saying. Shane was wearing the baby in the sling Brandt had made, and the blue made his eyes even sharper. Catching Brandt's gaze, Shane smiled wider and held Jewel's tiny hand to make her wave at him.

My people. Brandt's ribs ached as he inhaled, too much emotion flooding him along with the oxygen. And maybe equally necessary. He'd spent years avoiding dwelling on what he was missing, what he'd never had, right up until this moment when he had it and he wasn't sure how he'd lived without it. Reflexively, he waved back. Shane's eyes were nervous though, like he still wasn't sure he was supposed to be there.

Brandt wanted to go over to him, but there wasn't time for that with Hartman already going over the equipment for the audience. He took his spot next to Rich, gearing up way slower than usual as Hartman explained each step.

"See how Brandt and Rich check each other's connectors? We always double- and triple-check before a jump."

Check away. The memory of Shane's voice echoed over the months that had passed since their jump. Lifetimes really. But he could still remember those electric touches and Shane's laugh as they landed. Sex tended to rev Shane up like that too, make his voice all shot with adrenaline and pure wonder, but Brandt wanted to give him something outside of the bedroom that made him that loose and happy. He'd wasn't sure he'd ever obsessed over a birthday present this much.

Taking him on a jump was the obvious answer, but the new overprotective parent part of Brandt balked at the idea of both of them leaving Jewel behind on the ground. Simply because he knew how to do it safely didn't mean the risk was zero.

His back tensed as Rich checked him. These worries about the baby and what would happen to her if something happened to Brandt kept dogging him, arriving at the least opportune moments.

"Do you ever get scared?" asked one of the older kids, a girl in a plaid shirt.

"Nah," a younger smoke jumper answered. One of

Bronco's crowd, those too-cocky young guns who hadn't yet lost a buddy, hadn't really confronted near-death experiences.

Hartman made a scoffing noise and shot him a pointed look. "Of course we do. We're jumping out of planes. And fires are scary. It's only normal to be afraid. But it's what you do with that fear."

"Yeah," Brandt echoed weakly. Fear. That was what those worries were. And he well knew how deadly panic could be, but finding a balance between concern and calm was proving hard.

Somehow he managed to shove all those thoughts aside to demonstrate some basic air positioning, trying not to glance over at Shane too much.

"Now, why don't all of you wave goodbye to the jumpers who'll be taking that plane you saw earlier." One of the supervisors addressed the audience. "We'll continue your tour while they circle back around."

Shane made Jewel wave again as they followed Reid and the other supervisors out. *There goes my heart.* And it wasn't one of Shane's fanciful lines, but the truth. Brandt was as close to the two of them as he'd been to anyone else in years. And a few weeks ago, he would have laughed at the notion of getting attached to a tiny baby, but he was. Already she owned a huge chunk of his heart, and he hadn't thought he had one left to give. Kindness sure, good times certainly, but not all these deeper emotions that kept slamming into him at the least opportune time.

"Let's give them a good show," Hartman said as they boarded the plane.

"Will do." No more stray thoughts. No more looks back over his shoulder. Brandt had to stay focused. And he did. Triple-checking his gear one last time, listening closely for the signal.

Textbook.

Right up until the moment his chute didn't open.

Chapter Twenty

"Are they here yet?" One of Cameron's kids, Colt, a blond boy who kept asking to see Jewel, bounced up and down, kicking up a mini dust cloud as he did so. Shane shared Colt's impatience as they all waited at the edge of a clearing for the arrival of the jumpers. His stomach felt all slushy. Not dread precisely, but not excitement either. Cautious anticipation maybe.

"No. Obviously. We can't hear the plane yet." Tabitha, the other kid, a gangly tween girl, had made it clear she was not impressed with the goings-on at all. Both kids looked more like Cameron than her more weathered smoke jumper husband. Tabitha knew almost more about the smoke-jumping protocols than the people giving the tour, but she kept her knowledge to biting quips rather than her brother's boisterous outbursts.

"Watch the sky." Cameron straddled the line between sharing Tabitha's boredom and having admirable patience for Colt's endless stream of questions. The two kids were like a window into what the next few years could hold as Jewel grew into a kid. Would she be talkative? A showoff? Aloof? Smart? Waiting to find out made Shane almost as impatient as Colt. And he wanted to be there, wanted to see her go from baby to one of these little persons like the kids in the school group, full of personality.

"I don't see anything yet," Colt complained after ten seconds of sky scanning.

"Keep watching." Cameron ruffled his hair.

In Shane's pocket, his phone buzzed, but no way was he fishing it out now and missing the arrival of the jumpers. Whoever it was could wait.

The drone of a distant plane made Shane's heart speed up, hand tensing against Jewel's little back.

"Here they come!" someone called as a dark speck came into view. Then a few more dots, hazy on the horizon, gradually getting bigger. Shane's pulse sped up and he jiggled the baby a little. It was pretty cool, waiting for the moment when the parachutes took on recognizable shapes.

"Why is one parachute a different color?" he asked Cameron. On the ground, there was a flurry of activity from the other jumpers and supervisors watching the parachutes float down.

"Oh crap. Oh..." Trailing off, Cameron kept her mouth a tight line as she motioned Shane closer so she could whisper in his ear. "Someone had to use their reserve chute. That's why they're scrambling. In case there's a hard landing or a medical situation."

"Oh." All the excitement of watching drained away on the single syllable, replaced by clammy skin and a thumping heart. Even Jewel seemed tenser in her sling.

"Please be okay." Cameron's voice was barely audible, a whispered prayer as she kept her hand on Colt's hair and pulled Tabitha close to her. The little family looked so vulnerable that Shane's breath caught. Everything could change for them in the next few seconds. And

Cameron had to live with this worry day in and day out, fire after fire. He'd always appreciated first responders, but now he saw the toll that life took on the families too. This job asked so much of Cameron and the kids too.

Please don't be Brandt. Shane added his own prayer, then immediately felt guilty because no matter who it was, it was someone who mattered, and he didn't want to wish trouble on another family. *Please everyone be okay*, he amended his prayer.

The parachutes swooped lower, almost to the earth, and then right when it seemed they might hang in the air forever, the jumpers started touching down. There was so much activity on the ground that Shane temporarily lost sight of the differently colored chute. More of the support personnel raced past the crowd, including two people with big first aid kits.

"There's Daddy!" Colt pointed across the clearing to where Rich was untangling from his chute. Shane scanned more carefully now, trying to match the jumpers on the ground to the ones he'd seen ready to board the plane. No Brandt. He bit his lip hard enough to taste blood, trying to keep it together.

"I think it was Brandt," he whispered urgently to Cameron. A semicircle of jumpers and support personnel formed around the lighter colored chute. A hush fell over the crowd, the more experienced onlookers like Cameron undoubtedly sensing something had gone wrong.

"It's okay." Cameron squeezed his arm. "Breathe."

"I'm not sure I can," Shane admitted. He couldn't believe Jewel was still snoozing. She had to be able to feel the hammering of his heart. He'd never been this nervous before. No audition or show or recording studio had ever sparked this much terror in his gut. Brandt had to be okay because Shane had no idea what he'd do if the unthinkable happened. And not simply with the baby but with himself. He might never come back from it if something happened to Brandt, and that was sobering as hell, seeing exactly how deep into this thing he was.

All of a sudden, a cheer went up from the crowd as the semicircle parted and a very dusty Brandt holding his helmet emerged flanked by Hartman, the guy who had spoken earlier during the gear demo, and Rich. Brandt was walking slowly, and judging by the degree to which the others were hovering, he wasn't entirely steady. But he was up. Moving toward them.

Shane could breathe again, and all those long heart-beats without oxygen caught up to him in a rush, relief so potent that his head swam. And then Brandt was right there in front of him. He was vaguely aware that Rich was there too, greeting Cameron and the kids, but most of his senses were zeroed in on Brandt as he looked him over from his sweaty hair to his dusty nose and scraped-up cheek to his battered boots. He seemed in one piece, but Shane wasn't sure whether to trust it.

"Are you okay?" He didn't like how breathless his voice came out or how great the urge to touch Brandt was, to the point that he had to clench his fists.

"Yeah." Brandt rolled his neck side to side and wig-gled his arms, as if he too were still in shock that he was still standing. "Hard landing. Gonna feel it for the rest of the week probably."

"What happened in the air?" Shane almost didn't want to ask, but he also had a driving need to know exactly how close a call it had been.

Brandt shrugged. "Main chute wouldn't deploy. I had to use the reserve. It happens."

"Often?" Shane gulped. He had a feeling it wasn't the minor inconvenience Brandt was playing it off as.

"Some." Brandt took a deep inhale. Underneath the dust, he was still a little pale. "Not to me, maybe, but even with the most careful packing and prep and equipment checking, there are still risks."

"I know." But that didn't mean Shane liked this up close and personal reminder of exactly how grave the risks were. Needing to look away, he studied the baby's downy head instead.

"Hey." Brandt used his gloved fingers to tip Shane's chin back up. "I'm here now. I'm gonna be okay. You don't have to worry."

Yeah, he did. Worry felt like the only smart thing he could do, honestly. But he couldn't say that, could only nod. And judging by Cameron's raised eyebrows, Brandt touching him hadn't gone unnoticed. He'd said he wasn't going to keep Shane a secret, but Shane hadn't expected him to follow through on that. As Shane well knew, there was a difference between being honest with one's closest friends and being open with a crowd of strangers. But Brandt didn't seem to care, eyes still locked on Shane.

"Wilder! You're sitting the climbing demo, okay?" Reid, the big, ripped guy who had Hollywood action-hero vibes and had been their guide for a lot of the tour, strode over, followed closely by Hartman. If either of them had seen Brandt touch him, their easy strides and serious faces did a pretty good job of hiding it, projecting concern but not shock. "You got your bell rung pretty good out there. We don't want to risk your hard head any further."

Brandt opened his mouth like he was about to argue

that point, then glanced at Shane before nodding. "Understood."

"Sorry," Shane said as Hartman and Reid moved on. "I didn't mean to freak out on you."

"You had decent cause." Brandt exhaled hard, like all his adrenaline was whooshing out at once, shoulders sinking and jaw drooping. "I'm sorry I scared you."

"It's okay," Shane said even though it wasn't. He glanced over at Cameron. It wasn't fair, the worry and stress inherent in trying to make a family out of these risks. But he also was in zero position to tell Brandt to not do his job. "You're fine now, right?"

His own adrenaline drop made his hands shaky as he patted the baby, who had finally woken up and was starting to make unhappy noises.

"I'll be okay." Brandt's tone was weary and it wasn't the same as an emphatic *yes* at all. And even as tired as he looked, Brandt was still reaching for Jewel, releasing her from the sling before Shane could stop him. "Here, let me take her while we watch the demo."

"She slept right through all the commotion." Shane decided not to protest Brandt taking Jewel because she immediately calmed and surprisingly, so did Brandt, face softening, tension lessening in his posture.

"Good. Glad she missed it." Brandt's tone was surprisingly emphatic, but his expression was unreadable, eyes murky and not meeting Shane's. He kept holding the baby, even after transferring his helmet to Shane and accepting one of her bottles from the diaper bag. They followed the crowd to a climbing demonstration over at one of the outdoor training areas near a hangar. Brandt managed to look both tough and tender as he gave Jewel her bottle, big hand dwarfing the bottle and little pink blanket protecting her from the worst of his dust.

Shane's heart was in serious danger of not surviving this outing. Between watching the smoke jumpers demonstrate climbing maneuvers, he snuck a picture of Brandt and Jewel for later, both for them and also for himself, to remember the exact moment his heart escaped his chest, fragile and new. And inevitable, like they'd been building to this moment the last few weeks.

"Brandt?" The question escaped his lips before he could think better of it, but the need to say *something* kept poking at him.

"Yeah?" Brandt's attention was already split between the baby and the demonstration, and he didn't glance over at Shane.

"Nothing. Just that I truly am happy that reserve chute worked. And that you didn't get injured. Can't believe how relieved I am."

That got a sly smile from Brandt as he whispered back, "Because you have plans for me for later?"

Figured that Brandt would make this about sex. And Shane wished it were that simple, but there was nothing straightforward about all the feelings churning through him.

"That too." He kept his voice light. No point in giving away too much. "But also, the world needs you. Jewel needs you."

Shane needed him too, but there was a limit to what he could admit right then. Still, he wanted Brandt to know that his safety mattered.

"Thanks." Brandt's neck flushed and his gaze darted back to the baby.

"Now how about you explain to me what we're watching?" They'd probably both had all the emotional talk they could handle that day. His phone buzzed again with a message in his pocket, but he was too wrapped up in Brandt's narration of the demo, which had now moved on to some chainsaw action to care about his messages right then.

Brandt's eagerness sharing details was almost comical, and Shane had to laugh. "Five minutes of downtime and you're already missing being over there, aren't you?"

"I don't do well with time off." Brandt shrugged as he transferred the now-drowsy baby back to her sling and Shane. "And yeah, I like the job. Love it. It's hard to explain. But it's been there for me, a lot of years and a lot of times when nothing else was."

"I feel that way about music," Shane admitted. And in that moment, he understood why Cameron couldn't demand that Rich find a safer career. This life was a part of Brandt, woven into the fabric of who he was and what he stood for. And to care for him was to accept that, hard as it was. When it came right down to it, Shane wasn't sure how anyone could be strong enough to do this long-term.

Long-term. The word made the back of his neck chilly, equal parts longing and fear. Even with Brandt safe and sound and right by his side, the world had shifted. There was no shoving his feelings back, but hell if he knew what to do now.

Buzz. His pocket vibrated again. Oh yeah. His messages. He made a mental note to deal with his phone as soon as he got home and got Jewel settled. Whatever it was could wait while he tried to find his footing on this new terrain.

Chapter Twenty-One

Home. Seldom had Brandt been as glad to see a shift end, and as he let himself into the house, his body was already twitchy with anticipation, arms needing to hold Shane in the worst way. As it was, he'd probably come out to a few crew members today, touching him in front of everyone. Whatever. Nosy people could go fuck themselves because only the baby strapped to Shane's front had stopped Brandt from tackle-hugging the guy.

But now, hopefully, he could hug him until some of this ridiculous adrenaline drained away. It had been hours and still his pulse raced every time his brain jumped back to that moment of sheer terror when his primary chute hadn't opened. Years of jumping and never had his panic been that high.

"Shane?" he called softly, not wanting to wake the diva if she was sleeping. But that turned out to only be a hopeful dream as she was awake, in Shane's arms in the kitchen, and red faced and angry. Shane himself was pale, mouth a thin line, and eyes tight. Brandt's thoughts of what he needed himself fled in the face of such obvious misery. "Whoa. You look awful. What did the diva do to you?"

Groaning, Shane shifted the baby to his other arm.

"She didn't nap more than fifteen minutes at a stretch. She's so fussy that she even got angry at her bottle."

"She wouldn't eat?" There was that adrenaline again, heart thumping. He might not have memorized the baby book like Shane, but even he knew that not eating was a bad sign.

"She will, but not quite like usual. She drinks a little, cries, then tries again." Shane's tone was as weary as his face, and Brandt plucked Jewel from his arms even as he continued, "Maybe I shouldn't have taken her out. It was rather windy."

"It was." The wind conditions had undoubtedly played a role in his bad luck too. The emergency chute had deployed lower than a normal one and had been harder to control in the winds. He could still feel the tooth-rattling jolt of that landing. "But don't beat yourself up about bringing her. I asked you to come."

And now he had a fresh layer of guilt on top of that request. Bad enough Shane had had to witness his close call, but now Jewel might be sick. And that was on him way more than Shane. He was the dad, right? He should be able to keep her safe. Carrying the baby over to the couch, he sat down and laid her in front of him, trying to assess her for obvious signs of distress, similar to how he would a crew member. No injuries that he could see, and she wasn't particularly congested or other hallmarks of illness.

"I was debating calling Cameron for advice when you came in." Shane hovered nearby.

"Let me finish taking a look at Miss Fussy Pants first." He checked her sleeper. Not too tight and no tag or other itchy part. Only thing that seemed off was her angry face, but she was also a little more flushed than usual. "Huh. Does she feel warm to you?"

"Maybe a little." Shane reached down and felt her head. "Do we have digital thermometer?"

"I've got a first aid kit I keep in case I injure myself with power tools, but I'm not sure about whether it has a thermometer." Picking the baby up, he headed for the main bathroom in the hall. Shane was close behind him, and he looked in the kit under the sink while Brandt bounced Jewel to try to keep her from fussing more.

"Nope." Shane shook his head as he finished digging through the kit. "Nothing to take a temperature. Should I call Cameron?"

"Yeah. Use my phone. I saved her cell number in there." Juggling the baby, he managed to get his phone out of his pocket and handed it to Shane. He paced with Jewel as Shane made the call, trying to take some deep breaths, keep the cool head he was known for. Little kids got sick. She'd be okay. Except, what if she wasn't? What if he had to live with more of that helpless terror from earlier? Fuck. He hated things that were out of his control.

"Cameron says she's too little for this to be teething," Shane reported while still on the phone. "We've done most of what she's suggesting—check for bruises or signs of injury, make sure she's warm and dry and nothing is tight."

"Yeah, we tried all that. And sounds like you were dealing with this all afternoon?" Brandt didn't like having left Shane all alone with a potentially sick baby. The poor guy looked ragged, like he'd pulled a thirty-six-hour shift in the height of fire season.

"Yup. Cameron's saying that if nothing is working

that we might want to take her to the urgent care clinic so that we avoid a middle of the night ER visit. Could be a virus of some kind."

"Yeah. Let's do the clinic." Brandt didn't have to think too hard about the choice. If he and Shane couldn't fix the baby, then they needed someone who could. His back was already tense from hearing her cry. Not knowing what was wrong made his temples pound.

"Agreed. For myself, I'd tough it out with a virus, but she's so tiny..." Shane trailed off as he headed to the kitchen and started gathering supplies. "I'll get a diaper bag and some bottles together in case it's a long wait."

Working fast, they got ready in record time. Shane climbed in the backseat next to Jewel. "I'll ride back here, see if I can distract her from too much crying while you drive."

Despite the tense circumstances, Brandt appreciated how effortlessly they divided and conquered tasks, no arguing over who was driving or whose fault it was that the baby was sick. No, they had a common purpose, and that made it easier for Brandt to focus on the drive into Bend while Shane sang silly songs and kept Jewel's fussing from growing too loud.

The clinic was near the big regional hospital, a low, modern building with a big waiting room. About half the chairs were filled with more people than Brandt would have hoped for. And indeed, the line for the receptionist slowly crept forward, several minutes until it was their turn to explain why they were there. Shane was holding Jewel, so Brandt explained her symptoms to the receptionist, who wore pink scrubs and a pinched expression.

"She's not in the system." The woman frowned but

didn't look up from her typing. "Do you have a list of what vaccines she's already had?"

"No." And great, now he got to worry about those viruses too. He made a mental note to bump finding a pediatrician up his to-do list. "I've got her birth certificate though."

Brandt handed it over along with his license.

"So where's the mom? Or do you two have adoption paperwork too?" She gestured between him and Shane, who made a gurgling noise as he went even paler.

"Uh…" Shane made a gurgling noise. Nice to know how he felt about being mistaken for a couple again.

Like earlier, Brandt honestly didn't care. He wanted Jewel to see a doctor and if that meant Nurse Nosy here learned something about his personal life, so be it. He might not understand all the emotions Shane inspired, but he also wasn't ashamed of what they had going.

"The mom's not around. I'm the dad." Trying to keep his voice level, Brandt tapped on his ID. "My attorney has custody paperwork ready, but no court order yet. The baby will be on my insurance, but I don't have a card yet."

"Does Mom have insurance?"

"Probably not." Shane sounded as frustrated as Brandt felt. This shouldn't be so hard. And this was undoubtedly why Cameron had pushed them doing the court paperwork. Brandt knew full well how hard the system could make getting help.

"Is there any way to check?" The receptionist didn't seem any closer to being done with the questions, and Brandt had to grit his teeth as Shane answered that one.

"Not easily. I've got a phone number, but good luck getting her to pick up."

"All right." The woman sounded like she too was on the verge of losing patience. "Give me that number at least for the records."

"Are you going to be able to treat my daughter or what?" Brandt demanded after Shane supplied Shelby's number. His daughter. He hadn't really thought of the baby quite like that before. But she was *his*. And he *was* the dad, not simply in the legalistic sense of the word, but because of how much she mattered to him. "I'll pay cash if my insurance doesn't go through. And I'll get my attorney on the phone if you need documentation for the court stuff."

"No need to involve your attorney." The woman typed faster. Brandt must have said the magic word, because her voice sped up too. "Let's all take a deep breath. The insurance card for yourself should work if she was added recently. And yes, a nurse should call you back shortly."

"Good." Brandt managed to stay polite as they finally finished the paperwork and headed for the waiting area. Jewel was fussing again, and he held out his arms. "Here. Let me take her again."

"Thanks." Shane took the seat next to him before pulling out his phone. "Do you want me to try to reach Shelby? I'd be shocked if she had insurance, but I guess we should try to find out."

"Yeah. Send her another message, I guess." Funny how Brandt had gone from praying she reappeared soon to not wanting to deal with the hassle of involving her. But letting her know was also the right thing do, much as it made his neck tense.

"Message. Oh crap." Shane smacked his head.

"What?" Brandt shifted Jewel so he could turn toward Shane.

"Oh, nothing. Just that I've had a voicemail all day that I haven't checked. I meant to check after the demo, but then the baby was so fussy when we got home that I forgot. It's probably a telemarketer or something like that, but I'd better make sure it's nothing to do with Shelby."

"Yeah," Brandt agreed as Shane stood and paced a few feet away while pressing his phone to his ear.

Shane pursed his mouth and his eyes narrowed, then flashed like he was about to smile before clouding again. Finally, he wiggled his jaw as he typed something out on his phone. Brandt hated both how hard to read Shane was and how that made his brain gallop away with a whole list of dreadful possibilities.

"What is it?" he demanded as soon as Shane sat back down. "Shelby okay?"

"No, it was nothing about Shelby. I sent her a message though like you said." Shane dropped his gaze to Jewel, gently clucking her under the chin.

"But the other? Your voicemail?"

Shane gave a cryptic shrug. "It's fine. Something I'll deal with later."

Damn it. Brandt had zero right to inquire further, and this sudden urge to help Shane with whatever had arisen was unfamiliar and unsettling. He wanted to tell Shane that they could deal together. Wanted to at least pat his leg, tell him he didn't have to stew over this alone. But before he could find the words, a nurse came to the waiting room door.

"Jewel Wilder?"

Huh. It might have been the first time he heard the baby's name said like that, a glimmer of a future where she'd be a person with a name and a mind of her own.

But also carrying a piece of Brandt wherever she went. He had to swallow hard.

"That's us." He stood with Jewel and motioned for Shane to follow. Like or not, he was a part of this thing. And maybe Brandt needed him there. *Fuck*. That might be the scariest part of an already terrifying day.

Shane felt about as useful as mittens in July as he trailed behind Brandt and the nurse. He could have stayed in the waiting area, but something in Brandt's eyes had given him pause. A vulnerability maybe from a man who made a career out of cheating death. Shane would have followed that look anywhere, wanted to give Brandt what he needed. Hell, he wanted to *be* what Brandt needed, improbable though it was.

So if Brandt needed him to hold the diaper bag and help unwrap the baby from her blanket and sleeper so the nurse could get her vital signs, then Shane was going to be there with the assist. And if helping meant that he didn't have time to think about his phone message from earlier, well then so much the better.

"She's certainly got a mind of her own." The nurse laughed as Jewel didn't hesitate to let them know how much she hated the poking and prodding. Afterward, they took turns holding her until the doctor herself came into the room for the exam, which brought a fresh round of yodeling.

"Yup. There it is. Ear infection." The doctor took her scope away so Brandt could soothe the indignant baby.

"That's treatable, right?" Brandt bounced her from side to side as Shane laid out a fresh sleeper on the exam table.

"Oh, yes. Very treatable. And pretty common, especially in bottle-fed babies. Genetics may play a role too. Did you have a lot of them?" The doctor clicked around on her computer.

Brandt shrugged. "I don't know. Maybe. I remember a couple."

Shane's chest ached as he helped Brandt wrestle her back into her sleeper. Brandt had deserved so much better than to be little and in pain and in unstable circumstances.

"I had her outside a couple of hours today. Could the wind have caused it?" Shane asked. Brandt had tried to take that responsibility earlier, but Shane couldn't shake the guilt that he should have done something different. Brandt trusted him with the baby and that meant something, and he felt like he'd let them both down.

"Oh, I doubt that. She probably already had the bug." The doctor had sympathetic eyes as she looked up from the computer. "Being in the wind maybe didn't help, but it didn't cause the infection. Don't beat yourself up, either of you."

"What can we do to make her feel better?" Brandt held Jewel so she peeked over his shoulder.

"We'll get you set up with some antibiotics and fever reducers. Other than the meds, keep doing what you're doing." The doctor gestured at the three of them. "Lots of cuddles. She might wake up extra times tonight, but these infections tend to pass fast."

"Good." Brandt's relief was almost palpable, and Shane shared his sigh as they finished up at the clinic and headed to the pharmacy. The prescription wasn't quite ready, so they ended up wandering the aisle with the baby in her car seat, snoozing after the doctor ordeal.

"Everything good with you?" Brandt asked as they

stopped in front of a display of chips. He tossed a bag into the basket Shane was holding.

"Yeah. It's fine." Shane wasn't an idiot. Brandt was referring to the phone call earlier, but he wasn't ready to talk about that, not now with Jewel sick and Brandt needing him and his own feelings a tangled-up mess.

"You could tell me if it wasn't." Brandt's persistence was unexpected, but not entirely unwelcome. Maybe he cared more than Shane thought. They'd been the sort of friends who could unload after a long day for a bit, but Brandt voluntarily offering to hear Shane's problems felt significant somehow. And even more reason to not burden him with this.

"Thanks." He didn't elaborate but he did give Brandt what he hoped was a grateful smile. If they were alone, he'd touch his arm, but a family of four was a few feet away, as was an elderly couple browsing painkillers.

"Okay." Brandt nodded and headed for the cold case. He'd dropped the matter rather easily, and Shane trailed behind him.

"What are you doing?"

"You don't want to talk, but you're in a crap mood, and the doctor said we might have a late night." Brandt opened one of the freezer doors. "Ice cream might not help any of that, but it sure can't hurt."

"True that." They reached for the cherry chocolate chip at the same time, which earned him a lopsided grin from Brandt before the carton landed in the basket. Shane was officially not going to survive this man, who not only wasn't pushing but who was still trying to make things better, even amid all the worries for Jewel and his own trying day.

Shane didn't deserve him, that much was for sure.

Words tumbled over each other in his brain as he tried to sort out what to say that wasn't trite and wasn't too much.

"Wilder? Your prescriptions are ready." The pharmacy tech saved him from his indecision as she called Brandt's name. Which was also Jewel's and a nice reminder that the two of them were a unit, and Shane was the bonus helper who didn't entirely belong but also wasn't an outsider. It was a weird no-man's land of both wanting more and not being sure he could handle more. And it wasn't like he could name that want either, couldn't quantify it even as it weighed him down, made his shoulders slump and his step slow.

And his muddled thoughts continued even once they were back at the house, trying to get the medicine into the baby and then get her to sleep in her crib. They patted. They walked. They bounced. Shane sang and sang. Brandt rocked. And right when Shane was about to give up and propose Brandt at least go sleep himself, she settled and let them creep from the room.

"Wow. I think she's actually out," Shane whispered once they were in the hallway.

"Shush. Don't jinx it." Brandt put a finger on Shane's lips before heading down the hall and into the kitchen. "And we've absolutely earned that ice cream now. Your poor throat."

"There are certainly more fun ways to strain it," Shane agreed as he grabbed some spoons and bowls. God, he was so tired that even the thought of sex didn't rouse him. There was a serious risk of him falling asleep mid ice cream, let alone trying for any mouth action of the more fun variety.

"I can think of a few." Brandt's leer was similarly strained and he let out a long yawn. "Later."

"I feel you. So tired." Leaning against the counter, Shane stretched his neck.

"Come on." Not waiting for Shane, Brandt took the ice cream and headed back down the hall to his room.

"What are we doing?" Shane trailed behind him, stopping in the doorway as Brandt set the ice cream on the nightstand before pulling off his shirt.

"Ice cream in bed." Brandt said this like it was the most normal occurrence in the world, something they did nightly.

"Kinky." Barely managing a laugh, Shane followed Brandt's lead and stripped down to his boxers before joining him under the covers.

"Hardly." Brandt grabbed one of the spoons and offered Shane the other. "I bet we pass out before the pint is empty."

"I'll take that bet." Apparently, they were going to eat right out of the carton, making this even more cozy and domestic and sweet. So sweet he almost couldn't stand it. "And I'll take the wakeups. You've got an early morning. You sure you don't want me sleeping in there with her?"

"Nah. That bed in there is crap." Brandt caught a drip of ice cream with his tongue and suddenly Shane's dick wasn't so sleepy after all.

"So you're saving my back?" he pressed, that same urge from earlier driving him, wanting to matter to Brandt, wanting to be needed for more than a spare set of hands.

Brandt raised an eyebrow. "You need me to admit I sleep better with you right here?"

"Might be nice." Shane couldn't lie, not to him, not even when the truth made him look needier than he might like.

"Fine." Brandt let out a long-suffering sigh before popping a spoonful of ice cream in Shane's mouth. "I like you here. Even when you hog the covers."

"I'm sorry, who does what? Pillow thief." Swallowing first, Shane gave an exaggerated blink. Joking was so much easier than getting real about his feelings, about what this was and what he wanted it to be.

The teasing carried them through most of the carton of ice cream, but then Brandt sobered as he set the pint aside.

"Thanks for being there today." No joking, no silly grin, only honest gratitude, and Shane's breath caught, chest so full it hurt.

"Anytime," he whispered. And meant it. This was why he wasn't talking or thinking about that phone call. Brandt needed him. Jewel needed him. And he needed them. Everything else could wait.

Chapter Twenty-Two

Brandt was done being freaked out at his own domesticity, and instead, he marveled at his aptitude for it as he cleaned the counter, stopping as he heard Shane come in.

"What smells so good?" Shane asked as he set his guitar near the table. He'd missed dinner for another band rehearsal, which had also let Brandt execute his plan, such as it was. However, as Shane came closer, something in his speculative expression made Brandt start second-guessing himself. Maybe this was a silly idea after all.

"Baking." His tone came out all cagey.

"This a new talent of yours?" Shane's easy smile didn't help any either. He smiled more these days, which Brandt liked, but this time the tease felt like a barb. Damn it. Maybe he *had* freaked himself out with this whole thing.

"I'll have you know I can read a cake mix box as easily as anyone else." He moved so Shane could see the square cake on the counter. The kitchen hadn't had a round pan, but the box had directions for a sheet cake, and once spread with the canned frosting, it didn't look half bad. "And you might want to not poke fun at the effort if you want to have some."

"Cake? Man, you really do have a sweet tooth." Still smiling, Shane shook his head and brushed a kiss across

Brandt's cheek. And okay, that helped settle Brandt's nerves back down. He was much freer with affection than Shane, and it always felt like earning some sort of reward when Shane initiated contact. Made him want to do whatever it took to earn more little touches and kisses.

"Or maybe I had an occasion." Brandt gave him a pointed look as he hauled him closer.

"Occasion? What…" Shane blinked before his eyes widened. "Oh. *That.*"

"Come on. You can't tell me you forgot your birthday."

"Eh. It's just a day." Shane sounded exactly like Brandt himself had year after year. And why Brandt had this sudden urge for things to be different was something he refused to think too hard about, only that he couldn't let the day pass unnoticed. Still, though, his skin heated as Shane continued to study the cake, mouth pursing. "I really don't need cake."

"I know. But you're getting one." That Shane didn't *need* a big deal was maybe exactly why Brandt wanted to give him this. And honestly, the guy deserved so much more, more maybe than Brandt could give. But this? He could do a cake. "And before you start in on not wanting a fuss, you can say it's for Jewel's three-month birthday too."

Brandt gestured at the diva in her swing near the dining table. He'd strung two soft toys where she could kick at them, and she'd been happy enough to let him handle icing the cake without her in the sling. Maybe at her six- or nine-month birthday, they could let her taste a little frosting. Because she too deserved all the little celebrations that Brandt hadn't had. And aptitude or not, he was going to do his best to give her those moments. Because some day she'd have someone she cared about, and he wanted her to know what to do for that person and not have this ridiculous twitchy stomach over a cake.

"Thank you." Shane smiled at him, tentative, eyes soft and mouth crooked. That look made all this uncertainty worth it, made the heat creeping over Brandt's skin shift to something more pleasant.

"No problem." Brandt's voice came out gruff. "Like you said, I like cake."

"Well, it smells good." Shane brushed a light kiss over Brandt's mouth. "When do we get to eat it?"

"How about now before we try to get the diva settled for the night?" Brandt grabbed two plates and forks. "I have a feeling we're gonna need the boost."

"Was she still fussy?" Walking over to Jewel, Shane crouched in front of her to make a silly face.

"A little, but she's a lot better. Still hates the medicine, though." Brandt couldn't put words to the relief he'd felt that her illness had been very short-lived. He carried the cake to the table as Shane whipped out his phone. "What are you doing? Cake's not that pretty."

"It's for Jewel." Shane ignored Brandt's protest and snapped a few pictures of the cake and then baby in her swing. "So she knows we remembered when she turned three months."

"Good idea." Not that Brandt was likely to forget Shane's tender expression or the baby's gummy grin, but he liked knowing there would be pictures for Jewel to pore over later. After Shane got his pictures, Brandt served them both generous slices and took a seat at the table.

"How was practice?" he asked to distract himself from how hot Shane managed to look eating cake. Him licking the frosting off his fork made Brandt's dick take notice, but more than that, seeing him enjoy himself with Brandt's creation made his chest warm and light.

"It was okay." Shane shrugged and took another bite of the cake.

"Do you think this gig could turn into a regular thing?"

"Maybe." Shane stuck to the cryptic tone. Something had been going on with him ever since that phone call at the clinic, something that made his mouth tense whenever mention of his music came up. "Cake is good."

"I couldn't find candles. And I know better than to try to sing to a professional like yourself, but there's this." He slid a box closer to Shane.

"A present?" Shane's eyebrows went up. It wasn't a fancy wrapping job by any means. Brandt had marked "gift" on the online order form, and it had arrived in a slim blue box with a silver elastic band, which Shane fingered like it might be a detonator cord.

"You don't have to look like it might explode." And there Brandt was, getting antsy again.

"I'm not." Shane held up his hands. "I'm just surprised. In a good way. Thank you." Biting his lip, Shane lowered his gaze back down to the present, the color in his cheeks making Brandt wish he had done more.

"Might want to open it before you say that. It's not much."

Shane opened the box to lift out the slip of paper Brandt had slid in instead of a greeting card. "A get out of diaper duty coupon? I'll take that. And what's this?"

"Like I said. It's not much." Brandt gestured at the slim book Shane was turning over in his hands. He opened it to reveal the blank sheet music pages. "But I figured maybe you could use something better than those stacks of legal pads. I did a search on songwriter notebooks and that's what came up."

"It's awesome. Thank you." Blush deepening, Shane set the book aside and came around the table to kiss Brandt lightly. "I'll save it for my almost-done tunes that might be worth saving. First song I add is gonna be the one about your friend."

"Can't wait to hear it." Brandt pulled him in close for another kiss, this one longer. Shane tasted sweet but his hold on Brandt's shoulder was firm, like he too was trying to hold on to this moment for all it was worth.

"Now?" Shane asked as he broke away, glancing down at his guitar case. "I'm still working on parts of the refrain, but I could show you what I've got…"

"Yeah." Brandt reached over and plucked Jewel out of her swing. She'd been about to fuss, and no way did he want to miss this. "Sing us a song."

Shane sat back down, this time with his guitar and a folded piece of yellow paper, and he strummed idly while Brandt tried to settle the baby.

Humming softly, Shane turned slightly, so Brandt couldn't see his full face. Then he started singing, and Brandt was back in freefall, that instant when his chute hadn't deployed and the world had seemed to rush up with startling clarity. Every hundredth of a second had mattered.

Listening to Shane was like that. Riveting. Life changing. Every note mattered. And Shane had only jumped once, had never met Roger outside of Brandt's memories, and yet he *understood* on a level Brandt wasn't sure he himself had until Shane hit a low plaintive note.

A love song.

Shane had written a love song.

Not an ode to heroism as Brandt had ordered. Sure, it had the boy, his dream, and a terrain bigger than both, but it also had the singer who pined with a beauty Brandt wasn't sure he'd ever heard. Shane drew out the word *timber* until Brandt felt the note everywhere—behind his eyes, in his thighs and ass, down to his toes. Jewel's warm weight grounded him, kept him from melting to the rug as Shane finished his song with a little shrug, like maybe he'd surprised even himself.

"Wow." Brandt licked his parched lips. "Shane…"

"It's not much." Shane echoed Brandt from earlier but hell if there was any similarity between stationery and a song that already felt like a memory, lyrics he'd had printed on his soul, waiting for Shane to breathe life into, change from painful to beautiful.

"It's everything. You did him proud." He'd done Brandt proud too, but he wasn't sure precisely how to express that short of falling to Shane's feet. "You gonna add that to the playlist this weekend?"

"It's more of a cover band." Mouth twisting, Shane set the guitar aside. "Could have…never mind."

"What? Come on, man. Something's been on your mind." Brandt couldn't keep the hurt from his tone. "Can't you tell me?"

"It's not that. And it's nothing." Eyes going distant, Shane sighed softly. "But remember how Shelby found me in Portland? I was auditioning for a regional slot in a new competition show showcasing singer songwriters. That message the other day was them offering me a spot."

"You've got to take it." He didn't have to think about it more than a heartbeat. Didn't matter how the ground was rushing up to meet him or how inevitable the hard landing would be. "Tell me you didn't turn it down."

"Not yet." Shane's clenched hands and twisted mouth revealed the truth behind his indifferent tone. "But I will. I can't leave you in the lurch with the baby."

"You can't walk away from a chance like that." Brandt shifted Jewel to his other arm as he leaned forward.

Shane rolled his shoulders and loosened his jaw. "There will be other chances."

Liar. Brandt didn't believe that for a second. He knew full well that some things only came along once. "Not like this one."

"Exactly. It's not only a couple of days to go to Portland. If I win at the regional level—and that's a huge if—then I have to go to LA for who knows how many weeks to let the main part of the contest play out. I'm not sure what I was thinking auditioning, really. I'm not reality show material."

"Sure you are. You're hot, young, sing like you're trying to pull the audience's souls out, and you can take a story and turn it into..." Brandt still didn't have words, so he settled for making a sweeping gesture with his free hand. "That. Beautiful."

"It wasn't all that."

"It—"

Jewel cut him off with a hiccupy noise before he could tell Shane how he'd made Brandt see the truth of his own heart, both then and now. And that might be for the best, keeping those feelings to himself, so he didn't protest when Shane took the baby from his arms.

"We need to get her to bed." Shane headed for the kitchen, probably in search of the nighttime bottle.

"Okay, but we're not done talking about this." Would be nice if Brandt knew what more he was going to say, but no way was he letting Shane walk away from a chance like this.

Shane nodded, but in a way that wasn't necessarily agreement as he headed to Jewel's room with the bottle. They worked together in a silence that wasn't precisely strained but not entirely comfortable as they put the baby to bed. Shane broke the quiet as he softly sang the same older tune he reached for most nights, now familiar lyrics wrapping around Brandt's heart and squeezing tightly.

And just like that, the song was done, and Jewel was snoozing in her crib, leaving them to tiptoe out of the room.

"That was easy," he whispered.

"For once." Shane's smile was tight, an unreadable intent in his eyes as he stepped closer to Brandt. "Now, where were we?"

Brandt was still trying to decide how best to approach the prior conversation when Shane slid his mouth over Brandt's, slow and easy, like they'd been planning sex, not talking. And usually Brandt would be all over that idea, but he didn't want Shane to kiss his way out of an uncomfortable talk. Brandt wasn't letting him pass up this opportunity.

He moved his head before Shane could claim another kiss. "You're trying to distract me."

"No, I'm trying to thank you for a nice birthday."

"Last year's was probably better." Even now, Brandt could hear that laugh, that sound of pure joy. He was glad he'd been able to give Shane that, even for a moment.

"Not hardly." Serious now, Shane held his gaze. A lot passed between them in that look, all that had happened the past few weeks, all the little moments that maybe did add up to more memories than that one singular moment. "This one was special."

Shane said the last bit so softly that no way was Brandt denying him when he pulled Brandt closer, looping his arms around Brandt's neck and pulling him into a kiss that started as a sweet thank-you and morphed into a filthy promise.

Knowing he was fighting a losing battle, Brandt groaned as Shane used his lips and tongue to drive all his better sense away.

"Can we talk later?" Shane broke the kiss, damp lips still millimeters from Brandt's. "Please. I'm trying to think through everything. I am. But right now, I just want you."

Like Brandt could deny that request. "I suppose talking can wait. You are the birthday boy, after all."

"Yep." Some of the tension left Shane's eyes as he leered at Brandt. "Why don't you let me unwrap you?"

"Hey I thought I was the one with the cheesy lines." Brandt laughed even as he let Shane tug him the rest of the way toward his bedroom.

"What can I say? You inspire me." Already pulling at Brandt's clothes, Shane nipped at Brandt's neck. Yep. He was a goner. They should be talking, not fucking, but hell if Brandt could deny him a damn thing.

Chapter Twenty-Three

As far as birthday presents went, getting Brandt Wilder was at the top of Shane's list already. The cake. The music notebook. The expression on his face when Shane had sung. And now, him, half dressed and eager, everything Shane wanted, right here for the taking.

"Shirt off." He'd managed to push Brandt's loose pants down and off, but he'd rather not strangle Brandt with his T-shirt. He let Brandt pull it over his head then was immediately there to capture his mouth in a blistering kiss.

Brandt wasn't wrong. They needed to talk. But Shane needed this more. The world was tilting, everything on the precipice of change, and all he wanted was one more night exactly like this. Brandt was warm and urgent against Shane, all those gorgeous muscles rippling as he met Shane kiss for kiss, touch for desperate touch.

"Damn." Breathing hard, Brandt tilted his head so Shane had better access to his neck. "You're impatient tonight."

Shane looked up mid-nip at Brandt's collarbone. "The speed demon is complaining?"

"Not complaining." Brandt groaned as Shane followed through on the bite. "Trust me. But I want you naked too."

"Thought I was the one who got to make the wishes tonight?" Even as he complied and removed his clothes, he couldn't resist the tease. He was totally going to milk this birthday business as much as he could. He was so used to the day being an afterthought, even for his own parents. Brandt making him a priority was new and delicious and rather intoxicating.

"You are." Brandt stretched out on the bed, hair spilling over the pillow. He looked like a Roman god awaiting servicing, but then he moved his arms over his head like he was offering up all that power to Shane. "Whatever you want."

"I want you." Clothes off, Shane lay down next to him. That wasn't quite close enough, so he moved to straddle Brandt, who responded by undulating his spine, further putting himself at Shane's disposal. The perfect gift. Shane's breath hitched. "This. I want this."

He claimed Brandt's mouth, slow now, leisurely sips. If this was his present, he was going to savor it. And work until Brandt burned as brightly as he did. Sliding his lips along Brandt's bristly jaw, he then explored his neck, all the little places that made Brandt groan and gasp. Shane kept his touch light too, brushing over Brandt's arms and torso, finding future spots for his lips to land. Muscular shoulders. Dip between his collarbones. Sternum. Dusky nipples.

"Damn." Brandt was panting now, eyes glassy as his body shifted restlessly. "Can we go back to hurrying up?"

"Hush. Let me have my birthday present." He raked his mouth along Brandt's pec, capturing his nipple in a gentle bite.

"Fuck. Love your teeth." Brandt's groan had everything to do with getting the sort of friction he always seemed to like and nothing to with loving *Shane*, but still Shane's pulse skipped at that word. Brandt threaded his fingers through Shane's hair, grip just this side of too tight, like he wanted to keep Shane right there.

Keep me. Keep me. Shane's heart laid down a desperate beat, an unspoken wish that underscored every touch, every love bite. Finally, it was him, not Brandt, groaning and him who reached for the nightstand.

"Oh *yeah*." Lips kiss swollen and body wearing more than a couple of Shane's marks, Brandt already looked thoroughly fucked out as he widened his legs and grinned.

Shane had to laugh at that. "Guess that answers how you feel about fucking tonight."

"Have at me." Brandt stretched his arms to touch the headboard again, and Shane wanted a picture of him exactly like that, eager and needy and all for him. "Here. Let me flip."

"I want it like this." Shane stayed him by pressing down on his shoulders. And damn, wasn't that heady, pinning Brandt to the mattress. "Want to watch you come apart."

They'd fucked a few more times after that first time, and Brandt almost always flipped over to some variation of on his knees. Which was fine and hot as hell, but this time Shane wanted to see his face. Felt primal and possessive in a way that wasn't usually Shane's thing, but right then he wanted every piece of Brandt he could get.

"I'm not all that." Brandt, who was a walking, talking fantasy for a huge swath of the population, actually blushed. Damn. His uncertainty might be even more arousing than his usual cocky confidence.

"Yeah, you are." Stretching back up, he gave Brandt

a soft kiss before reaching for the stuff he'd retrieved from the nightstand. "And I'm gonna make you come without your hand."

"Fuck, yes." Brandt scooted back on the bed, eyes intent as Shane moved between his legs. "Do it."

Even with a clear invitation like that, Shane still wasn't going to skip the chance to play a little first. After he slicked up his fingers, he gently eased one in, knowing full well that Brandt was about to demand two. Making him wait was at least half the fun of this. But so was finding that magic spot inside Brandt that made Brandt rock up to meet his hand and made needy noises escape his throat.

"Damn. I still can't get over how much you love this." He went ahead and gave Brandt two fingers, working him more open.

Brandt's voice came out strained and breathless. "My offer to give you a demo still stands."

"Sometime." Seeing how much fun Brandt seemed to have bottoming had made Shane more curious, but his body had another agenda tonight. "Right now, I want this."

"Yeah. Me too." Head falling back, Brandt rode Shane's fingers like he was on a mission to get off in the next five minutes. "Damn. Do it already. Come on."

"Now who's impatient?" Laughing, Shane went ahead and took care of the condom and more lube.

"Me. Need you." Brandt's eyes fluttered open, a seriousness there Shane wasn't sure he'd seen before.

You. Oh, how he wanted that to be true. Not Brandt wanting someone to help with the baby and not someone to fuck and experiment with but wanting Shane specifically.

"You've got me." He meant it too, even given their earlier conversation. He couldn't give this up, not now. If Brandt needed *him*, then he was going to do his damnedest to be here, giving him that.

As he met Brandt's solemn expression, time felt especially tenuous though, like whatever this was might slip through their fingers any second. *No.* He refused to go there. He wasn't letting go. *Couldn't* let go.

All he could do was hold on. Hold on to Brandt and hold on to this precious, fragile thing between them. Hold on literally too, gripping Brandt's strong thigh, pushing it back as he moved into position between his legs. He loved how unexpectedly flexible Brandt was, belying his sturdy, muscular build. And he loved how Brandt always met him more than halfway, pulling his own legs up, body already surging toward Shane even before he lined up his cock.

Even with the earlier fingering, Brandt was tight. Almost too tight. But he always seemed to have some sort of cheat code where right when Shane was about to pull back, Brandt managed to relax and take him in. The way Brandt groaned and sank into the mattress felt like Brandt welcoming him with his whole body. That first time had also felt like this, familiar in a way that nothing had prepared him for. And again now, the sense of coming home as he slid in made him gasp right along with Brandt.

"More." Brandt moved with him, no patience for Shane trying to slow things down. "Please."

"God damn, I love when you beg." And no way could he deny the plea either. He thrust more purposefully now, aiming for that spot that made Brandt moan and curse as his eyes drifted closed again.

"Too fucking good."

"Yeah it is." Trying to figure out an angle that might let him sneak a kiss, he bent forward, which apparently did something good for Brandt because he met Shane's mouth with a hungry urgency.

"Fuck. Need…" Breaking the kiss, Brandt tried to work a hand between their bodies, but Shane batted it away.

"None of that. Wait for it." His voice had seldom been so demanding even as his own body struggled for control.

"Gonna kill me." Brandt's voice was pained, but the way he was meeting each of Shane's thrusts said he wanted all of this, including being pushed to wait.

"Hardly." Somehow he managed a laugh. "I like you too much to want to end you."

Like was an understatement, but even admitting that much had him finding Brandt's mouth again for a kiss, needing to block out all the warning lights in his brain trying to tell him that this was too much, too fast. Fuck that. Forget everything except this kiss right here, this driving need to be as deep inside Brandt as possible.

And Brandt must have liked that sort of desperation because he was groaning with every thrust now. "Yeah. Like that. More."

His cockhead was damp against his belly, bouncing every time Shane went deep. He had to be close now, and it would be so easy to grab his cock, send him over the edge. But Shane was determined to see if his boast could work.

"Fuck. Can't…" Brandt sounded equal parts frustrated and turned on.

"Yes, you can." Shane soothed him with a hand on his torso. "Promise."

"So close." All of Brandt's muscles went tense under Shane, including his ass, but then he made a frustrated noise. "Can't."

"Stop fighting it." Working on some new instinct, Shane hiked one of Brandt's legs up, taking further advantage of his flexibility to go deeper. "Let me get you there."

"Okay." The trust in Brandt's voice and eyes stole Shane's oxygen and was almost enough to make him climax. But not yet. Brandt first. Turning his head, he raked his teeth across Brandt's fuzzy calf.

"That's it." Brandt moaned, new level of keening. Damn. Shane wanted more of those noises and went harder. Faster. Fuck. This was going to be an epic race to the finish.

"Brandt..." He didn't know what he was asking, only that he might die if he didn't get an answer. His thrusts were fast losing all finesse, but Brandt must have liked that because his body bowed, tensing and holding. And right as Shane was about to give in and grab Brandt's cock, it pumped slippery fluid all over his abs as his ass clenched tight on Shane's dick.

"Oh, fuck." Shane wanted to celebrate what felt like a huge damn victory, but his body had other ideas, moving hard and fast until he was coming too even as Brandt was still shuddering under him. Felt like crashing through some invisible barrier, reaching a place he hadn't thought possible before fluttering back toward earth.

"That was something." Brandt sounded all dreamy as Shane withdrew as gently as possible. He took care of the condom before flopping next to Brandt, both of them still breathing hard.

"Something good?"

"You have to ask? Feels like I jumped without a chute and somehow still landed."

"Don't joke about that." Shane's voice went stern as his blood ran cold with the memory of those awful moments after the demo when he hadn't been sure whether Brandt was okay.

"Sorry. I won't do that again." Brandt pulled him close enough to kiss. "I'm safe. You know that."

"Yeah." Shane wasn't so sure about that. No one was ever safe, especially people in jobs like Brandt's. There were no guarantees he could make Shane, but Shane wasn't going to ruin the moment by arguing the point. Instead he burrowed into Brandt's chest, letting his steady heartbeat calm Shane's thready pulse.

"I'm just trying to say that you took me high." Brandt stroked Shane's hair before he yawned. "Hell. You fucked all my words out."

"It's okay. You rest."

"We were gonna talk…" Brandt ended with another huge yawn.

"Later," Shane promised even as dread chased the last of the pleasant hum out of his muscles, made him tense all over again. He didn't want a damn thing to change, but that seemed like a battle he'd already lost.

Shane's neck hurt. He was exhausted and still had hours of day to get through.

"So you're going?" And Brandt. Hours of him and his questions too. They'd been going around on this issue in whatever limited time they'd had together. And now Brandt had arrived back from his shift only to start in again as soon as he saw Shane in the dining area packing up his stuff for the show with the cover band that night.

"To this gig, yeah." Which Brandt damn well knew, having already decided to stay in with the baby rather than go out to watch again. Jewel still had a few days of antibiotics to get through, and the last thing they needed was her sick again. But the second last thing Shane needed was all this pressure from Brandt. "Quit trying to bully me into deciding on the Portland show."

Frowning deeply, Brandt buckled Jewel into her swing before turning back to face Shane. "You promised to think about it."

"And I have." Hell, he'd done little other than think ever since getting the call. Couldn't bring himself to cancel but also couldn't see himself going either. Any more thinking and his throbbing head might finally boil over.

"Why do I have the impression that you're just humoring me and still planning on turning this opportunity down?"

Busted. Shane shifted his weight from foot to foot, trying not to squirm in the face of Brandt's pointed look.

"Because maybe we both know that it's simply not practical right now?" He couldn't outright lie to Brandt, so he went straight to the conclusion he kept circling back to himself.

"Screw practical." Brandt's hazel eyes flashed as he stepped closer. "This is your dream."

"It's not that straightforward." *If only.* Shane had wanted one thing and one thing only for years now, right up until the minute he found something he wanted more. And he probably couldn't have that either, but he also couldn't ignore how his soul felt split right down the middle. "You don't have other childcare, and I'm not leaving her without a plan."

Or Brandt. He wasn't leaving him either, but keeping

the focus on logistics was so much easier than voicing everything else in his head and heart.

"Let me worry about the plan." Brandt touched Shane's shoulder, his hand warm through Shane's thin Western shirt.

"I know it's hard to believe but I've grown kind of attached." Relaxing into Brandt's grip, he tipped his head back, willing him to understand that he wasn't only referring to Jewel.

"I get that. She's easy to care about." And there they were, Brandt missing the point even as he rubbed Shane's shoulders and gentled his tone. "And I appreciate your help. But you need to at least do the Portland show. I'll figure something out for those days and then we can deal with LA if—when—that happens."

We. If Shane could let himself trust in that, this decision would be so much easier. But he knew all the way down to his boots that any *we* would evaporate the moment he left this cozy little bubble they'd built the last few weeks.

"Yeah. It's a big if."

"I've got some savings. I can see about a nanny rather than doing daycare if that comes to pass." Brandt certainly seemed to want to boil it down to money, schedules, and how easily replaceable Shane apparently was. Stepping free of Brandt's hand, he paced away.

"A nanny isn't the worst idea." If Brandt wanted to make this all about practicality, fine. Shane wasn't sure he had it in him to cling to something that clearly wasn't happening.

"It's not." Brandt flopped onto the couch. "But you still look like I'm suggesting you perform naked in a snake pit."

"Thanks for that visual." Shane had to laugh, even if it hurt. "And I don't know. I just…"

"What?" Leaning forward, Brandt made a frustrated noise. "I can't help if you don't tell me what's on your mind."

"You want to?" Turning on his heel, he studied Brandt more carefully now. The lines around his mouth and eyes were deeper, and his eyes held none of his usual joking.

"To help? Hell, yeah." Brandt scrubbed at his hair. Fuck. How far they'd come from the guy with the devilish grin who ran from responsibility. Shane's initial impressions seemed downright silly now, but he still had trouble trusting this new level of concern. "You think this is only about convenient babysitting for me?"

"Maybe," Shane admitted, because he wasn't sure of anything anymore.

"Well, it's not." Brandt's voice was firm, almost angry. "Perhaps at first, but we're well beyond that now, and I think you damn well know it."

He did. He so did. He was in so deep he no longer had any sense of direction, and knowing he wasn't alone in these murky waters wasn't much comfort. But Brandt caring also wasn't nothing, and if Brandt was going to be honest then maybe he could too. He stepped closer to the couch.

"That's just it. This isn't simply about leaving the baby. I'm not ready to say goodbye," he whispered.

"Then don't." Brandt flipped both hands palms up, like the answer was that easy.

"Don't what?"

"Don't say goodbye if you don't want to." Reaching for Shane, Brandt tugged him on to the couch, half on Brandt's lap which felt both ridiculous and comforting, especially when Brandt nuzzled his neck. "I meant what I said before we started this thing that I'm not gonna try to pin you down, but I'm also not shoving you out the door either."

"Felt like that earlier." Maybe that was what a lot of Shane's hurt was about, how eager Brandt had seemed about him leaving, how easily he could let go of the very thing Shane was pining for.

"Fuck it, Shane." Brandt's voice was angry, but his hands were still gentle as he pulled Shane closer. "This isn't a motel. I'm not flipping the vacancy sign on simply because you go to Portland or anywhere else for a couple of days."

"Oh." Still hung up on the idea that this was all an opportune fling for Brandt, he hadn't let himself dwell much on the idea of keeping this going after he left. Hadn't occurred to him that Brandt might want to try, that this might be as real for him as it was for Shane. His heart hammered faster, all the hope he'd been trying to keep in check rushing back in.

"Yeah. *Oh.* I—"

Bing. The doorbell interrupted whatever Brandt had been about to say, and Shane cursed low. They were far enough out in the country that other than package delivery, the bell seldom rang.

"I'll get it." Chill racing up his spine, he untangled himself from Brandt. Couldn't glance back. Couldn't dwell on what Brandt had been about to say. Could only open the door and—

"*Shelby.*"

Chapter Twenty-Four

Brandt should have followed Shane to the door. It was
technically his house, but he was trying to figure out
how to get Shane to see reason about this music opportunity of his. Shane could handle the package or whatever it was while Brandt sorted out what to say next.
They were dancing around some pretty big truths, and
his heart was still auditioning for a drum solo, hammering out a frantic beat.

"Shelby?" Shane's voice carried back to the couch.

Holy fuck. Brandt was on his feet before he even realized what he was doing, same reflexes that had kept
him safe from falling debris multiple times sending him
straight to Jewel's swing, positioning himself in front
of it. The pounding in his chest increased, adrenaline
heightening all his senses.

"What the hell are you doing here?" Shane asked as
Shelby entered the house.

"A nurse called. Said the baby was sick." Her hair
was longer than before, a little more scraggly, and her
face was more gaunt, high cheekbones slashing across a
paler face. Shelby's cut-off jeans and faded music festival T-shirt made her look younger than Shane, not older.

"She's fine now." Brandt crossed his arms over his

chest. Funny how only a few weeks ago he'd prayed for her to turn back up, but now his voice was hard. He was more than ready to fight to keep his baby safe.

"It was only an ear infection," Shane added. His jaw was tight like his teeth were grinding away at metal shavings. He'd seemed uncomfortable earlier, but it had been frustration, not anger in his voice then. His tone had shifted to something cold, anger rolling off him at a rate that Brandt wasn't sure he'd ever seen from the guy.

"I was worried." Shelby's voice wavered.

"Shouldn't you have been worried when you left your kid with me?" Shane's skin was mottled with red now, and he was back to wearing a hole in the carpet with his pacing.

"I figured..." Shelby started defiant, but then her face crumpled. "I don't know. I thought she'd be safer with you. Like I always felt. But then that nurse said she was sick and they needed to know what shots she'd had, and I didn't know what to do. Just started driving."

Brandt didn't cope well with tears on the best of days, and after this week, he was in even less shape to deal with the onslaught of waterworks.

"She's fine now," he repeated, gentler now, moving so Shelby could see Jewel.

"Oh. She's so big now." Shelby fell to her knees in front of the swing.

"Yup. It's crazy what a month will do." Shane continued to stare his sister down. Not liking their arguing, Brandt's stomach twisted. And it *was* crazy. Had it really only been a month? It felt like a lifetime, but not in a bad way, more that he was a different person now.

A dad. Ever since that night at the clinic, the title had seemed to fit more, like a shirt that had shrunk down to the right size at last. And now that he had that role, he wasn't giving it up. He spared a glance at Shane. He was something else now too, something that still didn't have a name, but hell if he was walking away from that either.

But right then, his top priority had to be Jewel, even if parts of him wanted to go to Shane, to soothe his anger and hurt.

"What do you want, Shelby?" Brandt crouched next to her, keeping his voice low, still wary and on edge.

"I don't know." She kept staring at the baby, not touching her but not looking away either. "Some lady lawyer has been leaving me messages…"

"Of course you don't know what you want. No surprise there." Shane sounded more tired than mad, but the bite was still there in his voice.

"Shane…" Having heard enough stories about Shelby and Shane's losing efforts to keep her out of trouble, Brandt understood where the anger was coming from, but Shane also wasn't helping anything either.

"I'm due on stage in forty minutes. I do not have time for this." Shane raked at his hair.

"Why don't you head to your gig?" Brandt suggested, trying to keep his tone neutral. "I can handle things here."

"Yeah, maybe I should go." Shane picked up his guitar case and bag.

"Do you need my keys?" Still keeping it light, Brandt dug in his pocket, but Shane held up a hand.

"I'll take the RV."

"Parking—"

"It's a big lot. I'll work it out." Shane's jaw was firm enough to sharpen an ax and his eyes were equally steely. He headed to the door, and Brandt stepped away from Shelby and Jewel to follow him.

"Be right back," he said to Shelby, who was still peering at Jewel. She didn't seem likely to move, let alone snatch her up, and Brandt couldn't let Shane leave with this head of steam.

"Don't." Shane shook his head as they reached the steps, door shutting softly behind them.

"I get it. You're mad."

"Mad?" Shane blinked. "She left Jewel. She didn't answer messages for weeks. And now she shows up, no warning, ready to ruin everything... *Mad* isn't even half of it."

"Maybe—"

"You're going to give her the benefit of the doubt? No. Defend her all you want, but I finished making her excuses a long time ago."

"I'm not making excuses." Brandt matched Shane's fed-up tone. "But from where I stand, I need her cooperation. A lot of yelling isn't going to get any of us what we want and what Jewel needs."

"Right. Your custody petition."

"Exactly. I can't kick her out, and I also can't risk her leaving with the baby. I need to talk to Cameron, and I also need to talk to Shelby. Talk. Not shout her down."

"I get it." Shane stepped down to the yard, then turned back. "I do. You're in a no-win situation. And I know you can't have her finding out about...everything."

"Maybe not yet," Brandt hedged. He hadn't gotten that far in his head yet, hadn't worked out what Shelby was likely to think about him and Shane knocking boots. "But regardless, I want you to come back here after your gig. Please. We need to talk more."

"Is there that much left to say?" Shane kicked at a dirt clump. "Fuck. I hate this."

"Me too." Fighting the urge to go to him, Brandt flexed his arms. "All I'm asking is for time to figure this out."

Shane exhaled hard. "You've got it. And better you than me."

"Shane—"

"I mean that." Shane made a sweeping gesture. "You're able to be nicer than I seem to be capable of right about now."

"You've got reasons for being upset."

"Yeah, I do. Good luck." Shane resumed walking to his RV.

And he wasn't kidding about running late. The last thing Brandt wanted was him speeding, so he couldn't stop him from leaving, could only call after him, "Drive safe."

That earned him a quick wave before Shane unlocked his rig. Damn. There was so much left unsaid between them. And he wanted to tell Shane that this didn't have to change a thing between them, but he knew in his soul that it already had.

Shane had had hard performances before. He'd been hungry any number of times. And sick more than once. Tired, that too. In bad weather and overwhelming heat both. He'd faced tiny crowds and last-minute changes. But he'd never had any gig as difficult as the one after Shelby showed up. What was funny, though, was that his awful mood didn't come out in flubbed lines or missed cues. No, it came out in the songs themselves, in the way they seemed to slice him open, the way his voice had a little more to it, until his throat ached every bit as much as his chest.

"Great set, man. Way to make them hurt." Clapping him on the back as they started packing up, Tim was all smiles even if Shane wasn't. Music was the best therapy he knew, but even it hadn't cured his dark mood.

"That's some instrument you've got there." Elaine handed him his share of the tip jar. "I swear you almost made me tear up a time or two."

"And that's hard to do." Tim bumped the drummer's slim shoulder.

"Thanks." Ready to get going, Shane pocketed the money. While he'd been singing, his brain had been too busy to dwell on what was happening at Brandt's house, but now that they were done, all he could think about was what havoc Shelby had likely wreaked.

"Are we going to get you again next weekend?" Tim asked as Shane snapped his guitar case closed.

"I'm not sure." Shane wished he had a better answer for the guy who'd been nothing but good to him. Hell, he wished he had a better answer for himself. "I've got a chance at a Portland competition show thing, but that's filming early in the week. Still not sure if I'm going to take it."

Tim's eyes went wide with approval. "Filming? Dude, you don't turn down a chance at video."

"Yeah." Shane nodded. He was going to regret it if he let the chance go, but nothing in his earlier conversation with Brandt had convinced him that taking the leap was the right thing to do. If Brandt cared like he said he did, Shane wasn't sure how he could walk away from that. But now Shelby was back in town, bringing with her a whole new set of doubts. "Not sure whether I'm cut out for reality TV."

"Ha." Tim let out a deep belly laugh. "Your life *is* a reality show. Two dudes and a little baby."

"Yep." Shane faked joining in with a chuckle.

Tim wasn't wrong. Shane's life had certainly been dramatic enough for some overwrought biopic. And comical, him and Brandt trying to take care of Jewel. Except they'd done more than okay. They'd kept her safe and watched her grow and loved her. They'd made more than just some punchline—they'd made a family, at least temporarily. They were good together, but as Shane well knew, all good things eventually ended. The town he'd liked, the teacher he'd enjoyed, the house with his favorite room—good stuff never worked out long-term.

And Shelby's appearance was proof of that. His brain continued to stew over what her showing up meant the whole way home. The little Toyota she'd arrived with was still parked at Brandt's, not that it made him breathe any easier, but at least that meant she hadn't left with Jewel. Quietly, he let himself into the house through the side door. The living area light was out, but he could make out a shape on the couch.

"Hey. You made it back." Brandt was already in the kitchen, near the window, like he'd been watching for Shane. He jerked his head in the direction of the hall. "We can talk in the sunroom."

On their way down the hall, Shane peeked into Jewel's room. She still looked so tiny in the crib. He might be all kinds of twisted-up over Brandt and his own future, but there wasn't much Shane wouldn't do for that baby.

"What's Shelby doing on the couch?" Shane asked once they were in the sunroom and could speak a little more freely.

"I didn't want to give her your room, all things considered." Brandt sighed like a guy who'd had a very long day. Shane hated seeing him so exhausted and tugged him over to the small couch in the room so that they could both sit, thighs touching. "I offered to take the couch myself, but she didn't want that. And she wasn't interested in that bed in the baby's room."

"Guess that makes sense," Shane said even though it really didn't. He supposed Brandt was being nice, not giving Shane's room away. At the same time, though, he'd slept almost all of the last few weeks in Brandt's bed, and he couldn't help but notice that Brandt wasn't keen on volunteering that information to Shelby.

"None of this makes sense." Leaning forward, Brandt twisted his fingers as he studied the worn floor.

"Yeah." On that they could agree. And no way could he see Brandt this distressed and not touch him. He rubbed Brandt's back lightly. "What are you going to do?"

"Hell if I know. Shelby wasn't exactly chatty after you left. I fed her some chicken and rice, but she barely ate before she fell asleep on the couch." Brandt dipped his head so Shane could continue his massage easier. "I called Cameron once she was asleep. She offered to meet with us tomorrow even though it's usually her day off."

"Think Shelby will go for that?" Shane kept working at Brandt's knotted muscles, trying to give him whatever relief he could.

"No clue." Groaning, Brandt grimaced.

"You sure you want custody?" That was unquestionably the best solution for Jewel, but he hated seeing the toll all this was taking on Brandt. If Shelby dug in her heels, this wasn't going to be easy on any of them.

"You have to ask?"

"No. Not really." Shane sighed because he had known the answer and because this was a long road Brandt was choosing. "You're a damn good dad, Brandt."

"Thanks." Turning, Brandt touched his forehead to Shane's.

"I want you to win," Shane whispered, taking the opportunity to hold his shoulders. "Regardless of what that means for us."

"Not sure there are any winners here."

There certainly were losers though, and Shane was likely to be one. He could accept that if it meant a safe future for Jewel, but he didn't have to like it.

Even as his chest ached even worse than earlier, he tried to keep his voice steady, not petulant. "You know what I mean. I want what's best for Jewel. And you."

"You matter too." Brandt gathered him close, strong arms coming around Shane and their cheeks resting together. Close enough to kiss, but that wasn't what this was about. Instead, they inhaled and exhaled in unison, long breaths where music swelled in Shane's head and all he could do was hold fast to Brandt, try to keep this moment as long as he could. But it couldn't last, and Brandt seemed to know that too, slumping against Shane.

"I think I'm going to head to Portland." He hadn't realized he'd decided until he said the words aloud. And maybe he'd known since Shelby's arrival that that was the only thing that made sense for him. But damn if it didn't feel like defeat, like heading off to lick his wounds while he settled for the thing he wanted second-best. Brandt needed space to work out his own future, and Shane's anger at Shelby wasn't helping anyone. So he'd go.

"Good." Sitting back up, Brandt nodded firmly.

"That eager to have me gone?" Fuck. This hurt even more than he'd thought it might.

"Don't be ridiculous. I'm gonna miss you." Brandt cupped Shane's face, calloused fingers rubbing against the stubble there. The truth of his words shone in his eyes, which were puddles of unhappiness, not of their usual humor. "But it's the best thing for you."

"I'd stay if you asked. If you needed me." A big part of him wanted Brandt to say yes, yes, he needed Shane. Staying might be as hard as going, but he'd do it for Brandt. *Need me. Want me.* His chest clanged like a cymbal, quaver running through his body like his heart had taken a direct hit.

"What I need is for you to go win." Eyes still sad, Brandt nevertheless managed a smile. Maybe he wasn't ever going to need Shane in the same way that Shane needed him. And Shane better get okay with that because the guy had enough stress. He didn't need Shane clinging to his leg.

"I'll do my best."

"You always do." Brandt traced Shane's lower lip with his thumb. "Don't look so sad."

"Trying. But it hurts," he admitted in a whisper.

"It doesn't have to." Voice way firmer than Shane's, Brandt moved his hands to Shane's shoulders.

"How do you figure that?" That Brandt wasn't more broken up about this was its own pain, how easily he could let go.

"You could try trusting that this thing between us can still work out." Brandt's mouth twisted around a heavy sigh. "Somehow."

"You're going to be the one advocating patience now?" There were certain depths of optimism that Shane couldn't reach and this was one. Brandt wanting it to work out made warmth race up Shane's spine, but there was a Crater Lake–size gap between wanting and having.

"Guess I am. I'm not giving you up that easily." Brandt stroked Shane's hair, and he leaned into the contact. Smart thing would be to pull away, to not chase false hope and to let Brandt go completely. But hell if he could do anything other than close his eyes and let Brandt pet him.

"The odds aren't great."

"Fuck the odds." Brandt's hand stilled and his tone hardened. "I've made a career out of taking losing bets and long odds. I'm betting on us figuring something out."

"Hope you're right." Only a foolish man would put money on that proposition. But what choice did he have? If Brandt truly wanted him to go, then he'd go. He'd sing what was left of his heart out because it was all he knew how to do. But trust? He wasn't sure he could do that.

Chapter Twenty-Five

"Where's Shane?" The sun was fully shining when Shelby finally migrated from the couch to the kitchen. She didn't wait for an invitation before pouring herself some of the coffee Brandt had started hours earlier. She was bleary eyed despite the hours of sleep and seemed more focused on doctoring her cup of coffee than paying attention to the baby hanging out in the sling on Brandt's chest. And she seemed more wary than concerned about Shane's whereabouts.

"On his way to Portland." He hadn't expected Shane to leave so soon after their talk the night before. He'd thought they might have more time. Hell, that was an entire mood right there. All Brandt needed was more time. More time with Shane. More time to figure out how to deal with Shelby. More time to work out his own future.

Everything was happening too fast. Including Shane's quick exit. They'd hung out, miserable together, in the sunroom, and he'd been about to say fuck it and tell Shane to sleep in Brandt's bed where he belonged when he'd said he'd rather stay in the RV, get an early start to Portland. But seeing as Brandt was the one loudly advocating for him to go, he hadn't felt he could argue with that. And when Brandt had woken up with Jewel at dawn, Shane was gone.

"He has a chance at a national TV competition." He pushed a bag of bagels Shelby's direction.

"Oh." Shelby made a perfect circle with her mouth before exhaling hard. "That and he's mad at me."

Huh. He didn't know how to respond to that. He really didn't want to start the morning with an argument, but he also couldn't lie. "He's not happy."

"I know. I screwed up." Ignoring the food, Shelby leaned heavily against the counter. She said it like it was an inevitable truth, but Brandt could see the trap looming if he agreed too readily. He took a long sip of lukewarm coffee and patted Jewel a few times while trying for a moderately upbeat tone.

"The nice thing about mistakes is that you don't have to keep making them."

"Not for me." Shelby made a sour face. "I always fuck up and make things worse."

"But you came back." And now they all had to deal with her presence, but maybe better now than later. And maybe this was her taking baby steps to making amends.

"I'm still not sure why I bothered." Shelby poked a hole in that theory with her gloomy tone. "You and Shane seem to have it all under control."

"It hasn't been easy." Damn. If she was jealous of their success at baby wrangling, he honestly didn't know how to educate her. All the late nights. All the times trying different things to keep the baby happy with short-lived results. All the drudgery—the bottles and diapers and endless changes. "It's a lot of work."

And now that he'd done it, he wouldn't trade it for anything, but he also wasn't having Shelby think he and

Shane had been having some sort of sitcom life either. Which she should know seeing as she'd been doing all that alone, while at least he and Shane had had each other.

"Yeah. *Work*." Shelby made another pinched expression. "I thought it would be fun, having a baby. But it was so hard. I didn't even make it eight weeks. Maybe my next try will go better."

Brandt's blood went Colorado mountaintop cold, heart slowing as he became hyperaware of each syllable Shelby had uttered. *Next. Try.* No. Shane had asked him if he was sure what he wanted, and in this instant of stark clarity Brandt had never been more certain of what he had to do.

"I want custody."

Shelby blinked and tilted her head, almost like she was seeing Brandt for the first time ever. "Like you want to watch her here longer for me?"

"This isn't babysitting." One possible future loomed in front of them, a lifetime of passing Jewel back and forth, never knowing when or where the kid might appear, never being able to predict or plan for handoffs. Brandt couldn't let that happen. "My lawyer has paperwork that will make it official who has responsibility and who makes which decisions."

"Wow." She whistled and her mouth stayed pursed. "Court. I didn't think…"

"Trust me, I hate involving the court too, but I have to think of Jewel's best interests here." Jewel had fallen asleep in the sling, and he rubbed her little back.

"And you think best interests means *you* keeping her?" Shelby sounded more confused than accusatory.

"Kids deserve a stable home. I know that more than most." He didn't want to get into his whole history with her, which was funny considering how easily he'd shared his past with Shane. This thing with Shane was so much more than sex. A huge part of their connection was how good it felt to talk with him. How right. Shane knew stuff about Brandt that people he'd worked with for years had no clue about, and he already missed him so much that it was hard to fully concentrate on what had to be done.

"Eh." She made a dismissive gesture. "Shane and I moved around so much I never bothered memorizing most zip codes. We turned out okay."

Brandt's brain supplied an image of Shane on his birthday, the way he'd been so surprised that Brandt had bothered remembering. The pained way Shane spoke about his past mirrored a lot of Brandt's own inner dialogue. And Shelby herself had certainly found her share of trouble. *Okay* was relative. Sure, they'd survived, but Brandt would hardly say they'd escaped unscathed.

"Listen, I don't want to fight you, but I'm going to do my damnedest to give Jewel what we didn't get."

"You're a parenting expert now?" Frowning, she broke one of the bagels in half.

Brandt had to take several shallow breaths so that he didn't snap back. Even after trying to calm himself, his tone still came out rather sharp. "I've learned a fair amount on the job, yes."

"I'm the mom," she whispered. Her hands were busy shredding the poor bagel. Like her hair, her nails were scruffy and uneven. Lots of little signs that she was struggling, and while Brandt's head pounded with worry for the baby, he wasn't unsympathetic to whatever she was dealing with.

"Yeah, you are." Brandt gentled his voice. "Nothing's going to change that. Just like I'm the dad. The DNA test proved it, but I don't want it to be only a line on a form."

"Guess that means we have to work together." She said it offhand, like she wasn't sure whether she liked that idea, but Brandt still nodded.

"We do. Which is why I'd like to get something in writing." He wasn't dropping that point. Not when fear of Shelby running off with Jewel made his stomach cramp and especially not when she didn't seem in any shape to parent on her own.

"Paperwork." She wrinkled her nose. "At least you've had help."

Help. It was true, but was that all Shane had been? He'd told Shelby that this wasn't babysitting for him, but he didn't think it was for Shane either. He was every bit as much a part of this parenting thing as Brandt.

And yet you sent him away. Told him you could manage without him.

Lies. Because he wanted Shane to make his dreams come true, but he also couldn't deny that he'd given Shane a firm push in that direction. And for what reason? Brandt was afraid of the answer there, and his brain was only too happy to gallop back to Shelby, who had apparently given up on waiting for a reply from him and finally taken a bite of the unmangled half of bagel.

"I couldn't have done this without Shane." He needed her to know that much, wasn't going to minimize Shane's role even if it might hurt his own case for custody to tell her.

"So you guys are like buddies now?"

Oh, how easy it would be to lie simply by agreeing. So easy. But also so far from the future he suddenly wanted with a fierceness that made all his muscles tense. He couldn't remember the last time he'd wanted something this much. "I like him. A lot. More than like."

"Oh." Dropping the bagel back onto the counter, Shelby narrowed her eyes. "Does *he* know that?"

That was a good question, and not one he'd expected. "I hope so."

He did hope. Hard. Shane had looked so wounded last night, and Brandt had thought his defeated expression was mainly for Shelby's reappearance, but now he wasn't so sure. Maybe he hadn't done a good enough job of convincing Shane that he'd miss him, that he wanted a way for them to work out.

"I don't know how I feel about that." Darting her gaze away, she licked her chapped lips.

"I'm not asking for your approval." Brandt truly wasn't. He was telling her because keeping it a secret served none of them, especially Shane, but he also wasn't up for a debate about the merits of falling for her brother. They had more important things to settle. "I'm asking you to think about what the best thing for Jewel is."

"That's just it. I'm not sure what I think right now."

Join the club. But of course Brandt couldn't say that. He was confused and missing Shane and worried he might have blown his chance there, but Jewel—and maybe Shelby too— needed him to be decisive and sure. He could deal with his own life soon enough. Shelby wrapped her arms around herself. Her face was creased with way more than just shock over the news that Brandt and Shane were involved.

"What do you need, Shelby?" he asked softly, not even sure if that was the right question.

"Nothing." Her face shuttered, features tightening up. "I should probably just go."

"It's okay to need help, Shelby." *Okay to need help.* It was a wonder lightning didn't sizzle right then at his failure to take his own advice. He needed Shane. Badly. Maybe even in this situation because as angry as Shane was, he still had way more experience with Shelby and what she might need. They'd formed a team these last few weeks, but Brandt hadn't wanted to admit it aloud how much he'd come to rely on Shane.

Shelby stayed quiet so long that he wasn't sure whether she'd heard him. "Let us help you."

That earned a scoff from her. "Us? You think Shane's coming back if he wins?"

"No. I think I'm going to him."

Chapter Twenty-Six

Are you okay?

Wasn't that the million-dollar question? Shane stared at the text from Brandt for long minutes, trying to decide if he should reply at all. Probably not, if he was being smart. But if Brandt were genuinely worried, there was no point in keeping him up at night simply because Shane was feeling petty. It was cold in the camper despite the summer weather, and he was still a little hungry after a skipped lunch and hurried fast food dinner.

Yeah, made it here fine and found a decent RV campground, he finally texted, not sure whether to expect a reply. However, the phone dinged almost immediately with the answer.

Good.

Huh. Single word answer. Now Shane was the worried one. He pulled the cover tighter around himself. Was *Brandt* okay? The baby? And yeah, Shelby too. If he were being honest, he'd been both curious and worried all day himself with a low-grade headache from thinking about all that could go wrong.

How are you doing? Baby okay?

This time Brandt's reply was a little slower in arriving. Yeah. Jewel's fine. Probably misses your singing. Shelby left.

Left? Shane texted back, finger shaking. With Jewel?

No, alone. Couldn't get her to go to the lawyer though. But it's fine.

Shane had a feeling that that *fine* was disguising a world of hurt and now his chest ached along with his head.

He typed and erased several texts about that being typical Shelby behavior, but none of that was helpful to Brandt in the present moment. He finally settled on, I'm sorry.

Me too. I think Shelby's depressed. She slept over sixteen hours by my count and still seemed sluggish.

Maybe, Shane had to admit. Shelby had looked pretty terrible when she'd shown up, and all that sleep wasn't like her either. But she'd always been rather moody and volatile, so it was hard to say what was illness and what was personality. Still, though, even as angry as he was about her leaving Jewel with him, he didn't want to miss more serious warning signs.

Do you want me to come back?

He already knew Brandt was going to say no, but needing to offer as he lay there alone in the camper, fighting the urge to go back regardless of what Brandt said.

No. I want you to win. Tell me which songs you're going to do.

And so he did, letting Brandt suck him into a discussion of which of his songs that Brandt had heard over the weeks might be the best fit to showcase both his voice and his songwriting abilities. He'd settled on the one he'd written last winter in Nashville, about being lonely in a crowd. The coffee shop crowd had liked it well enough, and it had gotten him the gig with Tim's group. Even after deciding, he kept texting back and forth with Brandt about silly stuff, neither of them saying a damn thing that mattered, until Jewel woke up, and Shane finally drifted off, feeling even more alone. He should have been there, helping Brandt get Jewel back to sleep.

Shane missed Brandt. And Jewel. But as he tuned his guitar in a quiet hallway of a Portland auditorium, it was Brandt he missed most. His smell. His taste. His laugh. The way he had of crowding into Shane and pulling him close, his nearness a form of affection. Right up until the moment he'd shown Shane the door.

Not that Shane blamed him exactly and not that Brandt had slammed that door shut. He'd said he wasn't shoving Shane away, and he kept talking about things maybe working out. However, Shane knew better than to trust those sorts of wishes. Brandt's priority had to be Jewel and what was best for that situation, and if he and Shane still got to hook up when Shane was back in town, well that was a nice bonus. True partnership seemed like a pipe dream.

Except for the part where Shane's head kept buzzing with a half-finished love song, lines that couldn't decide whether they were sweet or mournful. He'd known better than to fall for Brandt Wilder, yet he had. Hell, maybe it had been an inevitability from the first time he'd smiled in Shane's direction. Shane's hands ached from clenching the steering wheel the whole way to Portland, and his guitar strumming was tighter than usual, clumsy fingers missing notes that usually came as easily as breathing.

He'd suffered through a rehearsal where the celebrity judges weren't present, and he'd navigated the wardrobe and makeup folks. TV was a whole new ballgame for him, the number of people fussing over the competitors. The thing was probably rigged, with the showrunners already knowing who was going to get the nod to go to LA. He'd heard enough about these kinds of shows from others in the industry to be rather skeptical of his chances, even if he performed to his best, which in his current state of misery was doubtful. But he was still going to try. He'd promised Brandt.

Buzz. Setting the guitar aside, he fished out his phone. Not Brandt. The new messages were Tim and Elaine wishing him luck. He'd had an earlier one from Macy wanting to know if he'd seen Shelby and if she was safe. The saltier part of him had given serious thought to not replying, but the nicer part had sent a quick one that as far he knew she was still in central Oregon giving Brandt a hard time.

Still holding his phone, his thumb landed on his photo gallery. The last ones were from his birthday. Brandt's cake. And there was Jewel, looking so much bigger at three months than she had at two. Chubby cheeks now and a drooly grin. One of Brandt holding her as she reached for his hair. Who knew what tricks she'd be doing next time Shane saw her? The look in Brandt's eyes was new too, the softness there as he gazed at the baby. The only other time Shane had seen him look like that was…

That was something. Brandt all dreamy and sleepy post sex, the way he always gazed up at Shane like he'd performed some miracle. Maybe Brandt did feel something real for him after all, affection that lingered. But if that was the case, why was it so easy for Brandt to let him go? Shane looked down at the picture again, tempted to text it to him simply to have the excuse to make contact.

Between the two of them, they probably already had dozens of pictures of Jewel. Way more than Brandt had of himself—

Oh. Of course Brandt wasn't going to be the one to hold on. No one had held on to him. *Including you,* the voice in his head reminded him. *You went.* He'd assumed Brandt was only too happy to push him away, but that affection in Brandt's eyes wasn't something a person could fake. And here was Shane showing him yet again that people left simply because Shane hadn't wanted to trust. Still wasn't sure he could, but hell if he was going to be one more thing in Brandt's life that moved on.

I have to go back. The certainty he'd searched for the last few day arrived on a surge of adrenaline. He didn't have to let Brandt do this alone. He could—

Buzz. Another message, and this one he almost ignored, but he caught sight of Brandt's icon.

Changed my vote. You need to do the timber song.

Shane's throat tightened. Can't. It's not ready.
He wasn't ready either. Couldn't tell Brandt that.

Couldn't tell Brandt that he was about to walk away from all this either.

Fuck that noise. Brandt's reply came so quickly Shane could almost hear the retort. It's ready. I want to hear it again.

I'll play it for you soon, he promised, figuring Brandt could find out exactly how soon—

"No, play it now."

Shane whirled around to find Brandt standing feet away, wearing Jewel in the sling.

"What the—"

"Couldn't miss your big show."

"You came." He licked his lips. Shane didn't bother asking him how Brandt had gotten backstage. Brandt could charm his way anywhere on an ordinary day. Add in the adorableness of the baby wearing, and no one was turning him away.

"I did. And I want to see you do your best song."

"Yeah," he said faintly. "I know which one to do now."

And he did. Because Brandt had come. For him. He'd seen the stacked odds and come anyway because of course he had. He had the sort of courage Shane could only dream of. Shane had been such a fool to not trust him more. But maybe he still had time to fix everything as long as he quit playing it so safe.

"Good. Go big or go home." Brandt was dying to hug Shane, but he had a baby strapped to his front, and Shane had a guitar leaning up against one leg. He'd come this far and waited this long. He could wait a little longer, but damn was it good to see Shane in the flesh.

"I will." Shane nodded sharply. He looked paler than he had a few days ago. Meanwhile, his dark hair had a shorter cut and his jaw was scruff-free. He smelled good too. Something new and vaguely sweet. Brandt wanted to crawl all over him, trying to find the source and tasting everything in between. But that would have to wait.

"Nice shirt." He nodded at the blue Western-style shirt, which he hadn't seen before. "All fancy for TV?"

"Something like that." Shane's mouth twisted into a smile. "Can't believe you actually came."

"Me too, honestly," Brandt admitted. He'd wanted to. Intended to. But life had been complicated these past few days. And he hadn't realized exactly how much he'd been leaning on Shane for help until he had to do a three-hour drive north to Portland with the baby on his own. Yet they were here now and that was what counted. "I wanted you to have a cheering section."

Brandt lifted Jewel's arm making her wave at Shane, and to his surprise, she lifted the other one.

"Look at that. Your kid sure is brilliant." Shane laughed, but his eyes stayed warm, a tenderness there that was for Brandt alone. "And thank you, too."

"Anytime." Brandt held his gaze, trying to convey how far he'd go for Shane without needing to give voice to all the terrifying emotions ricocheting through him.

"Did Shelby come too?" Shane sighed like he was bracing himself for the answer.

"No. Can we talk about that later?" There were several conversations they needed to have, including more than one about Shelby, but Brandt wasn't going to ruin Shane's big moment with a lot of deep talk and big choices. "Filming starts soon, right?"

"Yeah. It does." Shane glanced away, back down the empty hallway. "I was about to go scratch."

Brandt blinked so hard he almost jostled the baby. "You were about to what?"

"Pull out—"

"I know what scratch means. Why would you leave this chance?"

"Because you need me." Leaving his guitar against the wall, Shane stepped closer, rubbing Brandt's biceps.

"I—" Brandt was going to deny it. Again. Because that was what he did. Even after his realizations while talking with Shelby, he still hated needing anyone. But he'd promised himself to be honest with Shane. And himself. "I do. But I want this opportunity for you too."

"Why?" Still holding on to Brandt, Shane tilted his head.

"Because the world needs your music. Because you making your dream come true makes me happy." He frowned because all that was rather trite and not precisely the reason either. "Because I'm falling for you— all of you, dreams and songs included. And it hurts, like physically aches to think of you not getting your shot."

Shane's whole face softened and his grasp on Brandt's arm tightened. "I—"

"Mr. Travis! There you are." A stern-faced young woman who was carrying a clipboard hurried down the hall toward them. "We're about to start."

Whatever Shane had been about to say could wait, as could the rest of what Brandt wanted to tell him. Stepping back, he motioned at Shane's guitar. "Go out there and make us proud."

"He will as long as he's not late." Still bustling with purpose, the woman turned her attention to Brandt and Jewel. "There's a green room where some of the other families are watching. We'll get reaction shots from them. You're welcome there."

Brandt didn't say anything because this had to be Shane's call. He knew that Shane generally kept his personal life private on the road, and while Brandt might have outed himself to his crew, Shane deserved space to make his own choice about what he wanted to show the camera.

Biting the corner of his mouth, Shane studied Brandt for a long moment. "Yeah. You're my family. You should be there."

"We are." Brandt wanted to say so much more, tell Shane how much it meant to him that Shane saw things that way and that Shane was willing to acknowledge their connection in some small way. But time was slipping away as the young woman strode down the hall, leaving them to scramble after her. She left Shane with a crowd of other performers and production assistants before showing Brandt to a big space that was probably ordinarily a rehearsal room, but now had a camera crew at one end and several rows of chairs in the middle.

A number of people had shirts supporting a particular contestant, and clumps of people milled around, good naturedly talking their person up. Brandt should have thought this through a little more because a Team Shane cowgirl onesie on Jewel would be too perfect.

"Your baby's adorable. Who are you here for?" A gray-haired woman in a purple T-shirt that said Go Regina! came up to him as he checked out the snack table off to the side of the space.

"Shane Travis. He's this cutie's uncle." He still wasn't sure how public Shane wanted to be in a romantic sense, but simply being here meant a lot.

"Oh, he's good. We've been following him a few years now. A bit tight to start a set, but man when he loosens up…"

"Yep. He's something." That pretty much described Shane's appeal in a nutshell—all sorts of tension simmering beneath a tight lid, but get to know him and his true complexity was revealed. He was quiet but deep, maybe as deep a person as Brandt had ever met. And he'd also never encountered this kind of pride, waiting for Shane to take his turn.

His own nerves jangled like he was the one about to perform. No way could he sit right then, so he stood, bouncing Jewel from side to side as he watched the first few performers on the large monitors in the room. All of the performers had the same backup band, and the stage had minimal decor with the show name featuring prominently behind the band. The three celebrity judges each had large golden buzzers in front of them, and if a singer received three votes, they were automatically through to LA on a "golden ticket" while a few others would get through on numerical scores at the end. Shane was early in the lineup, and while there had been a smattering of buzzers, no one had a golden ticket by the time he took the stage.

"There he is," he whispered to Jewel. "Come on, Shane."

Regina's relative had been right—Shane seemed a little stiff and wooden as he listened to the host, a fairly well-known comedian with a recent special that Brandt had watched on streaming. The host finished up the canned intro then invited Shane to say a few words.

"Thanks." Shane gave a tight half smile. Brandt could read his nerves even from here and tried to send calming vibes for whatever that was worth. "This is probably the most personal song I've ever written. And it's new. Maybe too new. But it's the one I need to share."

He started to strum, but it wasn't the opening chords to the timber song about Roger. No this was a different song. Brandt slumped into a nearby chair. He hadn't listened to Brandt after all, damn it. But wait...

This *was* a new song. One Brandt hadn't heard yet recognized instantly. It was *them*, weekend breakfast in bed, baby between them, laughing. A sliver of a memory turned into something beautiful and timeless under Shane's care. And however nervous he'd been to start, that wasn't showing now. His voice was as strong and clear as ever, each note seeming designed to hit Brandt square in the chest.

If the song about Roger had been a window into Brandt's past, this one was a snapshot of his present, each detail captured so that there was no escaping the big picture. This wasn't a fling, hadn't ever been a fling.

You're my family, Shane had said, and that exactly was what the song conveyed. They were a family, the three of them. They didn't need T-shirts or some group chant. Just a string of memories, and this unexpected, unshakable bond. And the song so perfectly captured all of that. It was a wonder that Brandt's heart didn't leap out of his chest right then and there, present itself to Shane for the taking, because it was his now, and there was nothing Brandt could do about it.

Not that he wanted to. Anyone would be lucky to have someone like Shane, someone who felt as deeply about them as Shane did. Oh, he didn't say the words, even in the song, but only something raw and powerful could inspire a song like this.

Love.

It was there in the harmony, and maybe there in that heart that was now Shane's too. Brandt wasn't sure because he'd never felt this before and was pretty sure no one had ever cared about him this much either. He held his breath on the final notes as his eyes burned.

Damn. Shane wasn't just something. He was everything. And now to see whether the judges agreed.

Chapter Twenty-Seven

That was something. Shane could almost hear Brandt's voice as he finished the song. His heart kept pounding even after the final chord, no longer with nerves but rather emotion. Felt like he'd run a four-minute mile and might never catch his breath again. And all he could think about was Brandt's reaction, if he'd truly heard everything in Shane's heart.

"Wow." The host guy came back out onto the stage with him. Oh yeah. Judging. He still needed a score. Shane supposed he needed to school his expression, some sort of made-for-TV eagerness maybe, but he was wrung out. Best he could manage was a nod for the host, who was continuing to dole out the compliments before turning toward the judging panel. "Judges, what say you?"

The first was a starlet more known for her social media empire than her movies, the sort of loud personality that reminded him of Shelby, or at least, how Shelby had used to be. For the prior contestant, the judge had been standing in her chair, and now with Shane, she was fanning her face with an exaggerated sad expression.

"You made me cry." She directed her critique right at Shane. And heck if he knew how to respond to that. "And I don't like to cry. Damn you."

"Sorry." He wanted people to feel, to hear his stories and be moved, but he didn't want anyone genuinely upset.

"Oh, don't be sorry. You're too pretty to be sorry." She waved her bejeweled and glittery fingers as the audience tittered. "And you better keep making me cry...in LA."

Pressing one of those well-manicured fingers to the big gold button, she hammed it up for the crowd, who whooped and hollered.

Shane let himself smile and say thank you, but she was only one vote. If he wanted a sure thing, the other two would have to agree.

"And Rita?" The host pointed at the next judge, an aging singer who'd been part of a hip-hop girl group in her teens that had been way more successful than her later solo pop efforts. She smirked at the host, who had to prompt her. "Do you agree?"

"Country's not usually my thing." Rita played to the audience, smiling at the smattering of boos. "And it's early in the evening. But the audience seems to love you..." That got an ego-raising roar from the audience and a laugh from Rita. "Thank you, Portland. I'm thinking..."

"Yes?" The host held the microphone out to the audience for more cheers when she drew the moment longer than necessary, hyping the audience further.

"Well, the crowd sure wants to see you in LA." She hovered her hand over the buzzer, getting more whoops and hollers. "Okay, okay. I can't hear a song like that and not hit this button."

Two. He'd gotten two golden buzzers. That was more than he'd expected, and his abs quivered.

"One more and you're through to LA." The host pointed out the obvious as the spotlight turned to the third judge. "But Graham's our toughest judge. Let's see what he has to say."

This guy was a producer with a string of hits to justify his lofty rep as a star maker. But he was also known for his biting wit on this show. He made a show of a big frown and a simmer-down gesture to the audience.

"Acoustic guitar is overrated. I'd like to see you take more advantage of the backup band. And loosen up a little when you intro your song. I was prepared for dental surgery, not that number."

"In other words, you liked it?" the host egged him on, all grins.

Shane couldn't smile though. This close to advancing, all of a sudden he didn't want to lose to his inability to make small talk with the audience. He seriously needed to start taking notes as to how Brandt so easily charmed people.

"I didn't hate it."

"Hear that, Shane? He didn't hate it." The host turned back to Shane as the audience laughed. "Anything you want to say to him to get him to press his buzzer?"

No would be the easy answer. No meant that he'd still be at loose ends, free to continue watching the baby for Brandt, and drifting through this thing they had going for as long as he could. No would mean fewer hard choices. But it would also mean disappointing Brandt, who was here and watching and who said he hurt with wanting Shane's dreams to come true.

"I sing to tell stories, and I've got a lot more stories in me. Give me a chance and I'll make you proud." He spoke to the camera and the judge, but really the words were all for Brandt. If Brandt was here because he felt something for him, then Shane was going to do his damnedest to make him proud. And he wanted to give this thing between them a real chance, even if that meant difficult decisions.

"Ah. A storyteller. Well..." The audience roared as he paused dramatically, eyes narrowing, voice somewhere between amused and scolding. "I suppose I'm curious. I'll give you that chance, but I'll be watching to see if you can deliver a show as well as you can write."

Buzz. The sound of the judge smacking the button seemed to reverberate through the whole auditorium and right through Shane's bones. He'd done it. Holy fuck.

"Thank you, sir." He managed to scrape together enough oxygen to speak. "And the rest of you. Thank you."

"And there you have it. Our first competitor with a ticket to LA."

The host waved him off the stage, where the same PA from earlier directed him through the maze of cameras and people.

"Congrats." She smiled up at him. "I bet the baby and your...guy are so happy for you."

My guy. God, Shane hoped that he hadn't fucked up everything that mattered with this win. "When do I get to see them?"

"We'll need you for some more pictures in a while, but I can send another PA to bring them to you. I'll see if the producer wants that reunion on film."

"No camera. Please. My kingdom if you forget to ask that question." He dug deep, trying to channel his inner Brandt, adding big eyes to his smile and conspiratorial nod.

"Okay." Despite her no-nonsense demeanor, she blushed. Whoa. The charm thing worked.

He was still reeling from that and the whole advancing thing when a different PA led Brandt and Jewel down the hall to him. No cameras followed, thank God, and the PA left quickly, leaving him and Brandt staring at each other, almost as if it were the first time all over again. Strangers and old friends and everything else, all at once.

"Well. I did it," he said, mainly because one of them had to say something and also because kissing Brandt senseless was probably a surefire way to draw the cameras.

"You did." Brandt kept looking at Shane like he'd produced a handful of stardust along with the win.

Not kissing him was damn hard when he made Shane feel that special. Fuck it. He took a step forward, then Jewel made a sleepy noise in her sling. Oh, yeah. No squashing the baby.

"Did she sleep straight through?"

"Nah. She saw you kill it out there. So did I." Brandt shook his head. "Damn, Shane. I thought nothing could top that timber song from you, but that one…"

"I wrote it for you guys. Didn't know if I'd ever find the courage to play it."

"I'm glad you did." Brandt licked his lips like he too had kissing on the brain. "Man. If I wasn't already crazy about you…"

"Yeah?" Shane had to laugh at the idea of wooing someone like Brandt, brash and fearless, with a mere song.

"Oh yeah. Told you. I'm falling for you." Brandt's gaze was so intense that Shane had to look away as emotion surged in his chest.

"Maybe you're not the only one falling." His voice was so soft, it was a wonder Brandt heard him.

"Good." Brandt's face softened like he knew what the admission had cost Shane. "I'm not sure I'm worthy of that song, but I'm sure as hell gonna try."

"Me too." This time he held on to Brandt's gaze as tightly as he would his body if they were alone, an entire ballad playing out between their eyes. It was the same song that had been rattling around Shane's brain earlier, the one that couldn't decide whether it was happy or sad.

"Shane. I—never mind." Brandt cut himself off as Shane's favorite PA scurried back toward them.

Damn it. Whatever he'd been about to say, Shane wanted to hear it.

"Mr. Travis? They need you for some publicity shots with the judges."

"Go ahead." Brandt made a shooing motion. "We'll keep. I promise. Take as long as you need. I got a hotel room nearby. I might go chill there with the diva while you take care of business. But after…"

"After," Shane agreed, so many promises in that one word. The song in his head shifted again, back to uncertainty. He could see those opening lines so well, but he had no clue where the music went from there, how to keep it a love song, not some mournful tale of regret. However, he wasn't giving up. He'd do whatever it took to find that elusive ending for their song.

Brandt had finally convinced the diva to sleep in her little portable cot and managed a shower for himself when a soft knock on the hotel room door sounded.

"You made it," he whispered as he let Shane into the room. Shane wore his weariness like an extra layer of clothing, tired eyes, slumped shoulders, and slack mouth, but he managed a small smile for Brandt.

"Yeah. Sorry it took so long." Shane set a backpack down before leaning against the door. Like Brandt, he kept his voice down. Brandt had set up the baby stuff in the far corner of the room, away from this entry foyer. "I had to wait through the rest of the show, and then there were a number of hoops to jump through for everyone advancing. I had to shoot some promo footage with the judges too. Graham doesn't like me. I bet I don't last long in LA."

"Hey now." Giving into the urge to touch him, Brandt clasped his shoulders. "That's no way to talk. You just had a big win."

"I know. I'm trying to not get my hopes up. That's all." Shane shrugged but didn't move out of Brandt's grip. His tone was almost morose, not nearly as hyped as Brandt had been expecting.

"Well, cut it out. You sound way too down for a guy who earned those cheers and that spot fair and square."

"Yeah. I get that. It's more…" Shaking his head, he dropped his gaze to his boots and Brandt's bare feet. "I'm going to miss you and Jewel when I go. I really am."

"I know." Brandt pulled him closer so that their foreheads touched. Shane being so worried about leaving them made Brandt want to hold him that much tighter. "Let's not get ahead of ourselves quite yet, though. No one's going anywhere tonight. You're exhausted and probably starving."

"They fed us. But I'd kill for a shower." Keeping their heads together, Shane rubbed his cheek against Brandt's.

"Let's keep you from doing damage then." Brandt steered him toward the nearby bathroom. "You go shower. I saved you one of the towels. I'll be here."

He meant far more than simply being okay with waiting. He was *here*. Here now and here for the future too, and he was still working out how best to express that to Shane. Hell, he wasn't even sure he could explain it to himself. He'd never had anyone he wanted like this. He'd taken more risks than any one human probably should, but he'd never taken one like the one he was contemplating here.

By the time Shane emerged from the shower, Brandt was still thinking, but he'd moved to one of the two beds, sitting up against the headboard. He'd never bothered finding a shirt after his own shower, leaving him in a pair of shorts as he lounged on top of the covers. Towel around his neck, Shane made a pair of boxer briefs look damn erotic, all his lean muscles and pale skin on display.

Brandt took a long moment to admire the view. "Better?"

"Yeah. You were right. I do feel more human." Shane glanced over at the other bed like he was trying to decide where to sit, like he belonged anywhere other than right next to Brandt.

"Don't even think about it." He patted the bed next to him. "Come here."

Shane nodded in the direction of the little cot in the far corner. Brandt had shielded it from the low bedside light with a chair, and so far, Jewel was snoozing away even with their low talking. "Not sure how I feel about fooling around with her—"

"I'm not talking about sex. Want to hold you." Brandt scooted over so Shane could stretch out, then spooned up behind him. "See? Isn't this better too?"

"Yeah." Tipping his head back, Shane relaxed against Brandt, pulling Brandt's arms tighter around him and dropping a kiss against his bare shoulder. "Being here with you, it's easy to pretend everything is going to work out."

"It is." *I hope.* Brandt had his own doubts, but even as new as this territory was, he'd also overcome far worse odds. Like he'd told Shane back home, he was betting on them. All in. And he wasn't going to let negative thinking ruin them before they even truly started.

"Hope so." Shane took a deep breath, like he was trying to inhale some of Brandt's confidence. Brandt squeezed him closer and kissed his ear as they lay quietly for several moments before Shane asked, "Did it work out with Shelby?"

Brandt groaned. Nothing like a hit of reality to crack their happy little bubble. "Not exactly. I couldn't get her to go with me to the lawyer. She... I might have told her about us."

"Wow." Shane whistled. "I'm betting she wasn't happy. You didn't have to do that."

"Yes, I did. You're part of this thing. I was rattled when she first showed back up, but then I realized that I couldn't try to keep us on the down low. Not if I want it to work out, like I just promised you it would."

"You're..." Shane's voice went even fainter. "Not sure I deserve you."

"Think that's my line. I never thought I'd be the sort of guy someone wrote a song about." Leaning down, Brandt managed an awkward kiss on Shane's lips.

"Oh, I could do a whole album on you." Eyes crinkling, Shane laughed before sobering again. "That would surely freak Shelby out even more."

"Well, it wasn't merely me telling her about us. I told her I want custody. And I also told her that I think she needs help. And between all those things, I guess I'm not her favorite person right now. She took off in that rattletrap of a car."

"Thank God she left the baby." The naked relief in Shane's voice mirrored Brandt's own, but she hadn't proposed anything like that, simply saying that she needed to think when Brandt asked again about going to his lawyer. She'd wandered out as abruptly as she'd shown up in the first place.

"Yeah. Even though I'm worried about her too, I was almost sick with relief," Brandt had to admit. He'd sat holding Jewel for a long time until his hands stopped shaking. "I told Cameron what happened, and she's filed an emergency order to give me formal full custody so if Shelby comes back, she can't simply take Jewel on a whim."

"Think Shelby's going to go for signing something?" Shane sounded as uneasy as Brandt felt about the idea of involving the courts, but he couldn't leave Jewel's future to chance.

"Not sure. Process server found her at a motel in Bend. At least she knows there's a hearing day after tomorrow. No clue whether she'll show though. Or whether she'll fight it."

"Tell me what you need." After rolling so they were face to face, Shane cupped Brandt's chin.

"You."

Shane frowned, but didn't release Brandt. "Don't be cute."

"I'm not. I need you." They were the three hardest words Brandt had ever uttered. Needing someone, being in a position to be hurt, utterly sucked, and yet, the alternative of a life without Shane in it was equally unbearable. "That's what I came to tell you. And to ask you to come with me to the hearing."

"Ah." Shane let go of him and glanced over at Jewel. "Because you need me to testify that you're a good dad?"

"No, because I need *you*. I mean, the other might help. But I need you." His voice shook, but Brandt pressed on. "Because I want you there, by my side. Because I can't do this on my own."

"You've got me." Shane pulled him close, let Brandt bury his face in Shane's shoulder. "I'll be there."

"Thanks." His words were muffled by Shane's body, but he waited several breaths before moving his face.

"If this doesn't go your way..." Shane trailed off, but his frown said he was still under the impression that Brandt's need had to do with the baby.

"If this doesn't go my way, I'm gonna need you even more," Brandt said firmly, meeting Shane's eyes. "Because I want you in my life regardless of who has custody."

"Thanks." Shane leaned in for a soft kiss. "Even if I'm in LA without you? I don't have to be there for another two weeks or so because they have more regional competitions first. But you seem hell-bent on me going."

"I am." Brandt took a deep breath that he didn't really need. Lying here like this, a lot of his earlier doubts and indecision faded. He knew what to do. "And don't assume that you're going to be all alone there."

"Oh? I don't want to date—"

Brandt growled. "You're not dating anyone except me. I meant don't assume that we're staying here when you go."

"You can't give up your job." Shane sat upright, keeping his voice down even as the bed shook from the jolt of his movement.

"If you go, I'm out someone I trust to watch—"

Shane held up his hands. "Which is exactly why I want to stay."

"I've been thinking hard about this." More like every waking moment. His eyes burned from the lack of sleep and his calves were probably nicely toned from taking up Shane's pacing habit as he'd tried to reason out a future for them. "If I win custody, I don't want to miss any big baby milestones. And I also can't take the sorts of risks that might put Jewel at risk too. That moment when the chute wouldn't open..."

"It was scary." Looking away, Shane twisted the comforter in his hand.

"I know. For me too. I've got tons of leave accrued and some savings. I can afford to take some time. Figure out my next move. I already took a few days to come here and to deal with the court stuff. The house is almost ready for the market. And Jewel's not going to be tiny forever."

"She's not." Releasing the blanket, Shane scooted closer again.

"And opportunities like this one for you, they don't come along every day either. There's plenty of air bases, but only one you."

"Sweet talker." Shane graced him with another quick kiss. "But your job is your life. Heck, it's your family too."

"Not anymore. You and Jewel, that's my family. That's where I want to be. If you want us." His heart started thumping all over again. He hated this need, hated being so dependent on Shane's answer. Old hurts mingled with fresh feelings, making him be the one to glance away, taking in one of the bland cityscapes on the wall.

"I want you. And if you asked me, I'd stay." Shane used his hand to make Brandt look at him again. "That's why I wanted to pull out of the competition. Because I want to be someone who stays for you. Someone you can count on."

Oh. Shane didn't simply want him, but rather he saw Brandt, all of him, those hurting, needy parts he tried so hard to bury, and he wasn't scared off by them. He wanted to stay even though Brandt had pushed him away. That meant something, something that had Brandt's eyes burning with a lot more than tiredness. "You are."

"I could be happy with watching Jewel and the cover band gig." Taking Brandt's hand, Shane squeezed it. "Wouldn't be a bad way to spend a summer. Or longer."

"I know you could do that." That he'd offer meant the world to Brandt, and he could see that life too, a path that wasn't without its appeal. But the house wasn't theirs, and the life wasn't meant to be Shane's. "I don't want you to have to settle for small-time success. Not when you've got a gift and a shot."

"All I ever wanted was to be heard. I thought I needed to hit it big for that to happen. But then I met you, and it turned out that what I really needed was the right audience. Someone to listen."

"Baby, I could listen to you for days." Brandt used their linked hands to draw Shane even closer. "But I want to share you with the world. Watching people's faces as they saw your performance tonight was so cool. I want more of that."

"You'd really come with me?"

"Think I'd follow you anywhere. You're going places, Shane Travis, and I want to see them from the front row."

"I'll get you tickets." Shane tumbled them both back on the bed.

"Hey now, don't make me a liar about not fooling around."

"G-rated. I promise." Laughing softly, Shane gave him a lingering yet relatively chaste kiss. "I… You believing in me, that means everything to me."

"And you mean everything to me too. You're—"

"—something," Shane finished with a tender laugh. "And you are too."

As he drew Shane in for another kiss, there were other words that Brandt wanted to say, but he might have used up all his courage for one night, flexing emotional muscles he wasn't sure he'd ever used before.

And the next few days loomed large too. They were one court date gone wrong for something so sweet to turn unbearably sour.

Chapter Twenty-Eight

"Do you want me to hold her?" Shane asked as they approached the courthouse in Bend. They'd had to park a few blocks away, and now that they were approaching the imposing stone building with its flags and official-looking plaques out front, Shane's insides were strangely quivery.

Nerves weren't going to help anything, particularly Brandt, who wanted him here, who'd said he needed Shane and for more than this hearing, and no way was Shane going to let him down. But at the same time, the truth loomed as large as the courthouse that this was a big deal and anything could happen.

"Nah. I've got her." Brandt sounded as tense as Shane felt, and the possessive way he was cradling the baby in her sling mirrored Shane's urge to gather her close. This could be his last chance to smell her powdery scent, feel her warm little body against his arm, and the desire to snuggle her was almost as overwhelming as the one to grab Brandt and Jewel and run away to somewhere the real world couldn't find them.

Except reality always did have a way of butting in. Even now, happy as he was about Brandt coming to his show and wanting a future with him, Shane was still bracing for the next bit of bad news. Brandt changing his mind. Shelby deciding she wanted to parent after all. Some state agency getting involved. Too many awful possibilities to count.

All the signs and notices on the door added to the doom cloud following them. This was real in a way that the last month or so hadn't been—the stakes that much greater as they moved from temporary emergency to something more permanent. And that was also true for him and Brandt as a couple. It was one thing to have a fun fling and another thing entirely to place his heart on the line.

"Think they'll make a baby go through the metal detector?" His joke fell flat as Brandt's face creased. God, Shane only had to look at him to know it wasn't even a choice anymore. He had Shane's whole heart, and the only question remaining was what he was going to do with that gift.

The bored-looking guard walked them through the security protocols, sending the car seat and diaper bag through the X-ray machine, while Shane walked through the metal detector. The guard used a handheld scanner to check Brandt and Jewel over before giving them directions to which floor they needed to go to.

"Oh good. You're early." Cameron greeted them from a bench outside their assigned courtroom. She wore a sharp suit, a far cry from the windblown mom she'd been last time they'd seen her. She'd recommended that they dress up for court too. Brandt wore a black dress shirt and nice pants that Shane hadn't been aware he owned, and had his hair neatly pulled back. Shane looked equally job-interview ready in a shirt he'd last worn in Nashville to a meeting with some record execs that hadn't panned out. Hopefully they all had better luck today.

"Any word from Shelby?" Cameron asked as Shane set the diaper bag and car seat down.

"No." Shane had leaped every time his phone buzzed the last twenty-four hours and had tried sending a few messages, but nothing. Ever since Brandt had raised the possibility of her being unwell, he was even more worried about his sister. Still frustrated, but also wanting to know she was okay.

"If she doesn't show…" Brandt frowned as he trailed off. He'd been as on edge as Shane this last day, and the lines around his eyes and mouth were deeper. Some of his usual cockiness was gone too, and Shane missed that brash confidence, hated the toll this was taking on him.

"We have a plan for that." Cameron touched Brandt's arm as he sank down next to her.

He was going to be gutted if things didn't go in his favor. No one who watched him with Jewel could doubt his care for her. Shane himself was guilty of being skeptical early on, but Brandt had proven himself over and over. He'd said at the hotel that he was going to need Shane even if he didn't end up with custody. Shane hoped that was true even as his back tightened. He wasn't sure he could bear it if Brandt pushed him away, because their connection went so much deeper than childcare for Shane.

As Cameron went over their game plan for the hearing, Shane continued to scan the wide hallway, honestly not sure what he was hoping for. Nothing about this was simple. His throat was dry, so he excused himself to go to the water fountain as they waited for their case to be called.

He got his drink at the end of the hall and was about to turn to head back when he spotted a familiar figure hunched over on a bench around the corner.

"Shelby?" He hurried over. "The hearing is—"

"I know where it is." She wore a red-and-white sundress, and her hair was more done than the last time he'd seen her, but she was too thin and pale for the Shelby he knew so well.

"Okay." He didn't wait for permission to sit down next to her. Experience had shown him that him looming over her with a lecture never ended well for either of them. "You came."

"Yeah." She rolled her eyes, undoubtedly already fed up with him pointing out the obvious. "Not sure why though."

Shane forced himself to take a big breath. And another. Brandt's chances here could be riding on what he said next and whether or not he could get beyond the anger already starting to bubble up again.

"Maybe because you care?" There. He managed to keep his voice Brandt-level gentle, not accusatory.

"Do I?" Giving a weary sigh, she rolled her slim shoulders. "I'm not sure. Like you said the other day. I left my kid with *you*. I did that."

"I kept her safe. You could have done worse." Thinking about that made bile rise in his throat, but maybe it needed to be said that she had tried to get Jewel to someone trustworthy, even if her methods left a lot to be desired.

"Yeah." She kicked at a gouge in the white linoleum, dark mark marring the otherwise gleaming surface. "You hate me now, I guess."

Why couldn't it have been Brandt who discovered

Shelby? Shane wasn't cut out for a pep talk. But he could speak from his heart, give her the truth. "I was mad when you showed back up. But I don't hate you, Shelby. I never have."

"You get tired of my shit. Being my keeper." Not looking at him, she dug the toe of her sandal into the gouge.

"Maybe patience isn't my strong suit." Shane owed it to all of them to admit to his own failings here. Shelby wasn't the only one with past actions to regret. "And maybe I wasn't there when you needed it most."

"You were this time. You got the baby to Brandt at least." Twisting her hands around her purse, she gave him a half smile that never made it past one corner of her mouth.

"Yeah." The last few weeks rushed by on fast forward in his brain—every late night and long look and little joke. All that had happened simply because he'd had nowhere else to turn. "He's a good dad. Thank you for leaving the birth certificate with her."

"I liked the name," she whispered.

"It's a good name. Think about what you want for everything else." Shane's throat was dry again. He was so out of his depth here, but he also couldn't stop trying to make things right, make Shelby see the full picture. "But he's so good with Jewel. She's lucky to have him."

"And you?" Finally meeting his gaze, she raised an eyebrow. "You lucky too?"

Figured that she'd want to focus on that particular detail. But rather than get angry, he went for honest again. If he was going to fuck this up, at least he could say he'd been truthful and hadn't let his temper win. "Yeah. I am."

"You and him hooking up was the last thing I expected..."

"Me too." Laughing, he turned his palms up. "Please don't hold that against him. Be mad at me all you want, but he loves that baby."

"Is that what you think I came to do? To punish him? And you?" Shelby's voice was sharper, each word a snare waiting for him to trip.

"I don't know." He wasn't lying. He honestly had no clue what was motivating her at that moment, and that more than anything made his heart speed up. "I hope not. You're a good person."

"Good person who abandoned her infant." She pursed her lips as her hand tightened its grip on her purse. "Says so in the court documents plain as day."

"That's the official legalese. I know you, Shelby." Taking a breath, Shane closed his eyes, picturing Shelby at eleven, all knobby knees and enthusiastic audience. She'd been trouble, but the fun kind. His constant companion, the one thing he could count on as they uprooted yet again. "I know the sister who used to share half her candy with me and who listened to my songs for hours and who made long road trips fun. You've got a good soul."

"You mean that?" Her voice was so soft that he had to strain to hear the question.

"I love you. And I love that baby." He was pretty sure he loved Brandt too, but this probably wasn't the moment to add that. Instead he took her hand, holding it tight. "I think deep down you know what the right thing to do is here."

"Brandt says I need help." Pulling her hand free, she shook her head. "But maybe it's just me. Screwing up, over and over. Same old Shelby."

"You've got a chance here to do something different. Change the pattern. I believe in you." Shane put all the

conviction he could into his voice. "And yes, get help. I want to help you. So does Brandt. A lot of people care about you."

"I—"

"We're about to start." Still wearing Jewel, Brandt came rushing around the corner, only to pull up short as his eyes went wide. "Shelby."

"Brandt."

So much meaning in those two words. It was impossible to read the tone of either of their voices, and silence stretched long and awkward until Cameron strode up.

"We need to head in now." Cameron gestured back at the courtroom. The previous group of people were streaming out and an official-looking person stood by the door. This was it. And hell if Shane had any clue what was going to happen. All he could do was hope that he hadn't made things worse, hadn't ruined Brandt's chances. Or his own.

Chapter Twenty-Nine

Brandt truly hated shirts with collars. They always rubbed weird on his birthmark and made him feel bizarrely vulnerable, like he was presenting himself naked for someone else's judgment. The last few years, the only real wear this shirt had seen was to funerals, and he was already counting down until this thing was over and he could take it off.

But not yet.

Now was the time to stand up straight next to Cameron as the clerk called their case. They'd filed a formal petition for sole custody, and this hearing to request a temporary order was the first step in the court case. He'd really wanted to avoid the court altogether, but that sheer panic he'd felt when Shelby had first shown up had changed his mind in a hurry. He needed something in writing, but that meant trusting that the court wouldn't screw any of them over. Brandt's inner kid had no such faith and kept looking at the doorway to the small courtroom.

The judge in her black robe strode to her seat at the front of the room, under a large state seal. She was younger than Brandt had expected, maybe only a couple of years older than Cameron. She motioned for everyone to take their seats before banging her gavel. The judge listened intently as Cameron laid out their request. Cameron had said that he should let her do most of the talking, and that was trust too, letting someone else speak for him, trusting lawyer-speak to actually work for once.

"In sum, your honor, petitioner has had sole physical care of the infant for over a month. During that time, there was no communication with the respondent, who was out of the country." Cameron was good at laying out the facts, but Brandt had to glance over at Shelby, who sat alone at the other front table, purse in front of her. He wanted this settled, but that didn't mean he didn't have sympathy for her. She stared straight ahead, expression so neutral as to almost be vacant. And she didn't flinch as Cameron continued, "She is a substantial flight risk, and as such, we're requesting the temporary order be granted today."

"Ms. Travis." The judge turned her head toward Shelby. "Do you have counsel?"

"A lawyer? No." She shot a sour look at Cameron.

"Do you require additional time to retain counsel to assist you?"

"I don't want a lawyer." Shelby's chin jutted out, a lot like Shane's when he got stubborn.

"All right. Did you review the petition and parenting plan submitted by Mr. Wilder?" the judge asked.

Shelby nodded.

"We need you to speak up for the record, please."

"Yes. I read it." Her voice was faint, and the judge leaned forward like she was trying to avoid making Shelby repeat herself.

"And you understand that Mr. Wilder is requesting sole physical and legal custody of the child? This order will be reviewed at the formal hearing for permanent custody, but an order today determines with whom the child will reside until that hearing takes place."

"I understand." Shelby swallowed audibly, and a dull pounding started in Brandt's temples. It was impossible to get a read on her tone of voice. He glanced over at Shane, who was similarly impassive, hands tightly clenched in his lap. Brandt wished he knew what Shelby and Shane had talked about, but there hadn't been time for anything more than a whispered "I tried" from Shane as they had entered the courtroom.

"Do you object to the petition?" The judge was all business, but not unkind. Hard to get a read on her too.

Shelby shook her head and fiddled with her purse strap.

"I'm going to need you to say it aloud. Do you have any objection to the court granting this order?"

There was a very long pause during which Brandt held his breath until Shelby finally spoke. "I guess not."

"You guess." The judge frowned. "Do you plan to contest the petition for permanent custody?"

"Probably not." Shelby's sigh echoed through the small courtroom.

"Ms. Travis, I'm going to need some decisiveness from you. Is there anything the court should know about Mr. Wilder's petition? Or his fitness as a parent? This is your chance to provide any relevant information to the court including anything about your relationship and/or your personal safety."

Brandt's spine tensed, vertebrae by vertebrae until his back was stiff as a two by four. This was probably where Shelby would reveal his connection to Shane and whatever other complaints she had.

"We don't have a relationship." A pink flush spread across her cheeks. "And I hear he's a good dad."

"Are you in agreement that Mr. Wilder's petition and parenting plan is in the best interests of the child? If you disagree with any part of the petition, the court may order mediation. The court can also appoint a guardian ad litem to represent the interests of the child." The judge's eyes narrowed.

Cameron had told him that the court appointing an attorney for the baby was a possibility, but Brandt still hated the idea of more investigation and more oversight. He had to remind himself that the judge was simply trying to make things clear to Shelby, especially since she wasn't being definite in her responses.

The judge tapped the top of her bench before continuing. "If you don't contest the petition, the court can grant the order and fast-track the case for a hearing on the permanent order."

There was another lengthy pause from Shelby as she studied her nails before raising her head. "I'm not going to object. I'm not… I don't really want to parent. This is the right thing to do."

"All right. The court finds all parties in agreement with the petition for a temporary custody order. The order is hereby granted. The hearing for the permanent order will be set…" The judge continued to go over the logistics, but all Brandt could hear was *granted*.

Relief. Not happiness and not joy, but relief rushed through him. It was hard to be happy about the situation, and putting Shelby through this had left a caustic taste in his mouth, but his baby was safe. *My daughter.* That was what mattered. And he was going to do everything in his power to keep her that way.

"We can leave now." Cameron touched his shoulder as everyone stood.

It was over. He patted Jewel, who had slept through the entire thing. Shane still had the baby gear, but he juggled it so that he too could place a hand on the sling.

"Well. That's done." Nodding, Shane followed the rest of them out of the courtroom. But once they were in the hall, Shane's mouth tightened further. "Be right back."

He hurried away, and Brandt wasn't too surprised when Shane caught up to Shelby. But the fierceness of their hug, now that was unexpected, as were the tears in Shane's eyes. He was whispering something to her, and she nodded as she clung to him.

Maybe Brandt needed to go over there. Say something. Make this hurt less for all of them. But as he turned, Cameron stopped him.

"Let them have their moment," she said gently. "There's a lot of big feelings right now, yours included."

"I hate that it came to this."

"I know. And you'll have a chance later to work toward something more amicable. But you did the best thing for Jewel here."

"Yeah." His chest still ached though, more so as Shelby continued to cling to Shane. This too was a type of trust, trusting that Shane could handle his sister, that he didn't need Brandt swooping in to save the day.

"Well, that was fast." Hartman, looking all spiffy in a dress shirt and tie, separated himself from the rest of the crowd in the hallway.

"You came?" Brandt had to blink. Not only did Hartman look like some sort of software ad, but he'd come to Brandt's hearing?

"Cameron said you might need a character witness

if your motion became contested." Hartman nodded at
Cameron, who was shuffling papers into her briefcase.

"Thanks. You didn't have to. But thanks." Brandt
lightly cuffed him on the arm.

"Of course I didn't have to. But I wanted to." Hartman
made a silly face at Jewel, who was awake now. "And I
wanted to check on you. Linc and I flipped a coin as to
who got to come. He's worried about you too."

"Appreciated." Brandt had any number of acquaintances, but he couldn't say as he had many others who
would show up for a court date. "And I'm okay."

"Good. As your friend, I'm happy for you that things
worked out today." Clucking Jewel under the chin, Hartman took a moment to make another face for her before
straightening. "And as your coworker, I gotta ask when
we can expect you back. Miss you, buddy."

Oh. Brandt should have anticipated this question. He
opened his mouth. Closed it.

"Or *if* we can expect you back."

"I'm gonna take some time." Brandt readjusted the
sling as Jewel started squirming.

Hartman nodded. "It's complicated, I get it."

"My chute didn't open." He kept his voice low. Shane
was the only person whom he'd told about the fear dogging him, how it was making it hard to concentrate on the
job, how it had brought all his priorities into stark focus.

"I know. Scary as fuck." Hartman fisted his hands.
Similarly, Brandt's neck was tight as rigging done right.
Talking frankly like this about the risks of their work was
damn hard. "You've got to think about your kid first."

"Yeah, I do. I might be all she's got." That wasn't precisely true. She had Shane and other people who cared
about her. But the court had given Brandt custody, and

he took that responsibility seriously. He rolled his shoulders. "I need some time to figure out what my next move should be."

"Makes sense."

Down the hall, Shane was still talking with Shelby. Brandt truly hoped Shane was able to convince her to get help if that was what she needed to get back on track.

"I might be spending some time in LA."

"That right?" Hartman followed Brandt's gaze to Shane. "Well, if you end up there long-term, I've got a contact on a helitack crew down there. If you start thinking about other jobs in the fire community, let me know. I'll hook you up."

"I'm kind of taken—"

"So's he." Hartman gave a dry chuckle. "I just meant any crew, anywhere would be lucky to have you, Wilder. And your kid is lucky too."

Brandt had to swallow hard. "You're not mad?"

"Nah. We've got a bushel of rookies all eager for airtime and jump reps. We'll be okay. And God knows you've earned the leave. Is this your first time off in ten years?"

"Pretty much." Brandt's paystub from the agency listed enough leave to have more than one payroll person call him to verify whether the number was a typo. The job had been everything for him for so long. Leaving it, even temporarily, wasn't easy. But he wanted to hold tight to what he'd found with Shane and Jewel.

"Well, enjoy it." Hartman's laugh sounded genuine enough, which loosened some of Brandt's tension. He hadn't liked feeling like he'd be letting people down by taking time off.

"I'll try." Again his gaze found Shane. His eyes were

weary, a certain heaviness to his shoulders and his steps as he walked back toward Brandt. They needed to get out of this place, out of these clothes, out of the stress of the past few days. Back to being them. Back to a place where he could show Shane how much he meant to Brandt.

Chapter Thirty

"Man. What a day." Shane emerged from his shower to find Brandt on the couch, no baby in hand. She'd been hard to settle after her long day, so Brandt had eventually waved him off so he could rock her in the dark. Looked like it worked.

"It was." Brandt stretched before motioning Shane closer. He looked older, like the court stuff had aged him. It had certainly taken a lot out of all of them. Brandt's eyes creased as Shane came nearer to the couch. "You okay?"

"Yeah. Just…long day." He couldn't help the sigh that escaped. He wished he'd been able to convince Shelby to stick around long enough to maybe see a doctor or counselor, but she'd said she wanted to get back to Macy's tour. She needed a better plan than that, but Shane didn't know how to force her to get help. She'd put the baby first though, so that was a step. Not enough. But something.

And the way she'd hugged him had stripped away years of uneasy feelings. He loved his sister. He wanted her to make better choices. He wanted her happy and healthy. Seeing her cry had been like taking a fist to the gut. He'd teared up too. Nothing about this thing was easy, and as relieved as he was for Brandt and Jewel, the finality of having a court judgment was also sobering.

"I'm worried about her too." Brandt nodded like he'd caught on to Shane's thoughts. "Today wasn't really a win for anyone."

"It was for Jewel." He didn't like how down Brandt sounded, so he forced out a more optimistic tone. "She gets some stability. And she gets you."

That got half a smile from Brandt. "Thank you for believing in me."

"Anytime." He let Brandt capture his hand and tug Shane onto the couch. He was too tall for Brandt's lap, but Brandt seemed to want him there anyway, arranging them this way and that until they were partially reclined together, him wedged between Brandt's legs. Not entirely comfortable, but he loved the nearness, especially when Brandt kissed the side of his head.

"Speaking of stable routines, at least she's asleep now. She was a bit fussy without your singing, but we managed."

"You do just fine on your own." Damn it. His dreary tone was back and that was probably not what Brandt needed. But he couldn't help it. He liked being valuable to Brandt, even for something like his lullaby skills. He'd even pulled on a pair of flannel pants after the shower and a T-shirt, to be ready for more bedtime duty.

"Not true." Brandt squeezed him closer, settling a hand over Shane's heart. "We need you. I need you."

"I'm not going anywhere. I'll help—"

"Not as a workhorse. Or a babysitter. You're more than that." Brandt spread his palm wide so that the heat of it seemed to melt into Shane's heart. Or maybe that was simply his words.

"Yeah?"

"You make this a family." Brandt's voice was as gentle as Shane had heard it. But strong too, like he truly believed his pretty words. "Without you, we're a triangle without its points. You connect everything up."

"Are we sure you're not the songwriter?" He tilted his head back further simply to watch Brandt blush.

"Hush." Brandt tapped Shane's lips. "I'm trying here."

"I know. And I appreciate that." Inhaling Brandt's familiar smell, he rubbed his cheek against the faded T-shirt Brandt had changed into after court. "I like having a family. Never thought I'd get one of my own though."

"Me either." A world of meaning passed between them, two less-than-ideal childhoods shaping their adult selves, the choices they'd made to keep themselves safe. Shane had assumed that stability simply wasn't in his genes, but Brandt sure as hell made him want to try, showed him what a family could be. What it should be. And maybe it made him a better brother too, made it easier to hold Shelby tight and wish her well. Like it or not, they were all in this together.

"I like it though," he admitted softly. "The other night at the contest...knowing you were watching, that made all the difference."

"We're gonna get shirts and pom-poms next round." Brandt jostled him with his leg, strong thigh rubbing against Shane's and making it so he didn't know whether to laugh at the ridiculous joke or moan at the contact.

Laughing won out. "Please don't."

"Don't lie." Tickling Shane's ribs, Brandt playfully nipped at his ear. "You love the idea."

"Ha." What he truly loved was this wrestling around like puppies. It made the heaviness that he'd carried all day evaporate. "I love you guys, but I draw the line at shirts with my face on them."

Brandt stilled his hand. "What'd you say?"

"No shirts—"

"Not that part." Brandt's voice was strangely bashful. "The other."

"I love you guys." Shane leaned back again, studying Brandt's pink face. "You didn't get that from my song the other night?"

"Eh. Songs are metaphors, right? Not literal. I wasn't about to take it to the bank just because you found some pretty words that fit your tune."

This man. This sweet, hot, confounding man was going to be the death of him. How someone so confident could doubt his appeal for even a second was almost comical.

"You. You fit the song." Nuzzling Brandt's neck, Shane hid his face. "I love you."

"Oh." Brandt formed a perfect circle with his mouth as he gave a soft exhale, eyes going half shut, clearly pleased. He didn't say it back, but that was okay because he dipped his head and was kissing him with an intensity that made Shane's feet curl against the couch. Awkward angle and all, they kissed until finally Shane's neck was about to give out.

"Damn, man. I was about to ask if you wanted a beer to unwind, but…"

Brandt's husky chuckle made heat lick at the base of Shane's spine. "I think we can find a better way to relax than that."

"I'm open to suggestion." Shane stretched suggestively against him before hefting himself off the couch.

They were both tired enough that he figured they better find the bed first.

"I've got plenty." Accepting Shane's hand up, Brandt joined him standing. Shane couldn't resist giving him another heated kiss. Bed. Soon. This first. He was never getting enough of this man's lips.

"Bet you do." After pulling away breathing hard, Brandt tugged him down the hall toward his room. Laughing, they both collapsed against the door for another kiss, hands still linked. Eventually, though, lips were not enough to quench the heat building between them. Skin. He needed skin.

"Get these clothes off." Brandt's command was a tease as he used gentle hands to pluck at Shane's clothing.

"You too." Shane leaned in for one more kiss. Then another as they undressed each other between kisses until they were both naked and rubbing together. Still wasn't enough.

But before he could voice that need, Brandt pushed him down on the bed. He was more aggressive tonight than usual, and Shane liked it. Ordinarily, his brain would be clamoring for him to take over and control the encounter, but right then he was more than content to soak in all Brandt's raw power, see what happened when he unleashed the full force of his confidence.

"What do you want?" Pinning Shane to the bed, Brandt loomed over him, hair spilling around his face.

"Y—"

"Don't go stealing my best lines now," Brandt scolded before dropping his head to kiss Shane's collarbone. "And you leave it up to me, we're gonna be here awhile…"

"You? Slow? I wanna see this." He stretched underneath Brandt, offering himself up.

"Be careful what you wish for." Chuckling, Brandt peppered him with more kisses. Shoulders. Jaw. Chest. It was new, lying back like this, letting Brandt explore, trusting him like this.

Using his hands as well as that devilish mouth, Brandt brought fresh awareness to all sorts of spots Shane had taken for granted. Behind his ear. His sides. His stomach. Closer and closer to his straining cock until Shane was a shivering ball of need. And curious. So very curious.

"I wanna know what it's like," he whispered.

"Yeah?" Brandt raised his head from Shane's stomach, one eyebrow going up.

"You keep boasting. Maybe you finally convinced me." He shrugged against the mattress, not wanting to make a big deal of this.

"It's not a flavor of soda. You don't have to." Brandt's voice was surprisingly serious.

"I know." It wasn't like he'd ever been totally opposed to bottoming. More like he hadn't felt ready on some internal level, a little twinge of uneasiness that sent his fantasies in other directions. But he was ready now, sexy speculation replacing that reluctance. "I wanna feel what you feel when I'm inside you."

"That's a tall order." Eyes sparkling, Brandt laughed as he made an expansive gesture. "I feel lit up. Like hundreds of little lights, glowing brighter and brighter."

That sounded perfect, all the heat inside him given purpose. He rose up on his elbows to stare Brandt down. "Do it. Light me up."

"Oh, I'm gonna try my best." Grinning wickedly, Brandt leaned up to brush a kiss across Shane's mouth before he reached into the nightstand. He tossed the lube on the bed, and some of Shane's curiosity took a left turn.

His body tensed even as he tried to talk himself back to that place where this seemed like the best idea.

"Relax, baby." Brandt pushed him back down, settling over him for another kiss, slow and possessive. "We're not gonna fuck tonight. You've never even fooled around. We're not going zero to sixty all at once."

"I don't need training wheels." He wasn't sure he appreciated being coddled even as part of him thrilled to Brandt's caretaking.

"But you do need this." In a single graceful movement, Brandt slithered down Shane's torso until his mouth was level with Shane's cock. Not giving Shane a chance to adjust to this most welcome development, he swallowed Shane to the root, making a pleased noise.

"No fair." Hell if he could think of any objections now. And he sure as hell wasn't going to complain about Brandt blowing him. Those hungry noises he made were almost as much of a turn-on as the warm heat of his mouth. Holding him deep, Brandt milked him with the flat of his tongue until Shane was moaning.

Right when Shane was about to lose his damn mind, Brandt released his cock with a wet, lewd sound before scooting lower. He teased Shane's balls with little licks of his tongue. More real estate Shane had clearly neglected far too long because each movement added little sparks to that heat inside of him.

"Fuck." His voice dropped to a whole new register as Brandt went even lower, attacking Shane's rim with his mouth. More of the same urgent noises he made when blowing Shane, and his obvious enjoyment of this smoothed over whatever awkwardness Shane might have had picturing this act, leaving only need. "More."

"Damn. So sensitive. Love it." Brandt met his de-

mands by tracing firm circles with his tongue before
going back to more flicks and teasing until Shane was
whimpering and shuddering. He was shameless now,
pulling his legs up and back to give Brandt better access.
The sparks of pleasure gathered, causing fireworks behind his tightly shut eyes. Damn. If this was what Brandt
felt, Shane was going to make a career out of doing this
for him too.

"So good." His feet dug into his thighs, muscles starting to tense. Unlike Brandt, he'd never had an orgasm
without friction on his cock, but his dick was drool-
ing against his stomach and thick, heady warmth swept
through his whole body. "Fuck. Fuck. I might…"

"That close already?" Sounding all smug, Brandt
backed away before Shane could beg him to finish him
off. He opened his eyes in time to catch Brandt slicking
up his fingers. "This good?"

"Yeah. Do it." If a mouth felt that damn good, he
needed to see what a finger could do. His ass tightened,
but in a good way this time, like his curiosity had turned
to outright need.

"Easy." Brandt's voice was soothing but that was almost more frustrating as Shane's body didn't seem to
know how to relax.

"Not sure…"

"Give it a chance." Rearranging himself slightly,
Brandt kept teasing Shane's rim with slick fingers as he
sucked his cock back into his mouth. It was almost too
much, sensation overload, and he groaned as he reflexively arched his back. The movement allowed Brandt's
finger to slip a little deeper. Didn't burn so much now,
and if he didn't get more of this hand and mouth duet,
he might die.

"More," he panted.

"Yeah?"

"It's better... *Fuck*." Any ability to talk fled as an electric current raced from his ass to his cock, up his abs, down his thighs. Fuck. Even his earlobes were burning hot as the wave of pleasure retreated. "Was that..."

"Fuck yes. Meet your sweet spot." Brandt's triumphant tone would be adorable if every cell in Shane's body wasn't clamoring for him to do it again.

"Stop. Teasing. Do it again."

"This?" Brandt returned his mouth to Shane's cock as he started fucking his finger in earnest, each stroke pushing purposefully against Shane's prostate.

"Yes. Yes. More." Perfect aim. Perfect pressure. Perfect suction of his mouth. Tension started coiling again, that hum of approaching climax, but despite the utter perfection of Brandt's onslaught, he couldn't quite slip over.

"It's okay," Brandt whispered against his cock. "Let go. I've got you."

Suddenly Shane was back in that airplane with Brandt, poised to jump, not sure whether he trusted Brandt to get him down to the earth. But he had. He'd made Shane fly that day. And now he was *Brandt*, and Shane trusted him with everything, including his heart.

Brandt added a second finger, and the pleasure was almost too much, too big, too scary. Shane had never been this high before, and it felt like he might rattle apart any second. He found Brandt's free hand, gripped it tight. And trusted. His heart expanded as his body bowed, and this time he leaped with the rising pleasure, cock pumping into Brandt's mouth, over and over.

It was a long way down, but a smooth, soft landing. "Damn."

"Damn right." Brandt grinned as he wiped his fingers on the towel that had been around Shane's neck earlier. After cleaning Shane up too, he came back up to lie next to Shane, gathering him close. "Did you light up?"

"I flew." Shane's voice was still full of wonder. It was a leap of faith, committing to this thing with Brandt, but if anyone was worth it, this amazing, confounding, special man was it. "You made me fly."

"Even better." Holding Shane tighter, Brandt rocked against him, hard cock trapped against Shane's hip.

"You can fuck me now." If rimming and fingering were that good, he could trust Brandt to make fucking even better, and doing it this boneless sounded marvelous.

"Oh hell no." Brandt gave him a stern look. "You don't get to make that call all sex drunk."

"Wanna make you feel good." Rolling slightly, Shane rubbed Brandt's arms and chest.

"You are." Brandt's breathing was already quick, like he'd been riding the edge the whole time. Sexy as hell. Shane stretched up to nip at his shoulder as he fisted Brandt's cock. He knew what Brandt liked, fast quick strokes and little bites on his neck.

"Fuck yes. Give me your teeth." Moving his own hand over Shane's, Brandt spurred him on as his head twisted to the side, baring his neck farther. He might not care about marks, but Shane tried to exercise some caution as he worked a line of love bites below where Brandt's collar hit.

"*Shane.*" Brandt fucked hard into their joined hands as he shot between them, creamy ropes that made them both even messier. And happier.

"You look like a vampire snack." It was Shane's turn to grin and sound smug.

"Good." Brandt gave him a sound kiss on the top of his head before wiping them both off with the towel. "I'd take being immortal if I got to do it with you."

"That's sweet. Volunteering to be undead just to keep me around." Shane pulled him back down so Shane could wrap himself around him.

"I mean it." Brandt rolled so they were face-to-face. "Love you."

Even as his heart sung, he frowned. This might not be a tune he could trust. "What was that about not making big decisions all come-happy?"

"Not a decision." Cupping his face, Brandt looked deep into his eyes. "A fact. Like the sunrise. I love you."

"You're something." Shane exhaled sharply as hope and love and fear all wrestled in his gut. But love was winning. This was Brandt. Brandt who made him fly. Brandt who he did trust, even with something terrifying like falling in love.

"Something you can keep around?" Brandt prompted as Shane continued to breathe like he'd marched days uphill. And maybe he had, everything, every old hurt and learning experience leading him here to this moment and this man.

"Oh, I'm going to keep you. For as long as you'll have me."

"Forever may not be long enough." Brandt's voice was a whisper, but the soft kiss he pressed on Shane's temple spoke volumes. And in that instant, Shane suddenly knew the end to the song that had been chasing him for days now. The one about Brandt that couldn't seem to make up its mind whether it was a happy tune or not. But now he caught the melody in full, stopped fighting it and let the notes fall into place.

Leap of faith. Wasn't that what Brandt had said on their first meeting? Shane wanted forever and if it meant going all in with Brandt Wilder, then that was exactly what he was going to do. He'd trust the music they made together, and he'd do everything in his power to give their love song the happiest of endings.

Chapter Thirty-One

Two years later

"More!" The audience roar was so loud that Brandt had
to clap his hands over Jewel's ears as the chants continued. "Encore!"

The shouts had Brandt smiling though, pride having
him both impatient and vaguely giddy.

"Okay, okay, twist my arm." Wiping sweat off his
forehead, Shane still had an easy grin for the crowd. The
venue was so tightly packed that Brandt bet he ended
up with two Seattle shows next tour. Shane took a long
drink of water before speaking more. "I guess I've got
one more in me."

That got a fresh round of cheers, and Shane had to
make the simmer-down gesture twice so he could continue talking. His ability to banter with the audience
had improved so much, and it was most evident in the
looseness of his muscles as he grabbed his guitar back
up again.

"And this is a special one. Going out to a special little
girl I can't wait to see soon."

"That's you," Brandt whispered to Jewel, holding the
toddler close. "They're playing for you."

"Dada sing my song?" Her whole face lit up as she did a happy humming noise. The song Shane had first performed the last time Brandt and Jewel surprised him was on constant repeat in Brandt's car, in the kitchen, and her most requested lullaby, even when it was Brandt doing the bedtime routine on his own. And he was a piss poor substitute for the real deal.

"Yup. Listen." He started swaying with Jewel as Shane's baritone filled the club. God, he'd missed that voice. It had only been a few weeks this time, but being home in LA without him had sucked. *Home.* Shane's winnings might have provided the down payment, and Brandt's tools made it livable, but it was the three of them who made it a home. A place to come back to again and again and a place to miss.

"We dancing." Jewel did a wiggle that made her pigtails bounce and almost launched her from Brandt's grasp. He missed the days of sticking her in her sling. Didn't miss the sleepless nights, but he was still getting used to this walking, talking little *person* at the center of their lives. Shane called her mini-Brandt with her blond fluffy hair and hazel eyes, but her pitch-perfect ability to hum along to her favorite song was not from Brandt at all. She had long musical fingers and high cheekbones and a temper all her own.

From their position offstage, he had a great view of Shane's profile as he launched into the final verse. Damn. It was just another Thursday, another stop in this mini-tour, but as always, he left a piece of his soul with the audience. And the way he felt each word never failed to stir Brandt's own emotions. He might know this song by heart, but Brandt wasn't ever getting tired of it.

"You ready to do our surprise?" he asked Jewel as the last notes sounded.

"Ready!" Jewel crowed. The keyboard player reminded the audience where to buy swag as the band prepared to leave the stage. Shane's friend Tim was touring with them this time and was Brandt's inside man for this operation. He had a wink for them as he said something to Shane as they all gave the audience one more wave.

"Here he comes."

"Dada!" Jewel's yell turned several heads, including the one Brandt most wanted to see. Uncle Shane just didn't seem to fit the sheer amount of parenting that Shane did, and Jewel herself was the one who'd started calling him "other daddy." And the look on Shane's face when she did it was all the proof Brandt needed that that was the right title for him.

Eyes widening, Shane broke away from Tim to hurry over to them. "What the—"

"Happy birthday, Dada!" Thanks to a lot of practice, Jewel delivered the line with a huge smile as she reached for Shane, stretching her little body toward him. Like Brandt, she'd missed him something fierce.

"Jewel." Shane scooped her up with a dazed smile. "What are you guys are doing here?"

"We you birthday present. Surprise." Her whole face glowed as she looked up at him. He was sweaty from the stage lights still and a little thinner and more tired than when Brandt had seen him last, but to Brandt, he never looked better than like this, holding their little girl with the same gentleness he handled her heart.

"You're the best surprise birthday present ever." Shaking his head, Shane looked down at her black T-shirt. "Hey. What's this? What did Daddy dress you in?"

"It's you." She preened, pointing to Shane's tour logo. Wild at Heart, they were calling this tour, and Brandt smiled every damn time he saw the logo, which was almost as good as the Wilder tattoo Shane kept threatening. The inside jokes between them were one of his favorite things, and Brandt hadn't missed the chance to wear a matching shirt, which earned him an eye roll from Shane.

"So it is. I'm so happy to see you both that I'll forgive the fashion choices."

"I'm happy too." Brandt held his gaze over Jewel's pigtails. "Don't worry. I'll change before I take you out for your birthday dinner. Can't have folks thinking I'm just another groupie."

"As if. And I'm not even gonna ask how you charmed your way in here." Laughing, Shane stepped aside as two roadies headed for the stage. Gone were the days when Shane did his own teardown. The record label that had signed him after his stint on the songwriting show made sure he had a good crew, and the roadies had a smile for Brandt and Jewel. Shane motioned down the corridor. "Let's get out of the way. My dressing room is this way."

He led them to a little room that had two guitars, a couple of chairs, mirrors, and a big basket of snack food, which Jewel made a beeline for as soon as Shane set her down.

"Ooooh. Snackies."

"Here." After shutting the door, Brandt riffled through the basket to find a toddler-friendly choice that might keep her occupied a few minutes. "Have some crackers."

"Thank you, Daddy." She had an angelic smile as she accepted the little bag of cheese crisps.

"Manners?" Head tilting, Shane laughed. "Man, what else have I missed?"

"Me?" Brandt settled himself in one of the chairs.

"Yeah, yeah." Shane kissed the top of his head before he took the other chair. "You too."

"I'm wounded." Brandt couldn't stop staring at him even as he joked, couldn't resist jostling his knee simply to have an excuse to touch him. "And she's got a bunch of new words now. Tried telling her to slow down the growing, but you know the diva."

"She looks bigger. And you look damn good yourself." Shane swept his gaze over Brandt, blatant appreciation that made Brandt acutely aware of exactly how many hours it had been since he last had Shane in his bed.

"Thanks." Brandt's voice came out all husky. Maybe Shane could be convinced to skip dinner.

"How long are you in town?" Shane took Brandt's hand, rubbing his fingers like he was trying to make sure he was really there. "I thought you had a shift this weekend."

"Benefit of still being part-time is it's easier to trade away hours. Ryland was happy to swap." That was the whole reason Brandt wasn't on this tour. Much as he'd liked being Shane's entourage and Jewel's dad, he'd missed the fire community a lot. So he'd gotten on with a hellitack crew, using his smoke jumper experience to get certified in short haul rescues. No more parachutes, but the ropes and rigging were plenty of an adrenaline rush. This early in the season, his main role was as a backup for other crew members, but come August and September he'd be closer to full-time as more fires cropped up. And as Jewel got older, the plan was to take on more hours as he could, especially when Shane wasn't touring.

"Tell him thanks."

"Will do. But no way were we going to miss your

birthday." Brandt squeezed Shane's hand. Jewel was still happy with her snack and was playing peekaboo with a rack of Western shirts. "We're here for this show and the Portland one, then taking you home with us. Wanted to see you close the tour out."

"Can't wait to be home." Shane exhaled hard and let his head fall on Brandt's shoulder. "Damn. Love the audiences we've been pulling, but I hate the road."

"Well, we're ready to have you home for a good long while." Brandt wasn't too proud to admit that he liked having Shane home best of all. He was super proud of Shane and the career he'd carved for himself, but their little house wasn't truly a home without him in it.

"Good. Because I fully intend to take my time with this new album." Swinging Brandt's hand, Shane gave him a meaningful smile.

"Got enough material?" Brandt waggled his eyebrows at him just to earn another smile.

"That you volunteering to be my muse?"

"Always." Not able to wait another second, Brandt leaned down and gave him a soft kiss that he was intending to be soft and friendly, but even the brief contact made heat pool low in his belly.

"Damn," Shane groaned and shifted on the chair. "Do not write checks your body isn't cashing in a hotel room with a toddler."

"I brought the nanny. She's enjoying some downtime and the pool at the hotel, but I got her and Jewel a separate room."

"Estelle's here?" Shane grinned widely. When Brandt had made the decision to return to part-time fire work, they'd needed more childcare help. Brandt's new friend Ryland had hooked them up with a cousin of his partner, a wonderful, energetic older woman who'd raised her own children and who was looking for a new challenge. And as much as Brandt loved being just the three of them, his little triangle of a family, he was also looking forward to a little alone time with Shane, who apparently felt the same way. "I really do love you."

"Love you too. And she's not the only tagalong. Shelby's supposed to meet us in Portland." He said the last bit of news carefully.

"You talked to her?" Shane's mouth quirked like he was trying not to frown. His relationship with his sister was still complicated, and like Brandt, he'd spent a lot of hours worrying over her.

"Yeah. I called to remind her you had a birthday, and she picked up for once. She sounded good. Healthy. Think this new counselor is helping."

In the months after Brandt's permanent custody petition had been granted, Shelby had bounced around a fair bit, but she'd finally decided to seek some mental health care. It had been a rocky road, lots of ups and downs, but she seemed to be in a better place lately.

"Wow. This is the best birthday—"

"You said that last year, too," Brandt reminded him, twirling the ring on Shane's hand.

"True. I did get nifty hardware out of that one." Shane gave him a fond smile. "You do have a way of making holidays memorable."

Funny how they'd gone from skipping most holidays to taking turns outdoing each other to make memories for Jewel. And each other.

"Says the guy who had me up to three a.m. building that play kitchen at Christmas."

"You loved it and you know it." Shane scooped up Jewel as she wandered away from the rack of clothes.

"Maybe I just love you," Brandt countered, dropping kisses on both Shane's and Jewel's heads. "I mean, I can't write an award-winning song about it—"

"It wasn't even a Grammy!" Shane acted like his best new entertainer award from one of the bigger music awards was no big deal. Brandt snorted because he knew under the modesty Shane was damn proud of where his career was heading.

"That's coming and you know it." Brandt believed. In Shane. In what they were building, the three of them. And in himself, in his ability to hold his little family together.

"As long as I have you guys here for it." Shane laughed as Jewel arranged herself so she was draped over both of them. Brandt wasn't sure his heart could hold the sweetness as she hugged them at the same time.

"I'm not going anywhere." Brandt wasn't ever letting go. He'd spent enough years running from attachment, but now all he wanted was to harness these two to him. Even when Shane was on the road, he was still part of Brandt's heart. Hell, he *was* Brandt's heart, the song that made it beat.

As he gathered Jewel and Shane into a tighter embrace, he met Shane's eyes. The love there made his breath catch. Yup. He'd hold tight to this, to their family, to this man who was everything Brandt had never known he needed, but now was the one thing Brandt wanted to hold on to forever.

* * * * *

Author Note

It was so exciting to return to my smoke jumping world for book four in this series. Like book one, rather than try to copy an existing smoke jumping base with its specific procedures, policies, ways of handling rookies and so on, I combined various parts of my research into many different bases into one fictional base and town. Some details relating to Brandt's work were simplified to allow the focus to remain on the characters and their growth and their story, but I did try to include as much realism as possible. Intrepid readers will recognize Linc and Jacob from book one and the brief mention of Tucker and Luis from book three.

I want to acknowledge the complexities of mental health care right now in the United States. Mental health awareness is a huge issue for me, and an area I continue to advocate for change in. For all the parents out there dealing with post-partum mental health issues, you are not alone, and help is out there. And likewise, mood disorders are a complex medical issue, and help is out there. If you or someone you love is struggling, please seek assistance and know that I am sending you my love.

As I wrote this book, over a million acres burned in Oregon in some of the worst fires in our state's history.

I loved writing this series, but never did I expect to be finishing the series while on red alert for evacuation. While my community was spared, many others were not so lucky. Across California and Colorado too, fires raged, and tales of great heroism emerged amid those of terrible tragedy. The human element of wildfire fighting was on display, and I felt new sympathy for the families who support the brave firefighters.

It was with this backdrop that I made the decision to not have any huge fires in this book. I didn't want a world where my beloved state burned and many amazing people lost their lives. Likewise, this book came through drafting and edits right as the world changed with the response to COVID-19. I very deliberately chose not to have these events affect the storyline, but I absolutely appreciate all our first responders and all that they do for our communities. My heart goes out to all those on the front lines, both firefighting and other key jobs from grocery store workers to truckers to all the health care workers.

Acknowledgments

As with all my books, I am so grateful for the team supporting me, especially at Carina Press and the Knight Agency. My editor, Deb Nemeth, gave me positive feedback at the exact moment I needed it most and saw this book's potential. Editing remains one of my favorite parts of the publishing process as that's where vision meets actuality. My revisions were also assisted by invaluable beta comments from Abbie Nicole, who helped make Brandt a better parent, and Layla Noureddine, who made the whole book better with her astute comments.

My behind the scenes team is also the best. My entire Carina Press team does an amazing job, and I am so very lucky to have all of them on board. A special thank-you to the tireless art department and publicity team and to the amazing narrators who bring my books to life for the audio market. A special thank-you to Abbie Nicole who is the best PA I could ever ask for.

My family is the center of my life and is so appreciated for their cooperation and assistance, especially as we all adapted to life in quarantine, online school, and other challenges. My life is also immeasurably enriched by my friendships, especially those of my writer friends who keep me going with sprints, advice, guidance, and commiseration. Thanks to Layla Reyne, Wendy Qualls, Gwen Martin, Karen Stivali, and Edie Danford among many other special people in my life. I am so grateful for every person in my life who helps me do what I love. And no one makes that possible more than my readers. I can't thank readers enough for their readership and encouragement over the years. Your support via social media, reviews, notes, shares, likes, and other means makes it possible for me to continue to write stories that mean the world to me, and I don't take that for granted!

About the Author

Annabeth Albert grew up sneaking romance novels under the bed covers. Now, she devours all subgenres of romance out in the open—no flashlights required! When she's not adding to her keeper shelf, she's a multi-published Pacific Northwest romance writer. The #Hotshots series joins her many other critically acclaimed and fan-favorite LGBTQ romance series. To find out what she's working on next and other fun extras, check out her website: www.annabethalbert.com or connect with Annabeth on Twitter, Facebook, Instagram, and Spotify! Also, be sure to sign up for her newsletter for free ficlets, bonus reads, and contests. The fan group, Annabeth's Angels, on Facebook is also a great place for bonus content and exclusive contests.

Emotionally complex, sexy, and funny stories are her favorites both to read and to write. Annabeth loves finding happy endings for a variety of pairings and particularly loves uncovering unique main characters. In her personal life, she works a rewarding day job and wrangles two active children.

Newsletter: *www.eepurl.com/Nb9yv*
Fan group: *www.Facebook.com/Groups/AnnabethsAngels/*

*Danger lurks everywhere for Central Oregon's fire
crews, but the biggest risk of all might be
losing their hearts...*

Read on for an excerpt from Burn Zone, *the first book
in Annabeth Albert's Hotshots series:
the emotions and intensity of Chicago Fire
with the raw, natural elements of Man vs. Wild.*

Chapter One

Six years ago, September

"Fucking wind." Linc had been shit out of luck plenty of times in all his years fighting wildfires, but being quite literally up a tree, dangling like a puppet, never got any easier to stomach.

"Hang tight, buddy. I've got you." Retrieving the cargo that had dropped along with the members of their smoke-jumping crew, Wyatt prepared to climb up after him.

Linc had been treed, parachute tangled in the branches of a massive pine, when the wind had pushed him off course. Even his years of skilled landings under pressure-filled circumstances hadn't been enough to keep him out of the tree.

It wasn't his first time being treed and probably wouldn't be the last time Wyatt had to save his bacon. That was the nature of their work on the front lines of forest fires—they'd saved each other's lives so many times, he'd lost track of the number, but never lost sight of this feeling, being helpless, waiting for his best friend to come bail him out again.

"Careful," Linc called when a branch creaked as

Wyatt started his ascent. "No stupid risks. May's counting on me returning you in one piece."

The fire season was winding down, lots of equipment checks and inventory for next year, and the occasional jump like this one, checking on reports of some spot fires from lightning strikes. Their job was to do what was necessary to prevent the spread of fire—hand digging lines, clearing brush, felling trees.

"She wasn't happy, having to take me this morning." Wyatt's voice was more strained than usual. Linc couldn't tell whether it was from the climb or the mention of May, who was pregnant with their first kid and had been full of worries all season long, the stress of being married to a smoke jumper getting to her. "Stupid truck's acting up again. She's on me to trade it in, get a four-door that can handle a car seat."

"Not a bad idea. Get me free from this mess and I'll come take a look at it tomorrow, see if I can get you running again for the short-term."

"Appreciated." Wyatt's tone was still clipped. Linc couldn't see him now, and he knew better than to twist too much. One wrong move and he could end up plummeting to the ground, which was enough of a drop to break some bones.

Ordinarily, Linc would be more proactive in getting free, but he'd tangled in a way that he couldn't get to the knife that was an essential part of their gear. Instead, he had to wait for Wyatt to reach him, trust that Wyatt wouldn't send him crashing through the branches, and that Wyatt would have enough sense to keep his own self safe. May—and Wyatt's mother, whom Linc loved almost as much as the memory of his own—would never forgive Linc if Wyatt went home with a broken leg or worse.

Working together this season was like shrugging into his favorite work jacket, worn and familiar, both of them more experienced this go-around. While Wyatt had stayed local after graduation, Linc had been gone as much as he'd been home, gaining experience on fire crews all across the West before finally duty called him back, roots as unavoidable as taxes. That Wyatt and this crew had been waiting was more than a reward for everything else he was dealing with.

Finally, though, he was free enough to grab Wyatt's hand, then use all his upper body strength to pull himself over the branch. Working together, they freed the chute. It was way too valuable and essential to their work to leave in the tree, so he breathed a little easier when it fluttered to the ground. Then they started their descent, tricky because of the weight of both of them. It was an old, sturdy tree, but Linc's attention remained on red alert for potential dangers until they were both on the forest floor.

Time to get to work, packing up the chute and rejoining the rest of the crew, digging fireline by hand, the wide dirt trails used to keep back any potential fire spread, until his arm and back muscles burned. This mission at least didn't involve an overnight in the forest, but it did have a long, arduous pack-out where they had to haul themselves and all their gear several miles to an extraction point.

"Careful!" Wyatt thrust an arm out right when Linc would have tripped over a large tree root. The others were some distance behind them, Wyatt setting a bruising pace as per his usual.

"Damn. You saved me. Again." Linc shook his head. They had been through hell and back, everything from fiery infernos side by side to pristine mountain mornings. Even in the years when Linc had been away for long stretches, they'd still shared every catastrophe and triumph from wading pools to wedding bells for Wyatt and every major life event in between. "What do I owe you?"

It was an old joke between them, but Wyatt's face darkened, eyes narrowing, voice hard. "Stay away from my little brother."

Fuck. Linc should have seen this coming, should have known that Wyatt had something more on his mind than May's worries. He'd probably been stewing all day, waiting to bring this up. That was how Wyatt got, even back when they were kids. He'd brood and brood and then his temper would flare.

"Me? What would I want with him?" Stopping, he turned to face Wyatt. If they were going to do this, he wasn't going to let Wyatt lecture over his shoulder like Linc was some ornery kid on a scout hike being called to task.

"Don't play dumb with me. I *know* you. Wasn't that me who didn't say a damn word when you took the number of that bartender New Year's Eve?"

Linc swallowed hard. He'd lay down his life for Wyatt, but he also wasn't going to let his best friend push him around either.

"Who I've taken to bed has zero to do with your brother. Zilch." On that point, he could be firm. That Wyatt disapproved went without saying—they might be brothers of the soul, but that didn't mean they always saw eye to eye. His skin prickled, old wounds he tried his damnedest to ignore.

"Fuck yes, it does. He came out. Told the whole damn family yesterday at Sunday dinner that he's gay."

"Bet that took some balls, standing up to all of you."

Somehow Linc managed a steady tone even as he wondered what in the hell Jacob had been thinking, coming right out and announcing that to his large, boisterous family that wasn't exactly known for open-mindedness, especially among the brothers. "Good on him, but again, nothing to do with me."

"Bullshit." The meanness was back along with a gravelly laugh. "He's been following you around two weeks now, doing all your crap jobs, ever since he got back from Vegas looking like a kicked puppy."

"He's been helpful." He kept his voice mild, not about to let on to any enjoyment of Jacob's presence, the way he lightened Linc's load far beyond hauling trash. And yeah, Jacob had been down, but some of that defeated air was starting to clear, leaving behind a guy with a quick wit, easy smile and strong back. "Not gonna deny I've been able to use him with the shit my old man left behind. It's a total—"

"Mess that ain't yours." Wyatt resumed their trek, not looking to see if Linc was following. Which he did. Like always. He might not like this conversation, but he owed Wyatt too damn much to just stalk off, even if part of him was tempted.

"I've been telling you," Wyatt continued as they crested a hill. "It's time you moved on. Let it go."

"Let it go to who?" This was an old argument, but Linc still took the bait, not liking the undercurrent of a message that maybe he should leave town again. "No real other family stepping up to the plate. Victor's dead. Dad's dead. Nah, man, it's on me. And Jacob's been a help. Stronger than he looks—"

Wyatt cut him off with a warning noise. "Did he tell

you anything about whatever shit went down in Vegas? You wouldn't keep that from me, would you?"

"Nah. He didn't say shit about his love life." But actually Linc might have kept quiet if he had. Not maliciously, but Wyatt wasn't good with a secret, and Linc... well, he had enough of his own. He could hold on to someone else's for them until they were ready to share.

However, something had gone down in Vegas, something big to send Jacob home, away from all his MMA friends, tail between his legs, looking as heartbroken as Linc had ever seen a guy. And, well, it didn't take an engineer to piece together the facts.

"How's your mom taking it?" he asked. Of all the Hartman family members, she was least likely to cast Jacob out. He was her baby, and Linc couldn't see her hurling hate at him, no matter what she might personally believe. And as she went, so would the rest of the family, Wyatt's homophobic ass included.

"Ha." Wyatt snorted. "Mom's playing this like she's known for years, but Dad just got real quiet, then went back to the TV in their room. I'm worried about his heart, man."

"Him? Strong as a fucking ox." Linc was more worried about Wyatt's liver these days than his robust old man's maladies. He knew the Hartman family, knew how much they doted on Jacob, even if he did try all their patience from time to time. The way Linc saw it, they'd survive this shock.

Wyatt might not.

"He ain't gonna make a hotshot crew, not now."

"He wants that?" Dread gathered in Linc's gut that had exactly nothing to do with Jacob's announcement or Wyatt's predictable meltdown. Something in him didn't like the thought of Jacob out here, doing the work that he and Wyatt had done for years, fighting forest fires. Jacob in the line of danger didn't sit right with him, not at all.

"He said he did. Other night. Who knows though?" Wyatt shrugged. "Says he's gonna go out for the volunteer crew first. But he's also yapping about trying college. You never know with that kid. Can't stick to anything worth a crap."

"Any ETA on the extraction?" Garrick and Ray, their other team members, came around the bend, huffing as they hauled their share of the gear.

"Nope. Gotta haul ass to get us back for a late dinner." Wyatt managed to sound upbeat, but later, once Linc was dropping him off at the small house he and May shared at the edge of town, Wyatt had one more warning. "And I meant what I said. Don't you start messing around with Jacob. We might go way back, but I'll lay you out flat myself, you and him start carrying on."

"No worry of that," he said, pitching his own voice low and calm, no trace of the junk heap of emotions piling up inside him. "Go on now. Don't make May walk out and see what's keeping you."

"Fine. Some uncle you're gonna be, the way you hover over her. Between you and Mom, kid'll come out rolled in bubble wrap."

That Wyatt considered him an uncle for the kid on the way didn't make him warm with satisfaction, the way it might have earlier in the day. Now, it just added to his guilt and uncertainty, feelings that didn't evaporate as he headed home.

There was a shadow on the porch as he pulled up, and his heart knew what it was even if his brain didn't want to admit it quite yet.

"Linc. I was hoping they'd bring you back early." Jacob's voice was low and urgent as soon as Linc stepped onto the porch. It was old and sagging, one of the many things that needed complete replacing, not just repair. No light either, another thing he'd need to add. Off to the side of the house was a junk heap, smaller now thanks to Jacob's help. The whole place had gone to ruin while Linc had bounced around, sometimes here, sometimes out in Idaho or Wyoming, trying to outrun…everything. But apparently he hadn't run far enough, pulled back by his father's death to this box of uncomfortable memories.

"What do you think you're doing?" He wanted it to come out stern, but his voice was weary, energy bled out from the argument with Wyatt and the long shift. And now this. In his tiredness as he'd pulled in, he'd missed seeing the little compact parked on the other side of the junk heap. The car had belonged to one of Jacob's sisters and was currently held together with little more than duct tape and hope.

"Waiting. For you. Figured you'd show up sometime before midnight." It was too dark to see much of Jacob's smile, but Linc could *hear* it. The pleasure in Jacob's voice sliced him to the core, spoke to everything he'd been trying so hard not to notice the past few weeks, like the way his pulse sped up just sharing the same oxygen. Trying to steady himself, he sank down on a five-gallon paint barrel, carefully positioning himself away from where Jacob was perched on the rickety railing. "Invite me in?"

Oh, hell no. Linc ignored that potential stick of dynamite and went for the real reason Jacob had probably turned up. "Heard you caused a bit of a ruckus with the family last night."

"They'll get over it." This new all-grown-up, super-confident version of Jacob had plagued Linc ever since he got back to town. Jacob was the kind of guy who didn't let life get him down long, bouncing back from what had to be a hell of a hurt, and Linc couldn't help but admire that quality. He still managed to joke around, smile, get under Linc's skin. Especially that last one.

He wouldn't say he missed the little kid Jacob had been, because he'd barely known him at all. Back then, he'd been just another little Hartman kid roaming around, getting underfoot to whatever real business he and Wyatt were about. But then he'd turned back up, all lean muscle and short blond hair and a come-get-me grin, no trace of that annoying toddler, and a whole lot more trouble.

"Anything in particular bring this on?" He told himself that curiosity was the only reason he was keeping Jacob talking.

"Friends of mine were sharing memes about coming-out stories."

Linc tried picturing a universe where he might... *Nah.* Never happening.

Jacob's sigh was far worldlier than his almost-twenty years would seem to support. "It's a social media thing. I know, I know, you're not big on that, but news flash, there's a whole world beyond Painter's Ridge."

"I've been around, remember?" He needed to remind them both that he was a good ten years older than Jacob.

"Chasing fires all over the West hardly counts as *around*," Jacob scoffed. "No cities. No smartphones. No friends beyond your hotshot crew guys."

"Hey now." Linc might be something of a loner, but he had friends. Might all be local or seasonal acquaintances elsewhere, but he wasn't the cranky hermit Jacob was trying to make him out to be.

"I'm just saying, you don't even make it up to Portland much."

"No need. Anyway, these…friends of yours, they pressured you into coming out?"

"No one *pressured* me." Jacob sounded outraged that Linc would even think he could be swayed like that. And there was the backbone Linc admired so much—strength, not just in his slim, fighting-honed body, but in his character. "It was in the back of my head though, all day. And then at dinner, Wyatt started in again on why I left Vegas, saying I couldn't hack it in MMA, even as Tyler's sidekick. And I'd just had *enough*. Enough of the pretending. Enough of the lies and not a damn person around here knowing the truth. I was just so fucking tired of his bullshit."

"I hear you." And Linc did, heard his pain and loneliness loud and clear. He knew something of that isolation, and while maybe he wouldn't choose Jacob's way out, he got the desperation that had driven his outburst. "And that was a brave thing you did, standing up to him. Telling everyone."

"I'm not looking for a head pat here."

"And I'm not handing them out." Linc could meet his irritation head-on.

"Wouldn't turn down a beer though. Fuck. That was *intense*."

"Another year and a half, I'll buy you one."

Nineteen, he reminded himself. *He's nine-fucking-teen.* Even if Wyatt hadn't warned him off, he needed to remember that the kid couldn't even buy a drink yet.

And thank the fuck that Linc had thrown out every last drop of alcohol in this place, first week back.

"Like you and Wyatt weren't drinking every chance you got, even in high school."

"Wyatt maybe," he allowed, stretching, trying to do something with the tension that kept gathering in his lower back, just from being here.

"Oh, right. I forgot. You're...like his guardian angel or something. Don't you ever get tired, being his designated driver? Cleaning up his messes?"

"Nope," he lied, far too easily. "He's my best friend. It's what friends do, take care of each other."

"I don't see him exactly returning the favor." Jacob flicked some stray leaf off the railing, narrowly missing Linc.

"You wouldn't know," he said testily, reminding both of them that he and Wyatt had a long history that Jacob had nothing to do with. "That man's done more for me than I can ever repay."

Jacob made a scoffing noise. "Maybe so, but you wouldn't know it from how he treats you sometimes. So, what's the deal? Can't believe Wyatt even told you about last night. He tell you to try to talk sense into me?"

"Fuck no."

"Oh?" Jacob's tone softened and he scooted closer. *Danger. Danger.* All Linc's proximity sensors pinged, brain squawking like a comm set when a fire wall shifted, coming straight at him. "I brought it up to make sure you were okay. That's all. Thought maybe you'd need to hear that your folks will come around. Give them time."

"Yeah." Jacob's sigh held a certain amount of wistfulness to it, which did something to Linc's insides, made

him want to be stupid and take his hand or something
else ridiculous.

"And for the record, I'm sorry about that Tyler kid.
He's a fucking idiot, but you okay?"

"I'm fine." Leaning forward, he rested a hand on
Linc's shoulder. "Totally and completely fine."

"Good." He didn't make a move to stand, couldn't, not
with Jacob's warm hand pressing him down, dangerous
sparks shooting all down his torso.

"But maybe I should make myself scarce for a few
days, let everyone calm the fuck down. You wouldn't
happen to know of somewhere with a spare bed now,
would you?" His tone was light, but there was no mis-
taking his meaning.

"You're not staying here." Even if Wyatt wouldn't flay
him alive, that idea was all kinds of trouble.

"No beer. No place to crash. You're no fun."

"Nope."

"I could be, though. Fun. The sort of fun you need.
And you know it." Jacob's voice had all the brashness of
nineteen to it, reckless confidence. "Don't tell me you
haven't felt it, ever since I started helping you here. I've
seen you looking at me."

Fuck. All those danger warnings shrieked again as the
car carrying his sanity went over the cliff. He worked
with any number of good-looking guys, had played four
years of high school sports, had been around locker
rooms almost two decades at this point, and it was going
to be Jacob who called him on sneaking looks? And the
worst, the absolute worst, was that he wasn't wrong. Linc
had looked. And that Jacob noticed said he was either
getting sloppy now that he'd hit thirty or that there was
something about Jacob…

And fuck it all, there could *not* be something about Jacob. No way, no how.

"No idea what you're talking about." For the second time that day, he played dumb, knowing full well Jacob wasn't going to buy it any more than his brother had.

"I get it. You're not out yet. But I've heard enough of Wyatt's stupid jokes when he thinks you guys are alone to know you probably swing my way, at least sometimes. And like I said, I'm not blind."

The words to deny Jacob's assumption rose in his throat, but wouldn't leave his lips. Something about Jacob indeed. Linc could lie about this by omission or necessity to just about anyone else. But not Jacob. From the start of helping Linc, he'd earned Linc's trust. And maybe his truthfulness too, because he simply couldn't make the lie come.

"You're not blind. It's no one's business but mine though."

"Good." Jacob drew the word out, sinful and seductive and more dangerous than fraying webbing on a jump rig. "I can keep a secret."

If only. But no. His bones still remembered with breathtaking accuracy how it had felt, dangling above the earth that morning, little pieces of rope and webbing all that separated him and a broken neck. The view might have been nice, but the fall would have been deadly, save Wyatt's intervention. Not unlike this moment here.

I've got you, buddy.

Stay away from my little brother.

"Doesn't matter. You're barking up the wrong tree. I'm not letting you stay here."

"Why? You think I'm on the rebound from Tyler? Or you think I'll out you? Or…" His voice hardened and his hand tightened on Linc's shoulder. "It's Wyatt, isn't it? Did he threaten you?"

"No." This time the lie came easy, both because he had to and because he didn't like Jacob's tone, like he was ready to go to war with Wyatt on his behalf. That sort of concern, an almost protectiveness, made him shift against the plastic bucket. He didn't need anyone playing champion for him.

Jacob's grip softened, massaging Linc's neck with a touch that had him stifling a groan. His hands were strong, calloused from hard work and years in the gym and felt better than a hot shower after a long day in the field.

"He wouldn't have to know. It could be just an itch we scratch this one time."

"Ha." Oh, to be nineteen and so damn sure of himself. And that right there was the other reason why Linc had to turn him down. There wouldn't be any one time only for him, not the way Jacob pulled him in even when he knew full well he had to resist. Jacob, who apparently saw what hundreds of guys he'd worked with hadn't. Jacob, who made him laugh even while hauling mountains of moldy magazines, a feat not many could manage.

But Jacob had all but said it himself—he was nursing a broken heart from Tyler, and Linc had no desire to chance everything just to be the rebound fuck the kid forgot in a month.

"Not happening."

"Not tonight, maybe, but—"

"Not now, not ever. There's plenty of fish your own age to fry. Go find one." He forced himself to pull away from that delicious torment, to stand up because his body was that damn weak that another few minutes and he'd be making all sorts of stupid choices. Better to be firm now.

"Your loss." The hurt in Jacob's voice as he scampered off the railing pierced Linc like a dart, a sharp, swift pain he'd do anything to take away. Anything, that was, except the one thing Jacob seemed to want.

"I'm sure it is." He wasn't trying to be flip. He absolutely was sincere—both sure that he'd regret turning him down and sure that he was doing the right thing. Jacob was simply a risk he wasn't ever going to be able to afford.

Don't miss Burn Zone *by author Annabeth Albert, available wherever books are sold.*

www.CarinaPress.com